THE FORGET-ME-NOT CHILD

Anne Bennett was born in a back-to-back house in the Horsefair district of Birmingham. The daughter of Roman Catholic, Irish immigrants, she grew up in a tight-knit community where she was taught to be proud of her heritage. She considers herself to be an Irish Brummie and feels therefore that she has a foot in both cultures. She has four children and five grandchildren. For many years she taught in schools to the north of Birmingham. An accident put paid to her teaching career and, after moving to North Wales, Anne turned to the other great love of her life and began to write seriously. In 2006, after sixteen years in a wheelchair, she miraculously regained her ability to walk.

Visit www.annebennett.co.uk to find out more about Anne and her books.

By the same author

ANNE BENNETT

THE FORGET-ME-NOT CHILD

HARPER

Harper
An imprint of HarperCollins*Publishers*
The News Building
1 London Bridge Street
London SE1 9GF

www.harpercollins.co.uk

A Paperback Original 2017
2

Copyright © Anne Bennett 2017

Anne Bennett asserts the moral right to be identified as the author of this work

A catalogue record for this book is available from the British Library

ISBN: 978-0-00-816231-3

Typeset in Sabon LT Std by Palimpsest Book Production Ltd, Falkirk, Stirlingshire

Printed and bound in Great Britain by Clays Ltd, St Ives plc

I dedicate this, my 20th book,
to my family for their love and
encouragement over the years.
I love and appreciate you all greatly.

ONE

Angela could remember little of her earlier life when the McClusky family lived in Donegal in Northern Ireland. As she grew she had understood that her name was not McClusky but was Kennedy, and she was the youngest daughter of Connie and Padraig Kennedy, and that Mary and Matt McClusky were not her real parents at all, though she called them Mammy and Daddy. She also learned that she had once had four older siblings all at school and so when Minnie the eldest contracted TB and Angela's mother realized it was rife in the school, she asked Mary McClusky, who was a great friend of hers, to care for Angela, then just eighteen months old, in an effort to keep her safe. Mary had not hesitated and Angela lived in the McClusky home, petted and feted by the five McClusky boys who had never had a girl in the family before.

However, before Angela was two years old she was an orphan; for her parents succumbed to TB too as they watched their children die one by one. Mary was distraught at the loss of her dear friend and all those poor young children. And Padraig too, for he was a fine strapping man and well able, anyone would have thought, to fight off any illness.

'Ah, but maybe he hadn't the will to fight,' Matt said. 'He'd watched his children all die and then his wife had gone as well before he developed it. What was left for him if he had recovered? I imagine he didn't bother fighting it.'

Whatever the way of it, there was a spate of funerals and though Angela attended none of them she was aware of a sadness in the McClusky family without understanding it.

Eventually Mary had to rouse herself for she had a family to see to, including little motherless Angela, and Matt had a farm to run. Mary did wonder if there was some long-lost relative who would look after Angela, but after the last funeral it was apparent there wasn't and Mary decided that she would stay with them. She knew there would be no opposition from Matt who had by then grown extremely fond of her, as they all had, and he just nodded when Mary said it was the very least she could do for her friend. Matt too had been badly shaken by the deaths of the entire Kennedy family and was well aware that a similar tragedy could have happened to his family just as easily. This time they had got through unscathed and he readily agreed that Angela should continue to live with them and grow up as their daughter.

'Angela will be your new little sister,' Mary told her sons. Not one of them made any objection but the happiest of them all was her youngest, Barry. At five years old, he was three years older than Angela and she was petite for her age with white-blonde curls and big blue eyes that reminded him of a little doll. She was better than any doll though for she seemed to have happiness running through her, her ready smile lit up her whole face and her laugh was so infectious all the McClusky boys would nearly jump through hoops to amuse her. 'I will be the best brother I know how to be,' Barry said earnestly. 'I was already fed up of being the youngest.'

Mary laughed and tousled Barry's hair. 'I'm sure you will, son,' she said, 'and she will love you dearly.'

And Angela did. Between her and Barry there was a special closeness though she loved all the boys she thought of as brothers and all were kind and gentle with her.

However the farm didn't thrive. A blight damaged most of the potato crop, and heavy and sustained storms left them with barely half of the hay they would need for the winter, meaning they would have to buy the hay needed from elsewhere, while many cabbages, turnips and swedes were lost to the torrential and ferocious rains that eventually flooded the hen house, resulting in many hens also being lost. That first bad winter they just about managed although empty bellies were often the order of the day and later Barry told Angela she was lucky not to remember those times.

Everyone looked forward to the spring after the second bad winter. Matt and his sons knew that if the spring was going to be a fine one nothing would go awry and with tightened belts they might survive. Matt had a constant frown between his eyes because the weather wasn't good. 'Surely this year will be better than last,' Mary said.

3

Matt's lips tightened. 'We'll see,' he said grimly. 'For if it's not a great deal better we will sink.'

In the early spring of that year a cow died giving birth and the female calf died, a fox got into the hen house and killed most of the hens, and one of the lambs scattered on the hillside was savaged by a dog and had to be put out of his misery. As their finances were on a keen knife edge these things were major blows. Matt knew he would have to leave the farm where he had lived all his life and his father before and his father. That thought was more than upsetting, it was devastating, but he had to face facts. One evening in late March after Angela and Barry had gone to bed and the dinner pots and plates had been put away, Matt and Mary faced their four eldest sons across the table and told them they didn't think they could survive another year.

There was a gasp from Sean and Gerry, but Finbarr and Colm, who helped their father on the farm, were not totally surprised. They knew as well as anyone how badly the farm had been hit, but they still thought their father might have a plan of some sort and it was Finbarr who asked, 'What's to do?'

'We must leave here, that's all,' Matt said.

'Leave the farm?' Sean asked.

'Yes,' Matt affirmed. 'And Ireland too. We must leave Ireland and try our hands elsewhere.'

That shocked all the boys for not even Finbarr thought any plan would involve them all leaving their native land, though Mary, heartsore as she was, knew that was what they had to do.

Finbarr glanced at his brothers' faces and knew he

4

was speaking for all of them when he said, 'We none of us would like that, Daddy. Is there no other way?'

'Aye, the poorhouse if you'd prefer it,' said Matt and he spoke with a snap because leaving was the thing he didn't want to do either. 'They have one in the town.'

At Finbarr's look of distaste, he cried out, 'Do you think this is easy for me? This is where I was born and where I thought I would die. It's my homeland but we can't live on fresh air.' Then he added with an ironic smile, 'Though we have made a good stab at it this year.'

Finbarr knew that well enough and didn't bother commenting, but instead asked, 'But where would we go?'

'Where Norah Docherty has been urging me to go this past year,' Mary said. 'And that's Birmingham, England. She's in a place called Edgbaston and she says it's not far from the city centre and she can put us up until we get straight with our own place and she says she can probably even help you all with jobs.'

Finbarr nodded for they all knew the Dochertys had left Ireland's shore four years before when they were in danger of having to throw themselves on the mercy of the poorhouse to save the children from starving to death. Then an uncle living in Birmingham had offered them all a home with him in exchange for looking after him because he was afraid of being put in the poorhouse too. It was a lifeline for the Docherty family and they had all grasped it with two hands and were packed up and gone lock stock and barrel in no time at all.

Mary knew Norah found the life hard at first for Norah had written and told her that the house was terribly cramped. Her uncle couldn't make the stairs and his bed had to be downstairs. But a man who lived just two doors down called Tim Bishop was the gaffer at a foundry in a place called Aston and he had put a word in for Norah's husband Mick. He had jumped at the job they offered him and Mary said he'd been tired coming home especially at first, for the work was heavy, but then a job was a job and with Birmingham in the middle of a massive slump, to get one at all was great. She said you really needed someone to speak on your behalf to have a chance at all and Norah's uncle had once worked at the same place as Tim Bishop and been well thought of and Tim Bishop approved of the family coming over to see to him in his declining years, for they all knew well the old man's fear of ending up in the poorhouse or the workhouse, as it was commonly known.

'This Tim Bishop Norah speaks of seems to be a grand fellow altogether,' Mary said. 'He had Mick set up in a job before he had been there five minutes. Please God that he may do the same for us.'

'Yeah, but what sort of job?' Colm grumbled. 'Don't know that I would be any good in Birmingham or anywhere else either,' he said. 'The only job I know how to do is farming.'

'Well you can learn to do something else can't you?' Matt barked. 'Same as I'll have to do.'

'We'll all have to learn to do things we're not used to,' Mary said. 'Life is going to be very different to the life we have here but that's how it is and we must all accept it.'

Mary had a way of speaking that brooked no argument,

6

as the boys knew to their cost, and anyway Finbarr knew she made sense and he sighed and said, 'So what happens now?'

'Well travel costs money,' Mary said. 'And that's something we haven't got a lot of, so we sell everything we don't need. Your father has sold all the cattle and even got something for the carcasses of the cow and young calf but it isn't enough. We'll sell everything on the farm because we can hardly take anything but essentials with us anyway.'

Sad days followed as the children watched the only home they had ever known disappearing before their eyes. The neighbours rallied, one took the cart and horse and another took the hens the fox hadn't killed and rounded up the sheep and yet another said he would have the plough and even the tools were sold. It was hard to get rid of the dogs and though Angela could only remember flashes of that time she remembered crying when Matt said the dogs had to go. All were upset. 'They are going to good homes,' Matt promised her and she remembered his husky voice and the way his eyes looked all glittery.

Barry hadn't liked to see the dogs go either but knew he had to be brave for Angela and so he said, 'We can't take dogs to this place Mammy said we're going to, Angela, so they have got to stop here.'

'They'd hardly like it in Birmingham anyway,' Mary said. 'Their place is here.'

'I thought mine was,' Gerry said.

'Gerry, you're too old to moan about something that can't be changed,' Mary said sharply. 'What can't be cured must be endured – you know that.'

'Who's having the table?' Barry asked.

'The person who has bought the cottage,' Mary said. 'That's Peter Murphy and he asked me to leave the table and chairs, my pots and all, the easy chairs, stools and settle, the butter churn and the press and all the beds. I was happy to do it and he gave me a good, fair price for them too.'

'Funny to think of someone living here when we've gone,' Gerry said.

'I suppose,' Mary said. 'But I'd rather someone was getting the good out of it than it just falling to wrack and ruin.'

They all agreed with that but when they assembled the following Saturday very very early that late April morning Mary looked at their belongings packed in two battered cases and two large bass bags and her heart felt as heavy as lead. She wasn't the only one. As they left the farmhouse for the last time they all felt strange not to see the clucking hens dipping their heads to eat the grit between the cobbles outside the cottage door, nor to hear the barking of the dogs. As they made their way to the head of the lane where the neighbour who bought the horse and cart would be waiting for them to take them down to the rail bus station in the town, they missed seeing the horse and cows sharing the field to one side and to the other side of the lane the tilled and furrowed fields, now bare with nothing planted in them. They missed seeing the sheep on the hillside pulling relentlessly on the grass.

Sad though they were to leave, the children were also slightly excited, but Mary's excitement was threaded through with trepidation for she had never gone far from home before, none of them had, and she looked at the youngsters' eager though slightly nervous faces and hoped to God they were doing the right thing.

All knew where the McCluskys were bound and even at that early hour some neighbours had come to see them off and wish them God speed and their good wishes almost reduced Mary to tears as she hugged the women and shook hands with the men and led the way on to the rail bus where she and Matt got them all settled in.

They were soon off, the little rail bus was eating up the miles, but it was only the start of the long journey to Birmingham. They would leave the rail bus at a place called Strabane and from there get a train to the docks at Belfast. Then a boat would take them across the sea to Liverpool where another train would take them from there to Birmingham. The rail journey to Strabane had begun to pall but they all perked up a bit when it was time to board the boat.

Mary was very nervous of going up the gangplank and once on deck the way the boat seemed to list from one side to another was very unnerving, but what worried her most was the safety of the children. Not the older boys, they should be all right, but it was Barry and little Angela she was concerned about. What if one of them was to fall overboard? Oh God, that didn't bear thinking about!

She didn't express her fears, she knew the boys would only laugh at her, but she said to Finbarr and Colm, 'You make sure you look after Barry and Angela. Make sure you keep them safe,' knowing they would more than likely want to explore the ship. Her gallivanting days were over and she was finding it hard enough to keep her balance now and they hadn't even set off yet.

'I don't need anyone to look after me,' Barry declared. 'I can look after myself.'

'You'll do as you are told,' Mary said sharply to Barry. 'And you mind what Finbarr and Colm say.'

Barry made a face behind his mother's back and Finbarr clipped his ear for his disrespect. 'Ow,' he said holding his ear and glaring at Finbarr.

'Never mind "ow",' Finbarr said. 'You behave or we'll not take you anywhere. We'll just take Angela because she always does as she is told.'

'Yes,' Colm said, 'you'd like to see around the ship wouldn't you, Angela?'

Angela wasn't sure, it looked a big and scary place to her, but she knew by the way the question was asked what Colm wanted her to say so she nodded her head slowly and said, 'I think so.'

Barry said nothing more because he definitely did want to see over the ship and Finbarr could be quite stern sometimes and he knew his Mammy would never let him go on his own. Anyway he hadn't time to worry about it because the call came for those not travelling on the boat to disembark and exhilaration filled him for he knew they would soon be on their way. Finbarr put Angela up on his shoulder because she couldn't see over the rail and from there she watched those wishing to disembark scurry down the gangplank to stand on the quayside and wave as the sailors raised the gangplank and hauled in the thick ropes that had attached the ship to round things on the quayside that Finbarr told her were bollards. Then the ship's hooter gave such a screech Angela nearly jumped off Finbarr's shoulder. The ship's engines began to throb and Finbarr lifted her down and Angela felt the whole deck vibrate through her feet as the ship moved slowly out to sea.

Matt and Mary joined the children at the rail as they watched the shores of Ireland slip away and Mary suddenly felt quite emotional, for she had never had any inclination to leave her native land. The sigh she gave was almost imperceptible, but Matt heard it and he put his gnarled, work-worn hand over Mary's on the deck rail. 'We'll make it work,' he said to her. 'We've made a right decision, the only decision, and we will have a good living there, you just see if we don't.'

Mary was unable to speak, but she turned her hand over and squeezed Matt's. It was hard for him too for farming was all he knew, but he was a hard worker and had always been a good provider, and she had a good pair of hands on her too. She swallowed the lump in her throat and said, 'I know we will, Matt, I'm not worried about that.'

And while the children went off to explore they stood together side by side and watched the shore of Ireland fade into the distance.

Mary was to find that she wasn't a very good sailor though the children seemed unaffected and wolfed down the bread and butter Mary had brought. It had been a long time since that very early breakfast, but Mary could eat nothing and Matt ate only sparingly. Mary thought that he had probably done that so that the children could eat their fill rather than any queasiness on his part.

Mary was very glad to leave the boat and be on dry

land again, but she was bone weary and it would be another couple of hours before they would reach Birmingham. All the children were tired and before the train journey was half-way through Angela climbed on to Mary's lap and fell fast asleep. She slept deeply as the train sped through the dusky evening and did not even stir when it pulled up at New Street Station. Oh how glad Mary was to see a familiar face as she stepped awkwardly from the train, for Mick Docherty was waiting with a smile of welcome on his lips. He was unable to shake Mary's hand for she had Angela in her arms. But he shook hands with Matt and the children one by one, even Barry, much to his delight.

He led the way to the exit and Mary was glad of that for she had never seen so many people gathered together. The noise was incredible, so many people talking, laughing, the tramp of many feet, thundering trains hurtling into the station to stop with a squeal of brakes and a hiss of steam, steam that rose in the air and swirled all around them smelling of soot. There was a voice over her head trying to announce something and someone shouting, she presumed selling the papers he had on the stall beside him, but she couldn't understand him. Porters with trolleys piled high with luggage weaved between the crowds urging people to, 'Mind your backs please.'

'We'll take a tram,' Mick said as he led the way to the exit. 'We could walk, and though it's only a step away, I should say you're weary from travelling. Yon young one is anyway,' he went on, indicating Angela slumbering in Mary's arms.

'Aye. And little wonder at it,' Matt said. 'We've been on the go since early morning and I'm fair jiggered myself.'

'Aye, I remember I was the same,' Mick said. 'Well you can seek your bed as soon as you like, we keep no late hours here, but Norah has a big pan of stew on the fire and another of potatoes in case you are hungry after your journey.'

The boys were very pleased to hear that. They had hoped that somewhere there might be food in the equation, but now they were out of the station on the street and no one said anything, only stood and stared for they had never seen so much traffic in the whole of their lives. Mary was staggered. She'd thought a Fair Day in Donegal Town had been busy, but it was nothing like this with all these vehicles packed onto the road together. Hackney cabs ringed the station and beyond them there were horse-drawn vans and carts mixed with a few of the petrol-driven vehicles she had heard about but never seen and bicycles weaved in and out among the traffic. A sour acrid smell hit the back of her throat and there was a constant drone, the rumble of the carts, the clip clopping of the horses' hooves sparking on the cobbles of the streets mixed with the shouts and chatter of the very many people thronging the pavements.

And then they all saw the tram and stopped dead. They could never have imagined anything like it, a clattering, swaying monster with steam puffing from its funnel in front and they saw it ran on shiny rails set into the road. Getting closer it sounded its hooter to warn people to get off the rails and out of the way and Mary found herself both fascinated and repelled by it. 'That's good,' Mick said as he led them to a tram stop just a little way from the hackney cabs, 'we've had no wait at all.'

13

'Yes,' Mary said, 'but is it safe?'

Mick laughed. 'It's safe enough,' he said. 'Though I had my doubts when I came over first.'

Mary mounted gingerly, helped by the boys because she still had the child in her arms. She was glad to sit for even a short journey though she slid from side to side on the wooden seat for Angela was a dead weight in her arms. It seemed no time at all before Mick was saying, 'This is ours, Bristol Street.' And once they had all alighted from the tram he pointed up the road as he went on, 'We go up this alleyway called Bristol Passage and nearly opposite us is Grant Street.'

Mary saw a street of houses such as she never knew existed, not as homes for people – small, mean houses packed tight against their neighbours and Mary felt her spirit fall to her boots for she never envisaged herself living in anything so squalid. The cottage she had left was whitewashed every winter, the thatch replaced as and when necessary and the cottage door and the one for the byre and the windowsills painted every other year, and she scrubbed her white stone step daily.

She could not say anything of course nor even show any sign of distaste. One of these was the house of her friend, besides which she didn't know how things worked here. Maybe in this teeming city of so many people houses were in short supply.

She hadn't time to ponder much about this as Norah had obviously been watching out and had come dinning down the road to throw her arms around Mary, careful not to disturb Angela, but her smile included them all as she ushered them back to the house. 'I have food for you all,' she said, but added to Mary, 'What will you do with the wee one?'

'I think she is dead to the world,' Mary said. 'I see little point in waking her. She'd probably be a bit like a weasel if I tried. She hates being woken up from a deep sleep.'

'Oh don't we all?'

'Yes,' Mary agreed. 'I suppose I'd hate it just as much. So if you show me where she is to sleep, I'll take her straight up.'

'That will be the attic,' Norah said. 'And you, Mick, get those boys sat around the table with a bowl of stew before they pass out on us.' The boys sighed with relief and busied themselves sorting chairs around the table as Norah opened up the door against the wall and led the way up the two flights of stairs to the attic. There was a bed to one side, a chest and set of drawers, and a mattress laid on the floor. 'That will do you two and Angela,' Norah said. 'The boys I'm afraid will have to sleep elsewhere for now.'

Mary was completely nonplussed at this though she knew Norah had made a valid point for she had four children of her own and the walls were not made of elastic. 'Where will they sleep then?'

'In Tim Bishop's place,' Norah said. 'You know I told you he got the job for Mick?'

'Oh yes,' Mary said as she laid Angela down on the mattress and began removing her shoes. 'Where does he live?'

'Just two doors down,' Norah said.

'I suppose it's him we shall have to talk to anyway about a job for Matt.'

15

'Of course, I never told you Tim died last year.'

That took the wind right out of Mary's sails because she had sort of relied on this Tim Norah had spoken so highly of to do something for them too and it might be more difficult for them than it had been for Mick Docherty. But a more pressing problem was where her sons were going to lay their heads that night. 'So whose house is it now?'

'His son Stan has it,' Mary said. 'Tim died a year ago and before he died he gave permission for Stan to marry a lovely girl called Catherine Gaskell. They had been courting, but they were only young, but unless they were married or almost married when his father died, Stan as a single man wouldn't have had a claim on the house. Anyway they married and sheer willpower I think kept Tim alive to see that wedding for he died just three days later and now Stan and Kate have an unused attic and the boys can sleep there.'

'I couldn't ask that of perfect strangers.'

'They're not perfect strangers, not to me,' Norah said. 'They're neighbours and I didn't ask them, they offered when I said you were coming over and I couldn't imagine where the boys were going to sleep. Stan said he's even got a double mattress from somewhere. Anyway I can't see any great alternative. Can you?'

Mary shook her head. 'No and I am grateful for all you have done for us, but I'd rather not have Barry there. He is only seven and for now can share the mattress with us and let's hope Matt gets a job and we get our own place sooner rather than later.'

'I'll say,' Norah said. 'And you can ask Stan about the job situation because he's the Gaffer now. Apparently

Mr Baxter who is the overall Boss said there was no need to advertise for someone else when Stan had been helping his dad out for years. So if anyone can help you out it's him.'

That cheered Mary up a bit. And she did find Stan a very nice and helpful young man when she saw him later that evening. He had sandy hair and eyes and an honest open face, a full generous mouth and a very pleasant nature all told, but Mary did wonder because he was so young whether he would have as much influence as his father had had.

Still she supposed if he agreed to put in a word for Matt and the boys, for only Barry and Gerry were school age, the others could work and if he could help them all it would be wonderful, but only time would tell.

TWO

Every morning for the whole of her short life Angela had woken early to the cock crow. She would pad across to the window and listen to the dogs barking as they welcomed the day and the lowing of the cows as they were driven back to the fields from the milking shed. When she dressed and went into the kitchen the kettle would be singing on the fire beside the porridge bubbling away in the pot and the kitchen would be filled with noise, for her father and brothers would be in from the milking after they had sluiced their hands under the pump in the yard and thick creamy porridge would be poured into the bowls with more milk and sugar to add to the porridge if wanted. It was warm and familiar.

The first morning in Birmingham she woke and was surprised to see Danny beside her for she couldn't remember that ever happening before and she slipped out of bed, but the window was too high for her to see out of. She wondered if anyone else was awake because she was very hungry. She wandered back to bed and was delighted to see Barry's deep-brown eyes open and looking at her. 'Hello.'

'Ssh,' Barry cautioned. 'Everyone but us is asleep.'

Angela thought Barry meant just their Mammy and Daddy and then she saw the children lying on the other mattress. She couldn't remember the Dochertys from when they lived in Donegal but she remembered Mammy telling her they had four children now. And so she lowered her voice and said, 'I'm ever so hungry, Barry.'

Barry didn't doubt it because Angela had had none of the delicious supper him and the others had eaten the previous evening and he was hungry enough again, so he reckoned Angela must be starving. 'Get your clothes on,' he whispered. 'Not your shoes. Carry them in your hand and we'll go downstairs.'

'What if no one's up?'

'They will be soon,' Barry said confidently. 'It's Sunday and everyone will be going to Mass.'

'Is it? It doesn't feel like a Sunday.'

'That's because everything's different here,' Barry said. 'Hurry up and get ready.'

They crept down the stairs quietly holding their shoes, but there was no kettle boiling on the range, nor any sign of activity, and no wonder for the time on the clock said just six o'clock. On the farm the milking would have all been done by that time, but in a city it seemed six o'clock on a Sunday is the time for laying in bed. And then he remembered there might be no breakfast at all because they were likely taking communion and no one could eat or drink before that. It wouldn't affect Angela, nor he imagined the two youngest Dochertys, Sammy and Siobhan, whom he'd met the night before. They were only five and six, but the other two, Frankie and Philomena, were older. He had no need to fast either for he hadn't made his First Holy Communion yet. Had he stayed in Ireland he would have made it in June, but here he wasn't sure if it would be the same. It did mean though he could eat that morning and he searched the kitchen, which wasn't hard to do since it was so tiny and, finding bread in the bin, he cut two chunks from one of the loaves, spread it with the butter he'd found on the slab and handed one to Angela.

But Angela just looked at him with her big blue eyes widened. 'Here, take it,' he said.

'It must be wrong,' she cried. 'We'll get into trouble.'

'I might get into trouble but you won't,' Barry assured Angela. 'But you must eat something because you have had nothing since the bread and butter in the boat dinner time yesterday. We had stew last night but you were too sleepy and Mammy put you to bed, so you must eat something and that's what I'll say if anyone is cross. You won't be blamed so take it.'

He held the bread out again and this time Angela took it and when she crammed it in her mouth instead of eating it normally Barry realized just how hungry she had been and he poured her a glass of milk from the jug he had found with the butter on the slab to go with it. 'Now you've got a milk moustache,' he said with a smile.

Angela scrubbed at her mouth with her sleeve and then said to Barry, 'Now what shall we do?'

'Well, it doesn't seem as if anyone is getting up,' Barry said, for it was as quiet as the grave upstairs when he had a listen at the door. 'So how about going and having a look round the place we are going to be living in?'

'Oh yes, I'd like that.'

'Get your shoes on then and we'll go,' Barry said.

A little later when Barry opened the front door Angela stood on the step and stared. For all she could see were houses. Houses all down the hill as far as she could see. She stepped into the street and saw her side of the street was the same. And she couldn't see any grass anywhere. There had been other houses in Ireland dotted here and there on the hillside, but the only thing attached to their cottage was the byre and the barn beyond that. There wasn't another house in sight and you would have to go to the head of the lane to see any other houses at all. To see so many all stacked up tight together was very strange.

'Where do you go to the toilet here?' Angela asked, suddenly feeling the urge to go.

'Down the yard,' Barry said. 'I'll show you. Mr Docherty took me down the yard last night, we need a key.'

He nipped back into the house to get it before taking Angela's hand and together they went down to the entry of the yard. As Barry had seen in the dark, now she also saw that six houses opened on the grey cobbled yard and crisscrossing washing lines were pushed high into the sooty air by tall props.

Barry said, 'Norah told us last night some women wash for other people. Posh people, you know, because it's a way of making money and they have washing out every day of the week except Sunday. And this is the Brewhouse where Mick says all the washing gets done,' he added as they went past a brick building with a corrugated tin roof.

The weather-beaten wooden door was ajar and leaning drunkenly because it was missing its top hinges. Angela peeped inside and wrinkled her nose. 'It smells of soap.'

'Well it would be odd if it smelled of anything else,' Barry said, 'and these two bins we're passing have to be shared by the Dochertys and two other families. One is for ashes, called a miskin, and the black one is for other rubbish.'

'Don't you think it's an odd way of going on?' Angela asked.

Barry nodded. 'I do,' he said in agreement. 'And you haven't seen the toilets yet, they're right at the bottom of the yard and two other families have to share them as well. They have a key to go in and you must lock it up afterwards. The key is always kept on a hook by the door.'

Angela found it was just as Barry said and as she sat on the bare wooden seat and used the toilet she reflected that Mammy had been right, they had an awful lot of things to get used to.

Stopping only to put the key back on its hook, the two started to walk down the slope towards Bristol Street and Barry wondered what Angela was thinking. He'd had a glimpse of the area as he had walked up Grant Street with everyone else the previous evening. He didn't think they looked very nice houses, all built of blue-grey brick, three storeys high with slate roofs and they stood on grey streets and behind them were grey yards. He didn't think his mother had been impressed either, but she had covered the look of dismay Barry had glimpsed before anyone else had seen it.

So he wasn't surprised at Angela's amazement as she looked from one side to the other. 'There's lots of houses aren't there Barry?' she said as they started to go down Bristol Passage.

'Yeah, but this is a city and lots of people live in a city and they all have to have houses.'

'Yes, I suppose,' Angela said.

'D'you think you'll like living here?' he said as they strode along Bristol Street. Despite it being still quite early on a Sunday morning there were already some horse-drawn carts and petrol lorries on the road and a clattering tram passed them, weaving along its shiny rails. There were plenty of shops too, all shut up and padlocked. Angela said, 'I don't know.'

'It's all strange here isn't it? Not a bit like home.'

'No, no it isn't.'

'Tell you what though,' Barry said. 'This is probably going to be our home now, not Mr and Mrs Docherty's house, but this area. So I'm going to make sure I like it. Don't do no good being miserable if you've got to live here anyway.'

That made sense to Angela but Barry always seemed to be able to explain things to her so she understood them better. 'And me,' she said.

'Good girl,' Barry said with a beam of approval and he reached for her hand as he said, 'We best go back now because we'll probably be going to an early Mass and we daren't be too late.'

Everyone was up at the Dochertys' and Mary asked

24

where they had both been and would have gone for Barry when he attempted to explain, but Norah forestalled her. 'It was obvious Angela would wake early,' she said to Mary, 'because she had her sleep out and it was good of Barry to take her downstairs and let us have a bit of a lie in.'

'But to take food without asking!'

'Well he couldn't ask me without waking me up first and that wouldn't have pleased me at all,' Norah pointed out and added with a little laugh, 'It was just a bit of bread and it's understandable that Angela would be hungry. Don't be giving out to them their first morning here.'

'I was starving,' Angela said with feeling.

'Course you were,' Norah said. 'You hadn't eaten for hours.'

Barry let out a little sigh of relief, very grateful to Mrs Docherty for saving him from the roasting he was pretty sure he had been going to get from his mother, and when she said, 'Anyway come up to the table now for I have porridge made for you two and Sammy and Siobhan,' the day looked even better.

St Catherine's Catholic Church was just along Bristol Street, no distance at all, and Norah pointed out Bow Street off Bristol Street where the entrance to the school was. 'I will be away to see about it tomorrow,' Mary said. 'I hope they have room for Barry and Gerry for I don't like them missing time. Wish I could get Angela in too because she's more than ready for school.'

'I thought that with Siobhan and was glad to get her

in in September,' Norah said. 'I think when they have older ones they bring the young ones on a bit.'

'You could be right,' Norah said. 'I know our Angela is like a little old woman sometimes, the things she comes out with.'

'Oh I know exactly what you mean,' Mary said with feeling. 'Mind I wouldn't be without them and I did miss the boys last night. Be glad to see them at Mass this morning.'

The boys were waiting for them in the porch and they gave their anxious mother a good account of Stan Bishop and his wife Kate, who they said couldn't have been kinder to them. That eased Mary's mind for her children had never slept apart from her in a different house altogether and she thought it a funny way to go on, but the only solution in the circumstances.

After Mass, Norah introduced them to the priest, Father Brannigan, and he was as Irish as they were. Mary's stomach was growling embarrassingly with hunger and she hoped he couldn't hear it. She also hoped meeting him wouldn't take long so she could go home and eat something, but she knew it was important to be friendly with the priest, especially if you wanted a school place for your children. Matt understood that as well as she did and they answered all the questions the priest asked as patiently as possible.

It might have done some good though, because when he heard the two families were living in a cramped back-to-back house with the older boys farmed out somewhere else, he said he'd keep his ear to the ground for them.

'Well telling the priest your circumstances can't do any harm anyway,' Norah said. 'Priests often get to know things before others.'

'No harm at all,' Mary agreed. 'Glad he didn't go on too long though or I might have started on the chair leg. Just at the moment my stomach thinks my throat's been cut.'

It was amazing how life slipped into a pattern, so that living with the Dochertys and eating in shifts became the norm. Gerry and Barry were accepted into St Catherine's School and went there every day with all the Docherty children and Angela was on the waiting list for the following year when she would be five. Better still, Stan Bishop said he could get Sean into the apprentice scheme to be a toolmaker and Gerry could join him in two years' time, and he could find a labouring job for Matt the same as Mick, so that by the beginning of June the two men and the boy Sean were soon setting off to work together.

Sadly, Stan could find nothing for the two older boys who were too old for the apprentice scheme, which had to be started at fourteen, and there was no job for them in the foundry. They were disappointed but not worried. It wasn't like living in rural Donegal. Industrial Birmingham was dubbed the city of one thousand trades and just one job in any trade under the sun would suit Finbarr and Colm down to the ground.

So they did the round of the factories as Stan advised, beginning in Deritend because it was nearest to the city centre and moving out to Aston where the foundry was.

They started with such high hopes that surely they would be taken on somewhere soon. 'The trick,' Stan said, 'is to have plenty of strings to your bow. Don't go to the same factory every day because they'll just get fed up with you but don't leave it so long that they've forgotten who you are if they have given you any work before. And if you're doing no good at the factories go down to the railway station and offer to carry luggage. It's nearly summer and posh folk go away and might be glad of a hand and porters are few and far between. Or,' he added, 'go to the canal and ask if they want any help operating the locks or legging the boats through the tunnels.'

'What's that mean, "legging through the tunnel"?'

'You'll find out soon enough if they ask you to do it,' Stan said with a smile. 'Just keep going and something will turn up I'm sure.'

They kept going, there was nothing else to do, but sometimes they brought so little home. Everything they made they gave to their mother but sometimes it was very little and sometimes nothing at all. They felt bad about it, but Mary never said a word, as she knew they were trying their best, and while they were living with the Dochertys money went further, for they shared the rent and the money for food and coal. But she knew it might be a different story if ever they were to move into their own place.

However, that seemed as far away as jobs for her sons, but life went on regardless. Barry did make his First Holy Communion with the others in his class, and not long after it was the school holidays and they had a brilliant summer playing in the streets with the other children. Mary wasn't really happy with it, but there was nowhere else for them to play. Anyway all the other mothers seemed not to mind their children playing in the streets, but she was anxious something might happen to Angela. 'You see to her, Barry,' she said.

'I will,' Barry said. 'But she can't stay on her own in the house. It isn't fair. Let her play with the others and I'll see nothing happens to her.'

'Don't know what you're so worried about,' Norah said. 'That lad of yours will hardly let the wind blow on Angela.'

'I know,' Mary said. 'He's been like that since Angela first came into the house, as if he thought it was his responsibility to look after her. He's a good lad is Barry and Angela adores him.'

'He's going to make a good father when the time comes I'd say,' Norah said.

'Aye. Please God,' Mary said.

Angela thought it was great to be surrounded by friends as soon as she stepped into the street. She had been a bit isolated at the farm. Funny that she never realized that before, but having plenty of friends was another thing she decided she liked about living in Birmingham.

Christmas celebrated by two families in the confines of one cramped back-to-back house meant there was no room at all, but plenty of fun and laughter. There was food enough, for the women had pooled resources and bought what they could, but there was little in the way of presents for there was no spare money. Many of the boots, already cobbled as they were, had to be soled and heeled and Mary took up knitting again and taught Norah. The wool they got from buying old cheap woollen garments at the Rag Market to unravel and knit up again so that the families could have warmer clothes for winter.

January proved bitterly cold. Day after day snow fell from a leaden grey sky and froze overnight, so in the morning there was frost formed on the inside of windows in those draughty houses. Icicles hung from the sills, ice scrunched underfoot and ungloved fingers throbbed with cold.

Life was harder still for Finbarr and Colm toiling around the city in those harsh conditions to try and find a job of any sort to earn a few pennies to take home. So many factory doors were closed in their faces and when the cold eventually drove them home they would huddle over the fire to still their shivering bones and feel like abject failures. No one could help and neither of them knew what they were going to do to help ease the situation for the family.

Slowly the days began to get slightly warmer as Easter approached. Angela would be going to school in the new term and she was so excited. She was just turned five when she walked alongside Mary for her first full day at school on April 15th. She was so full of beans it was like they were jumping around inside her. At the school she was surrounded by other boys and girls all starting together and they regarded each other shyly. When their mothers had gone their teacher, Miss Conway, took them into the classroom, which she said would be their classroom, and told them where to sit.

Angela was almost speechless with delight when she realized she had a desk and chair all to herself. After living with the Dochertys for months, she was used to sharing everything. She looked around and noticed what a lot of desks there were in the room, which was large with brown wooden walls and very high windows with small panes. There were some pictures, one with numbers on it, one with letters, and a map above the blackboard that stood in front of the high teacher's desk.

Another little girl was assigned the desk next to Angela and she turned to look at her, envying the pinafore she wore covering her dress. In fact most of the girls wore pinafores but her Mammy said funds didn't run to pinafores and she knew better than to make a fuss over something like that. The girl had straight black hair that fell to her shoulders and dark brown eyes, but her lips looked a bit wobbly as if she might be about to cry and her face looked as if she was worried about something, so Angela smiled at her and the little girl gasped. What the little girl thought was that she'd never seen anyone so beautiful with the golden curls and the deep blue eyes and pretty little mouth and nose. Spring sunshine shafted through the tiny windows at that moment and it was like a halo around Angela's head. 'Oh,' said the little girl with awe. 'You look like an angel.'

Angela laughed, bringing the teacher's eyes upon her. She thought maybe laughing wasn't allowed at school and she was to find that it wasn't much approved of.

Nor was talking, for when she tried whispering to the other girl, 'I'm not an angel, I just look like my mother,' the teacher rapped the top of her desk with a ruler, making most children in the room jump. 'No talking,' she rapped out and Angela hissed out of the corner of her mouth, 'Tell you after.'

And later, in the playground, she told the whole story of how she ended up living with the McCluskys, according to what Mary had told her. 'Funny you thought I looked like an angel,' she said. 'Because my real mammy thought so too and she insisted I was called Angela. All the others looked like my father.'

'And they all died,' the girl said. 'And your mammy and daddy as well?'

Angela gave a brief nod and the other girl said, 'I think that's really sad.'

Angela shook her head. 'It isn't really, because I can't remember them at all. Mammy, I mean Mary, has a photograph of them on their wedding day. It was stood on the dresser at home and I suppose it will come out again when we have our own house, but I have stared at it for ages and just don't remember them. And Mary and Matt McClusky have loved me as much as if I had been one of their own children and the boys are like brothers to me.'

'Huh,' said the other girl, 'I have no time for brothers. I have two, both younger than me, and a proper nuisance they are.'

Angela laughed and said, 'What's your name?'

'Maggie. Maggie Maguire and my brothers are called Eddie and Patrick. But I think Mammy is having another one and that will probably be a boy as well. I'd love a sister.'

'So would I,' Angela admitted. 'Shall we just be good friends instead?'

'Yes, let's.' And so a bond was formed between Angela Kennedy and Maggie Maguire from that first day.

THREE

Just after Angela began school, the priest heard of a house that would shortly be vacant due to the death of the tenant and Mary went straight down to see the landlord. She took her marriage lines with her and the birth certificates of the children and to prove her honesty she carried a recommendation from the priest and she secured the house, which was in Bell Barn Road and only yards from Maggie's house in Grant Street.

Mary was delighted to get a place of her own though she did wonder how she would furnish it, but when she said this to Matt he had a surprise for her. 'With the sale of the farm and land I had money over when I bought the tickets to get here,' he told her. 'Not knowing when I would get a job when we arrived, I put it in the Post Office and it's still there, so we'll go off to the Bull Ring Saturday afternoon and see what we can pick up to make the place more homely at a reasonable price.'

Mary was really pleased that Matt had kept the money safe and that he had kept knowledge of it to himself as well, or she might have been tempted to dip into it from time to time, and where would they be now if she had done that? They'd have a house but not a stick of furniture to go into it.

In fact it wouldn't have been that bad because the previous tenant had died and his family didn't want much of his furniture, so the house already had two armchairs, a small settee and a sideboard downstairs, and a bed and wardrobes were left in the bedroom upstairs. Norah went to inspect the house and agreed with Mary it needed a thoroughly good clean before anything else and they undertook that together. In the Bull Ring Mary and Matt bought oilcloth for the floor, a big iron-framed bed for the boys in the attic and two chests for their clothes. For Angela there was a truckle bed that was to be set up in the bedroom because Mary declared it wasn't seemly for her to share the attic with so many boys when she was not even officially related to them.

The purchases severely depleted Matt's savings and money from day to day was tighter than ever and Norah was finding it hard to make the money stretch. If some days they seemed to eat a lot of porridge it was because a pair of boots needed repair or there was a delivery of coal to pay for. Mary worried about the meals often. 'Men need more than porridge,' she said to Norah. 'If Finbarr and Colm do get a job they'll hardly be able for it and Matt works hard now and needs good food or he might take sick.'

Sometimes she would take Angela with her when she went to the Bull Ring on a Saturday afternoon and she would hide away and send Angela into the butcher's and ask for a bone for the dog. The butcher knew there was little likelihood of there being any sort of dog; most people had trouble enough feeding themselves. But he would be charmed by the look of Angela, her winning smile and good manners, and she usually came out with a bone with lots of meat still on it. Often the butcher would slip her something else, like a few pieces of liver, or a small joint because he would have to throw them away anyway at the end of the day.

And Mary would boil up the bones and strip them of meat for a stew along with vegetables and dumplings to fill hungry men. She would do the same with pigs' trotters if she had the pennies to buy them. She could make a couple of loaves of soda bread almost without thinking about it and if there was no money for butter, mashed swede would do as well. Cabbage soup was also on the menu a lot so though no one starved, the monotony of the diet got to everyone, but no one complained for there was little point.

Finbarr and Colm were filled with shame that they couldn't do more to help and knowing this, Gerry felt almost embarrassed to join Sean on the apprenticeship scheme in 1902 when he turned fourteen and left school. 'Don't feel bad about it,' Finbarr said. 'You go for it. I would do the same given half a chance.'

Both apprentice boys were full of praise for Stan Bishop and thought he was a first-rate boss, always patient with them if they made mistakes in the early days. 'He's a decent man,' Mary said. 'I always thought it.'

'He's a happy bloke, I know that,' Sean said. 'He's always humming a tune under his breath and he sings at home.'

'He does that,' Colm said. 'He's good, or it sounds all right to me anyway, and Kate has a lovely voice.'

'Well she's in the choir,' Mary pointed out. 'That's why they always go to eleven o'clock Mass. She sometimes sings when she is in the house on her own because I have heard her a time or two when I have been up visiting Norah. She has got a lovely voice, but then she seems a lovely person. She always seems to have a smile on her face.'

She had. It was evident to everyone how happily married they were and there was speculation why there had been no sign of a child yet, though Mary had confided to Norah that she thought Kate looked rather frail. 'I don't think it would do her good to have a houseful of children,' she said. 'It would pull the body out of her.'

'We none of us can do anything about that though,' Norah said. 'It's God's will. The priests will tell you that you must be grateful for whatever God sends, be it one or two or a round dozen.'

'I know,' Mary said and added, 'They're quick enough to give advice. But no one helps provide for those children, especially with jobs the way they are.'

'I know,' Norah said. 'And then wages are not so great either. I mean, my man's in work and I am hard pressed to make ends meet sometimes. At least Sean and Gerry are learning a trade, that's lucky.'

'Aye, if there is a job at the end of it.'

'There's the rub,' Norah said, because many firms would take on apprentices on low pay and get rid of them when they were qualified and could command far better wages, and take on another lot to train as it was cheaper for them.

'I'm not looking that far ahead,' Mary said. 'I'll worry about it if it happens. As for Kate Bishop, she seems not to be able to conceive one so easy, so I doubt they'll ever be that many eventually.'

'Don't be too sure,' Norah said. 'I've seen it before. They have trouble catching for one and then as if the body knows what to do, they pop another out every year or so.'

'Proper Job's comforter you are,' Mary said and added with a smile, 'Are you going to put the kettle on or what? A body could die of thirst in this place.'

There was no change in the McClusky household over the next couple of years. Sean, now halfway through his apprenticeship, got a rise, but it was nothing much, and Matt too was earning more so the purse strings eased, but only slightly. Towards the end of that year, Norah told Mary she was sure Kate Bishop was pregnant. There was a definite little bump that hadn't been there before. By the turn of the year Stan was nearly shouting it from the rooftops and though he was like a dog with two tails, Kate was having a difficult pregnancy and was sick a lot and not just for the first three months, like the morning sickness many women suffered from.

Many women gave her advice of things they had tried themselves, or some old wives' tale they had heard about, for all the women agreed with Mary that Kate Bishop couldn't afford to lose weight for she had none to lose. She was due at Easter and she hardly looked pregnant as the time grew near. 'God!' Mary said to Norah. 'I was like a stranded whale with all of mine. I do hope that girl is all right. I saw her the other day and couldn't believe it, her wrists and arms are very skinny and her skin looks sort of thin.'

'She's still singing every Sunday morning though,' Norah said. 'And she practises through the day, does her scales and everything.'

'I suppose it helps keep her mind off things.'

'Maybe. Can't be long now though.'

On the fifteenth of April Kate Bishop's pains began in the early hours and though Stan had engaged a nurse, it was soon apparent that the services of a doctor were needed and he booked an ambulance, and while he was waiting for it to come Kate had a massive haemorrhage and died.

Stan was distraught at losing his beloved wife and he couldn't cope with his new-born son. Both Mary and Norah were often in the house with Stan, mainly caring for the baby and making meals for Stan he had no appetite to eat. Sometimes he seemed almost unaware of their presence and both Mary and Norah felt quite helpless that they could do nothing to ease Stan's pain and were glad when Kate's older sister Betty arrived.

She was married to Roger Swanage and though they lived in a nice house that Roger had inherited from his widowed mother, still they had no children though Betty had been trying for years to conceive. She took charge of Stan's son and Roger took it upon himself to organize the funeral for Kate because Stan seemed incapable, though he did insist on choosing the hymns because Kate had favourites and he chose those.

Betty seemed surprised at the numbers who turned out for the funeral but Kate had been popular and very young to lose her life in that tragic way, so the church was packed, including many men, as the foundry was closed that day as a mark of respect. Even those not going to the Mass stood at their doorways in silence as the cart carrying the coffin passed, some making the sign of the cross, and any men on the road removed their hats and stood with bowed heads.

The Requiem Mass seemed interminable and Mary heard many sniffs in the congregation as Father Brannigan spoke of the grievous loss of the young woman leaving a child to grow up without a mother's love, and the loss would be felt through the whole community, but particularly by her grieving husband and her family, and the choir where she had been a stalwart member. Eventually it was over and the congregation moved off to Key Hill Cemetery in Hockley, as St Catherine's didn't have its own cemetery.

The wind had increased during the Mass and it buffeted them from side to side, billowing all around them, and when they stood by the open grave the wind-driven rain attacked them, stabbing at their faces like little needles – a truly dismal day. As the priest intoned further prayers for the dear departed and they began lowering the coffin with ropes, Stan gasped and staggered and would have fallen, but Matt reached out and put a hand upon his shoulder. 'Steady man. Nearly over.' The clods of earth fell with dull thuds on to the lid and they all turned thankfully away and walked back through the gusty, rain-sodden day to the back room of The Swan where a sumptuous feast was laid out, made by the landlord's wife and her two daughters.

Everyone seemed to think that it was right and proper

that Kate's childless sister should rear the motherless child. Even Father Brannigan saw it as an ideal solution when he called to see them a week after the funeral to discuss the child's future and baptism.

'And you are fully prepared to take on the care of the child?' he asked Betty, though his gaze took in Roger too.

It was Betty who answered, 'Oh yes, Father,' she said. 'Kate was my own younger sister and I'm sure she would wish me to do this, and how can I not love her child as if he were my own?'

'And have you children of your own?'

'Sadly no,' Betty said. 'The Lord hasn't seen fit to grant me any and we have a fine house waiting for a child to fill it.'

'Well I think that eminently suitable,' the priest said. 'What of you, Stan? Are you in agreement with this?'

Stan turned vacant eyes on the priest. He wondered how he could explain to the priest, without shocking him to the core, that he cared little for the tiny mite held in Betty's arms so tenderly, the mite his wife had died giving birth to. And he contented himself giving a shrug of his shoulders.

Father Brannigan saw the intense sorrow in his deep eyes and knew for Stan the pain of his loss was too raw to discuss things to do with the child, and so he thought it a good thing his sister-in-law was there. He turned again to Betty. 'And have you chosen names?'

'Yes,' Betty said decidedly. 'I want him called Daniel.'

Stan's head shot up at that and the priest was pretty certain he hadn't known of Betty's plan. And he hadn't, and though he and Kate had discussed names, Daniel hadn't been mentioned, yet Betty said Kate would approve of Daniel. 'It was the name of our late father,' she said to Stan.

Stan hadn't the energy to protest and felt anyway he had no right. Betty was going to raise the child, therefore she should have the right to name that child too. And Betty could be quite right – since it was the name of Kate's father she might have called him Daniel in the end. 'I don't mind what the child is called,' he said, 'but I want Matt and Mary McClusky as godparents.'

Mary was delighted to be asked but she noted the jealous way Betty held on to the child. While she was willing for Mary to take him from her and hold his head over the font so that the priest could dribble water over it, she took him back afterwards and would let no one else, not even his own father, hold him and Mary felt the first stirrings of unease. Stan on the other hand was pleased initially to leave everything to Betty and for Daniel to be taken back to their fine house in Sutton Coldfield after the christening.

'Where is Sutton Coldfield?' Mary asked Matt a few weeks later

'I'm not sure myself,' Matt said. 'I know it's a fair distance and a posh place, so Stan was telling me. He said Betty and Roger live in a big house built of red brick with a blue slate roof. And although it's not on the doorstep it's easy enough to get to because a little steam train runs from New Street Station and then the station in Sutton is just yards from their house.'

'He's going to see him soon isn't he?'

Matt nodded. 'This Saturday afternoon,' he said. 'He'll have been with them nearly three weeks then and he wants to see how he has settled down and everything.'

Later Stan talked to Matt about how it had gone. 'Tell you, Matt, when I saw him, I had the urge to grab him and bring him home where he belongs. But how could I care for him and work? Betty, on the other hand, already has the nursery fitted out for him, which is far more salubrious than any attic bedroom I could provide. There's also a garden back and front and I could see much better surroundings unfolding for Daniel if I left him there with his aunt and uncle, though I know he will probably call them mammy and daddy and will grow up thinking of them as his parents.'

'Like Angela did?'

'Ah but, the difference was she was told from the start who her real parents were and that they had both died, which was the truth, but Daniel has a father, though he will hardly be aware of that.'

'Why not?'

'Because Betty said it would confuse the boy if I kept popping up every now and then, and it wasn't as if I could offer him anything. She told me that if I cared for the boy I should stay out of his life and let them bring him up. The point is I know I can offer the child nothing, but I still wanted to see him, take him out weekends, you know, get to know him a bit, but Betty said if I intended doing that I would have to make alternative arrangements. She would only look after Daniel as long as I stayed away.'

Mary sighed when Matt told her that night what had transpired when Stan had gone to see his son. She wasn't totally surprised. She had thought Betty was the type

44

of person who wouldn't want to share her dead sister's child. In a way in her mind she was probably trying to forget he had parents and make believe that he was her own child she had given birth to.

In Mary's opinion secrets like this were not healthy and they had a way of wriggling to the fore eventually, spreading unhappiness and distrust. 'That's very harsh,' she said. 'I mean at the moment it's hard on Stan, but the longer Betty and her husband leave telling Daniel of his father, the greater the shock for the child. Stan might not be able to care for him and work, but that doesn't mean he can't be part of his life. I think he's a lovely man and I'm sure the child as he grows would benefit from knowing him.'

'I couldn't agree more,' Matt said. 'He said Betty was adamant. I think I might call her bluff in time. If she loves Daniel like he says she'd not want to give him up so easy, but Stan probably won't want to risk it.'

'Does he miss him?'

'I asked him that myself,' Matt said. 'I suppose that what you never had you can't miss but Stan said he always feels like something is missing and he copes because he knows Daniel will be happy and well loved, for Betty dotes on him and her husband does too, only slightly less anxiously. He said he would never have to worry that they would ever be unkind to him and he will want for nothing – no going barefoot with an empty belly for him. As long as the boy is happy that's all that matters to Stan.'

'That's what most parents want,' Mary said. 'Their children's happiness, and he is a decent man for putting the needs of his son before his own.'

Angela was unaware of what had happened to Stan's baby. She knew about the death of his wife giving birth to the child, that couldn't be hidden from the children, but the baby had just seemed to disappear. Even Maggie living only doors away from Stan Bishop knew no more. It was no good asking questions because things like that were not discussed in front of children so the girls concluded the baby must have died too. 'Shame though, isn't it, for Stan to lose his wife and baby.'

'Mm,' Maggie said. 'Though I don't think men are that good at looking after babies.'

'No, maybe not,' Angela agreed. 'I just feel sorry for him being left with nothing. Doesn't seem fair somehow.'

'My mammy says none of life is fair and those that think it is are going to be disappointed over and over,' Maggie said and Angela thought that a very grim way of looking at things.

FOUR

Stan seemed to get over the loss of his wife in the end as everyone must, but for ages a pall of sadness hung over him. Barry started on the apprenticeship scheme in 1907, the same year his brother Sean finished, and Stan's sadness wasn't helped by the news he had to impart to Mary. 'He was heartbroken when he came to tell me that the boys would have no job at the end of their apprenticeships,' Mary told Norah. 'Sean is out of work now like his older brothers and I suppose Gerry will be the same in two years' time. Stan said he could do nothing about it because it was the company's policy. It was a bit of a blow but not a total shock because that sort of thing is happening everywhere.'

'I know but it isn't as if they can get a job somewhere else using the skills they have learnt because there are no jobs.'

'Aye that's the rub,' Mary said. 'And now there'll be another mouth to feed on the pittance they will be able to earn. I mean you can only tighten a belt so far. And when Gerry is finished too in two years' time God knows what we are going to do.'

'I'm the same,' Norah said, 'and this has decided me.'

'What?'

'My eldest Frankie is just eighteen so half-way through his apprenticeship and my brother Aiden was after writing to me, offering to find him a job in the place he works. They're taking a lot of young lads on.'

'But Aiden is in the States?'

'I know, New York.'

'But . . . But surely to God you don't want your son going so far away?'

'Course I don't,' Nora said. 'What I want is for him to get a job somewhere local and meet a nice Catholic girl to marry and give me grandchildren to take joy from. But it's not going to happen, not here. I know when we bid farewell that will be it and I'll never see my son again but I can't deny him this chance of a future. I see your lads day after day worn down by the fact they can get no job. Unemployment is like a living death and how can I put Frankie through that when Aiden is holding out the hand of opportunity to him?'

She couldn't, Mary recognized that, but she knew Norah's heart would break when her eldest son went away from her. And though her own heart ached for her sons she couldn't help feeling glad that they had no sponsor in America.

Unbeknownst to her, though, Finbarr and Colm were very interested in Frankie Docherty's uncle's proposal. 'He seems very certain he will have a job for you,' Finbarr said.

'Yes he is.'

'What line of work is it?'

'Making motor cars.'

Finbarr stared at him. There were a few petrol-driven lorries and vans and commercial vehicles but personal motor cars were only for the very wealthy, they had taken the place of carriages, and Finbarr didn't think even in a country the size of America they would need that many. Frankie's career might be short lived when he got to the States.

Frankie caught sight of Finbarr's sceptical face and he said, 'My Uncle Aiden says that America is not like here and that everyone who is someone wants a motor car. They can't keep up with the demand. And they want to train mechanics too so that they can fix the cars when they go wrong.'

'Right,' Finbarr said. 'You excited?'

Frankie nodded eagerly. 'You bet I am,' he said, and added, 'I have to hide it from Mammy though.'

'I can imagine,' Finbarr said with a smile. 'Well I wish you all the very best and I only wish Colm and I were going along with you.'

'Wouldn't you mind going so far away?'

'Won't you?'

'Of course,' Frankie said. 'I expect to miss my family but that's the choice you have to make, isn't it. And you've got to deal with homesickness otherwise you will waste the chance you've been given.'

'That's pretty sound reasoning, Frankie,' Colm said. 'I imagine I would feel much the same.'

'And me,' said Finbarr.

'Maybe I can get my uncle to speak for you too,' Frankie said. 'He'll know your family for they were neighbours in Donegal and then Mammy helped when you first came over and my mother and yours are as thick as thieves now.'

'We would appreciate it,' Finbarr said. 'See how the land lies when you get over there.'

'Yes,' Frankie said. 'I won't forget. It will be nice for me to see a familiar face anyway. I'll write.'

So Frankie left a few days later. His mother cried copious tears and his siblings sniffled audibly. Even Mick's voice was husky and even Frankie was struggling with his emotions, and he hugged his family and shook hands with all the well-wishers gathered to wish him God speed.

'It will break my heart if Mammy is as upset as Norah was when we go,' Colm said.

'She will be,' Finbarr said. 'Worse maybe for there are two of us. But however sad she is, remember we are not just thinking about this for ourselves alone but also for Mammy and the others. All she has coming in now is what Daddy brings in and a pittance from Gerry and Barry's apprenticeship money, and Gerry will be out on his ear before long too.'

'Yeah I suppose.'

'We need to leave, Colm, and go as far as America if things are as good as Frankie's uncle says. The life we have now is no life at all, and even worse, we have no future to look forward to.'

It was sometime later Frankie wrote the promised letter and told them things were just fine and dandy for him in America and he was looking forward to them joining him. The even better news was that knowing the family personally from when they all lived in Donegal, their uncle was not only willing to sponsor them but loan them the £10 each needed for the assisted passage tickets, which would be easy to pay back from the good wages they'd be earning over there. Finbarr let his breath out in a sigh of utter relief, for he hadn't known how they were going to raise the money for the fare, and this generous man was coming to their aid. All they had to do now was tell their parents and he thought that was better done sooner rather than later and give them time, particularly their mother, to come to terms with it.

If Finbarr and Colm thought Norah Docherty was upset when Frankie left, that was before they had seen their mother's distress, for she was almost hysterical with grief. Never in her wildest dreams had she thought her sons would do what Frankie Docherty did and leave everything behind and travel to another continent entirely. She thought if nothing else, financial constraints would prevent them, for they would never raise the £10 needed to avail themselves of the assisted passage scheme. Aiden had paid for his nephew and it appeared he was prepared to loan her two sons the money needed and sponsor them too.

'We have no life here, Mammy,' Finbarr cried. 'There is no future for us, our lives are dribbling away.'

Mary continued to cry, but Matt had listened to his sons. Finbarr had a point, he realized, for he was twenty-four now and Colm twenty-three. They should be working at a job of some sort and have money in their pockets for a pint or two now and then, go to the match if they had a mind, court a girl perhaps, and all they could see in front of them were years of the same struggle. There was no light at the end of the tunnel because they were unable to procure some meaningful employment, so Matt's wage added together with a minute portion from his two sons still at the foundry had to keep them all. It was only Mary's ability to make a sixpence do the work of a shilling that stopped them from starving altogether.

The situation couldn't go on however, especially when there was every likelihood of the situation worsening when Gerry finished his apprenticeship in a year or two and subsequently Barry. His sons had the means of alleviating things for them and securing a future for themselves. It was bad that this involved them leaving home to move so far away but he didn't see any alternative. Though he knew he would be heartsore to lose them, for the good of them all it had to be.

Finbarr and Colm had their arms around their mother saying they were sorry and urging her not to upset herself, and her tears had changed to gulping sobs, and Matt waited till he was totally calm and then told Mary quietly the thoughts that had been tumbling around his head. As a pang of anguish swept over Mary's face Colm moved away so Matt could hold Mary's arm. Neither Finbarr nor Colm had been aware of Matt's thoughts and the fact that he had listened to them and understood their concerns meant a great deal since the one person their mother listened to and took heed of was Matt.

'But America, Matt,' Mary wailed. 'It's so far away. We'll never see them again.'

Matt gave a slight shake of his head. 'We might not and there will be a part of my heart that will go with them, but we can be content, thinking that we have given them the potential for a full and happy life.'

Mary was still silent so Matt went on. 'We left our native shores for a better life, remember.'

'We only crossed a small stretch of water though.'

'Never mind how long or short the journey was. We came for a better life,' Matt said. 'And for a time achieved it, but the system failed our boys and they are on the scrapheap. They want better than this and who can blame them? And if they have to go to America to achieve it, so be it.'

Mary gave a brief nod. Though tears shone in her eyes and she was unable to speak, she knew she had no right to deny a better life to her sons.

The rest of the family were astounded when they heard and more than a little upset, though they all could see why the boys had to go. Father Brannigan disapproved, but then he disapproved of so much, you wouldn't know what you had to do to please him.

'You will lose your faith if you go there.'

'Don't see why you say that, Father,' said Finbarr. 'They have priests and churches and plenty of Catholics already there.'

'It's a dangerous, lawless place.'

'Oh, have you been over there, Father?'

'No I haven't been,' the priest snapped. 'I wouldn't go to such a place if you paid me, but I can read the papers.'

'Even if it's as bad as you say,' Colm said, 'Fin and I wouldn't get involved in anything like that. We just want to do a job of work and get paid a wage that will enable us to enjoy life a little.'

'Frankie Docherty as been there some months now and he writes to us but never mentions any trouble of any kind,' Finbarr said and the priest was silent, because he had tried to talk Frankie out of going and he hadn't been dissuaded either.

The boys would not be going until the spring of 1908 as it was too close to the end of the year to cross the Atlantic, so Christmas that year had poignancy to it as they knew they might never ever be all together like that again. Stan came to wish them all Happy Christmas. He had grown fond of the boys and he felt a measure of guilt that he had been unable to help them in finding employment. Neither of the boys bore him any ill will however, and though they would undoubtedly miss their family, Frankie described New York in such glowing terms, they couldn't wait to see it for themselves.

Mary had got a battered case from someone, not that her sons had much to put in it – sparse sets of ragged underwear, everyday clothes holed and patched and the two jumpers Mary had knitted them both for Christmas, for she said from what she'd heard New York winters were severe. They would be travelling in the suits they wore for Sunday, though they were thin and quite flimsy now and the trousers shiny and shapeless, and the only boots they possessed they had on. They had no top coats or any money to buy them which was another reason for crossing the Atlantic in the spring.

The day arrived and the family assembled to say goodbye for there was no money for the fare to accompany them to the docks. Mary had thought of this day often and had shed tears each time she had thought of it, and now she held her sons tight, for it was a hug that would have to last a lifetime, and tears were also raining down Finbarr and Colm's face when Mary released them. Matt also hugged his two sons and wished them God speed. They bade farewell to Sean and Gerry and Barry and as he hugged Angela Finbarr said, 'You better behave yourself now I'm not around to look after you.'

'Huh, as if I ever took any notice of you anyway,' Angela said with a ghost of a smile.

Finbarr gave a watery smile back, glad of her lightening the atmosphere, even slightly, for the whole family had seemed steeped in misery, and it was hard to leave them like that, but they had a boat to catch. Mary stood on the pavement and waved till they turned down Bristol Street and so were out of sight. Then she came in, gave a sigh, plopped in a chair and burst into tears, wiping her eyes with her apron.

Finbarr and Colm's departure had left a gaping hole in the family and they maybe were aware of that but they certainly knew how their mother would worry and so they wrote a letter while on the ship just saying that they were well and quite excited and on course for America. They hadn't expected to be able to do that but it was a practice on some ships to encourage it, even providing the paper, envelopes and pens, since it was known it helped homesickness for many of the passengers, at least in steerage or third class, who were often not there through choice but forced through poverty and unemployment to make for the Brave New World.

The next letter came after they had met up with Frankie and his uncle and were taken to share a bedroom in Aiden's quite sizeable home. Finbarr wrote:

Before we came to America we had to go to a place called Ellis Island to see if we were free from disease. We were prodded and poked and examined and in the end the doctor said I was fit enough but needed more flesh on my bones. Colm was told the same and we were mighty glad because if you fail that medical you're sent back. We were asked questions, general knowledge sort of thing, and an account of why we have come to America and we found the Christian Brothers had beat enough knowledge into us for us to be able to give a good enough account of ourselves.

Colm wrote:

From Ellis Island you can see the New York skyline and all the skyscrapers some of the fellows on the ship had told us about. What a sight it was. And dominating the waterfront was the huge Statue of Liberty. Liberty that burns in the heart of every Irish man. This is truly the land of the Free and neither of us can wait to experience that.

'They seem happy enough anyway,' Matt said. 'So far at least.'

And they continued to be fine as they described the long straight streets of New York that had numbers instead of names and the shops and the buildings that towered above them till you could almost feel they were actually scraping the sky. They described the tramcars and the trains that run underground that the Americans called the subway and they talked of the job they did building motor cars.

Mary wished they wouldn't write in such glowing terms of the great life they were leading for she saw the same restlessness in her two younger sons, which intensified when Gerry finished his apprenticeship in 1909 and was immediately laid off. Angela knew that Mary was worried they would want to follow their brothers to America, but she also knew how tight the financial budget was. Maybe if she got a job and could contribute a bit and things were a little easier they would stay.

In 1910 Angela would be fourteen and could leave school but as her birthday was in early April it was after Easter before she could leave school and only then if she had a job to go to, otherwise she had to stay until July. From the experience her brothers had had she knew any job might be difficult to find.

'I don't like the thought of you in a factory anyway,' Mary said in early March.

'Mammy, I don't think I can be that fussy,' Angela said. 'Think of the way Finbarr and Colm searched for employment and they were willing to do anything and in the end they had to go to America to get a good job. Maybe,' she added with a grin at Mary, 'I should try that too?'

'Don't even joke about that,' Mary said. 'We'll keep looking. There must be something and we have got time yet.'

It was Norah who told her about the vacancy at George Maitland's grocery shop. It was a little out of the way for them, but she had gone visiting an old neighbour who had moved there and seen the card in the window.

'People around said he had a boy helping him but he caught rheumatic fever. They did think at one time the boy wasn't going to make it but when it was obvious he was going to recover George Maitland didn't advertise his position in case he wanted to come back to work, so my friend said. She said, "He's a decent sort that way, George." He even had his crabbed wife to help him a time or two but she insulted more than she served, my friend said, and if she was more in the shop in general and not just when he was short handed people would go elsewhere for their groceries.'

Angela wrinkled her nose. 'She doesn't sound very nice. But if the boy is recovering, I don't see why he's advertising now for someone new.'

'That's it,' Norah said. 'Apparently he is as well as he ever will be, but he's left with a weak heart and the doctor said the work in the shop is too strenuous for him, so as he can't go back there's a vacancy. Do you know the shop I'm talking about?'

Angela nodded, 'I'll go up tomorrow.'

'What about school?' Mary asked.

'I think this is more important,' Angela said. 'Jobs are snapped up these days and it's nearly holidays anyway and if I secure this job my school days are numbered and I'll be earning money almost straight away.'

Mary couldn't argue with that. 'I think you do right. We'll sort out the school later and I hope you get it.'

*   *   *

So early the next morning George Maitland turned as the bell tinkled and saw one of the most beautiful girls he had ever seen standing in his shop. She had white-blonde hair and the most vivid blue eyes and when she smiled at him it was as if someone had turned a light on inside her.

Angela in her turn saw an oldish man in his late fifties, if she had to hazard a guess. He had a pleasant face rather than a handsome one for he had a large nose and a wide and generous mouth set in slightly sallow skin. He had plenty of hair but it was a bit like pepper and salt in colour and matched his big, bushy eyebrows. Beneath those eyebrows were the softest kindest eyes she had seen in a long time and he said, 'Can I help you?'

'Yes, please,' Angela said. 'I've come about the ad.'

'The ad?'

'Yes it's in the window,' Angela said. 'About a shop assistant.'

'You want to work in the shop?' George said. He had never thought about employing a girl before but there was no rule against it and he realized he would like to see that pleasant and attractive face every day.

'It's five and a half days a week,' he said. 'All day Saturday and half day Wednesday, that all right?'

'That's fine, sir,' Angela said, hardly daring to believe that this man was going to employ her. She could go home and put a smile on Mary's face, because it was nearly the holidays so she could start work straight away. 'Thank you, sir,' she added and wondered if it was bad form to ask about wages. She needed to know, but wouldn't like to scupper her chances.

George wondered if she knew how expressive her face was. He was surprised she hadn't asked straight away what she was to be paid when he told her the hours she would be working, but knew from her face she was working up to do it now.

And so he forestalled her. 'And the wages are ten and six a week,' he said, knowing if he had employed a boy he would have started him on twelve and six.

However, Angela didn't know that and ten shillings and sixpence sounded fine to her, especially when George added, 'And a basket of groceries every Saturday.'

George readily agreed to write a note for the school so that Angela could be released from school early and she began in the shop at the start of the Easter holidays. She was a hit with most of the customers and soon he didn't know what he had ever done without her. She loved serving in the shop and it showed. She greeted every customer, even the awkward ones, with a bright smile and if someone had a sick child they were worried about or a doddery mother or chesty husband she would remember and enquire about them. Added to that, she was quick and efficient and could reckon up faster and more accurately than any boy he had ever employed.

He felt quite paternal towards Angela. She could easily have been his daughter and how he wished she was. He had thought by the age he was now he would have sons to help him in the store and carry on after his day, as he had done with his father, and maybe a daughter or two to gladden his heart.

But it was not to be, for Matilda didn't like that side of married life. That hadn't worried him at first for girls of her class were not supposed to like sex and as they were heavily chaperoned during their courtship he was unable to ask or reassure her about it. In fact they had both been so constrained and had such little time totally alone thatt he knew no more of Matilda when he married her than when the courtship had begun.

She was completely innocent of sexual matters or what you did to procreate a child. In that she wasn't unusual of her station; very often it was expected that the husband would teach a girl what was what on their wedding night. So George imagined that he would talk to her about sexual matters and any problems could be sorted out.

However, she didn't even like discussing such things. She said it was 'dirty talk' and was completely disgusted when he explained how they might conceive a child together. She threw him from her with such force that he almost fell out of bed while she screamed at him that she was surprised at such dirty words spilling from his mouth and she never wanted to hear a word about it again. So nothing was sorted out at all.

Matilda agreed to share a bed and often lay beside him as stiff as a board, but that was all. She wouldn't allow George to touch her in any way. He had initially thought she might come round in the end, but as time went on her attitude became more and more entrenched. He begged and pleaded, cajoled, but Matilda wouldn't budge an inch. 'But don't you want a child, my love?' he'd asked in desperation and frustration one night.

'A child!' Matilda had shrieked as if she had never heard of such a thing. 'No I don't want a child. I have no desire to find myself lumbered with some smelly, bawling brat.'

George felt a stab in his heart as he realized he had fallen for a beautiful face, for in her youth Matilda had been a stunning beauty and he had been overawed that she had agreed to walk out with him. Her parents made no objection to their courtship for though George was 'Trade' he was known as a steady, sober and easygoing sort of chap who would inherit the shop after his father died.

What George got was a shell instead of a real flesh-and-blood woman. One who looked good on the top but with nothing underneath. He was heartbroken that his dreams of a family to fill the rooms above the shop would only ever be dreams and never become reality. However, he believed marriage was for life and if you made a bad choice you had to live with it, and as he wasn't the sort of man to force himself on a woman he settled for a loveless and a sexless marriage.

He felt ashamed that his wife spurned him so totally and he threw himself into the shop, knowing there he was in charge and a success, but it was a sterile success for he was working only for a woman who had no interest in it and was only interested in the profit made.

And now Angela had brought brightness to his days he was almost content.

Angela could have told him he had brought contentment to Mary with the groceries she took home each Saturday. In fact it was more than contentment. In fact that first Saturday, as she unpacked the bag and laid all the articles on the table, Mary burst into tears and wiped her eyes on her apron as she felt the worry of making nourishing meals for them all slide from her shoulders.

And so when Angela gave her her wage packet unopened she extracted sixpence from it and gave it back to Angela. 'I don't want it, Mammy,' Angela said. 'The money is just for you.'

Mary shook her head. 'It's right you keep something, for the men hold back their ciggy money, so you should have something.'

'But I don't smoke.'

'I should think you don't,' Mary said. 'But there might be something else you want. Save it if you can think of nothing just now, but you can rely on sixpence coming your way every week.'

'Thank you Mammy.'

'Yes, and talking about smoking, I wish your father didn't do so much of it,' Mary said. 'He has that hacking cough and smoking can't help. Smoking less might help his stomach too.'

'What's wrong with his stomach?'

'Oh I don't know,' Mary said. 'Indigestion most likely. It only seemed to start when you started bringing the food from Maitland's. His stomach's not used to good food, too rich for him.' And then she added as she saw Angela's brow creased in concern, 'But don't worry yourself, Angela. If that is what's upsetting him he'll get used to it in the end.'

FIVE

Mary thought life had finally reached a more or less even keel. She had no idea what the future held, but just for the moment things were going along nicely. True, like their elder brothers, Sean and Gerry could find no permanent jobs, but that wasn't so important now that Angela was bringing in ten shillings a week and a big bag of groceries. Barry, now two thirds of his way through his apprenticeship, had had a raise and he was able to also tip up ten shillings a week and Matt earned three pounds and kept little back for himself. It meant if Sean and Gerry had earned anything it was a bonus and if they hadn't managed that, it didn't matter.

Barry knew that wasn't how his brothers viewed things because he had discussed it with them. They felt failures and they viewed the lives of their brothers in America with unbridled envy. 'I don't think I'm asking a lot,' Sean said. 'I want a job of work that pays enough for me to live independently, pay rent and bills with enough over to buy some much-needed clothes, or have my leaky boots mended, or go out for an evening and have a few beers. Now I call that living a life.'

'Well you can't do that here,' Gerry said. 'Just at the moment a person needs to go to America to live at all.'

'Well why don't you go then?' Barry asked.

'Basically because of you, mate,' Gerry said.

'Why me?'

'Because we're dropping you in the mire.'

'How?'

'Well we can't all swan off and leave Mammy and Daddy on their own.'

'They won't be on their own,' Barry said. 'I have no yen to go to America and how will you not going to America help any of us?'

Both boys had to admit it would make little difference, but Gerry still felt bad about leaving Barry to shoulder all the responsibility of their ageing parents on his own, but Sean said, 'At least Angela loves our mammy as much as we do, so there will be no problem when you wed.'

'What d'you mean when we wed?'

'Well you will wed won't you?' Gerry said. 'Everyone knows that you are crazy about her. Plain as the nose on your face.'

'Yes but Angela is little more than a child. She's not even sixteen until the spring and I don't know if she feels the same about me.'

Sean laughed. 'Course she does. The love-light's shining in her eyes every time she looks at you. Think Mammy's aware of it and I reckon nothing would please her more because she loves Angela like the daughter she never had.'

What Sean said was true. Angela had no memory of her earlier life with her birth parents but the memories that were rock solid for her were of Mary cuddling her tight and tucking her into bed at night with a kiss. Angela knew she was truly loved by the whole family and especially Mary and Matt, and she loved them in return. Barry knew she loved him too and always had, but she was so young. It might be a childish love she had for him and not yet the love of a woman for a man, a love that would last a lifetime and stand strong and true against all that life might throw at them. He couldn't ask such a young person to make a commitment like that, it wouldn't be fair. He decided to stick to his original plan and wait until she was eighteen and he was through his apprenticeship before admitting how he felt about her and hoping she felt the same. So Barry never spoke to Angela but the boys wrote to Finbarr and Colm and said they wanted to try their hand in America.

The elder boys were delighted their younger brothers wanted to join them and they recommended that they travel in ships on the White Star line for there was more comfort for the third-class or steerage passengers.

Finbarr wrote further:

If I were you I'd take the train to Southampton and sail on the Titanic. *I've been reading up about it and it's the largest passenger ship in the world. It's been made in Belfast and it has its maiden voyage on 12th April, a grand time to cross the Atlantic. There are electric lights, you sleep four to a room, three meals a day is all included and served in one of two dining saloons and there is running water in the shared bathrooms. And best of all it's unsinkable. Just say the word and I'll book you two places now if I can because lots might want a place for her maiden voyage. Our journey across was comfortable enough but it didn't have the facilities like the Titanic. I wish Colm and I had been able to travel on it, but we'll be here to meet you on the dockside.*

Sean and Gerry were terribly excited to be given the chance to travel on such a magnificent ship and they read up all they could about it. Mary was absolutely astounded that her two other sons wanted to go to America too. 'You'll be next I suppose,' she snapped at Barry.

Barry knew she wasn't cross but frightened and he said gently but firmly, 'Not me, Mammy. I've no yen to go travelling.'

'What if they lay you off when you finish your apprenticeship?'

'Shall we cross that bridge when we come to it?' Barry said. 'But even then I promise I am going nowhere.'

Mary let out a sigh of relief, but she didn't want Sean or Gerry to go either, but what could they do? The slump seemed deeper than ever in Britain. There was a slump in America too but Finbarr and Colm seemed immune to it and they had guaranteed they could get their brothers jobs as soon as they came over. Matt could see the lads' point of view though he too would miss the two of them sorely. Mary could see it, though wished she didn't have to, and Angela felt a deep sadness that two more brothers were going to live an ocean away from her.

The boys did their best to reassure their mother. They showed her a picture of the ship and told her about all it had on board and everything, but as Mary said to them, there was always the chance they might fall ill or something. A few years ago the people in Ireland were leaving in droves for America and so many perished in the ships they began calling them coffin ships.

'I know,' Barry said. 'Things are much improved now. I mean Fin and Colm gave a good account of their journey and the *Titanic* is supposed to be the best of its kind.'

They were travelling down to Southampton on Tuesday 9th April, which was Angela's sixteenth birthday. Fin and Colm had paid for their train fare to Southampton and booked them into a lodging house near the docks and they would board the *Titanic* from there the following morning. 'Get a good night's sleep,' Finn advised, but Sean and Gerry were far too excited to sleep. This was the start of the greatest adventure of their lives and they didn't want to waste the whole night sleeping, and spent most of the night talking of the journey which they were looking forward to and of arriving in America where their lives would really begin.

On Monday 15th April a very excited woman arrived in the shop with news that the unsinkable *Titanic* had gone down in the Atlantic Ocean, sunk when it hit an iceberg. Apparently the news had appeared on an American newsreel and her aunt in America had sent a telegram to her as her son had been due to sail on the *Titanic*. But he had been taken ill and had to cancel.

The blood had drained from Angela's face and eventually the woman noticed. 'God, Angela, you've gone ever such a funny colour.' Then she clapped her hands over her mouth and said, 'Oh me and my big mouth, blurting it out like that. Your brothers were on it weren't they? I remember talking about it when my Tom was due to go too.'

George had heard every word too and he said consolingly to Angela, 'There will be lifeboats to get the people off, don't worry. A big new boat like that will have enough to cope with any eventuality. And the ship might not even be fully sunk, people might still be on it.' Then he turned to the woman and said, 'Did it say anything else about those rescued, the survivors?'

The woman shook her head. 'Don't know if there's any more to tell yet, not that you can get it chapter and verse in a telegram.'

'No, course not,' George said and he turned to Angela and said, 'You should go home. What this woman has heard others can hear. You should be with your mother and send for Barry and his father. You need to be together.'

Angela went round for Barry before going home, for if Mary had heard any inkling she might need their support. When she told Stan what she had heard that morning he was upset himself and fully agreed Barry and Matt needed to be at home and when they were sent for she told them both what she had heard that morning. Matt gave a sharp intake of breath and his face drained of colour, but he said only, 'This will hit your mother hard, Barry.'

It would hit Barry hard if anything bad had happened

to them. They were his big brothers and he loved them. And yet he said to his father, 'We know nothing concrete yet, Daddy. We must hold on to that.'

'You're right, Barry,' Stan said as they left. 'Sometimes these snippets of news are anything but helpful. Come and tell me as soon as you know anything definite. I was very fond of those young men.'

They walked home almost in silence, each busy with their own thoughts, but all were relieved to find Mary knew nothing, and they were able to tell her gently and hold her as she wept.

A telegram arrived the followed day from Finbarr. He didn't know if the news of the sinking of the *Titanic* after hitting a massive iceberg had reached British shores so he explained that first and explained another ship called *Carpathian* had picked up survivors and was estimated to be arriving in New York on 18th April. The news gave everyone renewed hope. The men returned to tell Stan, who relayed the news to the work-force. Angela went to tell George, and neighbours hearing of the sinking of that gigantic vessel with two of the McClusky sons on it came to say how sorry they were, and they too went home cheered that survivors had been picked up by another ship.

They existed in a kind of limbo for a couple of days. Norah Docherty, knowing the same fate could have happened to her son, was great company for Mary in keeping her spirits up and Mick took Matt to The Swan for a pint. In fact, Matt, the very moderate drinker, had far more than one pint since many of the men wanted to buy him one – their way of showing sympathy – and it ended up with Mary and Angela helping the very drunk

Matt up the stairs to bed. As they lowered him on to the bed, Angela said, 'Are you going to undress him?'

'I am not,' Mary said emphatically. 'I'm not even trying to move his hulk around to get him more comfortable. I'll just remove his shoes, that's all, and I'll tell you, I'd not have his head in the morning for a pension, and yet I can envy him because for the last few hours he has been able to stop worrying about those lads.'

'They'll be all right,' Angela said. 'They probably had a fright and might have got a bit wet, but they are big strapping lads and know how to look after themselves.'

'Of course they do and you are right,' Mary said and Angela so hoped she was right as she followed Mary down the stairs.

On 18th April just before eight in the evening, Finbarr and Colm had stood just outside the harbour in New York and watched the *Carpathian* sail in. And once the *Carpathian* had docked, the two young men surged through with the rest to check the list of survivors to see if their younger brothers had been among the lucky ones. A sailor from the rescue ship, seeing their anxious scrutiny of the lists pinned up, asked who they were searching for, and when they told him he said that few men had got off. 'I heard as how there weren't even enough lifeboats for everyone.'

'Not enough lifeboats?' Finbarr repeated almost in disbelief.

'Well wasn't it supposed to be unsinkable?'

Finbarr nodded. 'That's what they claimed wasn't it, Colm?'

'Yes,' said Colm in agreement. 'I mean, that was one reason we encouraged them to travel on the *Titanic*.'

'Well it hit a gigantic iceberg, see. Most of an iceberg is below the water, you only see a bit of it, and whatever way it happened, it hit the iceberg and started to sink. I heard this from the sailors we pulled onto our ship,' the *Carpathian* sailor said. 'One of them said when the iceberg was spotted there wasn't time to turn such a large ship to avoid it. He said if they hadn't tried to avoid it and had hit it head on it probably would have been all right but, as it was, it crashed into the side and the iceberg ripped straight through it and it started to fill with water.'

'What were you doing picking up sailors when more passengers could have been in the lifeboats?' Finn asked.

'They were the sailors chosen to row the lifeboats,' the *Carpathian* sailor said. 'If they hadn't rowed away from the ship as quick as possible when it sank it would have pulled the lifeboats down with it. Then we'd have had no survivors at all to rescue. There were a few other men as well. Travelling first class, some were let on the boats straight away, but then the crew found out how dire the situation was and after that it was women and children only that were loaded into the lifeboats.'

'And the rest of the men?' Finbarr asked, though he knew the answer.

'They went down with the ship,' the sailor said bluntly. And then, looking at the clothes Finbarr and Colm had on, which marked them as working men, the sailor went on, 'Would your brothers be travelling steerage?'

'They were,' Finbarr said. 'What of it?'

'Nothing,' the sailor said. 'That is, nothing good. It's just that these sailors told us that few steerage passengers, carried in the bowels of the ship, made it to the lifeboats anyway, not even the women and children. One told me some hadn't even got to the deck when the ship sank without trace.'

'People wouldn't have been picked up by other ships, would they?' Colm cried, desperate to find some glimmer of hope. 'Like if they were clinging to some wreckage or something like that to keep afloat?'

The sailor shook his head. 'Sorry, mate. First off, there were no other ships in the area. Ours was the only one who answered the distress call, so probably any other ships were too far away to be of any use. And secondly, even if someone had managed to hang on to wreckage, how long do you think they'd last in water cold enough to have huge icebergs floating in it? One minute? Maybe two, but no more than that before they froze to death.'

Colm staggered at the news. They bought papers on their way home and read the reports of the collision that sank a ship claimed to be unsinkable on her maiden voyage. It was news that shocked the world, and their brothers had died, and the way they died was horrendous, and Finbarr in particular felt as guilty as Hell for urging Sean and Gerry to follow them.

When they returned to their lodgings they decided to say nothing to their mother and father about the things the sailor from the rescue ship told them. 'It would serve no purpose and only upset them further,' Finn said. 'Anyway, it's not the thing to put in a telegram, and that's what we must send first thing tomorrow and we can write them a fuller letter later.'

Colm agreed, 'Aye and it will be hard enough to cope

with the loss of two sons and enough to be going on with.'

And so the bare telegram just said that neither Sean nor Gerry were among the survivors on the *Carpathian*. They had been waiting for the telegram and yet Angela's fingers shook as she took it from the telegraph boy. 'Any message?' the boy asked.

Angela shook her head. 'No message.'

She shut the door and turned and gave the telegram to Barry, for she couldn't bring herself to open it. Barry took it from her and read the few bald words out to them all as his own voice was breaking with emotion, and tears sprang from his eyes as he felt the aching loss of his brothers. Angela did too, but she pushed aside her heartache to deal with Matt and Mary who were in pieces.

She knew that until the arrival of the telegram Matt and Mary would have hoped it wasn't as bad as they feared. They had encouraged this. They had all hoped themselves because it's what people did. But now all hope was snuffed out, Sean and Gerry were gone and she would never see them again, and if she felt the pain of that loss so keenly, she could only imagine what it was doing to Matt and Mary, and the anguish etched in both their faces tore at her heart.

Even after the telegram Barry and Angela couldn't understand the scale of this tragedy and in the papers Barry had brought in they had both read about the proverbial unsinkable liner, on its maiden voyage, that had indeed sunk and sunk so quickly when it struck an iceberg that though 705 had managed to get into lifeboats and so were saved, 1,517 perished. Most of the fatalities, the papers claimed, were steerage or third-class passengers and any that were rescued were women and children. The lack of enough lifeboats for all the passengers was also discussed, and the fact that a lot of the lifeboats were not full when they pulled away from the ship, for the *Titanic* sank quicker than anyone thought it would.

The newspapers made grim reading and Angela hid the papers away in the cellar with the kindling for the fire, intending to burn them when she got the chance, for she and Barry both thought dealing with the death of their sons was quite enough to be going on with, without constantly reading about such a disaster. But that was hard to do without Matt or Mary catching sight of the headlines and so on, because they seldom left the sitting room.

Coming into the room the evening following the arrival of the telegram, Mary had sobbed afresh as Angela helped get her ready for bed. Angela said, 'I understand Mammy's distress really because I suppose the telegram snuffed out the last glimmer of hope that she kept burning in her heart. I know it did for me, for I loved them just as if they had been my true brothers.'

'Yes,' said Barry with a sigh. 'I know you did and they knew it too. And I know the casualty figures are shocking, but knowing that two of those left to die are your own flesh and blood is hard to take. But that is what happened, and they are dead and gone, so that neither of us will see them again. But that's how it is and we must deal with it.'

Everyone felt sorry for the McCluskys and many understood the spiral of depression Matt and Mary had sunk into when the telegram arrived, cutting off all hope that either of their sons might have survived. So they continued to pop in and out as they had when the news first broke and didn't usually come empty-handed. Unable to do anything to ease the situation, they brought a bit of stew they had left over and cakes they'd made, and Angela marvelled that these people, some of whom had little enough for themselves, were willing to share with them. Norah also visited, and Stan were always popping in and out.

The priest, Father Brannigan, came too, purporting to show support and sympathy in their loss, but managed to turn it round to slight condemnation against Matt and Mary for letting the boys go in the first place. While he drank two cups of tea he ladled three sugars into them and ate all the scones that one of their neighbours had brought round for them earlier that day.

Eventually, annoyed at the implied criticism Angela knew Mary and Matt were unable to cope with, she said, 'Sean and Gerry had no permanent work, Father. They had to go each day to the factories to pick up a few hours' work if they could. Often they arrived home empty-handed.'

'Many work that way.'

'But maybe they haven't an alternative,' Angela said. 'But Sean and Gerry had two brothers already in America who could find them good jobs and have them lodging in the same house as themselves. It was a wrench for them to go for all of us, but I know they felt bad when they could contribute nothing at home. They saw themselves as a drain on the family and could see no future for themselves. No-one did anything wrong and yet Mammy and Daddy have lost two sons and maybe prayers, rather than censure, would be more helpful at this point.'

Had Mary and Matt been thinking straight they probably would have been surprised at Angela talking to the priest that way, but it all went over their heads and even Father Brannigan didn't come back with a sharp retort as he would normally, for he was unused to any form of criticism from his parishioners. However, Angela's words had hit home and he had seen the sadness lurking behind her eyes that glittered with unshed tears, and so they all knelt and said the rosary together and before the priest left he promised to say a Mass for the repose of the boys' souls.

That comforted Angela a great deal but it didn't seem to sink in to Mary and Matt. As the loss turned into a manageable ache, Barry had to go back to work, for they had to eat, and Matt made no effort to return. Mary seemed incapable of caring for the house or cooking anything and so Angela tried to give up the good job she had at Maitland's grocer shop to look after them both.

However, Mr Maitland wasn't happy losing his assistant who worked so hard and was a favourite with the customers because she was always so cheerful, and he said it had been a terrible tragedy and it was unreasonable to expect the parents to get over the loss of two sons straight away, and he gave her another week before he advertised for someone else. Barry was glad about that because he was the only one working and he hoped Angela could return to work before too long because money was so short.

However, the extra week was drawing to a close as

one day slid into another with no change, and that night as Barry made his way home from work he'd made a decision, but first he had to talk to Angela. He had a bit of a wait but he was a patient man. Angela had cooked liver and onions and Barry tucked in with relish, glad that Angela was such a good cook and an economical one. His parents, he noted, had eaten little and he knew if they were to recover from this, he had to give them something to look forward to.

Eventually, with Mary and Matt helped to bed, Angela sat down on the settee before the hearth opposite Barry with a sigh. 'Tired?' Barry asked.

Angela nodded. 'A little but it's the emotional part of it that wearies me most.'

Barry shook his head. 'I don't know how you put up with it day by day.'

'Well I owe your parents my life and love them dearly anyway. But I could cope much better if I could see some light at the end of the tunnel and for their sake more than mine.'

Barry suddenly moved to sit beside Angela and caught up her hand, something he hadn't done since she'd been small and she wasn't sure how to react. But she had no time to think because Barry looked deep into her eyes as he said, 'What do you think of me, Angela?'

Angela looked at the dear and familiar face and his intense dark eyes and felt her stomach turn over like she had butterflies fluttering inside and her mouth was dry enough to make her voice husky when she said, 'Wh . . . What d'you mean?'

'You know what I mean,' Barry said almost impatiently.

'But if you are shy of saying so I will tell you what I think of you. That all right?'

Angela gave a brief nod and Barry went on, 'I love you, every bit of you. I think I've loved you from the moment I first saw you with your blonde curls, your lovely blue eyes. But those eyes in the early days were sad and confused, and I wanted to help you and so I was determined then to be the best big brother I could be.'

'And you were,' Angela assured Barry. 'But you were more than that. You were my protector, my knight in shining armour. I wouldn't have got on half as well without you and I loved you too.'

'As a brother?'

Angela swallowed deeply and said, 'Yes, as a brother.'

'You were a child and I was a child,' Barry said. 'But my love for you has changed and deepened and now I love you as a man loves a woman and I need to know if you feel the same.'

Angela didn't answer straight away but then what she did say was, 'I think it's wrong for me to feel towards you any other way than as a brother.'

'Why?'

'Well we were brought up as brother and sister.'

'Yes but we are not brother and sister. There is no blood between us and that's what counts,' Barry said earnestly. 'Look, I had no intention of speaking of this, not because I was unsure of my own feelings but because I know you are only just sixteen and I am only nineteen. I intended leaving it two years till my apprenticeship is over and I'm earning decent money.'

'You might be in an even worse state financially then,

if you are laid off when you turn twenty-one as your brothers were,' Angela said.

'Yes and I'm afraid it may well be,' Barry said and it did worry him that he would end up the same, but there was nothing he could do about that. He shrugged. 'It's a chance I must take,' he said. 'But whatever happens I'll want you by my side, loving me as a woman with a love strong enough to withstand anything life throws at us.'

He hoped she felt the same, for he would not force her, and so he said almost tentatively, 'Angela, could you love me even a little bit?'

Angela had been having strange yearnings flowing through her body when she was near Barry, or sometimes even when she just thought of him for months. She wasn't sure what they were and she had tried to ignore them, pushing them down into her subconscious, certain the Church would say they were sinful. Most enjoyable things were.

But Barry's words and passionate eyes boring into hers had unlocked her feelings and so she answered, 'No.' She saw his face fall and she added with a smile, 'There's no way I can love you a little bit, I can love you an enormous big bit.'

Barry felt as if his heart had stopped in his breast and he looked at Angela incredulously. 'You mean that?'

'I most certainly do. I can't say when I stopped loving you just as a brother; I just know that I tried to push the feelings down, but the thought of not having you in my life fills me with fear. But now we have admitted our feelings for each other I think we will have to keep them secret from Mammy.'

'Well my brothers seemed to think she knows already.'

'Oh, she's maybe guessed a bit but she won't know for definite,' Angela said. 'I think we must hide our happiness for a wee while.'

'Why?'

'Well, out of respect, I suppose.'

'You knew Sean and Gerry as well as I did,' Barry said. 'And if it is as the priests say and they are in a better place and can look down on us, knowing them well, do you think they'd be happier in Paradise if we lamented long and hard and went round with faces that would turn the milk sour?'

'Yes but . . .'

'Angela, don't think me heartless,' Barry begged, 'for I'm really not and there's not a day goes by when I don't miss my brothers, but they would want me to get on and live life. Besides, I'm not just thinking of me in this but of Mammy too, particularly Mammy, for if we wed soon she will have to take a grip on herself because there would be a wedding to plan and the thought of grandchildren to gladden her heart. It will give her something to look forward to, something to live for.'

Angela wasn't at all sure that Barry was right in his assumptions, but now they had admitted their feelings for each other she doubted they could continue to be discreet, and anyway, she didn't want some hole-in-a-corner affair. Barry had at least convinced her that they were doing nothing to be ashamed of, so she didn't want to go skulking around her own home and perhaps lying to Mary and Matt, for that wouldn't be showing either of them any respect at all. No, it had to be out in the open. 'You're right Barry, it's only right that they be told as soon as possible.'

'Yes,' said Barry. 'I'll speak to them tomorrow after dinner.'

SIX

The following evening Angela had made an excellent stew from a selection of vegetables and a scrag end of mutton she had queued for hours in the Bull Ring to get. She wanted to make something a bit special for she knew Barry was intending to speak to his parents that night and in their present lethargy and sadness she wasn't at all sure how they would react to it.

As they sat at the table Angela thought Mary looked just a shade better. There was a spark in her eyes that she hadn't seen in a long while and she was pleased to see that Mary at least had got her appetite back, for she attacked her dinner with relish. Small signs of recovery, surely, and she couldn't help feeling that what Barry was going to say might knock her right back again. When everyone had finished, Angela cleared away and made a cup of tea.

Normally they would take the tea to drink before the fire, but Barry asked them to sit at the table and drink it because he had something he wanted to say to them. Angela saw Mary gazing at Barry fearfully. Angela's mouth went suddenly very dry and she watched

Mary's face with apprehension as Barry explained that the brotherly love he had always had for Angela had changed to real love and just the previous day Angela had admitted she felt the same way. 'So now we know we truly love one another, we want to get married,' Barry said.

Mary smiled wryly and she wondered if her young son thought he was telling her news because she'd seen how it was for the young people some time before. They had betrayed themselves in just the way they gazed at one another in odd moments. His brothers had been aware of it too, for she had overheard them discussing it and she couldn't have been happier, for she had prayed for just such an outcome in her nightly prayers for years.

Before she was able to say this however, Matt spoke and as he hadn't spoken since the arrival of the telegram, Angela was pleased that their discussion seemed to have got through to him, even though his words were ones of censure. 'Talking of marriage when your brothers are barely cold?' he said to Barry and his voice was almost a growl and the words seemed wrung out of him. 'At best it's unseemly and disrespectful. I'm ashamed of you, Barry.'

'And not getting married will bring the boys back, will it?' Mary demanded, before Barry had a chance to speak.

Angela looked at Mary her in astonishment. Mary caught the look and with a sigh admitted, 'I've been thinking for a while that maybe I have been selfish, wallowing in self-pity.'

'Ah no, Mammy,' Angela contradicted. 'You haven't a selfish bone in your body.'

Mary shook her head with a sad smile and said, 'I am no saint, my dear, and you have done your best to shield me from what happened on that tragic boat. But today when you were in the market, your father was feeling a bit chilly and so I went down to the cellar to get the makings to lay the fire and there I saw the old papers you kept from me and I read that entire families were lost on that ship and . . .' Mary's voice faltered and stopped as she recalled her shock and horror reading the words Barry and Angela had sought to protect her from. The anguish in her heart had forced a cry from her and tears stood out in her eyes for her own lost sons. And yet she knew they weren't the only sons lost, there were also husbands, fathers and brothers lost. All no doubt beloved members of families who would always miss them, because even the relatively few passengers from steerage that had been rescued were women and children, the lucky ones.

Remembering this now she said to Barry, 'Were there no men at all from steerage saved?'

'Well it was women and children first,' Barry said. 'In the papers I read it said that at first, when the sailors began loading the lifeboats, it was first-class passengers first and there were men too. When they realized how bad the situation was, the men were refused and they only took women and children.'

'Well I read in one paper that there weren't enough lifeboats for all on board anyway,' Mary said. 'I think that a scandalous state of affairs.'

'It was supposed to be unsinkable,' Barry pointed out. 'I imagine Finn and Colm feel bad because they encouraged Sean and Gerry to go on that ship.'

'Because it was supposed to be the safest way to cross the Atlantic,' Mary said. 'And yet nothing changes, for aside from the men, most of those who were left to die in the icy sea were steerage passengers. Women and children, even wee babies.'

'It was a dreadful thing to happen,' Angela said. 'I was beginning to think you would never recover from such tragedy.'

'I was beginning to feel that way myself,' Mary said. 'But even before I found the papers in the cellar I had told myself that I must get over it. I mean I don't think there will be a day goes by when I'll not miss those boys and wish with all my heart they hadn't died and certainly not in that awful way, but had they not died I was hardly likely to see them again, for few people ever return from America, and so it's as if they are dead in a way.

'Oh, they could have written as Finn and Colm do and I am pleased they have such good jobs and, please God, one day they will write and tell me of the girls they intend to marry and later the birth of children I will never see. It is hard rearing children who are unable to find any sort of future in the country where they were raised so that they have to go so far across the foam, but the reality is four sons have already been lost to me.'

Angela's heart bled for the abject sorrow on Mary's face because every word she spoke was the truth. And then Mary gave a sigh and went on, 'However, some in that fated ship lost all belonging to them, while I still have one son left and I have Angela, who is as close as any daughter. For the two of you to wed is what I have longed for and though both of you are young, life is uncertain and I think we should go ahead and plan the wedding.'

'I see you are determined upon it,' Matt said. 'Going on as if our sons had not existed.'

'If they lived they would applaud us,' Mary said. 'And I doubt they'd feel any different dead. They knew the way the wind blew between Barry and Angela probably before they realized it themselves. I know you are hurting, for I am myself, but we can't undo this terrible tragedy. Sean and Gerry died a painful death and that will stay with me always. But this is a new start for us all and if you can't see that then you're a numbskull.'

'Oh, it's a numbskull I am now, is it?' Matt said, affronted.

'Yes you are,' Mary said unabashed. 'If you can't see that this is the way forward, the only way, something in life to look forward to and in time rejoice in.'

Matt was quiet and Angela could tell he was thinking over Mary's words as she knew he often did. She was astounded at the rapid turnabout Mary had made and wondered if they'd been right to try to shield her. She was a lot stronger than either of them had given her credit for and this truth was compounded when she turned to Angela and said, 'Now weddings cost money and I know there is precious little to spare so how about trotting off to Maitland's Grocery tomorrow morning and seeing if you can have your old job back. Didn't you say he was keeping it open for you?'

Angela nodded. 'Till this Monday.'

'Well tomorrow is Saturday, so if he has kept his word your job will still be there for you.'

'Shall you be all right?'

Mary nodded. 'I might be better if I have less time to think.'

'Shall you mind going back?' Barry asked.

'No,' Angela said with a laugh. 'Why should I mind? I loved my job and I know the money is needed. I can't wait to start if you want the truth.'

'Good,' Mary said. 'That's settled then.'

The next morning Angela set off for Maitland's Grocery Store early, fairly certain that George Maitland would be there getting ready for the first customers, and when she tapped on the door he opened it with a beam. 'Am I pleased to see you,' he cried, throwing the door wide. 'Come in, come in and give me the news.'

'Well the first thing is I would like my job back, please,' Angela said.

George sighed in relief as Angela explained that she now felt able to leave Mary and Matt to fend for themselves and return to work. 'They are much improved,' she told George when he enquired after them. 'At least,' she added more honestly, 'Mammy has improved. I think Daddy will never really get over it and I think he sort of blames Fin and Colm for encouraging the two younger ones to go. Mammy doesn't and she says that tomorrow she is going to write and tell them so because you know they write regularly and we expected a letter from them after the telegram but we have heard nothing. Barry thinks they might be a little scared to write and he could be right, but anyway if that's the case Mammy intends to remedy it.'

George nodded. 'She's a great woman, Mary.'

Angela nodded. 'She is indeed and I know that more than most.'

'But Matt hasn't got much better you say?'

Angela shook her head and added, 'You would hardly know what he thinks, because he seldom says anything at all and none of it good since the arrival of the telegram.'

'No sign of him getting back to work?' George asked. 'That might help him get a grip on himself.'

Angela shook her head vehemently. 'He's not fit,' she said. 'Not physically I don't mean, though he's thinner and frailer than he was because he eats so little and has started having pains in his stomach again, but he's had those pains for ages. Mammy thinks it's indigestion. But I'd be more worried about his emotional state. Barry thinks he might never work again.'

'It must be hard for you financially with Barry not out of his apprenticeship yet.'

Angela shrugged. 'It has been hard but we have managed just about. Needs must and all that.'

'Well I'm delighted you're back. The customers have been asking for you. Mrs Maitland has had to come and help me at busy times.'

Angela wrinkled her nose, for Matilda Maitland had scarcely set foot in the shop since she had been working there. 'Bet that didn't go down too well.'

George didn't speak, but shook his head with a smile before going on to say, 'Well this has decided me. I have thought about it time and enough. I am putting your wages up two shillings to twelve and six.'

Angela gave a gasp. 'Oh Mr Maitland. Are you sure?'

'Quite sure, my dear,' George said. 'And I will pack

you up a big bag of groceries to take home with you today and every Saturday night after we close.'

Tears were standing out in Angela's eyes and she brushed them away impatiently and determinedly swallowed the lump in her throat as she said, 'Thank you so much, Mr Maitland. You are very kind.'

George Maitland's voice was gruff as he answered the girl he had grown so fond of in the two years she had been working at the shop and he said with a twinkle in his eye, 'Not at all, my dear. I'm looking after myself, that's all. It's just a ploy to get more hours' work out of you, for people can work harder if they are not hungry.'

Angela knew it wasn't that at all but she didn't bother arguing, but instead began removing her coat. 'Shall we make a start then?'

'Now? You mean start right now?' George asked.

'Why not now?' Angela said. 'I have to start sometime and it might as well be today as Saturdays were always busy and usually needed two of us.'

Angela spoke the truth as George knew well. He'd actually thought that morning that he'd probably have to ask his wife to lend a hand before the day was out. He hated asking her, because she detested serving in the shop and made that abundantly clear and was so short and abrupt when she served people that she upset some of his best customers. And now here was Angela offering him a solution. 'Well if you're sure?'

'Course I am,' Angela said. 'Looks like I'm needed too because there's already a queue forming outside waiting for you to open up.'

There was and George hurried to open the door. The

people poured in, most only too delighted to see Angela behind the counter again.

The day passed swiftly as busy days often do. Though she assumed the family would know why she hadn't returned home after seeing George Maitland, she found a small boy in the street who agreed to go and tell them for two ounces of monkey nuts. She had no dinner with her, but Mary realized that and sent a sandwich back with the child. Angela was very grateful and ate it in the store room as she always did.

When George returned to the shop he appeared pensive. 'What are you thinking about so intently?' she asked with a smile.

'I'm thinking that it's madness for me to go upstairs for my dinner every day while you sit in the store room eating a sandwich.'

'Why is it?' Angela asked. 'I don't mind. I've done that since I started here.'

'I know, for that's how Matilda wanted it,' George said grimly. 'But you will feel more able to do a full afternoon's work with a good dinner inside you and Matilda is a good cook, I will give her that.'

Angela was quite happy with a sandwich and knew that however good the food, she wouldn't take full enjoyment of it in the stilted atmosphere there would be, because she'd only be there on sufferance. But then she knew it would save money for them all if she was to be given her dinner at the shop. She would only need a light tea and a meal only had to be cooked for Barry when he came in from work. She knew Mary would as usual see to herself and Matt at dinner time and then they could have tea with her. That surely was more important than Matilda Maitland's bad humour. And yet she said, 'Mrs Maitland might not like it.'

'You leave Matilda to me,' George said. 'From now on you will eat dinner with us. Agreed?'

'If you say so, Mr Maitland,' Angela said with an impish grin. 'You're the boss.'

'Glad you realize that at least,' said George, but he had a smile on his face as he turned the sign to OPEN and unlocked the door.

Mary cried when she unpacked the two shopping bags George had filled with groceries for them all. There were three loaves of bread that George said would only go stale if they stayed in the shop, a block of lard, and another of butter and a chunk of cheese. There was the ham and corned beef that had been left at the end of the day and a side of bacon left on the bacon slicer and a dozen eggs, and then he had added a jar of jam and a packet of biscuits. Mary could see the makings of many meals with the food George Maitland had given them and when Angela told her about the raise and the new arrangement Mary felt the nagging worry slide from her shoulders that they wouldn't have enough to eat, heat the house and pay the rent.

'You must take a little more for yourselves,' she said to Angela.

Angela shook her head. 'I don't want anything.'

'Listen to me,' Mary said. 'You think you know all there is to know about Barry, but you know him as a brother. You need to get to know him as the man you will spend the rest of your life with and, please God, as the father of any children you may be blessed with and for that you two need to get out more on your own.'

'We haven't the money for that sort of thing.'

'With your increased wages and Barry's money we have enough,' Mary insisted, 'especially if you are guaranteed a hot dinner every day and George sends home groceries every week. Anyway you don't have to spend a lot. Now and again you could maybe go to the cinema, or the Music Hall, or if money was tight you could just go for a walk, or go down the Bull Ring on a Saturday evening where there is great entertainment to be had I've been told.

'And another thing,' Mary went on before Angela had time to form any sort of reply, 'tell everyone about your impending marriage so the two of you can openly go down the street hand in hand, for you are doing nothing wrong.'

'I know that,' Angela said. 'I wasn't sure about it myself at first, you know, with Barry nearly a brother to me, but he convinced me that it was all above board to feel as we do.'

'Hmph, and he might have to do some more convincing before he is much older.'

'What d'you mean?'

'Why did you think it might be wrong?'

'Well I suppose because we had been brought up so closely,' Angela said. 'I knew Barry loved me. He said that when I arrived at your house first, though, he couldn't understand much of it, but he felt sorry for me because he said I looked so sad and he was determined to be the best big brother he could be. And he was and I always loved him. I loved you all of course but there was always a special place in my heart for Barry, my big brother, so when those feelings changed I thought they must be sinful, so sinful I nearly told it in confession.'

'But you didn't,' said Mary with a smile.

'No I didn't because to give voice to it would make it more real,' Angela said. 'At the time I was trying to convince myself that I was imagining things. And I suppose I was sort of ashamed.'

'Well all I'm saying is that others may feel as you did at first,' Mary said. 'In fact some around the doors think you are brother and sister. We came here as a complete family and I thought of you as my daughter by then, and you were a wee sister to all the boys, and so many will think these feelings you have for each other very wrong indeed. And so I don't want you to hide away as if you were guilty of some crime. Hold your heads up high.'

SEVEN

How wise Mary was, Angela often thought in the weeks that followed that little chat, for there was open condemnation from neighbours. George Maitland had been slightly alarmed when she told him as well as being surprised, though he knew they were unrelated because Angela had told him when she first came to work in the shop how it had transpired that she was living with the McCluskys. But he knew what people were like and many he knew would take a dim view of this state of affairs, and the customers in the shop were shocked at first and it didn't entirely stop when Angela told them she wasn't Barry's sister, for some still considered it bordered on an incestuous relationship.

Added to that was what they saw as a lack of respect shown to their two boys drowned in the Atlantic Ocean. 'There was no decent period of mourning at all,' women muttered among themselves around the doors.

'And that cock-and-bull story of her not being related to the McCluskys at all doesn't ring true to me.'

'Yes they're all the same family as far as I'm

concerned,' another agreed. 'I'm surprised Mary doesn't put a stop to it.'

'Wait till Father Brannigan gets to hear. He'll roast the pair of them alive.'

Some women showed their displeasure initially by refusing to be served by her. Angela found the animosity hard to take for she had never encountered it before; she'd always thought she was well liked.

Mary told her to take no notice, that their news would be a seven-day wonder, that was all, and then it would be someone else they turned their attentions upon. Angela knew that that was probably true, but meanwhile she found it hard to approach a group of chattering women, who fell silent as she grew near and ignored any tentative greeting she offered, and she felt their eyes boring into her back as she walked away. 'Miss hoity toity,' someone called after her as she passed. 'Marrying her brother with no respect for the dead.'

Barry seemed not to notice, or at least not to care. 'Why worry?' he asked Angela one Saturday night as they made their way to the cinema. 'While they're pulling us to pieces they're leaving some other poor devil alone.'

But it was almost a fortnight since the news that Angela intended to marry Barry McClusky became public, and just that morning a woman had refused to be served by Angela. She dreaded the day when George Maitland would ask her to leave and although the money she earned as well as the groceries given ensured their survival, she would still be glad not to face the bevy of scornful, judgemental women day after day. She turned to Barry now and said, 'Don't you care what they are thinking about us and what some are even saying?'

Barry gave a little laugh as he shook his head. 'Slides off me like water off a duck's back,' he said. 'It would matter only if it were true, but it isn't. You and I are doing nothing wrong and you must really believe that, or it will taint the time we have together.'

Angela knew Barry was right and cuddling up tight against him as they walked, she felt safe and secure and it was easy to tell that she cared not a jot for the opinion of the neighbours.

After a while the animosity calmed down a little when George eventually took his customers in hand and assured them Angela was no blood relation to the McCluskys and far from showing lack of respect to the two boys that drowned, they decided to marry early to give Mary some reason to go on, to give her something to look forward to, for she was in danger of falling into depression.

Most customers accepted that. Many of George's customers were Catholics and went to St Catherine's and knew the McCluskys to be a respectable family, and no wonder Mary was so very desolate, losing two sons like she had. Giving her a reason to go on would seem to be a good idea. However, over three weeks later another customer, one Edith Cottrell, known for her caustic tongue, still refused to let Angela serve her.

Angela turned away with a sigh and George Maitland saw the tears in her eyes and it angered him. He knew there were plenty of shops on Bristol Street that people could go to if they decided to boycott his shop. And yet he felt that he could no longer stand by and allow Angela to be treated so badly by some of his customers and so he faced the woman and said, 'Angela must serve you, because I'm busy.'

The woman was affronted. 'I'm a respectable person I'll have you know,' she said. 'And I am particular and I will not have that hussy serving me.'

Angela's head shot up and her eyes were no longer full of tears. Instead they flashed fire and her face was flushed as she demanded angrily, 'Who are you to call me a hussy? Let me tell you my foster mother Mary McClusky would likely wash my mouth out with carbolic if she heard me using that word about another person, especially if it was totally unfounded as yours is. I called Mary McClusky my foster mother because that's who she is and the fact that people think she is my mother speaks only of her generosity of spirit that allowed her to take into her home the orphaned child of her dear friend, my mother. She cared for me and gave me as much love as she did her own sons. My name is Angela Kennedy, but soon, when I marry Barry, I will be called McClusky and will be proud of that.'

'Hmph,' Edith Cottrell snapped irritably as she added, 'And does Barry McClusky know what a she-devil you are and one with an evil temper?' She swung round from glaring at Angela to face George Maitland and said, 'You should take care who you employ, or you'll find decent people won't come in here. I'll go elsewhere and I'll spread the news, never fear.'

Angela knew by giving way to that outburst, however justified she might have thought it was, she had alienated one of George Maitland's customers and she knew the knock-on effect that could happen from that. She bitterly regretted risking making life more difficult for such a kind man who had helped her, and therefore the family, a great deal. So she gave a small sigh before saying to

Edith Cottrell, 'You needn't bother going anywhere because it's me that's leaving.' And she removed her apron as she spoke.

'What you doing?' George cried. 'Put that apron back on!' And he leaned across the counter and said, 'Angela will not be leaving, Mrs Cottrell, but you will, for I don't want your sort in here abusing my staff for no reason and, if any of your friends are of like mind, they can stay away too. Good day to you.'

Edith Cottrell looked from Angela biting her bottom lip in anxiety and still clutching her apron in her hands to the resolute George and she said, 'I hope you know what you are doing.'

'I do absolutely,' George said. 'And as I said before, good day to you.'

Edith Cottrell had no option but to leave and as she flounced through the door and shut it behind her with a slam Angela looked at George and said, 'Oh Mr Maitland. What have you done?'

'Something I should have done a while ago. Never could stand the woman anyway.'

'But won't she destroy your business?'

'She may try,' George conceded. 'But the woman isn't liked whereas you are, by many people, and so I think the majority will have more sense than to heed her. Mind,' he added with a little chuckle, 'they may have a peep into the shop to see this she-devil I have working for me.'

'But, George, they should know me,' Angela protested. 'I've been working here ages now and, to be honest, I was surprised anyone had any sort of negative reaction when I told them about me and Barry.'

'It was shock, that's all,' George said. 'And some who moved here after you probably did think that Barry was your brother, for you were all brought up like one big family. Most now, knowing the truth of it, are fine, but you always get the odd ones, like Edith Cottrell, who see sin when none exists. Take no heed of her.'

Angela tried to do just that and it was easy enough to do as Edith never went near the shop. Others did though, for George was right. Whatever it was Edith told them, a stream of women entered the shop over the next few days to buy sundry items, but really to see if Angela had overnight turned into the screaming she-devil virago Edith Cottrell probably described.

They found her unchanged and thought it wrong of Edith to bad-mouth her so, for the girl was doing no harm at all. In a way Edith did Angela a favour because after that everyone behaved as they always had towards her and many even offered their congratulations.

Some expressed concern that she was very young to marry but then others put in that it wasn't as if they didn't know one another. And it wasn't as if Barry and Angela would be totally alone starting married life for they would live with Mary. Barry had made that abundantly clear and Angela didn't seem to mind that either. Truly, if Barry had suggested leaving she would have done her best to dissuade him, for she couldn't bear Mary to be left alone with Matt, who was so still and silent it was as if the lifeblood had been sucked from him.

There was just about enough money to buy everything needed in the house, but little slack and Barry suggested to his mother that she should see if Matt was entitled to anything as he was unable to work.

Mary shook her head. 'There's nothing for the likes of us Barry,' she said. 'If you don't work you starve.'

'No,' Barry cried. 'There's something called the National Insurance Scheme that looks after you when you're sick. Dad has been paying in for a year or so. I don't know much about it because it doesn't apply to apprentices, but the Gaffer – you know Stan Bishop – said to tell you and for you to have a word with him, like. He's been on about it since that last time he called to see Dad.'

Mary knew Stan was an honest man who would put her right about things and she went see him expecting nothing, only to find Matt, like all workers, was in a scheme where he paid four pence a week, the employer three pence and the government two pence, which en- titled him to seven shillings for fifteen weeks, but he had to be deemed unfit to work in the first place by a doctor. It might have ended right there because Mary hadn't money to spend on a doctor who might say there was nothing wrong with Matt at all, and then they would get nothing and still have a doctor's bill to find, and this was what she said to Stan.

'Oh, you don't have to pay for this doctor, Mary,' Stan assured her. 'He's on the panel. That means part of the scheme and paid out of the contributions.'

'And what if they find nothing wrong?' Mary asked for in her heart of hearts she thought Matt was suffering from extreme sadness, because she was suffering from that too, only she had forced herself to get on with life for the sake of the two left to her and the sadness receded slightly to a constant but bearable ache. She had tried talking to Matt who would look at her with rheumy, anguished eyes and just mumble, 'I can't, Mary. I just can't.'

'I think he'll find Matt is too sick to work,' Stan said. 'It hasn't got to be anything physical, but there again he's not a well man, Mary. When I called to see him last time I was shocked at his appearance. He was skin and bone.'

Mary shook her head. 'I know, he won't eat.'

'Well, there is something radically wrong when a fit man shrinks away to nothing,' Stan said. 'Let's get the doctor to have a look at him shall we?'

Matt didn't want to see any doctor and it took the combined efforts of them all to convince him to agree to it, but when the doctor called Mary was on her own, because Barry and Angela were both at work. The doctor was as aloof as most of them were, but he wasn't there to be a friend but to find out if there was something wrong with Matt, or just the loss of his sons that had caused this malaise and weight-loss. She had to admit that the doctor seemed to know his stuff and he checked Matt all over and asked him loads of questions and then he faced him and said directly, 'How long have you known?'

'Known what?' Mary demanded. 'What you on about?'

Matt ignored Mary and it was the doctor he addressed as he said, 'Not long all told.'

Mary looked from one to the other and said, 'Will someone please tell me what's going on?' And then all of a sudden the men's faces were so grave she didn't know whether she wanted to hear what they were going to say. But even as she mentally backed away she told herself it was yet one more thing to be faced. She swallowed the nervous lump that had formed in her throat, faced the doctor and said, 'Go on.'

'Your husband, Mrs McClusky, has a tumour in his stomach,' the doctor said gravely.

Mary wasn't totally sure what a tumour was, but it didn't sound a great thing to have and so she said, 'So can you take it out?'

'I'm afraid not.'

'So what happens now?'

'Nothing happens,' the doctor said, and went on to say to Matt, 'I can give you something for the pain.'

'You never said you were in pain,' Mary said to Matt almost accusingly.

'I was, but I was in such agony at losing the boys anyway,' Matt said. 'That hurt so much, any other pain didn't seem to matter. And then you were suffering too, so how could I load it on you?'

'And were you in a lot of pain?'

Matt shrugged, but the doctor said, 'A great deal of pain, I would have said, judging by the size of the tumour now.'

'Aye,' Matt said. 'The pain was bad enough at times but still nothing to the loss of two sons drowned in the Atlantic Ocean.'

The doctor raised quizzical eyes to Mary and she said, 'Our two sons were lost at sea, making for America to join their older brothers. They travelled on the *Titanic*.'

Everyone knew about the loss of life on the *Titanic* and Mary saw the doctor's eyes widen in sympathy and he quite knew why the man before him had ignored the pain he must have had for some time. Not that it would have made any difference to the outcome, but maybe he could have made him more comfortable.

'Is that really all you can do,' Mary said, 'just give him painkillers?'

'The man can't work miracles, Mary,' Matt said. 'I've come to the end of the road and that's all there is to it.'

Mary had not realized the doctor would be able to do nothing. Doctors were important and powerful and to seek their advice usually cost more money than she ever had, and what was the point if they could offer no cure? Matt on the other hand seemed to accept his fate and he just asked the doctor, 'How long have I got?'

'It's impossible to be absolutely accurate, Mr McClusky,' the doctor said. 'However, the tumour has grown very large and seemingly quite quickly, so I would say months rather than years.'

Mary gave a gasp of shock as she realized that soon she would lose her man, who had been by her side for many years. They had shared in good times and lean ones and she knew she would miss him a great deal.

Matt looked across at her and gave a wan smile as he said, 'Best tell our Barry and Angela to get a move on planning that wedding if they want me at it.' And only Mary saw the tears glittering behind his eyes.

Angela and Barry were devastated to hear what the doctor had said when Mary told them as soon as they arrived home from work. Angela felt tears spring to her eyes because she loved Matt and she would miss him very much. She remembered when she was small and he was fit and strong he would lift her up onto his broad shoulders and carry her around the room. He had a special smile just for her and called her his wee little lassie. However, she didn't let the tears fall because she knew it would be worse for Mary and felt she had to be strong for her, but Mary had had time to come to terms with the doctor's prognosis. Her tears were spent, helped in part by Matt who had urged her not to take on so. He said everyone has to die some time and he'd had a fairly good innings.

And because Matt accepted his imminent death so well, everyone in the family took their cue from him. The Gaffer could hardly believe the report the doctor left with him and he came to see Matt and was sad to see that he had deteriorated further since he'd last seen him. Matt though had accepted his fate and so they chatted together about old times and the years they had worked together.

When the Gaffer left Matt he sought out Barry in the factory. 'Sorry to hear about your father.'

Barry was touched by the Gaffer's such obvious concern and he said, 'Thank you. It was bad news, you know. We thought he was just still grieving over my brothers. Mammy said she feels bad she didn't see how ill Daddy was, but she was distracted by the loss of the lads as well. Neither of them were thinking straight at the time.'

'Of course not,' the Gaffer said. 'That's quite understandable and Mary is not to blame herself in any way. Now this is something else I don't want to load onto her either. With the doctor's diagnosis she is entitled to money but there are forms to fill in and I called at the

107

Post Office on my way back here and got them. But they are so detailed I think they might flummox your mother.'

'I'd say so Gaff,' Barry said. 'Mammy can barely read, let alone fill in forms. Angela and I will see to them.'

'Yes,' Stan said. 'You'll soon be head of the house, young Barry. You must look after your mother.'

'You haven't really to remind me of that, Gaffer, I would do that anyway,' Barry said a trifle stiffly.

'Of course,' Stan said. 'No offence intended.'

'None taken either.'

'Good,' Stan said. 'Good. Now if you pop into the office before you leave here tonight I will give you the forms.'

EIGHT

News of Matt McClusky's illness was sweeping the factory and many patted Barry on the back and said they were sorry to hear it and asked him to pass on their best wishes to his father. When he came home and said this Mary shook her head as she said, 'I know there are no secrets in the back-to-backs, but how they have heard of this so quickly beats me. I mean, two women asked me if it was true that Matt was very sick when I was at the grocer's.'

'I had a customer quiz me too,' Angela said. 'And Maitland's is a step from here.'

'Ah well, you know the three quickest ways to spread news?' Matt said.

'Yes, we know,' said the other three, for they'd heard it often. And they chorused together, 'Telephone, telegraph and tell a woman.'

They laughed gently for it was Matt's stock phrase and Mary marvelled, but was pleased to see Matt taking part in family things again and realized it was probably pain that had paralysed and exhausted him. Now with the strong pain-killers prescribed by the doctor, the life that he had left was more bearable and her conscience smote her afresh for not realizing how sick Matt was.

Mary didn't say this, but what she did say was, 'Well this woman has said nothing about your illness and yet I know it will be common knowledge across the county by the morning, and the one who probably doesn't know yet is the priest, and if he gets the news from other people's tittle tattle, when he does come I will be given a lecture. We need to see him anyway to bring the wedding forward.'

No one asked why. They had decided on a six-month mourning period before marriage out of respect for the two drowned boys and so as they had declared their feelings for one another in May their wedding was set for mid-October. Now there was a real chance that Matt might be dead by then.

And so the following day Mary went along to see the priest and told him about Matt and saw by his face he hadn't known, and he said how sorry he was to hear it, and Mary wished that she could believe one word coming out of his mealy mouth.

When she said they had decided to bring the wedding forward she saw his eyes narrowed in suspicion and he said, 'Is there another reason for this untimely haste? Barry and Angela are very young as I said initially.'

Mary bridled and though usually she was respectful to the priest she was angry enough to forget that as she snapped, 'If you're implying what I think you are, then all I can say is you've got a mucky mind. My Barry and Angela love one another, but they know right from wrong. I have just told you that my man is dying, the man is father to both of them and they love him dearly and they want him at their special day, and it is Matt's

110

dearest wish that he walks his daughter up the aisle and that, and only that, is the reason for bringing the wedding forward.'

The priest was outraged. 'Mrs McClusky!' he almost roared. 'That is no way to speak to a priest.'

Mary was completely unabashed. She shrugged and said, 'Maybe it isn't, but it can't be right implying that our young people have been up to something they shouldn't.'

'I was merely asking . . .'

'No you wasn't,' Mary contradicted. 'You was judging and there isn't anything to judge.'

Suddenly she lost patience with the man and said, 'Now I haven't time for this. Are you going to marry Barry and Angela or aren't you, because if it offends your sensibilities then I'll pop along to St Chad's and ask them to do it?'

She didn't mention this altercation with the priest at home nor did she say that she had rendered the priest almost purple in the face with rage. And he was angry with her for he knew if she did go to St Chad's and said he refused to marry two of his own parishioners it would reflect badly on him.

Mary watched his face working and guessed many of the thoughts running round his head and knew she had him over a barrel. No need for anyone to know that and she said only that the wedding was rescheduled for mid-August and that didn't leave them much time to organize anything and it was a good job they wanted nothing lavish.

Mary was right, the news spread like wildfire. There was a constant stream of visitors to the house for Matt had been a very popular man, and with the wedding of his youngest son Barry to add to all that had happened to him, there was a lot of feeling in these visits. Father Brannigan was less welcome than most and he was stiff with Mary initially, but when he saw Matt, he knew he should have come to see him sooner or at the very least enquired after him when he hadn't been seen at Mass and excused Mary for her outburst, thinking she had a lot on her plate. As for Mary, she was surprised how little it mattered to her that the priest was friendly with her or not.

However, she knew they would soon need the services of a priest so she tried not to antagonize him further and so the visit passed well enough and he promised to call again and possibly hear Matt's confession if he'd like that.

Matt gave a wheezy laugh, 'If you want, Father,' he said. 'And I know it's your job and all, but sitting here day after day has been the most sinless time in my life. I think my soul must be only the slightest bit grey at the moment.'

Mary was smiling as she opened the door for the priest and even he had a grin on his face and she was glad she had kept details of their disagreement from the others so that Matt was able to behave quite normally towards him.

Angela thought it was very hard for her to get totally excited about her wedding. As spring gave way to summer, which was proving to be a warm one and mostly dry, she was aware that as each passing day was one day nearer the day she longed for, when she became Barry's wife, it was also nearer the day when Matt would breathe his last and she would say goodbye to the only father she had ever known.

Barry too was affected by the imminent death of his father and he was also terribly worried about finance. He didn't earn that much as an apprentice, but it was better than nothing and he was concerned that when he qualified he might be laid off as his brothers had been, and if that happened he didn't know how they would survive. At the moment they were all right with Angela working at Maitland's shop and bringing home a pile of groceries every week as well as her wages. And the extra seven shillings a week they had been awarded due to Matt's illness was a godsend, though Mary saved most of it, knowing it was money she could not rely on, but it did mean she could afford to get the medicine to make Matt's life a little easier and dull the pain that he said was like a wild beast tearing his insides out.

Angela knew that Barry was worried about money and so when they went for a walk one sunny evening in late July, she assured him her job at Maitland's would be safe even after she married because George had told her so. 'He said he can see no problem at least till the babies come.'

'Huh, not too many babies I hope,' Barry said. 'God, Father Brannigan would scald me alive if he heard me, but I have no desire to see the body pulled out of you with a baby every year.'

'Barry, I long to hold your child in my arms,' Angela cried.

'I know,' Barry said, slipping his arm around her. 'And when you do I will be the proudest man in the universe. And I want to be the best father in the world and see that the child wants for nothing, and how can I guarantee that if we have too many mouths to feed?'

'But doesn't the Church say that we must be grateful for what God sends?' Angela said, quoting the Church's mantra. Planning your family if you were a Catholic was expressly forbidden.

'I know what the Church says but the Church hasn't to provide for them,' Barry said. 'And you haven't seen the ragged-arsed urchins running the streets. I mean, when I was growing up I was always adequately fed, but some of these children look as if they have never had a square meal in their lives. Their arms and legs are like sticks and they beg for any leftover food at the factory gates when we leave at night. Some get their wives to put up extra and share what they have left but it's so little and there's so many of them. It breaks your heart to see them.'

'Ah, it must do,' Angela said. 'Poor wee children.'

'Yes and I never want my child to suffer like that,' Barry said almost fiercely. 'You've no idea Angela. One chap was telling me he lives near the coal yard and every day at the crack of dawn a gang of them are there with their buckets because when the lorries come out laden with coal, some falls off when they go over the cobbles and they scrabble around and fight each other for these scrappy bits of coal. I never want our son or daughter to be forced to do that either.'

'But how will you stop babies?' Angela asked. 'If we love each other and show that love, don't babies just come from that?'

'Yes, but there are ways of preventing that without spoiling the fun altogether,' Barry said with a coy smile.

'What ways?'

'Don't you be worrying your pretty head about that.'

'I bet it's something the priests wouldn't approve of.'

'Almost certainly,' Barry said. 'And if you knew more you would just worry over it.'

'And you won't?'

'I won't give a tinker's cuss,' Barry said. 'Look, you'll be my wife and we will decide when we'd like to add to our family, not some unmarried priest. Agreed?'

'Yes Sir!' Angela said with a mock salute and a cheeky grin, and Barry caught her up around the waist and spun her round and Angela felt she might burst with happiness.

The days folded one into the next and the kindness of people came to the fore, like the women down the yard who pooled resources to make a cake. A girl she barely knew from Grant Street, who'd got married the previous year, was willing to loan Angela her dress. And Mary took some of the money hoarded from the seven extra shillings a week she was getting from the Insurance and took Angela down to the Rag Market in the Bull Ring on the Saturday before her wedding, set for 17th August. George had given Angela the day off as the Rag Market sold fish through the week and it was only Saturday when it sold clothes, but it was definitely where the bargains were to be found, and Mary bought the softest, loveliest underwear, a silk nightgown and stockings and the prettiest white shoes.

Angela had never owned such lovely things, and thanked Mary as they walked home. 'You don't get married every day of the week,' Mary said. 'And because we went to the Rag Market it wasn't a big cost all together. You are getting married on a shoe-string, my girl, and it wasn't what I wanted for neither of you, nor Matt either. We wanted more of a big splash.'

'Oh I'm not interested in all that sort of razzmatazz,' Angela maintained. 'The important thing is that I am marrying someone I love and that's Barry.'

'It does my heart good to hear you say that because you truly are made for each other.'

'I'm just glad that Daddy has come round about it now,' Angela said. 'It would have put a blight on the day if I was aware of his disapproval.'

'I know,' Mary said. 'I think much of his testiness then was due to the pain he was in, he has admitted as much to me. But I didn't know that and really went for him about the way he was when you announced how you felt about one another, which was no surprise to me and shouldn't have been to Matt if he had eyes in his head. Mind, he did say it's hard to think that just four months after two of our sons' bodies are lying in the Atlantic Ocean we are going to be celebrating a wedding, almost as if their deaths were of no account. And yet his greatest wish in the world is to walk you up the aisle which will be the last act he will do for you.'

Matt seldom walked far now, for the tumour had grown so big it made walking difficult and the way it was positioned made breathing difficult too. 'D'you think he'll manage it?' Angela asked.

Mary shrugged. 'Who knows,' she said. 'I have the offer of the loan of a wheelchair and if he will agree to get into it to be pushed to the church, he has a chance but . . .' and she spread her hands helplessly and added,

'I think we'll just have to wait and see how he is on the day.'

'Yes,' Angela said. 'That's all we can do.'

Angela was such a beautiful bride it brought a lump to Mary's throat. The two had gone up into the bedroom the morning of the wedding so Mary could help her dress. They had given themselves plenty of time because there was something special Mary had to give to Angela. But first there was the dress and no matter that it was loaned, she looked a treat and Mary told her so as she stood before the mirror, now hardly able to believe her reflection.

Mary smiled at the look on her face as she said, 'Now, you must have something old, something new, something borrowed and something blue.'

'Well something new are all my fine underclothes and my shoes are new too,' Angela said. 'And I borrowed the dress and veil and I have the blue lace handkerchief George presented me with, but for something old . . .'

'I have that,' Mary said. 'Something old and very beautiful and it belonged to your mother.'

Angela gasped. 'What is it?'

'It's this,' Mary said and she peeled off the tissue paper from the article in her hand and there in her palm lay a beautiful silver locket. 'When your mother gave you into my care she said that if anything happened to her, then I must give you this on your wedding day, because she received it on hers, as it was a present from your father.'

'It's beautiful,' Angela said, slightly awed to be holding

something that had once belonged to her mother. 'Is there anything in it?'

'Why don't you look?' Mary suggested, holding it out to her. 'It belongs to you now.'

Angela took it from Mary and pressed the catch and the locket opened. In one side was a miniature of the picture that stood on Mary's sideboard that she said was a picture of Angela's parents on their wedding day. She remembered as a child spending hours staring at the picture trying to remember something, anything about her real parents, but there wasn't even a glimmer of memory there. But now she would carry them near her heart always for she vowed then and there she would never take it off.

'That's your hair,' Mary said and in the other half of the locket there were three tiny, but absolutely perfect ringlets tied up with a red silk thread. Angela lifted them out gingerly. 'Was my hair really like that?'

'It was,' Mary said. 'Like a little doll you were. Connie always intended to have a photograph of all of you and a miniature from that for the other side of the locket, but that sort of thing is expensive and when you have a fine houseful of children there is always plenty to spend any spare money on.'

Angela could well understand that but wished it had happened for she had no idea what her siblings had looked like. All she knew was that they were nothing like her because they had all taken after their dark-haired, brown-eyed father, so Matt told her, and she alone took after her golden-haired, blue-eyed mother.

Angela thought of all the times when money must have been tight and she thought of the grinding poverty that had driven them to England in the first place. Though she couldn't remember those austere times herself, Barry had told her how it had been for them and she was amazed that, due to a promise made to a friend, Mary had never felt tempted to try and sell the locket, or at the very least pawn it.

So her gratitude was heartfelt. 'Thank you, Mammy,' Angela said. 'Thank you for keeping it so safe, I will treasure it always.'

The lump in Mary's throat was back and to prevent the tears lurking behind her eyes trickling down her cheeks she said briskly, 'Come, we must be away, for though it's fashionable for a bride to be late, you can't be so late that Barry thinks you're not coming at all.'

Angela gave a gurgle of laughter as she said confidently, 'Barry would never think that.' She hurried nevertheless and when they entered the room Matt was rendered speechless for a moment and then he said with awe, 'Oh, my darling girl, you're beautiful, so you are.' He was immensely glad he had agreed to be pushed to the church in the wheelchair because it meant he might be able to walk the length of the church to the altar, to walk Angela down the aisle. This was terribly important to him for he couldn't have loved her more if she had been his own and as her father he had to do this one last thing for her. He remembered how tickled pink he had been to have a wee girl in the family, when in the aftermath of the tragedy of losing an entire family he had known and liked so well he had realized Angela was theirs for keeps. She was so different to the boys and would love to climb onto his knee, wind her arms around his neck and kiss his leathery cheek. The boys had seldom done such a thing and it always gladdened his heart when Angela did it.

It was only a short walk to St Catherine's Church and a pleasant one that warm, sunny summer's morning. It was far enough for Matt though, and Mary was well aware of that, and she padded the chair with cushions to make it more comfortable for him. As the wheels rumbled over the cobbles neighbours not going to the Nuptial Mass stood in the doorways and cheered them on their way.

The priest was waiting for them in the porch and told them Barry and his best man Stan Bishop were already there. Angela had known Barry had spent the night with Stan so he wouldn't catch sight of the dress, and Stan had assured Angela he would get the groom to the church well ahead of her, and he was a man of his word.

In the porch Matt was eased out of his wheelchair and, biting his lip against the pain, he stood with his arm through Angela's as the Wedding March began. Angela was aware that every step was agonizing for Matt and so their pace was slow down the aisle of that packed church. Barry slipped from the pew and stood before the altar with Stan and by the time Angela and Matt reached them, there wasn't a dry eye in the place.

Matt sank thankfully into the wheelchair Mary had brought for him. Angela stood beside her husband-to-be and threw back her veil. Barry looked at her and saw the radiance in her face and felt his heart miss a beat, and Angela felt her mouth was suddenly very dry and her own heart was hammering in her breast and she knew she loved Barry McClusky more than life itself, and she reached for his hand and squeezed it tight, for soon they would be as one, man and wife.

The wedding had taken a great deal out of Matt but there was no opportunity to rest once they reached home, for in their absence the neighbours had been busy and the house was decorated and the table was groaning with food, adding to the things Mary and Angela had prepared. The two-tiered cake was in the centre and Angela marvelled that people who had so little themselves would go to such lengths to make their day a special one.

And it was so special. Even the weather was kind to them, which was a bonus for the previous few days had been unsettled. 'Ah well,' said Barry when she commented on this, 'The sun shines on the righteous.'

'Oh you, Barry McClusky,' said Angela, giving him a push.

'D'you see that, ma?' Barry said in an appeal to his mother, though he had a great grin plastered to his face. 'Not five minutes married and she's abusing me already.'

'Oh I saw it and I'd say she had reason,' Mary said. 'Sun shines on the righteous indeed.'

The weather did make a difference though because they were able to spill onto the street from the cramped little back-to-back which couldn't hold one quarter of all those who wanted to share in Angela and Barry's special day.

Later when everyone had gone home as it got dark, Mary said she was dropping with tiredness and so Barry helped his father to bed, and Mary followed suit, and Barry and Angela were alone for the first time, and

Barry led Angela to the settee and sat beside her and said, 'Hello Mrs McClusky.'

'Hello Mr McClusky,' Angela replied in like vein.

Barry smiled and put his arm around her and kissed her lips and though the kiss was a chaste one, he felt the blood coursing round his body and heard his heart thumping against his ribs, and he knew he wanted to pick Angela up in his arms, carry her upstairs and ravish her, but he knew he would have to proceed a lot more slowly.

He didn't even know if Angela had any idea what went on in the marriage bed and he asked her gently. Immediately she felt a crimson flush flood her cheeks as she said almost in a whisper, 'I know a little bit Mammy told me. I know about coming together to make a baby. She said it may hurt.'

Barry nodded. 'The first time it may hurt a little, but I'll try to hurt you as little as possible. We'll go up now and I may do things you might think are wrong, but they're not, not now we're married.'

Angela was looking at Barry with large, apprehensive eyes and he laughed gently. 'Don't look at me like that. You trust me don't you?'

'Of course I do, Barry.'

'Come on then,' Barry said, getting to his feet and pulling Angela up next to him and hand in hand they climbed the stairs. They elected to sleep in the attic as they both agreed the bedroom would be more comfortable for Matt and Mary at the moment.

It was a novel experience for Angela because she had never slept in the attic and she had slept in the corner of the bedroom with Mary and Matt, which Mary had curtained off as she grew, for privacy.

Barry was no stranger to the attic and he led his young wife across the oilcloth laid on the floor to the double bed Mary had insisted on buying for them, and he laid her down and began to slowly undress her until she lay naked, shivering and slightly embarrassed. She reached for the silken nightgown she'd laid ready, but Barry took it from her. 'You have no need of this, my love,' he said, as he threw off his own clothes, snuffed out the lamp and got in beside her, 'I will warm you. Lie back now and let me love you properly.'

And Angela did just that and was glad Barry had warned her, because his hands were all over her body stroking and caressing her most intimate parts. Even worse was the fact that she was enjoying it too. She wanted him to go on and on and when a little moan burst from her it was too dark for her to see the small smile of satisfaction that flitted across Barry's face, for he knew he was awakening her sexuality. Angela had an ache inside that she didn't fully understand and when she pleaded, 'Barry, please . . .' she didn't really know what she was asking for.

And then Barry entered her and there was one short, sharp pain but that was followed by waves and waves of exquisite joy that flowed all through her. And when it was over and she lay spent, she thought, so that's sex. The one thing you must stay away from until you are married and no one ever even hinted that it could be so enjoyable. 'Are you all right?' Barry asked, a little concerned by the silence. 'Did I hurt you?'

'Oh no, my darling you didn't hurt me at all,' Angela said. 'You loved me properly, that was all, and it was

123

the greatest thing I have ever experienced and oh, Barry McClusky, I love you more than life itself.'

'And I love you too my darling girl and let's hope we have years ahead of us when I can show you just how much.'

NINE

The following morning, the glowing look on Angela's face told Mary that whatever happened in the marriage bed the previous night had pleased her and she was relieved. She hadn't been able to discuss such things with Barry, for it would have just embarrassed the pair of them, but she had hoped he would go slowly as Angela was so young and quite naive about sexual matters. Maybe he had worked that out for himself though! He seemed delighted as he walked to Mass that morning holding his wife's hand, a wide grin plastered to his face.

They were congratulated by many both before and after Mass that morning, especially by Angela's friend Maggie that she didn't see so much of now they were both working except for meeting after Mass. Maggie threw her arms around her friend and then Barry and wished them many many congratulations. Others were lining up to shake Barry by the hand and hug Angela and some even kissing her on the cheek, causing the familiar crimson flush to flow over her face.

The wedding had taken it out of Matt and anxiety

about him was draining Mary and yet she urged Barry and Angela to enjoy the lovely summer's day. 'Soon you will both be back at work,' she said. 'So make use of the time you have together. Looks like the sun is still continuing to shine on the righteous, as Barry maintains.'

Despite her words though, Angela saw the lines of strain pulling Mary's mouth down and she said firmly, 'We will take a walk out this afternoon after I have eaten the dinner I will help prepare and I am quite determined on that.' Mary didn't argue as she well might have and protest she was all right and would manage fine, and Angela knew she would be glad of her help though she'd probably never admit it, so the women worked amicably together as they had done many times before and Barry sat beside his father and read snippets out of the paper to him.

So it was much later as Angela and Barry walked through Cannon Hill Park that Angela said, 'Do you think we should have let your father go to the wedding?'

'Doubt we could have stopped him,' Barry said. 'He wanted to go so much he agreed to be pushed in a wheelchair, that's how important it was, the prerogative of all fathers to walk their daughters down the aisle and to all intents and purposes he is your father. He'd have probably felt a complete failure if he hadn't been able to do that.'

'But he's ill,' Angela cried. 'I mean he has gone downhill so fast, overnight, for he was a different man yesterday.'

'He was putting on an act yesterday,' Barry said. 'It was our wedding day and he wanted nothing to spoil it.'

'I suppose,' Angela said, and added, 'Your mother has seen the deterioration in him and she's worried. She told me that though he says nothing she knows the pain's worse and she's going to get the doctor tomorrow.'

'Mammy does right calling in the doctor,' Barry said, 'for he said he'd keep Daddy pain free as long as possible and it is all they can do for him now. And that's really the point,' he said to Angela. 'We have to face the fact that my father and your foster father is dying. He has a few months at best and we cannot change that in any way. Now if I was the one dying . . .'

'Oh don't . . .'

Barry smiled at Angela's horror-struck face and said, 'Just imagine if I was, I'd rather be let do things I wanted to do even if it shortened that life, because if you lay in bed and did nothing you would still die anyway.'

They began to make their way back and Angela was assimilating Barry's words when he put in, 'You know if you were to ask Daddy now, I bet even though he feels rough today, he won't regret what he did yesterday. And it wasn't just walking you up the aisle, though that was a big thing for him to do, but added to that was the party that followed the wedding that meant he didn't get any rest at all.'

'He seemed to enjoy that,' Angela said. 'Everyone was so pleased to see him.'

'Yes, they were and he did,' Barry said. 'So if he pays for it now then he does. But the doctor should be able to make his life a little more comfortable.'

The doctor did come the following day and upped Matt's morphine and it eased the pain, but made him drowsier. But Mary wouldn't let Barry and Angela waste their holiday sitting with him now when he slept so much of the time.

Barry still hesitated and Mary gave him a little push. 'Go on,' she urged. 'I will be fine, honestly . . . You just go on and enjoy yourselves while you have the chance.'

They hadn't any money but the weather was kind to them and Angela didn't care where they went as long as they were together, for she was loving Barry more with every passing hour. They could only go where they could walk to and thinking it was no good going to the town looking at things they couldn't afford to buy, they went the other way. Calthorpe Park was a favourite of hers anyway and they walked beneath the avenue of trees still in full leaf though there were a few leaves already littering the ground. She said, 'On a warm day like this it's had to think of these trees stripped bare in the winter.'

'It's hard to think of winter at all,' Barry said. 'I don't know who does like the dark and the cold and the leaden skies, so let's not think about things to come but enjoy this glorious day, which is ours to share and I am here with the most beautiful woman in the world, my wife.' The words and the way he looked at her as he said them caused Angela's stomach to give a lurch and her heart to begin hammering in her breast, and so when Barry drew her into the shadow of some nearby trees and kissed her, she melted into his arms and responded eagerly. They could have easily gone further for they both wanted to, but they controlled themselves with difficulty and Barry knew he had got himself a treasure, a woman he loved who enjoyed sex as much as he did.

And long may it continue, he thought and it had a

chance if Angela wasn't having a child every year. Bringing babies into the world, she might struggle to cope and finding enough for them to eat would be a constant headache . . . What woman in that situation would enjoy sex when at the end there might be yet another mouth to feed?

'Penny for them,' Angela said.

'Oh they're not worth a penny,' Barry said dismissively. 'I was just thinking how much I want to ravish my lady wife but will have to contain myself till tonight.' Angela laughed and Barry grabbed her around the waist and whispered huskily in her ear, 'But it will be all the sweeter for the wait.'

'Barry!' Angela protested. 'Stop it, you are getting me all of a fluster. Hold my hand while we go round the flower beds and try and control yourself.'

With a broad grin on his face, Barry did as Angela asked but she wasn't really cross, rather she felt wanted and desired by the person she loved most in the entire world.

The next day Barry took Angela to the canal. He was no stranger to the canal for he had learnt to swim in there like his brothers before him. Most boys learnt to swim in the 'cut' as it was called, but it was skinny dipping so nice girls didn't go near. Angela had been one of the nice girls, Mary had seen to that, and she'd looked at the dirty, torpid oil-slicked water that smelled quite rank and thought she hadn't missed much not being allowed near the canal. And she also knew that whatever inducement had been offered, she wouldn't have gone into that water for a pension and she was glad she was a girl and would never have been expected to.

However, it was very pleasant walking along the towpath and periodically stepping out of the way of the shaggy enormous-hooved horses that pulled the highly decorated barges through the water. 'Why are they decorated with elephants and roses?' Angela asked.

Barry shrugged. 'Don't know,' he said. 'Always have been so maybe no one remembers the reason why now. Dad told us lads that what the boat people really don't like is being called river gypsies.'

'Why?'

'Cos they aren't I suppose,' Barry said. 'Dad said they were farmers and thrown off the land when the railways came in. I suppose this was the only way of earning a living and giving them somewhere to live as well.'

'I suppose,' Angela agreed. 'Really that's what life is all about isn't it, making enough money to live on?'

She felt sorry for the boaties, as Daddy said they were known, and she had heard many talk of them in a disparaging way. They wore a uniform of sorts, thick boots, cord trousers, cotton shirt, a waistcoat and always a cap. The women wore dark dresses nearly to the floor though often their boots could be seen peeping out beneath them. Their shawls though were more colourful and their bonnets were trimmed with lace. Their children in comparison were very scantily clad in a variety of items and usually barefoot and skipped nimbly from boat to towpath and back again with ease, helping their parents operate the locks.

She had found the whole thing fascinating and she had enjoyed their couple of days off. They couldn't afford any more time off work however and so the next day Angela was back in the shop and customers found that though she'd always been a happy person before, now it like she had a sort of glow about her, for though she was still young she had become a woman like them. Something else gave her more self-assurance than before and that wasn't totally due to being loved up so effectively by Barry – it was to do with her feeling of belonging.

The McCluskys had welcomed her freely into their home and treated her as one of the family and though she loved them all and she couldn't have loved Mary and Matt more if she had been born to them, as she grew up it had bothered her that her name was Kennedy for Matt and Mary had not adopted her in the normal way, but just took her to live with them. She had not been lacking in love and it shouldn't have mattered what her name was. It did, however, and she wasn't sure why it did, and she could never have told Matt or Mary, for they would never have understood and would undoubtedly have been upset. However, now legally she was a McClusky and Barry's parents were hers too and that made her very happy and contented.

Life continued as it always had. Some days Matt was quite bright and other times very ill. Barry reminded her that each day was a bonus and on days when Matt was well, Barry often spent most of the evening reading snippets out of the paper for him and they'd fall to discussing the articles. Mary liked to see Barry showing so much concern for his father and giving him some time, for Mary said he looked forward to Barry coming home because time hung heavy on him.

None spoke of how long Matt had, though they all

knew it couldn't be long and privately Angela wondered if he would see Christmas.

When December arrived, however, Matt was still with them, though he slept most of the day and it was Angela who was feeling under the weather and when she was sick in the chamber pot a few mornings running Barry was beside himself with worry. 'You're doing too much in that bloody shop,' he railed. 'Caught a chill, most likely as well, going out at the crack of dawn. You'll have to tell him it's too much for you.'

Angela knew that Barry was more anxious than angry and she hid her smile because she was fairly certain she knew what ailed her. She hadn't had her monthlies either and she knew they stopped when you were expecting a baby, Mary had told her that, and part of her wanted to catch up Barry's hands and tell him he was going to be a father and dance him around the room at the delight of it all. But she hesitated to say anything because Barry had gone on about the body being pulled out of her if they had a lot of children too close together. He might think this pregnancy too soon, though he must have known there was a good chance of her becoming that way with the sex they enjoyed nearly every night.

Mary couldn't understand her. She had noticed the absence of rags steeping in a bucket of disinfected water every month and heard Angela being sick in the morning and wondered why there had been no announcement. She knew Angela was excited and yet it was a muted excitement and Barry seemed to be totally unaware, at all, and so it was about halfway through December when she said to Angela as she came in from work one evening, 'Isn't there something you need to share with Barry?'

Angela stared at her. 'You know!'

'Course I know,' Mary said. 'I've got eyes and ears and a brain in my head, but apart from all that there's a sort of look about you, oh I don't know how to describe it, just something different, but men don't see these things. Barry doesn't know does he?'

Angela shook her head.

'But why haven't you told him?' Mary asked.

Then Angela told her about Barry wanting to space any family they might have so that she wasn't worn down with it.

'Well, 'Mary said, 'I don't know how he intends to do that. I think you just must be grateful for whatever God sends.'

'I thought he might feel it was too soon.'

'Now, listen to me,' Mary said. 'All that planning your family rubbish is for the future surely. This is your first child and I'll tell you if I know my son, he will be tickled pink at the news and I should not delay telling him. Oh,' she added, 'and when you do don't let on that you've mentioned it to me first. It's important that the husband is the first to know.'

Mary was right, Barry was so delighted he didn't know what to do with himself and he picked Angela up, spun her round, declared she was a clever girl and kissed her passionately and the next thing he said was, 'Who else knows?'

'No one.'

'No one?' Barry repeated. 'Not even Mammy?'

'No one,' Angela assured him, 'Though maybe your

mother guesses something's up. We'll tell her together tonight.'

Barry suddenly clasped his hands to his head and cried, 'God, I can scarcely believe I'm going to be a father.'

'You'd better because it's going to happen,' Angela said.

'My darling you've made me the happiest man in the world,' Barry said, holding Angela tight.

Angela laughed lightly and said, 'Especially when I deliver a son for you.'

'Son or daughter makes no odds to me.'

'I thought all men wanted a son?'

'I am not all men,' Barry said. 'And how could I not love a baby you and I have made with love?'

'Ah, Barry,' Angela said and she melted into his arms.

Barry was so concerned about Angela's pregnancy that he began to irritate everyone. He would barely let Angela lift a finger and said that she definitely had to give up her job. In the end, Angela told him to stop fussing. She wasn't ill and now that she was over the sickness she felt as fit as a fiddle. 'And as for giving up my job, don't you think I will be giving that up soon enough and then won't we miss my money and the bags of groceries I bring home every week?'

Barry knew Angela spoke the truth and seeing the sense of her words said grudgingly, 'All right, keep your job if it means so much to you but I don't want you climbing steps or on chairs to reach things.'

'George wouldn't let me do anything like that,' Angela said reassuringly. 'He's almost as bad as you.'

And he was, Angela was being honest, but he wasn't

that happy about Angela's pregnancy because he knew that he was soon to lose her and would have to get someone else in to help him. He had thought and hoped, being so young, it might be some time before they began a family.

Angela liked George and they got on well together but she often sensed an inner sadness in him that seemed to make him a more caring person and he was extra solicitous towards Angela once he knew of her pregnancy and she told this to Barry to set his mind at rest. Barry was relieved but as he held Angela close he told her what he really wanted was to earn a decent wage so that he could provide for them all.

TEN

Even before Angela announced her pregnancy Barry knew he would have to get Angela's old bed downstairs for his father, because now he was too ill to make the bedroom on his own and the stairs were so narrow, it was difficult for Barry to carry him. It was even more cramped in the small living room with the bed in place but no one bothered complaining, there was nothing else to be done. Now someone would have to sit with him all night too, dozing as well as they could in the chair. 'That will be my job of course,' Barry said.

'Why you of course?' Angela said.

'Because it's not a job for you,' Barry said. 'Not for women, particularly you and my mother. It will be too much for her.'

'Isn't that for me to say?' Mary asked her son. 'And let me tell you, I have more experience of spending the night in a chair and taking what rest I can, for when three of your brothers got the whooping cough I stayed up night after night so Matt could get his rest, for he had a job to do. And so if you think you are doing this by yourself you are mistaken, for you will not be fit to do your job if you were to do that. And remember, Matt is my husband, so my responsibility.'

Barry shook his head. 'Not totally, Mammy,' he said. 'He is my father and if he was of right mind what d'you think he'd say to me letting you sit up with him night after night and me seeking my bed as if he was nothing to me?'

'Why don't we take it in turns then?' Angela said. 'And before anyone says a word, Matt is my father too and this way we will only have to do it every third day and we still won't be leaving him alone.'

And so it was established and when she told Barry of her pregnancy he did balk a bit at her missing sleep and spending her nights in an uncomfortable chair, but he was overruled by Angela and Mary. In this way they limped through Christmas as Matt took a downward turn. He was slipping in and out of consciousness and everyone knew one time he wouldn't wake up again. The neighbours came to see if they could help but there was little they could do, and when the priest saw the state of him he said he should have been told how ill he was and he needed to administer the Last Rites, and it didn't matter a jot that he was unconscious. Mary was greatly comforted when the Last Rites had been given to Matt who, she knew, would soon meet his Maker. The doctor also popped in periodically and when he came just after Christmas, he told Mary Matt was holding on by a hair's breadth and he could go any time.

That was not news to any of them and yet Mary was very glad that she was the one with Matt when the end came in the early hours of Tuesday 8th January 1913.

Matt had been restless that night and so Mary had been unable to settle and was sitting beside his bed wishing she could do something, anything to ease his passing, when he suddenly opened his eyes. Mary was startled because she hadn't seen his eyes wide open like that for a while and they weren't rheumy and pain-riddled, but seemed quite clear and she was even more amazed when he fastened those eyes on her and said, 'We were a good team, Mary,' for Matt had said nothing except the odd unintelligible mumble for some time. However she replied in like manner, 'We were, Matt, a very good team indeed.' They weren't a couple to show affection for one another. It wasn't their way, but uncharacteristically Mary leant forward and kissed Matt's dry paper-thin cheek. She saw his lips turn upwards in a slight smile before his eyelids slid shut again. Mary sat back down in the chair and held Matt's hand firmly and eventually his rasping gasps for breath slowed and she knew he was nearing the end even before she heard the death rattle in his throat.

The room was suddenly very still and Mary knew Matt was gone. With a sigh Mary got to her feet and pulled the sheet over her husband's face before going upstairs to wake Barry.

Barry had thought that because he knew his father was dying, had known for a while, that when he eventually did it would be easier to bear, but he found that wasn't the case at all. 'I suppose it's because death is so final,' he said to Angela.

'I suppose so,' she replied brokenly. 'Oh God, Barry, I will miss him so very much.'

Both Angela and his mother seemed awash with tears and Barry envied them those tears because what he wanted to do was throw himself on the floor and howl his eyes out. But he knew that was a luxury he couldn't allow himself for everyone was relying on him. He was a bit at sea himself and very grateful to Stan Bishop who had told him when his father was diagnosed with terminal illness he would help him with the arrangements for the funeral and so forth if he wanted him to. Barry did indeed need his advice. He had to see him anyway to take a few days off and Stan proved to be a tower of strength.

As was the custom, the neighbours had a whip-round for flowers and though Mary accepted the flowers with good grace, she told Angela she wouldn't be surprised if Matt was turning in his grave. 'Couldn't abide flowers on a grave that would just wither and die in no time at all,' she said. 'He always said if the one who died is the man of the house and maybe the sole breadwinner any money collected should be given to the widow to buy food or to help with the rent. No one can eat flowers.'

Maybe not, but a good send-off was considered of great importance so on the day of the funeral the wreath from the neighbours was laid on the coffin before the altar at St Catherine's alongside the family flowers. It was also fairly littered with Mass Cards, which were sent by Catholic relatives and good friends, including Matt and Mary's two sons in America. They both sent loving letters of condolence and each had folded a ten-dollar bill inside the envelope which they said was to 'help' with things. It was more money than Mary had ever seen in her life and Barry advised her to put it straight into the Post Office where they would change it to sterling.

The day was a keen one and it was cold enough in the lofty church during the long and mournful Requiem Mass, despite the fact that it was packed. Angela dreaded the walk to Key Hill Cemetery in Hockley in such cold and as they stepped out of the church their breath escaped in wispy trails from their mouths and they were assailed by a biting wind sending flurries of ice-laden snow that fell from a leaden sky.

The coffin was pushed before them on a cart as they walked in a procession, led by Father Brannigan. Barry came after him, with his arm around his mother and Stan Bishop took care of Angela. Everyone else followed behind and stood dithering at the graveside while Father Brannigan intoned prayers for the dear departed.

Eventually it was over, the prayers said, the coffin lowered, the clods of earth thrown on top and the crowds turned thankfully to make their way to the back room of The Swan public house on Bell Barn Road where Mary and Angela had made enough food to feed the masses, helped greatly by George Maitland who had donated a great deal of the food and willingly gave Angela time off to be with Mary and help her through this dreadful time. Mary shed tears at George's generosity and only wished she could thank him in person but it was Saturday, and that was his busiest day in the shop and though he would have liked to close to attend the funeral he knew he would let a lot of people down if he did that.

Many people marvelled at the spread the two women

had managed to conjure up in those austere days. They certainly appreciated it and Angela watched the food they had taken days to prepare disappear faster than the speed of light. She couldn't begrudge them, though, for by coming to the funeral they were showing respect for Mary, and Angela knew if Mary thought she had the support of the neighbours it would help her cope better.

And the neighbours did gather around Mary after the funeral which meant Angela could stop worrying about her and mourn Matt herself. But life must go on and she returned to work the day after the funeral and accepted condolences from George and many customers, knowing that the pain at the loss of Matt would eventually settle to a bearable ache and she would be able to look forward to the birth of her baby who she thought would help them all.

However before the birth Barry came home one day in March with good news. He was just a fortnight away from his twentieth birthday and Stan had called him into the office because he had a proposal to put to him. Although Barry couldn't officially finish his apprenticeship for another year, Stan had seen the chap in charge of the apprentices and he said that there was really no more he could teach Barry and that he was a good and conscientious worker and so Stan decided to finish his apprenticeship a year early. It needed the approval of the management, but the death of Matt who had worked for the firm meant that Barry was now the sole breadwinner and had glowing praise from his superiors, so they decided to stretch a point. And so from his birthday his wage would rise to £3 a week which had been what his father earned. The women were very pleased, particularly Angela who had been concerned at how they would manage financially when she had to give her job up at Maitland's shop.

George was pleased at her news though he had to admit to himself that part of him had hoped that finances would ensure Angela stayed working for him, leaving Mary to care for the child. Now he knew that wasn't going to happen. Not only was Angela a good worker, she was also like a ray of sunshine and he knew he would miss her greatly. But he didn't betray his inner thoughts in any way and congratulated Angela and said to pass on his good wishes to Barry before going on to say, 'You surprise me, though, for most employers I know of are not generally concerned with the welfare of workers unless it affects their ability to work hard and make them plenty of profit.'

'I think that it's Stan that made a difference,' Angela said. 'He was very fond of Matt and suffered alongside him when the boys were drowned, and when he saw how ill Matt was he was shocked and came to see him many times and sorted out the sick pay and everything. He felt guilty about Barry's two brothers who were laid off as soon as they were through their apprenticeship.'

'That's what I mean,' George said. 'That's common practice.'

Angela nodded. 'I know,' she said. 'But then those boys decided to try their hand in America and perished in the sea. It made me wonder if they would have been so keen to go if they were regularly employed. And if I thought that, I bet it crossed Stan's mind too. He told Barry that his hands had been tied over that, but he would ensure it never happened to him, and now this news.'

'I know. It's almost unbelievable.'

'Stan thinks it's likely there's going to be a war.'

'A war?' George repeated. 'What gives him that idea?'

'I asked Barry that and he said it's because of all the unrest in Europe.'

'There's always upset in Europe,' George said dismissively. 'If we bothered about everyone we'd never be away from the place. Very volatile, the Europeans are, generally. Anyway, what happens over there doesn't affect us.'

'No I suppose not,' Angela said. 'Stan asked Barry if there was a war, would he go, enlist you know? Barry said, not likely, not unless he was forced to, that is. He said he had to look after his mother and me and our baby and that was enough to be going on with. Stan said he was glad Barry was so sensible and he wished all young fellows felt the same.'

'I'd agree with him there,' George said. 'Some young fellows are hot-heads altogether. So let's hope England doesn't allow herself to be pulled into a war that is really no concern of ours and we keep our young fellows at home, where they belong, until they mature a bit.'

'Ah, yes indeed,' Angela agreed.

According to Iris Metcalf, who was the woman most neighbours called on when their babies were due because few used the services of a doctor unless in an emergency, Angela's baby was due towards the end of May, maybe 24th or thereabouts, and so when March drew to a close Barry told Angela she should think about giving in her notice. However, Angela felt incredibly well and with Mary doing the lion's share of the housework and cooking, she didn't see the necessity.

However, someone else was concerned about Angela continuing at the shop, or maybe incensed might be a better name for it. Matilda thought, even assumed that Angela would give in her notice as soon as she became pregnant. It was after all what any decent woman would do, but George said the family needed her wages to survive. And so she continued to come and flaunt herself. Matilda had told George it wasn't seemly to have Angela at the front of the shop serving people and he reminded her that he made the rules in the shop, not her.

In all other ways in the home and even the marriage Matilda held sway and got everything she wanted, but from the first George had made it clear that the shop was his domain, as it had been his father's and before him his grandfather's, and he made the decisions. This suited Matilda mainly because it gave them a good living and she had no desire to enter the smelly shop let alone work there. She had once hankered after a terrace house in some grander area far away from the cramped houses in the mean little streets, but George always said it was more practical to live in the flat above the shop. 'It's plenty big enough for us two,' he'd said the first time she had asked him and he had stuck to it like a mantra and in the past would often go on, 'I mean it isn't as if we have a house full of children.' He had stopped using this as another stick to beat her with because she couldn't help not liking children. And she really thought what women had to endure to conceive was too disgusting for words and she was having no truck with that. But George's paternal feelings had been turned on when Angela McClusky came to work in the shop. He was more than just fond of her and that was like a thorn in Matilda's side and she begrudged every mouthful of the dinner she took as her right because George said so. But she knew Angela couldn't go on much longer. So when she was still there the first week in April she said to George as they sat eating their evening meal, 'I just hope you have honed up your midwifery skills, that's all I can say.'

'What?'

'I think you heard,' Matilda said testily. 'I hope you know just what to do when Angela McClusky goes into labour in the shop in front of all the customers.'

George blanched at the thought, but said firmly enough, 'That won't happen.'

'And how are you going to ensure that, pray?' Matilda said. 'According to what I hear, babies have an annoying habit of coming unannounced whenever they please and the more inconvenient the time the better. Tell you what,' she added, 'I am surprised that young husband of hers has not been up to see you before now, because you are putting Angela at risk, not to mention their unborn child if she carries on like this. And you can't even use the excuse that they need the money any more because from what I hear he is on good money now.'

Matilda's words hit home for George knew a lot of what she said was right and he thought himself selfish and insensitive not to encourage Angela to leave, just because he was dreading not seeing her again. But he may have put her at risk. Pregnant women should rest, he had heard, and though Angela had never said she wanted to leave, he knew he should have insisted and before he could talk himself out of it, then and there he went down to the shop, packed a bag of groceries, and went down to see Angela with two weeks' wages in his pocket to tell her that for her own sake she mustn't come to the shop any more.

Both Barry and Mary were relieved that Angela was released from the shop and she could rest more, and though Angela missed the shop and had never complained, the ponderous weight she was now carrying around did wear her out, so she knew it was probably for the best.

Now that money was easier Barry gave Angela money to buy some things for the baby and she went to the Bull Ring with Mary. They wandered around the stalls comparing prices and chose what to buy with care. Eventually they bought some soft sheeting to cut into squares to make nappies and they also bought rubber pants. 'A marvellous invention,' Mary called them. 'There were none of these sorts of things in rural Ireland when mine were growing up,' she said. They added long nightdresses, little vests, a couple of crocheted matinee jackets, a bonnet, bootees, a couple of warm wool blankets and a shawl. 'Now,' Mary said, as they set off for home, 'we're all ready. All we're waiting on is the baby.'

'Oh yes,' Angela said. 'I hope it's soon. Nine months is such a long time.'

'It's no time at all to grow a new life,' Mary said. 'Don't fret, your baby will come when he or she is ready and that's how it should be.'

ELEVEN

Angela's pains began in the early hours of 24th May. It was Saturday and Barry worked half a day and so Angela said nothing to him. Although she longed to meet the baby she had carried for so long, she was nervous of the birth and Mary understood this and so gave her some idea of what to expect. 'A first baby usually takes its time,' she said. 'After that it's as if the body knows what to do. But the labour with a first is usually longer and when your pains start they are little more than a grumbling, not unlike the pain you sometimes get with your monthlies.'

And lying in the bed that morning, Angela thought Mary had been right, for the pains were like the drawing pains she'd had each month before she became pregnant, when she would search out the cotton pads she always had ready in the cupboard. 'Best thing in the early stages is to keep moving,' Mary had advised and Angela knew that she was probably right about that too, but she could hardly leave her bed so early and walk the floor.

All that would do would be to wake Barry and then once he realized what was happening he would probably not want to go to work but stay at home fussing all around her and worrying himself into an early grave. No, it was better Barry was kept in ignorance for a wee while yet and she closed her eyes and tried to rest, drawing her legs up to ease the pains slightly.

Next to her in the bed, Barry was awake though he kept his eyes shut. Since Angela's time drew nearer he had tended to sleep more lightly and so he had been aware of her slight movement when the pain woke her first and was aware of her beside him now with her knees pulled up and sometimes giving small gasps that she tried to smother. Angela was right that he was anxious, for as his darling wife had grown bigger and ungainly he realized what he had done and what Angela would have to go through to give birth to the child.

He loved Angela more than life itself, but she was young, surely too young to start having babies when she had scarcely finished maturing. He had said as much to his mother out of Angela's hearing and she had said, 'Tell you the truth, Barry, I have thought the same myself. But see, Son, what's done is done. Angela might be small and young, but she's strong enough and I have sounded out Iris Metcalf and you know she's helped the birth of nearly every child in this street, so she knows her stuff. We just have to put our trust in God, that's all.'

It wasn't that reassuring and Barry hadn't the same belief in prayer as his mother and he felt totally helpless. But he reasoned there was no need for him to lie there when Angela was obviously in pain and trying to cover it up, so he whispered, 'Angela.'

150

'Oh I'm sorry,' Angela whispered back. 'Did I wake you?'

'I was awake anyway,' Barry said. 'Are you all right?'

'Right as rain,' Angela said and then gave a gasp as another pain gripped her.

'Doesn't sound it to me,' Barry said. 'Shall I fetch Mammy?'

'No,' Angela said firmly and added, 'Look Barry, it is the baby coming but your mother assures me that first babies take ages.'

'Even so, I won't go in today,' Barry said. 'They'll understand I have to stay with you.'

'To do what exactly?'

'What d'you mean?'

'I mean what is the point of you staying away from work?' Angela said. 'I told you your mother said it takes ages and she meant hours, not minutes, and you can do nothing during that time. You might not even be let in the room. I know your mother thinks it's no place for a man when a woman is giving birth and it's more than likely the midwife will feel the same way. You'd just be kicking your heels and worrying more than ever.'

'I feel so useless.'

Angela gave a wry smile. 'I imagine most men do,' she said. 'Your work is over until the baby's born and then you can prove that you are the best father in Christendom.'

'I will be that all right,' Barry said fervently. 'But can I do anything for you now? How about me making you a nice hot cup of tea?'

Angela knew there was going to be no further sleep or rest for either of them that night and said, as she attempted to get out of bed, 'Your mother said it was best to move around.'

Barry pushed her gently back onto the pillows and said, 'Don't care what my mother said. I am going downstairs now to make a cup of tea for my lady wife because it is all I can do for the woman who is soon going to make me the proudest man on earth.'

Angela's eyes filled with tears at Barry's lovely words and she knew it was important that he made that tea. 'Are you sure?' she asked.

'Course I'm sure,' Barry said, slipping his trousers on as he spoke. 'If only to prove to you that I'm not bloody helpless.'

He pushed his feet into his boots, gave Angela a kiss and left the attic. And Angela heard the clatter of his boots on the stairs in the still night and knew it was unlikely Mary would sleep through it and would probably work out why Barry was going downstairs so early.

Angela was right and a few minutes later she heard Mary's laboured breath as she ascended the stairs. She was wearing an old robe wrapped over her nightdress but Angela was pleased that she had the warm slippers on her feet that she had bought her for Christmas. 'Is it time?' she asked Angela, but she was in the throes of another contraction that answered her question.

'And where's his Lordship off to?' Mary asked. 'It was like a herd of elephants going down the stairs.'

'Angela smiled. 'I know,' she said and despite the fact she felt bad about waking Mary it was very reassuring to have her there. 'He's making me a cup of tea,' she told Mary. 'He insisted. He said he feels useless.'

'Well he will,' Mary said. 'Most men are useless when

it comes to the birth. But making a cup of tea won't hurt him and drinking it won't hurt you. After he is packed off to work I want you to move down to the bedroom where you will be more comfortable and that will be your room from now on and I will relocate to the attic.'

'Are you sure?'

'Course I am,' Mary said. 'It's right now for me to move to the attic. But I must try and protect the mattress by covering it with some rubber sheeting I got hold of.'

'Barry did threaten not to go in today,' Angela said to Mary. 'He wanted to stay with me.'

'Stuff and nonsense!' Mary said impatiently. 'Men are neither use nor ornament when a woman is giving birth and I wouldn't have him, or any other man cluttering up the bedroom, so going to work is the only sensible thing to do and I shall tell him that when he gets here with the tea.' And Mary did tell Barry and in a tone that brooked no argument though he did try.

Mary went down to see to the bed and when Angela had finished the tea Mary and Barry helped her down to the bedroom, and Mary told her to rest between contractions while she followed Barry downstairs and cooked him breakfast. It was too early for him to go to work so Mary asked him to top up the coal scuttle with coal from the cellar and also fill the kettle and the large pan with water from the tap in the yard, and Mary hung those over the fire so there would be plenty of warm water when it was needed.

As soon as Barry left Mary cooked porridge for Angela to give her strength for the ordeal ahead. She took it up to her to find her in quite a lot more pain.

She didn't really want the porridge, but ate it to please Mary, but she was grateful for the second cup of tea she brought.

Despite Mary saying it was better to move around in the early stages Angela found it hard to stand and with each contraction she had the desire to crouch. When she told Mary this she said, 'You might surprise us all and give birth quicker than I imagined. Will you be all right if I pop along to tell Iris you've started?'

'No I'll be fine and I'd really like to see her,' Angela said for she liked the doughty little woman. She felt safe in her hands; she knew what she was doing and she was clean.

When she said this to Mary she agreed. 'Some dirty ones about. Most around here have Iris now, but before she moved here about ten years ago women would get who they could to help if they had no handy relatives, and the tales they have told me about some of these old hags, gin sodden many of them and completely useless! I've heard some right horror stories. There's none of that sort of carry-on with Iris. Anyway I won't be a tick.'

Mary was much longer than a tick. But then she brought Iris back with her and Angela was relieved to see her because the space between the contractions had shortened considerably and the pains were much stronger. 'Let's have a little look, ducks,' she said throwing back the bedclothes. She gave a grunt of satisfaction as she stood up again and said with a smile to Angela, 'You're almost ready. Not be that long till you're holding your wee baby in your arms.'

Angela felt a thrill of excitement run through her even though Iris went on to say, 'Still a wee bit of work

154

to do yet, I need to see everything is going well inside, but I need to scrub my hands well before I do that.'

'I have warm water ready,' Mary said and led the way downstairs. Iris was very gentle in her examination and declared everything was as it should be and they just had to wait. And that's what they did while Angela's pains grew in intensity. Mary made tea for them all and when Angela began to writhe in the bed, trying to escape the wild beast tearing her insides out, Iris tied a towel to the bedhead for her to pull on when the pains got bad. 'They are bad already,' Angela wanted to say but she wasn't able to say much as a massive contraction disabled her and then there was a sudden rush of water from her body. 'That's your waters gone,' Iris said. 'Won't be long now.'

Mary positioned herself at Angela's head and suffered with her though every pain as she bathed her face, which was shiny with sweat, and she offered her sips of water and encouraged her gently. 'Come on, my bonny lassie,' she said, using the endearment Matt always used. 'You can do this. Ride the pain, lassie.'

Sometime in this maelstrom of pain and discomfort Barry came home from work. Mary would not let him see Angela who she said wasn't fit to be seen and also said she had work in the room above and if he wanted anything to eat he had to make it himself. Such a thing had never happened before to Barry, and yet this was a special day and, please God, at the end of it he was going to be a father.

That exhilarating thought coursed through his body and he had no intention of sullying the day with any trace of ill humour and so he said, 'I'll knock up a sandwich for myself, never fear. Go back to Angela. I'd say her need is greater than mine.' Mary scurried back upstairs and took her place again at the head of the bed and she hadn't been there that long when Angela said she wanted to push.

This last stage of the birth was what had worried Mary the most, thinking Angela might tear herself badly, or even haemorrhage if the strain on her slim young body was too great. Iris knew what Mary was concerned about because she told her that morning as they walked to the house and so she examined Angela swiftly. 'She's wide enough,' she said reassuringly to Mary and to Angela she said, 'Push away, ducks. This baby is anxious to be born.'

Now Angela understood the reason for the towel which she pulled on so hard she threatened to pull the bedhead down on top of her because she had never experienced such pain. She felt as if she was on fire and was trying to give birth to a red-hot cannon ball and her low moans had turned to shrieks. And Mary and Iris were encouraging her to give one more push and yet one more. She wanted to tell them to shut up but hadn't breath left to do it.

Just when she really thought she could do no more Iris called out, 'I can see the head! Come on, Angela, give it all you've got.'

Angela gathered all her strength and pushed with all her might. 'Good girl,' Iris said approvingly. 'Give another like that.'

Angela did but then she lay back on the bed and said, 'I can't do any more.'

'Every woman feels like that,' Iris aid airily. 'Have a

156

breather and when the urge to push comes again then go with it and push with all your might. One more decent push might do it.'

The urge to push couldn't be ignored and when it came Angela's whole face was contorted as she pushed with all the strength she had left. There was a sudden extreme pain and her breath left her body in a scream and then she felt something slither between her legs and newborn wails filled the room.

'Oh Angela, you clever girl,' Mary said and her voice was husky with unshed tears as she went on, 'You have a beautiful little daughter.'

'Oh let me see her,' Angela said, struggling to sit up.

Iris wrapped her in the shawl Mary had ready and placed her in Angela's outstretched arms. She gazed into her beautiful face and the milky-blue eyes flickered shut as Angela rocked her gently. She felt such a powerful tug of love for the child that she gave a gasp. 'I didn't think it was possible to love a child as much as this,' she said in awe. 'I love Barry but this is . . .'

'Mother love, that's what that is,' Iris said. 'I think it's the most powerful emotion in the world.'

'I agree with you,' Mary said. 'Matt always said it was nature's way of ensuring that mothers would protect their young.'

'Yes, fortunately human beings don't have to do much of that,' Iris said. 'Now where's that young husband of yours, for I'm sure he would like to get acquainted with his new baby daughter?'

'Don't know where he is,' Mary admitted. 'Thought he'd be wearing the floorboards out in the room below to be honest. I best seek him out.'

In the end there was no need to do that. Barry had been pacing the room like a caged tiger but each time he opened the door to the stairs he heard his young wife's moans and it tore at his heart-strings. He wanted to run up and see what was happening to her but he knew his mother and the midwife wouldn't let him in.

So, as he could do nothing to help her, he had to be somewhere where he couldn't hear her suffering and the only place was outside and so he went out. He needed to keep moving, to walk, but he didn't intend to go far from the house and so he was walking aimlessly along Bell Barn Road, down Bristol Passage to Bristol Street and back again.

He was approaching the house when a neighbour sitting on her doorstep taking the air said as he passed, 'Hope everything's all right, Barry. Your Angela gave out such a scream a few minutes ago.'

The blood ran like ice in Barry's veins and he tore down the street to the house, wrenched open the door of the stairs, leapt up them two at a time, yanked open the bedroom door and just stood and stared at the woman he loved so dearly holding a baby, their baby, in her arms as if she had done it every day of her life. He had eyes for no one else and his eyes were so full of love and amazement it was beautiful to see.

Iris whispered to Mary, 'Let's go and have a cup of tea. I'll have to clean the baby up later and check she's all right, but it can wait. I think those two need some time to bond with their baby.'

Neither Angela nor Barry were really aware of Mary and Iris leaving the room and Barry continued to gaze at his child as if he couldn't believe his eyes. 'It's a girl,

Barry,' Angela said gently. 'Are you disappointed that I haven't given you a son?'

'Disappointed?' Barry repeated as if he couldn't quite believe his ears. 'My darling girl, what are you thinking of? Between us we've created this perfect child and she'll grow to be as beautiful as her mother, inside and out, and gladden our hearts with every passing year, and you ask if I am disappointed? I am not, not in the slightest and I don't care if I never have a son.'

Angela sighed with relief. 'The next one will be a son,' she said.

'Son or daughter will make no odds when the time comes,' Barry said. 'But I meant what I said before this one was born. I want you fully recovered from the birth and to have a few years enjoying our daughter before we give her a playmate. Have you a name for her? You would never discuss it before the birth and as you did all the work it should be your decision.'

Angela smiled. She had never discussed names with anyone, thinking it unlucky, but she had decided almost from the time she realized she was pregnant what to call a girl and she said, 'I would like her called after my mother and yours, Constance Mary. D'you like it?'

'I love it,' Barry said. 'And it's right that you should honour your mother in that way and my mother will be over the moon.' Barry leant forward and kissed the baby's soft, soft skin gently and said, 'Hello, Constance Mary McClusky, welcome to our family.'

And Angela thought she just might burst with happiness.

*　　*　　*

Neighbours had streamed into the house those first few days after Connie's birth all carrying a gift of some sort, a rattle or teething ring, a small cardigan or pretty nightgown, and they all admired the child who they said was the image of her mother. Even George came and Angela was delighted to see him and he brought a complete pram suit for the baby to wear as she got older when the winter set in. Barry's brothers sent a couple of beautiful dresses trimmed with lace and bedecked with ribbons that they said were all the rage in the States.

'And they might well be too,' Mary said. 'But they're not very practical. When you are out of your lying in we'll take a dander up to the Rag Market for more everyday clothes for Madam here.'

However, before they could do this Mary opened the door to see Maggie outside with a pram full of baby clothes. 'What's all this?'

'Hello, Mrs McClusky,' she said, 'I've come to see Angela and the baby and these are from me mother. She had a clear-out and thought you might like these old baby things and the pram because she doesn't need that either.'

'How kind of her,' Mary said. 'Is she sure?'

'She is,' Maggie said with an emphatic nod of her head and added with a grin, 'She said she is giving up all that sort of nonsense now and said my father must tie a knot in it. I think Mammy is glad to get rid of the stuff for wee Maurice is six now. And it's too cramped in the attic to keep clothes she has no use for. She said take them and welcome.'

Angela was very grateful for the bag of clothes, which

were lovely and she lifted one after the other with a cry of delight. 'There's a christening gown at the bottom,' Maggie said. 'It's well-worn for we have all been christened in it.'

It didn't look at all well worn, Angela thought as she peeled back the tissue paper it had been wrapped in and sat gently stroking the silken fabric. 'It's so soft and so white,' she said. 'It looks brand new.'

'Oh that's Mammy,' Maggie said. 'She has this thing that the gown shouldn't ever look second-hand and so every time it's worn she washes it in that soft Lux soap and whitens it with Becket's Blue in the final rinse water and when it's dry she wraps it in tissue paper and stores it in a drawer in her room because the bedroom is not as damp as the attic.'

'Well it worked, will you tell her, and I am very grateful,' Angela said.

'I will,' Maggie promised and added, 'She's sent over her old pram as well, that she was glad to be shot of I think.'

'Oh I will be so glad to have that,' Angela said fervently, her face a big beam of happiness because she hadn't known how they were going to afford a pram and though the baby would be fine in a shawl for now, when the winter came she would like her tucked up warm and cosy.

'Hey,' Maggie said suddenly, 'can I have a wee cuddle?' Angela smiled as she lifted the sleeping baby from the cradle at her side of the bed and placed her into Maggie's outstretched arms. The baby just wriggled a little, protesting at being disturbed, and then she settled and her breathing became steady as she slumbered on. Over the child's head, Maggie's smiling eyes met those of Angela and she hugged the baby a little tighter and said, 'Oh isn't she just lovely? You are so lucky, marrying the boy of your dreams and having this beautiful baby and still just seventeen. Everyone is envious of you.'

'Oh I hope you're wrong about that,' Angela said. 'Being envious is not a good thing to be.'

'It's not said in a horrible way,' Maggie assured Angela and went on, 'People are pleased for you. I suppose it's because you had such a bad start and people are just glad it has turned out so well for you.'

'I never felt I had a bad start really,' Angela admitted. 'I mean, I know I lost my entire family and that might be thought of as sad, but I was too young to remember them and I was lucky enough to be given a whole new family, the McCluskys. I never lacked love or care and that's really what matters to a child. And as for Barry, though I love him dearly I never think of him as the boy of my dreams, he was just always there and I always felt safe when he was around.'

'But you don't think of him as a sort of brother, do you?'

'Not now I don't,' Angela said. 'Anyway, what about you and Mike Malone?

Maggie gave a shrug. 'Oh he's just a neighbour, a friend that's all.'

'No great passion then?'

'No,' Maggie said, but a smile played around her mouth and Angela could make a good guess that Maggie would have liked Mike to be more than a friend. She liked him too because he was a really nice lad and as

162

he was the same age as Barry, they had been firm friends when they had been at school together.

So Angela said, 'You don't know that your feelings won't change. They often do as you grow. I mean, look at me and Barry, I only thought of him in a brotherly way for years. But then I began to realize that I loved him in a different way and now our love has deepened and become stronger.'

'There's still hope for me then,' Maggie said.

'I'd say.'

'And you do truly love Barry now, I mean properly like a husband?'

Angela smiled as she said, 'Yes, well it isn't as though I've had a plethora of other husbands to practise on, but for example we didn't get young Connie there from holding hands.'

Maggie's peal of laughter caused the baby to jump slightly before settling again to sleep as Maggie said, 'I never thought for one moment you did. But didn't you miss your mother more when you had a child of your own?'

'How could I miss what I never had?' Angela said. 'This is all I have of my parents.' And she opened the locket she always wore around her neck for Maggie to see. 'This was given to me on my wedding day. It was my father's present to my mother when they married and it will be Connie's on her wedding day. I look at that picture sometimes and try to remember, but it's still all a blank to me. I have named the baby Constance after my mother, though, and Mary as well after Barry's mother.'

'Constance Mary,' Maggie said. 'They're good names'

163

'Glad you like them,' Angela said, 'because I'd like you to be Connie's godmother.'

Maggie was astounded because it was the last thing she'd expected, but she was obviously pleased. She grabbed at Angela's arm and cried, 'Oh my God, do you mean it? I would be so thrilled . . . Oh I never expected that. Oh Angela I am so thrilled.'

Angela was quietly amused by Maggie's reaction because she had thought of Maggie straight away and Stan Bishop was to be godfather.

'I take it you'll accept? she said.

'You bet I accept,' Maggie said. 'You couldn't have said anything that would please me more.'

And so, a few days afterwards Constance Mary McClusky was baptized at St Catherine's Church. Even Father Brannigan seemed a little more human. At Mass he announced the baptism that would take place that afternoon and a great many people congratulated Angela and Barry outside the church. When she saw Maggie Angela said quietly, 'Did you see Father Brannigan? He almost had smile on his face.'

'No,' Maggie said. 'I thought so too at first, but I think it was just a touch of wind he had.'

Angela bit her lip to stop a giggle escaping for she could see Father Brannigan making his way towards them and she remembered Maggie had whispered things like that to her before at school, causing her to laugh at inappropriate times and get into trouble, and she could hardly laugh in the priest's face. 'All ready for this afternoon?' he asked Angela.

'I think so, Father.'

'I do think the names you have chosen eminently

suitable,' the priest said. 'It's right that you honour the woman who gave birth to you and the woman who reared you.'

Angela nodded. 'I thought that, Father, and Mary was so pleased to be included and she deserved to be for she was a wonderful mother to me. Now she is so much looking forward to having a baby in the house again.'

'And you having Maggie here to look after her spiritual welfare.'

Maggie gave a grin and said impishly, 'I'll do my best, Father. And I will have Stan Bishop to help me so, between the two of us, we'll endeavour to ensure that Connie McClusky turns out a good little Catholic.'

Father Brannigan frowned slightly, not sure that Maggie wasn't making fun of him. It wasn't the words she said, but her manner, yet her face looked innocent enough and he decided he might have imagined it and he turned back to Angela. 'So I look forward to seeing you all this afternoon at four-thirty sharp.'

Angela thought how different a church is with so few people in it. Voices seemed to carry further and had an echoing sound and even shoes sounded loud on the marble floor and despite the fact that it was now early June, it was chilly in that stone edifice with its vaulted ceilings.

Connie bawled her head off when she was roused from her slumber by some strange person pouring cold water on her head. Mary said it was good to yell, it was getting the devil out of her. Angela looked across at the baby in Maggie's arms and thought she was innocent and pure and had no devil inside her, but now was not the time to argue about it. Everyone, including Father Brannigan, was going back to the house for a bite to eat for it was a special day and she had helped Mary make a fair few fancies as well as lots of sandwiches. Connie behaved angelically once the water-pouring was over and in the house she was passed from one to another with barely a murmur. 'Isn't she a little star?' Barry said that night as they undressed for bed with the baby slumbering in the cradle beside them.

'She is,' Angela said and added with a grin, 'Takes after her mother there.'

'Ho! And one who thinks a lot of herself as well,' Barry said and gave Angela a playful tap on the bottom and then he turned her around and kissed her.

Angela felt frissons of desire run through her body and when Barry said huskily, 'My darling girl, you have made me the happiest man in the world,' she answered, 'If you come to bed, I know a way to make you happier still.' And Barry lost no time in getting beneath the covers and cuddling up to Angela and she sighed in contentment.

TWELVE

Angela never forgot the wonderful summer of 1913. The whole family doted on the child. Just to look at her made Angela's heart melt and she wasn't the only one, for she helped to mend Mary's heart, which Angela thought had been broken when she lost her sons and badly bruised too at the death of Matt.

In fact, Connie's birth helped everyone because she was a sunny, happy child and Angela took her out every day, pushing the pram proudly. She went to see George when Connie was just over a fortnight old and he had tears in his eyes as he gazed at her.

The lack of any child of his own to follow after him hit him afresh. A grocery shop was cold comfort next to a living, breathing child to hold in his arms. So though he was pleased for Angela, he was also envious of the love shared between her and Barry, which was obvious from her radiant smile and the softening of her voice when she spoke of him. And most of all George envied her the child that she was so clearly besotted with and he knew she would hardly relish leaving her and returning to work in the shop again.

He had tried two assistants since she had left and both had proved useless and he was limping along on his own. He did tentatively mention coming back to Angela, but she was vehement in her refusal. 'I don't think Barry would like it,' she said. 'He earns well enough now and we can manage and though Mary isn't old, she's too old to start looking after babies. She's done enough of that and anyway I would miss my wee girl if I didn't see her all day, every day. Unless there is no alternative I don't see the point of having children and giving them to someone else to rear.'

'I do quite understand my dear,' George said. 'It was just a thought.'

'And kindly meant I'm sure,' Angela said. 'You were always very good to me, all of us really and if I had to have some form of employment I would be back here like a shot.'

But that wasn't likely to happen and George knew he had to accept it and move on as Angela had. She bade goodbye to George as customers appeared, but it wasn't so easy to leave because they all wanted a peep of the baby and they oohed and aahed over her and said she was a darling wee dote.

Angela didn't mind because she was immensely proud of her baby, but later as she was making her way home she was a little anxious about George. It was common knowledge that his wife wasn't an easy woman. She was a fine-looking woman still and must have been a stunner in her youth, but Angela doubted she had a kind or loving bone in her body.

'It's often the way with very beautiful women,' Mary said when Angela mentioned her concerns about George when she got home. 'The men have their heads turned and Matilda Maitland would have made a play for George because of the shop.'

'But she doesn't like the shop.'

'Doesn't like demeaning herself to serve in it, but I bet she likes the living it brings in,' Mary said and added, 'Women like that seldom have children. I wouldn't be a bit surprised if George is lacking in that area as well, and you know what I'm talking about.'

Angela did but she was still young enough to blush discussing even mildly intimate things. But she thought Mary was probably right and it might explain how emotional George had become when he saw Connie. She felt sorry for him, for he was a kind and generous man and she was sure he would pay Matilda back a thousand-fold for the merest scrap of affection.

'It wouldn't happen in the Catholic Church for the man would have the priest out to give the wife a talking to, but he's Church of England and likely they don't do that kind of thing.'

'No I suppose not.'

'And I know what you think of George and I am fond of him myself,' Mary said, seeing Angela's woebegone face. 'But there is nothing you can do and there is a saying that he has made his bed so he must lie on it, so if I were you I would try to put George's problems out of your head and get ready to feed Miss Connie for she's stirring in her pram and will be hollering in a minute.'

Mary was right, she thought as she lifted Connie from the pram, really what ailed George was none of her business and she could do nothing to help him and

169

she sighed as she sat down and began unbuttoning her blouse.

Connie was almost five weeks when she smiled for the first time and Angela thought for a moment her heart had stopped beating and she lifted her up in her arms and held her tight and called to Mary to come and see. And she did see because now that Connie knew how to smile, she seemed to do a lot of it.

'Wait till her Daddy sees that,' Mary said. 'He'll be turning cartwheels, so he will.'

Angela laughed. 'He might well,' she said. 'For he's one proud father. I think as she grows she will wrap him around her little finger.'

'I believe it's the way with fathers and daughters,' Mary said. 'And sure, didn't you have Matt where you wanted him? He never cuddled the boys as he did you.'

Angela knew Mary spoke the truth and she smiled wistfully. 'I would have loved him to see Connie,' Angela said with a sigh.

'Then he would have wanted to live long enough to see her grow up,' Mary said. 'Anyway, if we believe the priests that there is something after this life, he might well be looking down on us just this minute.'

'Do you doubt there's an afterlife then?'

'No,' Mary said. 'Not really. I can't afford not to believe for then I would never see my boys again, or Matt of course. As it is I can hope that all those I've loved and lost will be waiting for me at the other side.'

'And my parents and siblings,' Angela said. 'Comforting thought that, isn't it.'

'It is,' Mary said with an emphatic nod. 'And so I will believe it until I'm proved wrong.'

'And so will I,' Angela said and she removed the baby from her breast and sat her up, rubbing her back to get her wind up. Connie sat groggily, almost replete and then she gave an enormous burp. 'I hope that's not an opinion, young lady,' Mary said in mock severity and both women burst out laughing.

Angela relished every day and took delight in every milestone Connie passed like the first time she rolled over, or a tiny tooth peeping through the swollen red gums, often after many fractious and fretful nights. Then there was the first time she held a rattle in her hand without dropping it, and a few days later she could pass it from one hand to the other. Barry was absolutely delighted when she shouted 'Dada' one day as he came through the door and she learned to clap her hands and sit up unaided without a pile of cushions around her in case she fell over.

'She'll be walking soon and then she will be one body's work,' Mary remarked one day. 'So you best get ready to run after her, because my running days are over.'

Angela knew that only too well. She could never linger at Mass nattering to Maggie now because as Connie became more mobile, she went to the early Mass at nine with Barry while Mary minded the baby and she had to hurry home so Mary could go to the one at eleven and Angela did the dinner for them all. So the girls agreed to meet on Saturday mornings as they did their shopping and Connie loved her Auntie Maggie very much. 'Tomorrow's Barry's favourite day in the week,' Angela said as they were wandering around looking for something cheap but tasty for Sunday dinner.

'Why, because he gets a lie in?'

'No he doesn't have one of those, he wakes the same time, which is just as well, as Connie thinks six, or sometimes before six is a grand time to get up. No, he looks after Connie while I get on with the dinner. He says it's the only time he has her all to himself and they do have some fun together.'

'He's good to do that,' Maggie maintained.

'I suppose,' Angela said. 'He always said she's his baby too.'

'Well that is true, but some men think looking after a baby is beneath them, women's work. He doesn't go for a drink then on Sunday morning?'

Angela shook her head. 'Nor at any other time in the general way of things. He earns enough to pay the rent, the gas, put good food on the table, have a cellar full of coal in the winter and buy clothes for Connie as she grows and for us all to have good boots on our feet. Many aren't as comfortable as we are but there is little slack. If there is any money left he tends to put it in the Post Office, so there is always something put by for that proverbial rainy day.'

'So he doesn't go to the football either?'

Angela shook her head and Maggie said, 'Angela you have got a good man there.'

'You don't have to tell me that,' said Angela.

It was coming up to Christmas, which hadn't been fully celebrated the year before because of Matt's terminal illness, but Barry said they must do the works with a child in the house, although she was far too young to know anything about it.

Mary had made the cake some time ago with Angela's help and they had all had a stir of the pudding. Now with just a fortnight to go Barry and Angela got the tree, streamers and decorations down from the attic where they were stored while Mary made mountains of mince pies. 'Mammy, you're not feeding an army,' Barry complained good-naturedly.

'Well Stan's coming too isn't he?'

This was true. Barry had asked the Gaffer when he found out he would be spending Christmas on his own, again. He had spent every Christmas alone since his wife had died, but unless they had been related Barry couldn't have asked him while he was an apprentice. People might have thought he was sucking up. 'Stan is only one more person, Mammy,' Barry said.

'I know,' Mary said. 'But I want to make plenty so he can take some home with him and I know you when you get started on mince pies.'

'It isn't my fault,' Barry said. 'You shouldn't make them so tasty.'

'Hmm, the term "greedy guts" springs to mind.'

'Oh come on, Mammy,' Barry protested. 'Christmas is one day in the whole blessed year when you can indulge yourself.'

'You're right and so that's why I'm making so many mince pies.'

Angela listened to Barry sparring with his mother with a smile on her face because it was all play acting. Mary would cook them a wonderful Christmas dinner and not stint on anything so that they would be hardly able to move after it. The mince pies would be for the tea along with chicken sandwiches, sausage rolls and pickles and slices of Christmas cake. And then Stan Bishop would go back to his lonely house.

'It is a shame Stan Bishop would be by himself if you hadn't asked him to our house for Christmas,' Angela said to Barry as they scurried home from Mass the Sunday before Christmas. The day was icy so wisps of vapour surrounded her mouth as she spoke and her feet crunched on the frosty ground and she cuddled closer to Barry as she went on, 'He is such a lovely, considerate man, I'm surprised he's still single. I mean his wife has been dead some years now. I couldn't remember all of it because I was just a child, but Mammy told me all about that and I could sort of remember the funeral. It was ever so sad and then to lose the baby as well.'

'He didn't lose the baby,' Barry said. 'Not in the way you mean. He's been brought up by his wife's sister.'

'So why isn't he spending Christmas Day with him?'

Barry shrugged. 'I don't know,' he said. 'He never mentions him.'

'Never mentions his own son? That doesn't sound like the Stan I know.'

'Well he's pretty good about keeping things close to his chest is Stan,' Barry said. 'Maybe you should ask him.'

'Oh I don't know that I'd like to do that,' Angela said. 'There night be a good reason for him not mentioning him. I am intrigued, though, because I always thought he would make a good father, a bit of a doting parent, you know?'

'Yeah, I would have thought that too.'

What Barry had told Angela about Stan made her feel differently about the man. She felt incredibly sad for him, but the subject wasn't broached again until they were sitting round the table eating their Sunday dinner, Connie on her father's knee. Angela said Barry had told her about Stan's son that she thought had died and that he never mentioned.

'He's not let see him,' Mary said. 'So I suppose there's nothing to say.'

'Not let see him?'

'No,' Mary said. 'You have to see the situation as it was then. First of all, I have never seen a happier couple than Stan and Kate, and they had a bit of a wait for Daniel because he wasn't born till 1905. And then tragedy. I wasn't surprised Stan was so distracted, they were so kind and loving the pair of them. Awful it was and when Kate's sister Betty came with her husband Roger, I really think Stan saw her as a Godsend, at first. Anyway, even when she took the baby to live with her, because he was all at sixes and sevens and wasn't in any fit state to look after a baby, and he knew he couldn't look after him and work.'

'Yes,' Angela said. 'But if he had kept in contact with Daniel and got to know him a bit, he might have come back to live here with him in the end when he was older.'

'I doubt that,' Mary said. 'If he was brought up in the lap of luxury as he is, according to Stan.'

'No he'd never settle to life here,' Barry agreed. 'And why should he? His home, his life, his friends, his school and his doting parents are there. Why would he want to leave all that?'

'Anyway, that wouldn't be at all the way Betty would want it. I met her at the funeral and didn't take to her at all. She wasn't a bit like her sister Kate. She was quite a lot older and she has never been able to have children.

'Now I am not saying she wasn't sorry her sister died and she did mourn her, but the consolation for her would have been the newborn child. She was certainly one of the first ones to hold him, she could almost have given birth to him. She was possessive about him and only begrudgingly handed him over when I was at the font and took him back straight afterwards. I think she wants to pretend the child is hers and Roger's and doesn't want Stan in his life. She wants all the child's love directed towards her.'

'I don't think that's a healthy way of looking at things,' Angela remarked.

'It isn't and the losers are Stan and his son.'

'He's still a decent bloke though,' Barry said. 'And a good boss. I know he was upset when my brothers were sacked when they finished their apprenticeships, but look how he fought to keep me on.'

'Yes, I often wondered about that,' said Angela.

'It was a bit because of my brothers,' Barry said. 'Apparently, Stan told them that it was unlikely the boys would have gone to America if they had been kept on in regular work at the factory and they ended up being drowned at sea. And then with Dad taking sick and dying, he said they had to bear some responsibility.'

'Even though all Stan said was true,' Mary said, 'I'm surprised they took any notice. Places like that are not generally noted for their charitable gestures.'

'You're right, they're not,' Barry said. 'But just at the moment they needed experienced workers like Stan and to a lesser extent even me.'

'Why?'

'Well it's a bit hush hush,' Barry said, remembering too late that Stan advised him not to say anything just yet. 'Don't tell anyone, will you?'

'What sort of anyone?' Mary commented dryly. 'I don't know many Russian spies and the people I do know will not, in the main, be the slightest bit interested and I think Angela would say the same. Your secrets are safe with us.'

'Well it's just that we are starting up new lines. It means employment for some, and that's the good news, and it means all the qualified men have to learn how to work the new machines so we can train the new ones.'

'Is that all?' Mary said. 'That's what all that cloak and dagger stuff was about?'

Barry nodded as Angela, watching his face, said, 'So what are the new lines?'

'We have a whole new section starting up and the people working there will be making bullets. There will be about fifty jobs going.'

'Bullets!' Mary echoed. 'What would we want with so many bulllets?'

Barry didn't answer, he just said, 'And that's not all, because two of the forges are having new dies fitted in the new year to make long narrow tubes, and they will be the barrels for rifles, and batches will be sent along to the gun quarter to be assembled.'

'But what's it all about, son?' Mary asked. 'It isn't as if we are at war or anything.'

Barry was suddenly very still and Mary said, 'You think there's going to be a war don't you?'

'I don't know,' Barry admitted. 'But Stan thinks we might be dragged into that business in Europe.'

'How could we be?' Angela asked. 'It's miles away.'

'I know,' Barry conceded. 'But the company must know or suspect something, or they wouldn't go to all this trouble and expense, and if we do go to war then I'd like to think that we were semi-prepared. We can't wait till the bullets are flying to make our own.'

Just at that moment Connie started shouting and wriggling and Angela had to take her from Barry so he could eat the rest of his dinner in peace. She put her arms out to Connie who rewarded her with a smile that nearly split her face in two and Angela's heart constricted with the love beyond measure she felt for this child. As she took her in her arms she knew without a shadow of a doubt, however hard life might be, she would never give her child away for someone else to bring up.

THIRTEEN

That Christmas was a magical one for Angela and she was woken by Barry kissing her lips very gently. 'What is it?' she asked him drowsily.

'Nothing,' Barry said. 'I mean, that is, nothing bad. I just couldn't wait one more minute to give you my Christmas present.'

She fully understood Barry's impatience when she sat up in bed and opened the large box he handed her, for he had bought her a good, warm coat in navy with a fur trim and matching hat. 'Oh, Barry, it's wonderful,' she cried as she lifted it out of the box.

She knew few women had a coat of any description and none would have one of this quality and she did wonder how Barry had managed to afford it, but she couldn't spoil the moment by asking him. It was much later when she found out he'd seen it in the Rag Market and Stan had bought it for him and he had paid him so much a week, cutting down his cigarettes to do so. She had been further moved when she heard that, but on Christmas morning she was looking forward to wearing it to Mass.

Oh how proud Angela felt as she stepped out for Mass that crisp, cold Christmas morning. She barely felt the icy chill of the day, wrapped in her warm coat and hat. Even her hands were covered with thick, black, woollen gloves which had been Barry's present to her the previous Christmas.

She had her hands on the handle of the pram because Connie had to go along with them that morning as they were all going to nine o'clock Mass. Angela made sure though that Connie was wrapped warmly, from her flannelette vest and petticoat beneath her winter-weight dress and cardigan to the pram suit covering all that, one of the two from her two brothers in the States. They said in the letter sent with them that they were all the rage in America, made to protect babies from a harsh New York winter. One was a sort of royal blue and one dark red and Angela had chosen the red one for that morning.

Although there were pram suits in Britain they were woolly, knitted ones but the American coat, leggings and bonnet and even mittens and bootees were made of some sort of fleecy material. The bonnet was trimmed with lace and Barry thought Connie looked enchanting with the lace framing her pretty little face, tendrils of blonde curls escaping at the sides and over her forehead. More important than how she looked though was how warm she would be and with the fleece suit on and tucked into the commodious pram with a couple of woollen blankets she would be as snug as a bug in a rug and with a bit of luck might sleep all the way through Mass.

Just before they left for Mass Barry had gone upstairs for his overcoat and as he was coming down again he saw Angela holding Connie in her arms and he felt such love and pride for them that his heart stopped beating for a moment and he wanted to wrap his arms around them and never let harm come to them.

He remembered that when Connie had been born, her hair was so blonde it looked as if she had no hair at all if a person didn't notice the down on her head. But now she was seven and a half months old she was developing the curls Angela had as a child. Mary always said she was the image of her mother at the same age and Barry could plainly see why Angela's mother named her so because angelic was the word that sprang to mind whenever he looked at his daughter.

He loved them both with an intensity that almost frightened him, for times were precarious for the working classes, because diseases were rife and people were fragile and sickness spread like wildfire in the cramped, insanitary hovels they lived in, and women like Stan's poor wife could also die in childbirth and he knew he really wouldn't want to go on if he lost them. 'Barry,' Angela called and Barry realized he was still standing on the stairs caught up in reverie. 'Are you all right?'

'Fine. Just thinking.'

Angela laughed. 'You don't want to do much of that on Christmas Day,' she said. 'Leave that for every other day of the year.'

'I will,' Barry promised. 'I will close my mind from this moment on and not think of another thing for the rest of the day.'

'You are a fool,' Angela said, but fondly. 'If you get your coat on we're ready.'

181

Angela loved going to Mass on Christmas morning. She liked the church all ready to celebrate the birth of Jesus, the white and gold altar cloths, the flickering candles lighting up the whole altar, the figure of Baby Jesus put into the manger at last completing the nativity. And when the priest came to begin Mass she knew his vestments would be white and gold too and he would carry a candle set in a golden candlestick that would gleam and glisten and behind him would be four altar boys in red cassocks and white surplices keeping pace with the priest.

She also enjoyed meeting friends and neighbours and wishing them Happy Christmas, but as they neared the church Angela noticed a lot of the poorer women looking at her coat with envy and she felt so sorry for them, because a good few had only a threadbare dress, a thin shawl and down-at-heel boots to keep out the cold of the day, and for a moment the joy went from her.

Maggie voiced what many of the women who passed Angela in the porch might have wanted to say. She grabbed Angela by her two wrists and spun her round. She cried, 'Well will you look at the set of you. Tell me, is this all from Santa?'

'It is,' Angela said with a broad grin in answer to Maggie's pleasure.

'Well then, my girl, I'd have said you have been thoroughly spoilt,' Maggie declared.

Angela agreed with her, but she wasn't the only one spoilt that Christmas, for Santa had left Connie a truck full of coloured bricks and a number of board books courtesy of Maggie's mother. 'Wouldn't take a penny piece for them,' Mary said. 'Was a bit offended I had offered. She said she was glad to see the back of them, but it has certainly made Christmas for Madam here.'

And her Christmas got better for that morning Maggie had given her a monkey on a stick and when Stan arrived just before lunch, he had a large bag with him and from it he pulled out a big soft brown teddy bear almost as big as Connie. 'He's lovely,' Angela said, taking it from Stan and stroking his soft fur. 'But you needn't have bothered, you only had to bring yourself.'

'Not at Christmas,' Stan said. 'And it gave me great pleasure to buy a present for a child.'

Angela could say nothing to that but, 'Well thank you, it was very kind of you.'

'You and Mary have not been forgotten either,' Stan said. 'I thought most women like perfume, but there is so much of it I hadn't a clue what to buy. But the girl advised me.' And he took from the bag two small packets. 'I got them different so you could share,' he explained. 'The girl told me the younger women go for this one,' he said, handing one to Angela. 'April Violet,' she said, opening it up and revealing a little bottle, then dabbing some on her wrists. Even the bottle was beautiful and the perfume inside looked deep purple.

'Mary this is yours,' Stan said and handed Mary a yellow packet. 'Tiara Bouquet,' Mary read. 'Oh I can't wear this unless I have my tiara on.'

'Won't get much wear then,' Angela said with a laugh. 'Come on, stretch a point because it's Christmas and dab some on your wrists and we can compare. Thank you, Stan, for such lovely gifts.'

183

'Oh yes, thank you, Stan. That was such a thoughtful thing to do and we never expected it.'

And neither woman said that they had never had proper perfume in the whole of their lives. Even at Christmas and birthdays, it was too expensive to contemplate and now Angela had got perfume she didn't know when she'd use it for the only place she went was church for Mass. But surely even the Church couldn't object to a dab of it. It would seem criminal not to use something Stan had spent so much money on.

Stan hadn't finished however and out of the bag came a bottle of whisky and cigars for Barry that caused his eyes to open wide with delight. 'Oh you couldn't have done better mate, I love a drop of whisky.'

'Do you?' Angela said. 'I didn't know that.'

'That's because I don't allow myself to indulge in it,' Barry said. 'As for cigars I don't think I've ever tasted one, but my Dad used to speak of them with reverence. Not that he ever had many, just like this, a few bought at Christmas.'

'Well you seem to have pleased everyone in the room,' Mary said. 'Makes my presents to you seem a bit mundane and ordinary.'

'I didn't expect a present from you at all,' Stan said in surprise. 'You'll be giving me a fine dinner and the chance to celebrate Christmas with your family and that is present enough for me. My gifts were just to say thank you.'

'I only bought you socks,' Mary said. 'In my experience men are very bad at shopping for themselves and no one can have too many socks.'

Stan laughed. 'Well,' he said, 'they may seem like mundane presents to you, but I am immensely grateful because you are right, I am bad at buying things for myself and I don't think I own a pair of socks that haven't holes in them somewhere, so new ones will come in very handy.'

'Mammy,' Barry said suddenly, 'the smell of that dinner cooking is making me feel light-headed, for I hadn't much breakfast after Mass, to make room for it.'

'Get away with you,' Mary said. 'And you know the best thing you can bring to a dinner table is a good appetite. But we have the soup first anyway and that's just to be heated up so it will be ready in a jiffy.'

'Right, I'll sort out the table,' Barry said.

'And I'll cut the bread,' Angela said, sitting Connie on the mat in front of the guarded fire, her truck full of bricks beside her.

'What shall I do?' Stan asked.

'Nothing, you're a guest.'

'Oh please, that makes me feel uncomfortable and I'd rather be doing something.'

'All right then, I have a very important job for you,' Barry said and he jerked his thumb towards Connie as he spoke, 'and that is to entertain Madam there.' Stan felt panic rise in him. He would rather do any job but that one, for he wasn't any good with kids. He turned his gaze almost with dread towards the baby who was regarding him with large blue eyes. And then Connie smiled and the smile was so wide and radiant Stan felt his heart give a flip and the next he knew he was on his knees beside her on the rug and building a tower with the bricks. Connie crashed it down with a cry of delight and chuckled at the very dismayed look on Stan's face.

Her laugh was so infectious Stan built another tower which had the same reaction, and another, and was almost sorry to be called to the table despite his hunger. Angela had caught sight of his face as he got to his feet after playing with Connie and thought Betty hard and unfeeling to keep him apart from his son.

Maybe he couldn't be a father in the normal way, but he certainly should have been given the chance to build some sort of relationship with him. The fact that Betty and Roger were not Daniel's real parents would eventually come to light as these things inevitably do, and Angela wondered if the boy would resent the pair of them for separating him so totally from his natural father.

Still, she told herself, it really was none of her business and anyway, it was Christmas Day and no sad thoughts allowed. There could be few sad thoughts around the table with Connie there. She could understand little but seemed to delight in everything and her infectious chuckle and her evident pleasure that caused her to clap her hands with glee amused everyone and chased any mournful thoughts away. So it was a cheerful meal and Angela thought Stan such good company she thought he might easily become a regular guest at Christmas.

The meal was fabulous and after it the women washed up while the men sat before the fire and smoked a cigar and kept an eye on Connie. And when it was all done and put away, Angela remarked, 'Not the weather for a walk today,' for icy sleet was falling from a sky the colour of gun metal.

'No,' Stan agreed. 'Not the day at all.' And then he added, 'I suppose we could always have a sing-song. I used to sing a lot at one time.'

'Did you?' Angela said because it was the last thing she had expected Stan to say, but his word tugged a memory for Mary who said, 'Oh my goodness, that struck a chord. You used to sing with your wife, Kate. She had a lovely voice.'

'Did you do it professionally?' Angela asked.

'Good Lord, no,' Stan said. 'We'd just do it for our own selves though Kate used to sing in the choir at Mass, so we'd sing any new hymns she had to learn at home and it would help her remember the words and then we might do others we both knew well just for fun.'

'I'd hear you,' Mary said. 'Anyone passing would hear you and Kate used to sing even if you weren't there.'

Stan nodded. 'She used to sing to the child she was carrying, who turned out to be Daniel,' Stan said. 'Some people thought she was crazy. She used to sing him lullabies because she said he could hear and he would know the songs when he was born, and when she would sing them to him he would remember and know how much she loved him. I have never sung a word since the day of Daniel's birth. Even at her funeral I chose her favourite hymns and found I couldn't open my mouth.'

There was a sudden silence as Stan stopped speaking because they had all been hanging on every painful word. There were tears in Angela's eyes and in Mary's and Barry had an unaccountable lump in his throat. Even Connie sitting on the rug watching them all was silent, feeling the solemn atmosphere.

Suddenly, Stan got a grip on himself and said, 'I don't know what came over me. I'm sorry. Here I am, a guest, and this is how I repay your hospitality, doing my best to put a damper on Christmas.' He gave a sudden sigh and almost immediately launched into 'O Little Town of Bethlehem'.

It was too much for Angela. She had been moved by what Stan had said and now his rendering of the carol and the look on his face, showing what it had cost him to sing again after all this time, caused the lurking tears to start to trickle down her cheeks. To cover herself she lifted the baby onto her knee and began to sway in the chair in time to the music. There was a spontaneous burst of applause when Stan had finished, with Connie joining in enthusiastically, much to everyone's amusement.

'You have a fine voice,' Barry said and the women agreed.

Stan went very red in the face, he was not used to being praised, and he held up his hands.

'Oh, stop please,' he cried. 'And it's not that I am ungrateful, far from it, and I found it very hard and very emotional to sing that, for it was Kate's favourite carol and I never sang it on my own, we always sang it together. You know, it would help me if you all join in.'

And they did and sang all the carols they could remember. Some time into the singing, Angela realized Connie had fallen asleep and she laid her in the pram in the room knowing the bedroom would be icy.

'She's a lovely child you have,' Stan said. 'I'm usually useless with kids.'

'I'm sure that isn't true,' Angela said.

188

'Oh I assure you it is,' Stan said. 'You all know I have a son?' They nodded and Stan continued his story. 'Kate's sister Betty is bringing him up and she doesn't want me around. When I got to think about it when I thought I was more or less over Kate's death, well maybe not over it, but coping better at least, I wanted to get to know my son and I booked the weekend off work and I went to Betty and said I wanted to have Daniel for the weekend and get to know him a bit.'

'How old was he then?' Angela asked.

'Not very old,' Stan said. 'He was just over two and of course didn't know me from Adam and he didn't like my house and wanted to go home. I took him to the park and spent hours pushing him on the swings and roundabouts and kicked about with a ball I'd bought, and we had fish and chips for dinner but the child still wanted to go home, wanted his "Mammy and Daddy". I tried to soothe him, but he wouldn't be soothed, so I picked him up and he started to scream as if he was being murdered and then he was screaming that he hated me. He squirmed, kicked and punched me so I had to put him down and he curled himself in a tight ball and wouldn't uncurl himself, or speak one word to me, and I was worried to death.'

'I bet you were,' Angela said. 'But Daniel was only a very little boy and he was probably confused and frightened. So what did you do then?'

'I tried to think what Kate would want me to do and I knew she would want me to do what was best for the child, so I repacked the little case he had brought with him and the child uncurled himself quick enough when I told him I was taking him home.

'As we approached I saw Betty was looking out of the window and I thought she was probably bewildered and maybe a bit anxious because I was supposed to have Daniel for the whole weekend and here we were, back already. Betty hadn't been keen on the idea of my taking him for the whole weekend anyway because she said that was a long time for a small child to stay with someone he didn't know that well and she was dead right. She knew Daniel far better than I did.

'Anyway she came out to meet us to find out why I was bringing Daniel back so soon. Daniel gave a cry as he saw his mother approach and he pulled his hand from mine and ran down the road towards her and into her waiting arms. When she lifted him up he wrapped his arms tight about her, buried his head in her neck and burst into sobs.'

'Ah poor wee boy,' said Mary.

'Aye,' Stan agreed. 'I saw that after. But at the time, I couldn't speak and if I'd tried I would have bawled my eyes out too. So though I saw Betty looking at me quizzically I could only shrug my shoulders and spread my arms wide.

'And then Daniel sat away from his mother's embrace, scrubbed at his eyes with his sleeve and pointing at me he said, "Don't make me go with that nasty man again, Mammy. He is horrid." 'Course, Betty accused me of doing something to the boy and I could only shake my head and then I just handed Betty the case, turned on my heel and left. I have seen neither of them since that day and it was five years ago.

'Betty and her husband applied to adopt Daniel about a year after that. By then I was feeling like a real rubbish

190

father.' He looked at them all listening to him and he said, 'The hardest thing in the world after the death of my wife was to hear my son screaming out over and over that he hated me. I really thought Daniel would be better off not knowing anything about me and I signed the papers, so Betty and her husband are Daniel's parents legally. His name is Daniel Swanage and I have no part in his life.'

'I think that is one of the saddest things I have ever heard,' Angela said. 'If his adoptive parents really love him, Daniel will survive this. I am testimony to that, but it's you that will be hurting and you that have lost the most.'

'And don't think a little boy meant those words,' Mary said. 'If you had got to know him first, defied Betty and gone to see him every weekend and took him out and gave him a fun time, the outcome of that weekend might have been different.'

'I know, I have thought that myself,' Stan said. 'And the beggar of it is, it's too late.'

'Aye,' said Mary. 'That's the rub.' She got to her feet and said, 'Throats need lubricating after all that singing,' and she got up to make tea, but Barry waved away her offer of tea for him and Stan. 'We've got something more interesting,' he claimed and got up and brought bottles of beer he had got in for the festive season and the bottle of whisky Stan had brought him and put them all on the table as Stan got a deck of cards from his pocket.

He showed them some card tricks first and they were amazed at his skill. 'D'you know any card games?' Barry asked. 'I never had a pack of cards because Daddy didn't approve of gambling.'

'I don't approve of gambling either,' Stan said. 'My money is too hard-earned to lose it all on a game of chance. I do it just for fun and it's great entertainment for a winter's evening.'

Mary still looked doubtful. 'Do you think it right though to play cards on Christmas Day?'

'I can't see that we are doing anything wrong,' Stan said. 'Honestly I can't. As long as no money changes hands it's just a game. Let me teach you all to play whist and you will see how harmless it is.'

'All right,' Mary said and Angela was glad because she too wanted to learn a few card games. In fact the McCluskys picked up the rules of whist very quickly and thoroughly enjoyed themselves.

They had played four games when Connie woke. 'I best get tea,' Mary said and everyone groaned for no one was hungry, but Mary insisted. 'Well I'll put it out and cover it with tea towels and you can please yourselves. Connie will probably be ready for something anyway.'

'Shouldn't bank on it,' Angela said, holding the baby in her arms. 'She's had a good plate of her own mashed-up dinner and then a fair few forkfuls of Barry's because he had her on his knee and he of course gives her anything she wants.'

'You can't be giving out to the child,' Barry said. 'It's Christmas Day for goodness' sake.'

'Who's giving out to the child?' Angela said to Barry. 'It's you I'm giving out to. You'll have her spoilt. If you're not careful.'

'Fathers always spoil daughters,' Barry said. 'It's their prerogative. Anyway my own Daddy used to say better that way than the other way.'

Angela well remembered hearing Matt say that and she smiled at the memory. And it was true and she was glad that Barry loved Connie so deeply and was not afraid to show it. 'Hand her over,' Barry said to Angela. 'Me and Stan will keep her amused while you're busy.'

'I need to change her first,' Angela said. 'Unless you would like to do that too?'

'No,' Barry said, giving Angela a cheeky grin. 'Women are much better at that type of thing. I'm more than ready to admit that.'

'Oh I bet you are,' Angela said, but she laughed as she took Connie upstairs to make her more comfortable, for she had to agree with him, men didn't change nappies. And if any did, and it was found out, they would be a laughing stock. In fact most of the day-to-day care was down to the women, but Angela considered that right and proper.

When she returned to the room though and handed Connie to her father she said, 'Don't throw her around much, you may drop her.'

Barry stared at Angela as if he didn't believe his ears and then asked incredulously, 'Why would I drop her? I have never even come close to dropping her before.'

Angela knew that but she also knew how many beer bottles had been emptied and vast inroads had been made in the whisky too and she was a bit concerned because Barry was unused to alcohol and she doubted Stan was a big drinker either generally.

However, her words fell on deaf ears and Barry and to a lesser extent Stan were soon tossing Connie in the air and spinning her round the room till she was breathless. There was no doubt that she enjoyed these games for she was screaming with laughter and shouting for more although Angela's heart was often in her mouth.

It meant though that Connie was far too wound up to eat much tea yet, despite this, Angela put a veto to any more rough-and-tumble games with Connie after tea lest she lose the bit she had eaten.

Undeterred, the men carried her over to the rug for more tower building. As the women washed up they could hear Connie's squeals of excitement as she sent the towers crashing and Mary remarked to Angela, 'You'll never get her to bed tonight.'

'Well not till Stan goes home,' Angela agreed. 'Her father is as bad, but I can manage him. But I think Stan has had a good day, don't you?'

'He would be a hard man to please if he hasn't,' Mary said with a smile. 'And I don't think for one minute that he's an unreasonable man.'

Stan had had a wonderful Christmas with the McCluskys and though he was usually quite a sober man, he had imbibed a little too freely and Mary thought him too unsteady to go home on his own, clutching the parcel of goodies Mary had packed in his bag along with his socks. 'Go along with him, Barry,' Mary urged. 'See he gets home safe.'

Barry was almost as drunk as Stan was and had no desire to go out into the cold and the wet, and Grant Street was no distance away. But then he surveyed Stan standing swaying slightly as he bid them goodnight and knew when the cold night air hit him he could easily overbalance. What if he did that and hit his head or something? He said to Angela, 'All right if I go up with him?'

'More than all right,' Angela said and she hitched Connie further up her hip as she said, 'Little Miss here will settle easy if you two are out of the way.'

Barry grinned at her for he knew she had a point and he said, 'Wait on Stan. I'll come along with you. I'll just get my coat.' And Angela gave a sigh of relief when the door closed after the men.

FOURTEEN

'Happy New Year,' Stan cried, bursting through the McCluskys' door holding aloft the bottle of whisky. He also had with him a lump of coal and half a crown, because he was first footing. The first foot of the New Year had to be a man with the darkest hair and so that had to be Stan rather than Barry, as that ensures good luck for the family. The whisky is to signify the fact that they would never go thirsty, the coal that they would never be cold and the money so that they might have enough to last them all year. It was a custom the McCluskys brought with them from Ireland and though Stan had never done it before, he played his part beautifully, sneaking out just before twelve o'clock and as the hour was struck and some factory hooters sounded and people banged dustbin lids together he went back in to wish a Happy New Year to one and all.

Everyone had such high hopes for the New Year. For some time there had been unrest and clashes in Europe, though none had affected Britain and no one seemed to think Britain should get involved in countries so far away. They should deal with their own affairs.

Nearer to home though there was unrest among workers striving for better working conditions and living wages, and some workers had gone on strike. These strikes usually achieved very little and didn't last long as the people couldn't exist for long without their wages, however meagre they were. Barry had great sympathy for them for he knew that but for the grace of God and the goodness of Stan Bishop he could have been one of them, and he understood the desperation of Gerry and Sean to sail to America where Colm and Finbarr were making such a good living. He sincerely hoped that some of those problems could be solved in 1914.

Then there was the Home Rule for Ireland supposed to be brought into being this year. He knew it would be marvellous if it ever came to pass because freedom from the yoke of England beat in the heart of every Irish Catholic who thought Ireland, being a separate island, should have a separate government and not be under British Rule. He knew too the Ulster Unionists would oppose the Bill, but if it became law there would be nothing they could do about it, surely.

'Oh I think they'll likely have something up their sleeves,' Mary said when Barry said this to her. 'They'll not give in without a fight. We just must wait and see.'

They hadn't long to wait before England began to unravel. In the early spring of 1914 some bricklayers began agitating for reform and the unrest began to spread to other towns and cities. And then the management's response in London was to lock the bricklayers out of their place of work.

'That will cause severe hardship and sooner rather than later I'd say,' Barry said one evening as he threw down the paper down in disgust and added, 'The Boss said they're probably taking a hard line in London to dampen down the protests in other places.'

Angela nodded. 'He could be right, but you'd think they would at least listen to the workers' concerns, possibly compromise a bit.'

'I don't know why you're so surprised,' Mary said. 'Since when have these top-notch people given a tinker's cuss for the rest of us?'

'It is a bit short sighted though isn't it?' Angela said. 'I mean, factories and so on need workers. I'm sure if they treated them right, even if they couldn't meet all they demand straight away, they would work harder.'

'Maybe,' Mary said. 'But the bosses can behave how they want really, because there are so many on the dole queues now, they can easily replace whoever proves troublesome enough.'

However, after three weeks there was no sign of any softening on either side, but Angela knew the strikers would have to give in in the end because they were starving and so were their wives, and worse, their children.

Angela hated reading the paper for she imagined the despair of the bricklayers striving for a living wage and watching their children cry with hunger. God, she thought it would tear a man to bits, yet she felt she had to read it and when she said this to Barry, he admitted he felt the same way.

'That's what I'm on about, I suppose,' Barry said. 'There are people working here in Birmingham at various places full-time and yet not being paid enough to feed their families. Now we're seeing even more stick-thin, barefoot kids in the streets. I always leave something from the dinner you put up now, for somehow it's even worse than it was before. Lots of us do it now, because it's hard to see such abject desperation on a child's face and not be moved by it. But you can only help one or two and some days there's so many of them.'

'From now on I will make you extra,' Angela promised, 'and if all wives with husbands in work did the same at least we could help more of them.'

'Yes we could,' Barry said. 'What makes me mad is if these blokes who have no job just give a mate a hand, say by helping out on a stall down the Bull Ring a time or two and the dole office get to hear of it, they stop the money altogether.'

'It's the wives that come to the rescue,' Mary said. 'I've seen them taking in washing, sometimes two loads as well as their own, and they beg for old orange boxes and the like, and chop them into sticks in the cellars to make up bundles of kindling they sell around the doors of the posh houses. It's them that ask for tick in the shops and they are seldom away from the pawn shop.'

What Mary said was true and it depressed Angela and she thought it was small wonder that there was such unrest in the country. 'And that Lloyd George seems to think more of foreigners than us,' Angela said, jabbing at the paper. 'All this happening in his England and he's more worried about the "build-up of weaponry in Europe". He calls it "organized insanity", but who really cares?'

Barry thought they might be made to care a great deal before too long because no one built up weaponry for the sake of it and yet, on the other hand, there were always skirmishes and England had always kept well clear of any involvement, so this was probably the same. Anyway they could do nothing about anything other than making extra sandwiches to stop the children starving to death and thanking God that their daughter wasn't suffering the same fate. For he knew it must tear the heart from a man when he couldn't provide for his family.

Meanwhile he took such joy in his own child for she seemed to learn something new each day. She had 'Mammy' and 'Daddy' off pat and Mary she dubbed 'Ganny, and she was making a stab at Stan and Maggie but was not quite there yet. But then she would surprise them by suddenly saying 'door' or 'bed' and shouted 'more' and 'again' if she wanted another game, or more food. And then one day at the beginning of February Connie, who had been getting on her hands and knees for a week or two, crawled across the floor for the first time and pulled herself up by the guard surrounding the fire and hearth. The three adults looked at each other knowing that Connie would no longer stay where she was put. 'We'll have to make sure the door to the stairs is kept closed at all times,' Mary said.

'Yes,' Barry agreed, 'and I'll get some wood on Saturday to make a gate for the cellar steps, because I definitely don't want her falling down there.' The gate was in place and secure by Saturday evening and a good job too, for now Connie had mastered the art of crawling she could go across the floor in seconds, and what fascinated her were the places she hadn't been allowed before, and one of those was the cellar. 'Oh wouldn't she just love to be down there playing with the coal?' Mary said with a chuckle as she removed her from the gate yet again and brought her into the room. 'Told you it's one body's work when they're at this stage.'

And no doubt about it now, they were at that stage. Connie wasn't prepared to sit in the pram while Angela did the washing, and she had to take her with her and make sure the door was shut when she did the bedrooms, and ironing had to be done when she was in bed and safely out of the way. And yet Angela wouldn't change a thing, for her love for the child was immeasurable and she felt privileged to watch her developing into a real little person.

'And won't it be lovely when the spring comes?' Angela said to Mary one day in late February as she stood at the window and watched the rain lashing the grey pavements. 'I will be able to take Connie to the park and let her crawl all over the grass!'

'I think we could all do with some warmth in our bones,' Mary agreed. 'And it's a pity we can do nothing to hurry it along.'

But the spring hadn't really taken hold when the Home Rule for Ireland Bill was passed in Parliament. But there was a clause for those opposed to the break-up of the union. The Conservative opposition leader Bonar Law issued pledges to all the Ulster Unionists who opposed Home Rule for Ireland. In the end Antrim, Armagh, Derry and Down had the majority of pledges necessary to use the clause the government had put in place to opt out of Home Rule for six years. 'Six years, sixty years,' Mary said disparagingly. 'They are already watering down what they promised us. We will never have a united Ireland now, mark my words.'

'Maybe it was a way of avoiding civil war,' said

Angela. 'I think the Unionists are ready for it because in the paper it said that the Ulster Volunteer Force is over 100,000 strong and they did that military exercise last month in Tyrone. That surely was to show the government what it could do if it wished. It's a bit like bullying really.'

'It's a lot like bullying,' Barry said. 'But the damage is done now.'

'Yes and I think the Government have their hands full with them suffragettes,' Mary said and she glanced at Angela and added, 'Good job you haven't taken up with all that nonsense.'

'No, it's not all nonsense,' said Angela. 'The point is I agree with much of what they say, because if men have the vote, we should have it too.'

'Why?' Barry said. 'Surely you would vote the same way I did?'

'No,' Angela said. 'Not necessarily. If you have the vote it is your right to choose and I wouldn't vote the same as you if I didn't believe in that party. That's what it's all about. Someday I think we will be very grateful to the Pankhurst women and all the other suffragettes who have gone through a great deal and I even understand their frustration too. It's just another example of governments not listening, but I can't agree with their methods.' And Angela had a point because the suffragettes had begun to set fire to empty houses, railway stations, sport stadiums and had vandalized golf courses.

'Good job,' Barry said with a forced little laugh. 'What would Connie do if you were sent to prison?'

Really Barry was quite shocked. He'd always thought Angela would follow his lead, as head of the house, if women ever did get the vote and that idea had been turned right on its head. After a few moments though his thought patterns changed and he was proud of Angela and it showed she was a woman of integrity, saying what she did. Even the way she spoke showed she had a thinking brain and had thought things through. Surely he wasn't thinking of her not using that brain? He realized that though he loved Angela, he had thought of her as his wife and Connie's mother, not as a person in her own right as she so obviously was.

'D'you think it will ever happen that women will get the vote?' he asked. Angela shook her head. 'Couldn't tell you, but some women have died or been made very ill for the cause, usually because of the harsh treatment they have received in jail and I would hate to think their sacrifices were for nothing.'

The protests went on and more sacrifices were made but Europe and Ireland were in such turmoil all over that the British government weren't as shocked as they would normally have been when the following month in London, a suffragette named Mary Richardson took a meat cleaver to a Velazquez painting in the National Gallery. No one knew how or when the violence was going to end and suffragettes were viewed as just another headache for the government. Barry said he couldn't see why the government couldn't just give women the vote and be done with it.

Angela agreed with him, but she was not that bothered about politics. Her concern was keeping Connie as healthy as possible and she took advantage of the warm spring weather to push Connie to the park every fine afternoon. Barry fully approved of Angela taking the child out of the unhealthy streets and on Sundays he would join them on their jaunts.

Mary was invited, but she always refused. Barry was concerned about this, especially if they were going further afield, but Mary encouraged them to go, waved them off cheerfully enough and always had a meal waiting when they returned. 'She will never come with me either,' Angela said. 'Sometimes I think the walk might do her good and it isn't as if anyone can gallop along pushing a pram. I have told her this but she always says her gallivanting days are over.'

'She doesn't seem to mind,' Barry said.

'I really don't think she does,' Angela said. 'Between you and me I think she gets tired. She wouldn't admit it in a thousand years, but I think she finds Connie a bit of a handful. She loves her to bits, no doubt of that, but children are very wearing at this age. With us out of the way she can put her feet up and have a wee nap.'

Barry nodded his head. 'Yes I think you're right.'

'So while there's no harm in asking her along, and you never know, she might surprise us one day, but if she says no then we have to accept that she prefers being left behind,' Angela said. 'And knowing Mammy as I do, the last thing she would want would be us wasting the day worrying and fretting over her, so let's set out to enjoy ourselves. And she's always keen to know what we've done and where we've been isn't she?'

And enjoy themselves they did. Sometimes they went to nearby Calthorpe Park, or Cannon Hill a little further away, or they visited the Botanical Gardens or walked down to the canal to see the brightly painted barges pass, or they'd go for a dander down the Bull Ring, always a colourful place with lots going on while the constant banter between the barrow boys and potential customers and between the barrow boys themselves always made Angela smile.

Returning from an outing to Calthorpe Park one day Angela said, 'D'you think Connie would appreciate a tea party for her birthday next week?'

'I think she'd love it, but who would you invite?' Barry asked.

'Well as she's only a year old she hasn't a wide circle of friends just yet,' Angela commented drily. 'But there will be us, and I'm sure Maggie and Stan would like to be asked, and it falls on Sunday so it couldn't be better. And there will be a cake and a candle, though one of us will have to blow that out this year at least, and lots of little cakes and fancies and presents. What else does a twelve-month-old child want or need?'

So the party was planned for the following Sunday and during that week Angela bought a pram second-hand for the rag doll she knew Maggie was buying and Mary made a mattress and little blankets for the pram. However the best present of all was brought up from the cellar by Barry. He had been working every night that week and he had made a rocking horse, which he had painted white and red. It was an incredibly beautiful horse and Connie's eyes opened wide in surprise and delight. She had stood up holding on to the guard and she suddenly loosed hold of it and set off walking, on her own, across the room towards the rocking horse. She only managed half-way before collapsing and made the rest of the way on her hands and knees, but Angela knew her baby girl was on her way and though she knew she would have to develop eyes in the back of her head, her heart rejoiced.

Less than a week later Stan called Barry into the office. 'I wanted to sound you out,' he said. 'Just so you know, if the balloon goes up I'm enlisting.'

'Balloon goes up, what you talking about?'

'If war is declared.'

'You said this before and nothing happened,' Barry said. 'You sure you're not just scaremongering? I mean, I agree that those Europeans seem a fiery lot and they have spats all the time and get over them. We rightly don't get involved in what is really their own business, so why should we get involved now?'

'I think we will be dragged into it this time, that's all,' Stan said. 'The government can't see what's staring them in the face. All their energies seem directed on stopping the Irish killing one another.'

'Look Stan, I can't leave Angela, my mother and baby daughter to fend for themselves and join in a war I have no interest in.'

'You don't have to,' Stan said. 'I will and you can take my place in the factory. I have put in good reports about your work over the years and I will recommend you. They take more notice of my opinion now. So if the call-up comes, you can claim exemption because you will be in a reserved occupation. The factory is taking on war-related work now.'

'But why should you do that?'

'Why not?' Stan said. 'Think about it. I have neither chick nor child belonging to me.'

'What about your son?'

'Huh, he doesn't even know I exist,' Stan said bitterly. 'And if he did ever find out, what would he think of me, sitting pretty here while others risk their lives?'

Barry shrugged. 'So what of my child?'

'That's totally different,' Stan said firmly. 'As she grows, Connie will understand that you had her to care for and her mother and grandmother. She would never blame you, but I'm not brining my son up and in fact have no rights with regard to him because I signed them away. So no one will mourn me if I don't make it.'

'Well that's not true,' Barry said. 'Haven't you ever heard the saying that you are stuck with your relatives and thank God you can choose your friends?'

'Yeah I've heard it.'

'Well then you've got friends who'd miss you. Mammy thinks the world of you, you know she does. She's never forgotten what you did, letting my four older brothers lodge with you when we first came here, and she never will, and Angela also thinks the world of you. As for Connie, you are her favourite uncle and a damn sight more use than her real uncles who she'll probably never see. And you might be a right silly sod at times but I am quite fond of you myself.'

Stan was forced to laugh. 'All right then,' he said. 'So you'd miss me if I wasn't here?'

'Like Hell I would,' Barry said. 'So let's hope this latest skirmish comes to nothing and blows over like it has other times and you won't have to go anywhere.'

Stan said nothing for he saw that was how Barry wanted to deal with what he'd said. There was little point in arguing about it because it wasn't as if he knew

208

anything definite, just a feeling in his bones that Europe was building up to something big, like a big melting pot of unrest with old rivalries and resentments bubbling to the surface and he felt certain it would soon overflow.

There was another reason for him wanting to keep Barry safe that he never let himself think about in the day, but there were thoughts that disturbed his sleep at night, and that was the fact that he loved Angela. He knew however Angela viewed him only as a friend, a good friend, but that is all he would ever be, a good friend of Angela McClusky because the love of her life was Barry. They were soul mates and he wanted Angela's happinesss above all else and so if any of these skirmishes turned to a war England was dragged into, he wanted to keep Barry safe for Angela's sake.

FIFTEEN

Barry said nothing to either Angela or Mary about the conversation he had with Stan for he saw no reason to alarm them, but he started bringing in two papers on his way home from work. The *Birmingham Mail* dealt with mainly local news, but the *Daily Mail* he scrutinized from cover to cover and he saw that Europe was not a comfortable place to be in at that time. He was glad that he was in Great Britain although even there it was hardly comfortable with half the country on strike for better pay and conditions.

And then on Sunday 28th June, the heir apparent to the dual monarchy of Hungary-Austria, Archduke Franz Ferdinand, was assassinated in the Bosnian capital Sarajevo by a Serbian nationalist called Gavrilo Princip. The Archduke Ferdinand's wife Sophie, Duchess of Hohenberg, who tried to protect her husband, was shot in the stomach and she also died. Barry knew with a sinking heart that something big would come from this. It was splashed all over Monday's papers and he knew he couldn't protect his mother or Angela from news like this so he read the article out to them as they sat having a drink before bed.

They were both understandably shocked and then Barry added, 'Apparently, they weren't very popular, particularly in Budapest and Vienna.'

'They weren't very popular,' Mary repeated and added, 'I would have said that was a barbaric sentence to pass on someone whose only crime appears to be one of unpopularity. Besides which, if you did away with all the people you didn't like the look of, or the way they went about things, the world would be near empty.'

'Yes it would,' Angela agreed. 'And however unpopular they were, no country can stand by and let the heir of their emperor be killed in that way. What's likely to happen now?'

Barry shook his head. 'I'm not sure,' he admitted. 'I suppose this Hungary-Austria alliance could attack Serbia.'

'Well that won't affect us,' Mary said complacently.

Barry opened his mouth but closed it again without speaking. He had said enough for the time being. He would say more when he knew more.

Barry didn't know much more for nearly a month, except for finding out that Princip was an Austrian subject. Stan was right, the British Government had their eyes completely off the ball and so were unaware that the Emperor Franz Joseph wanted to attack Serbia in retaliation as the assassination had taken place on Serbian soil and he had asked the Kaiser for help. Russia came in on the side of Serbia and mobilized 1,000,000 troops and when they wouldn't withdraw Germany declared war on Russia on the 1st of August and two days later declared war on France. Italy decided to keep out of it and Belgium's neutrality was assured by a treaty signed in 1839 by Britain, France and Germany. When German troops went into Belgium on 4th August, breaking that treaty, Britain was plunged into war the following day.

In a way it was so quick and unexpected because Britain had been unaware of it until it was too late to even try to prevent it. Mary and Angela were extremely worried by the news. 'Shall you be called up?'

'I don't know if there will be a call-up but anyway I am safe,' Barry said and told them of Stan's proposal. Angela couldn't help but be pleased that Barry would be safe, but worried about Stan. 'Suit me if we could keep them both out of it,' Angela said. 'What do they know of war?'

'What does any ordinary person know?' Mary said. 'And I bet young lads will enlist in droves, like it's some big adventure they're going to.'

Mary was right and the very next Sunday just as they were finishing dinner they heard the military band going along Bristol Street. 'I wonder where they're making for,' Angela said.

'Let's go and find out,' Barry suggested.

'Oh I can't,' Angela said. 'There's the dishes to see to.'

'I'll see to the dishes,' Mary said. 'You go and see what it's all about.'

'Are you sure?' Angela asked.

'Course I'm sure,' Mary said firmly. 'And I bet young Connie here would like to see the soldiers marching behind the band, wouldn't you, pet?'

Connie nodded her head emphatically for she had heard the band and loved music. 'Let's away then,' Barry said, scooping Connie from her chair and on to his shoulders in one movement.

'Wait,' Angela cried. 'She needs her coat.'

'Not on a day like this she doesn't, woman,' Barry said. 'Hurry up or it'll be over before we get there.'

They weren't the only ones setting out for when they stepped out of the door they saw many doing the same thing and all making their way to Bristol Passage, which led down to Bristol Street. And what they saw when they reached the main street stopped many in their tracks.

A man in full regalia led the band. He had a cap with a shiny peak pulled down so low, Angela doubted his eyes were visible, but what was visible was his dark, curling moustache above his resolute mouth. He was wearing white gloves and in one hand he carried a twirling ornamental stick. He looked neither right nor left but straight ahead and his boots rang with each precise step on the cobbles and set the beat for the musicians to follow, reinforced by the big drums at the back.

The band were followed by the regular soldiers, khaki bags slung across their bodies, rifles over their left shoulders and all perfectly in time. A cheer rose in the air and rippled through the watching crowd and small boys ran whooping and cavorting along the pavement, caught up in the excitement of it all.

Behind the soldiers were civilians, many mere boys, younger than Barry, and he could well understand the lure. For the band and the spectacle were a promise of a more exciting life than one played out on those mean streets where they mightn't even have employment. Even from the people standing with them, one or two broke away and joined the motley crew following the army. 'Shall we follow them and listen to what they have to say?' Barry asked.

'You . . . You won't be tempted to join them?'

'Are you joking?' Barry said. 'I'm not a boy to be swayed by a few marching soldiers. I'm a married man with responsibilities and in the job I do, I'm helping the war effort, so I'm doing my bit that way.'

Relieved and reassured, Angela let out the breath she hadn't been aware she was holding and said, 'We may as well then.'

As Barry and Angela had guessed, the army marched into Calthorpe Park and a man with a bristling moustache and a shiny peaked cap, like the one the band master wore, leapt up onto the steps of the stadium. The band played on and the man made no effort to speak while the people were still streaming in through the entrance.

Eventually, a large crowd had assembled in front of the stadium, the band had stopped playing and laid their instruments down, and the man began to speak. He spoke first of what a privilege he'd always thought it was to serve his country, as he had done for many years in the British Army, and the finest way to serve any nation was to fight for them if that's what had to be done, especially in a war situation.

'So now our country is at war again, but it is an honourable war to bring freedom and justice to oppressed nations. The British Army's aim is to rid the world of brutal aggressors, for they are our enemy and we must crush them so that innocent men and women can live in peace. Many have already answered the call and come forward to help in this task. But we need more to ensure we win this righteous war. Which of you young men have the courage to join us? Who amongst you will be able to wear the British Army uniform with pride knowing they have been part of making the world a safer place?'

It was stirring stuff, Barry had to admit, and despite his words to Angela his feet seemed to want to move of their own volition. He planted them firmly on the ground and he knew fighting in a war would be bloody and dirty and probably quite frightening at times and he might be injured or killed. And then where would that leave his mother and Angela and his baby daughter? He might not see her grow up so he was glad that wasn't in his life plan anyway, and yet he couldn't help wishing desperately that he could be part of this honourable war.

He wasn't a bit surprised though when young men and boys began peeling themselves away from the crowd to join the ranks of those who had followed the army. At first it was one or two that went, but that became a trickle and then a flood until a great many young men were there to sign on the dotted line and be part of the great British Army.

'Shall we go now?' Angela said for she had seen the zeal in her husband's face and, for all his assurances, it had disturbed her. 'Unless you want to see if Stan is here. I did look but didn't spot him.'

'Oh he won't be here,' Barry said. 'He has already

216

been to see them at Thorp Street Barracks. He's already in.'

'Oh,' Angela said and then she exclaimed, 'Look, there's one that isn't in yet, but looks as if he's about to rememdy that.' For a little way ahead of them in the crowd was Maggie and she had her arm linked with Michael Malone and as they watched he stepped away from her and joined the other boys and young men waiting to join up. 'It's Michael,' she said. 'Thought he would have more sense.'

'Maybe sense has less to do with it than lack of money,' Barry said. 'He was laid off six months ago and hasn't really earned a penny since then. In fact that may be why a lot of boys are joining up.'

'Dangerous path to tread.'

'Needs must,' said Barry.

The weeks that followed were strange ones. All the young fellows at the foundry gave notice as they said they were joining up and the only people applying for the jobs were women. The factory was noisy, greasy and grimy and a lot of the work was heavy and Barry didn't think it was a place for women to work and took the problem to Mr Baxter who was the manager of the whole factory. 'I think you must get over that prejudice against women, young Barry,' he said when he'd heard him out.

'It's not prejudice, sir,' Barry protested. 'Or at least not in a nasty way. I'm thinking of them, sir, for the work is really not suited to women.'

'So what's to be done?' Mr Baxter said. 'Those orders have to go out for they are for the war effort. How are we to expect our soldiers to face the enemy with no weapons or rifles?'

'Well no.'

'Look, Barry,' Mr Baxter said, 'ours will not be the only factory to be nearly empty of all its young man. You need a great deal of men to fight a war and have a chance of winning. You also need a great deal of ammunition too, so if there's no men to make it there's only the women left. Give the jobs to the women, Barry, and believe me they'll tell you if the work is too much for them.'

Barry was very surprised as the weeks passed. The women came in overalls with scarves wrapped turban-style around their heads. They were a cheerful lot, full of laughter and fun, and they changed the atmosphere of the factory floor, though the noise of the machines prevented them from talking a great deal when they were working, but they made up for it in the canteen when they were at their dinner or tea break when the noise level was sometimes very high indeed. But Barry put up with that because in all other ways they were no trouble. They arrived promptly and worked hard and never complained about the job as the young lads were wont to do and Barry had to revise his opinion of the work a woman can or should do.

He was further astounded when he saw women as conductresses on the omnibuses and trams, but completely flabbergasted when he saw women driving them, and they were driving horse-drawn wagons too and petrol-driven ones. He heard they were working in factories all over the country, leaving their homes and families some of them and taking lodging in the bigger houses. Cramped back-to-back houses usually had no space to accommodate these intrepid souls who took work where they could, in drop forges, or steel works or Dunlops making tyres for military vehicles. Then there were many types of weaponry made in special munitions workshops and it was women now who assembled and tested guns in the gun quarter.

All these used to be men's jobs, but there were few fit men about and Barry often felt he stood out like a sore thumb, for those he did see were all in uniform. Angela could have told him of the askance looks she had from some neighbours when she explained that Barry wouldn't be enlisting because he had exemption as he was in a reserved occupation. Some of the women went further and made snide remarks about him sitting pretty while others fought his battles, and others snubbed her completely. Although it hurt her because she would have said that she was well liked, Angela understood some of their reactions for they all had loved ones, husbands, brothers, sweethearts who had enlisted without a thought.

She said nothing about it to Barry, for it wasn't as if he could do anything about it and it would only worry him. She knew Mary had taken a bit of stick too because she mentioned it one day when she came in from shopping. 'What did they say?' Angela asked.

'Oh what I might have expected,' Mary replied, 'jibes about keeping my little lambikin safe and similar stuff.'

'Oh, Mammy I'm so sorry,' Angela said.

'Don't know what you're sorry about,' Mary said. 'T'isn't your fault. Anyway don't you worry about me. Their abuse rolls off me like water off a duck's back.'

'I suppose it will all be sorted out when the men are

219

back home again and the war's over,' Angela said. 'It can't last for ever anyway. Some people at the shops were saying it might be all over by Christmas.'

'Nice if it was,' Mary said. 'But I doubt it. There are too many countries involved for it all to be wrapped up so quickly.'

'So we just live with the insults?'

'That's about the shape of it,' Mary said. 'Count to ten or bite your lip or whatever. Don't say anything you might regret because when the world is back to normal you will have to live alongside these people.'

Angela didn't argue with Mary. She was very wise and Angela hated confrontation anyway, but she avoided her neighbours as much as possible.

A very welcome letter came from Stan in late October. He had a spot of leave and there were no people he would rather spend it with. He said he would be staying in his old house because the neighbours had been keeping an eye on it for him and he was keeping the rent up to date so far.

Mary wrote and welcomed him warmly, only sorry that she couldn't offer him a bed too. 'I bet it's in a bit of a state as well,' she said to Angela. 'Looking after a place is all well and good but it's sure to be damp not being lived in, especially now the cold weather is setting in. His bed could easily be damp too.'

'Well he can't sleep in a damp bed,' Angela said. 'He'll go down with pneumonia.'

'What say you and I go and look at the place and maybe light the fires to warm it up before he gets here?' Mary suggested. 'He left me one of the keys for safe keeping.'

They went up together leaving Connie at Norah's to mind but when they surveyed Stan's house however they knew they would have to do more than light a fire and check the sheets for dampness. The house had an unloved look about it and a sour smell lingered in the air. Dust was thick on every surface and cobwebs festooned the corners of the room, the fender was dull and the grate badly needed black leading.

Because Stan had plenty of coal in the cellar they first dealt with the hearths and the one in the bedroom too and when that was clean and tidy Mary lit fires in the living room and the bedroom before tackling the rest of the house. It took some time and they were very glad of the cups of tea Norah brought round when they had been hard at it for a couple of hours. 'This is just the job,' Mary said as she accepted a cup gratefully. 'My throat's that dry.'

'And mine,' Angela said. 'It's the dust. What have you done with Connie?'

'The wee angel went to sleep on my knee and so I put her in the pram,' Norah said and she looked around the room. 'You two have done wonders. I'd love to see the look on his face. When does he arrive?'

'About half ten Saturday,' Angela said. 'Barry's taking the morning off to welcome him.'

Stan arrived at the McCluskys' first but he wouldn't stay because he had all his kit with him and he said that it would be better to dump it all in his house first. So Angela left Connie with Barry and went up with him and Mary followed her because they wanted to see his reaction to what they had done to the house. And when he opened the door he stood on the threshold and just stared. He had never seen the house so clean and tidy, gleaming with polish and a cheerful fire burned in the black-leaded grate behind a shiny brass fender with extra coal in the scuttle on the hearth.

'I got you a few bits,' Mary said. 'Not a lot because you'll be eating most meals with us, a small loaf and butter, tea, sugar and oatmeal to make porridge for your breakfast if you want to. I didn't leave any milk because it would only go sour but you can bring some from our house, I have a can you can use.'

'You are so very kind,' Stan said, his voice husky with emotion at their thoughtfulness. He tried to get a grip on himself as he valiantly tried to swallow the lump in his throat and stop the tears trickling down his cheeks and thoroughly embarrassing everybody.

'It was nothing, really,' Mary said and then as she turned to go she suddenly said, 'Oh and don't worry about the sheets being damp, Angela here has had them warmed up with hot water bottles.'

'Like I said, I'm overwhelmed.'

'It's been no trouble honestly,' Angela said. 'We've lit the fire in the bedroom too so that the place will be cosy and warm for you.'

'I don't know what to say,' Stan said. 'Thank you seems so inadequate.'

A catch in Stan's voice caused Angela to look up and she spotted a tell-tale tear seeping from Stan's left eye and knew he would hate them to see him crying and she said 'There's nothing to say. It's obvious you appreciate all that we've done for you and that's all that matters. We'll leave you to get sorted and come down when you're ready.'

Stan just nodded.

'D'you know,' Mary remarked as they walked down Grant Street, 'Stan Bishop is one of the nicest and most generous people I know and yet I don't think he has ever had much kindness shown to him. Look how he reacted over what we had done.'

Angela agreed, 'You could be right, so let's make sure he has a good leave and we'll be as kind to him as we know how.'

'Aye,' said Mary and the two women were smiling as they went in the house.

Stan hadn't seen Connie when he had just called before going to his own house and when he arrived about lunchtime he was astounded at the change in her in just a few months. But one thing hadn't changed and that was her love for her 'Uncle Stan' which she attempted to say, and Stan hugged her tight and said to Angela later as they sat to eat the delicious meal that Mary had cooked, 'I thought she would have forgotten all about me.'

'What,' said Angela in mock horror, 'forget the finest tower builder in the universe? I'd say not.'

'Yeah,' Barry agreed. 'Ideally children need more than their parents in their lives and Connie's a bit short on real relatives and she picked you as her pseudo uncle.'

'Suits me,' Stan said. 'Shame I'm not going to be around much in the near future for this is embarkation leave. God knows when I'll get leave again.'

Barry nodded. 'I guessed it was embarkation leave,' he said. 'I might not know much about the army, but I know that much.'

'And how are you finding training?' Mary asked.

'Oh I have no trouble with the training,' Stan said. 'It is after all what I joined up for.'

'Are you ready to go?'

'Is any man ever ready for war?' Stan said. 'Although I have sometimes been as angry and frustrated as any other man, I have never wished to inflict harm on another human being. And yet most of our training was about that, learning all the different ways one man could kill another.' He paused slightly and then continued, 'We were told about these "Pals Regiments" they've set up so people from small towns and villages will all be together. The cities will be split into areas so, for example, there are a number of Birmingham Pals Regiments and I shall be in one of these.'

'Isn't that a good thing?' Angela asked. 'Isn't it better to have someone you know and trust at your back in battle?'

'There is that of course,' Stan said, 'and probably that was the idea behind it, but it means that the men will know one another, might be related even. We are told that even if their brother falls before them, they must step over him and go on.'

Angela gave a slight gasp, for she was quite shocked at Stan's words, though she thought she had no right to be for she wasn't a fool, but when she had used the terms 'going to war' or 'in conflict' she didn't immediately think of the human cost of it. But in actual fact, in brutal terms that's what war boiled down to, killing more men than your opponent so as to be declared the winner, and Stan, watching her face, said, 'I'm sorry. Have I upset you?'

Angela shook her head. 'No, not really. It's just I've

224

never thought of it that way before and now I have, I don't think I could ever kill anyone.'

'I could kill anyone who threatened my family,' Barry said, vehemently.

'Well all right,' Angela conceded. 'But the Germans aren't threatening us.'

'No, but they have invaded Belgium,' Stan said. 'And Belgium signed a treaty some time ago that they could claim neutrality.'

'Why?' Angela asked. 'I mean why just Belgium?'

'I don't know,' Stan admitted. 'Maybe because they're only a small country and have little in the way of defences in the event of being attacked by other countries round about and Germany ignored that treaty.'

'But why did they do that?' Angela cried. 'Did anyone think of asking them why before beginning a war that will undoubtedly kill many people?'

'D'you know Angela?' Stan said. 'I don't think anyone thought of that. I saw this coming for some time though because Europe was so volatile, our government seemed to be taken on the hop. I suppose many of the countries in Europe had had various skirmishes and squabbles amongst themselves so many times and got over them without our involvement and they must have thought or hoped this would be the same. I had a sort of premonition that this might be different. Mind you, I didn't envisage all the other countries joining in too. I thought it might be some major skirmish we might be pulled into and maybe it would have been like that if it hadn't been for the Archduke being killed, giving the Emperor a reason to attack Serbia and asking for the Kaiser's help.'

'According to the paper, Germans are committing gross atrocities in Belgium as well,' Barry said.

'We might almost expect behaviour like that,' Stan said. 'I would have said many invading armies intent on taking over a country don't treat the people so well.'

'Yes I think the same,' Barry said. 'It's a way of establishing control from the start. Anyway, whatever could have been done to avert all-out war wasn't done and now it's too late.'

'And I'm fed up of war talk,' Mary said. 'And such things shouldn't be discussed in front of Connie, for most of it goes over her head. Doesn't it pet?' she said, tousling Connie's curls.

Mary was rewarded with a beautiful smile, for though Connie didn't understand all the words said, she picked up on the atmosphere and knew all about serious faces and solemn ones, and she was glad when her Daddy smiled at her and it appeared to be over. To Mary he said, 'Sorry, Mammy, you're right of course.' He looked across at Angela and said, 'We could take Connie to the park if you like. That's if Stan wants,' he finished, glancing across at his friend.

'I can't think of anything I'd like better,' Stan said.

'That's settled then,' Barry said. 'Shall we take the pram?'

'No,' Angela said. 'She'll be tired on the way back and if she's in the pram she'll sleep and then I'll never get her to bed tonight.'

'Righto,' Barry said and he fastened Connie into her coat before going out the door holding her hand.

'That won't last long, her walking on her own,' Angela said. 'A few yards along the road and she'll have her hands up to be lifted onto Barry's shoulders.'

'And he'll oblige of course?'

'That doesn't even need saying,' Angela said. 'He would have her totally ruined if I didn't watch him.'

'Ah well,' Mary said, 'better than taking no notice of her at all.'

Angela didn't argue for she knew she was lucky that she had a husband in a million and one who loved spending time with his child. She knew some men had no time for the babies once they were born but when she said to Barry how much she appreciated the help he gave her, he said Connie belonged to both of them and he missed enough of her growing up away at work all day. 'Not all fathers feel that way,' Angela said.

'I know it,' Barry said. 'And they are the losers because they don't know what they're missing.'

The sad thing was, Angela thought as she washed up the pots from dinner, Stan was one in the same mould as Barry and his son was as lost to him as if he had died.

There was no point in saying anything though because it wasn't as if talking would make a ha'p'orth of difference. She gave a small sigh and standing on tiptoe gave her husband a kiss on the cheek. He was pleased, but surprised and with a smile on his face he said, 'I'm not complaining or anything, but what was that for?'

'Does there have to be a reason to give my husband a kiss?' Angela asked. 'Let's just say it's because I know how lucky I am.'

SIXTEEN

The next day as Stan joined the family for Sunday dinner he said, 'They are recommending that all men who haven't already done so should make a will before they are sent overseas.'

Angela gave a shiver and Stan said, 'Just because I have been asked to make a will doesn't mean that anything is going to happen to me. It's a precaution to help your loved ones if anything did happen.'

'Well no good me making a will,' Mary said. 'For I would have nothing to leave.'

'Ah but I have a son,' Stan said. 'A son that I have had no hand in rearing. Meanwhile I have been given a good salary over the years and only me to spend it on and I am not a great drinker, do not gamble, only have the one packet of fags a day and for years now any money left over from my wages has been put in the Post Office for Daniel. I want to make sure he will get it if anything happens to me though I will put in a codicil that the money be kept in trust for Daniel until he is twenty-one. My commanding officer helped me when I admitted I didn't know the least thing about making a will. He told me the firm to go to in the city centre too. Apparently they do a lot of military wills.'

'But do you really need a will when Daniel is with family?' Mary said. 'Surely Betty would make sure the boy got the money?'

'How would Betty explain it?' Stan asked. 'I signed all rights to my son to Betty and her husband and have no contact at all really because she said it would just confuse him.'

'Don't see how it could,' Mary said. 'Betty was wrong to ask you to do that. You were still mourning your wife.'

Stan nodded. 'My head was all over the place in the beginning and I couldn't have coped with Daniel. I was glad of Betty then.'

'I know you were,' Mary said, for she remembered it well.

'Didn't give her the right to steal your son,' Barry said. 'You couldn't have been in your right mind when you signed those papers because I could never sign my child away.'

'Aye, Barry,' said Angela. 'But we have had Connie eighteen months, think if you were faced with a newborn baby and a dead wife?'

'Yes,' Mary said. 'Stan was very vulnerable then and Betty took advantage.'

'And the plus side of all this is that Betty and Roger love Daniel,' Stan said. 'I know that they will love and care for him as if he was their own son and that's what Betty wants him to be. How then will she explain the money? I don't think for one moment that she will steal the money from him but she could very easily say it was a gift from them, her and Roger. I want a solicitor to deal with it and so I intend writing Daniel a letter explaining everything to him.'

'And what will that do to the lad?' Mary asked quite sharply.

'What d'you mean?'

'Well if Betty has her way, Daniel won't know you even exist,' Mary said. 'And then out of the blue when he's twenty-one he gets money from a stranger and a letter, and in that letter the stranger claims to be his father. If he thought Betty and Roger were his parents he is bound to be upset they've lied to him, upset that he never got to know you when you were alive. Whatever way he takes it, he is bound to be disturbed in some way.'

'You think I should say nothing?'

'No,' Mary said. 'I think there has already been too much secrecy in this whole business. If Daniel had been told Betty and Roger had adopted him as soon as he could understand and especially if you were a fixture in his life, then he would be able to take this in his stride long before he reaches twenty-one. If you didn't survive the war he would be upset and would mourn, but because he loved you and knew you loved him, the strength of that love would enable him to go on with his life and he probably would be grateful to Betty and Roger for caring for him so well. But this way . . .'

'Someone is bound to get hurt,' Stan said. 'And I'm afraid it's going to be Daniel, the person I would cut off my right arm for.'

Angela felt so sorry for Stan and yet she knew every word Mary spoke was the truth. She couldn't see how anyone could make things any better. But then Mary said, 'There is only one thing to be done, you must write to Betty.'

Stan shook his head, 'No communication, that was the deal.'

'War changes everything,' Mary said. 'Tell her you have enlisted and what arrangements you have made for Daniel when he reaches twenty-one, if you do not survive the war. Don't look like that,' she went on, seeing the look of protest on Stan's face. 'Betty won't be able to touch that money or the letter if you wrap it up legally. That way if you don't survive the war she would be a fool if she didn't tell Daniel the truth about his parentage. It will still be a blow but better than receiving that bomb- shell with no warning on his twenty- first birthday.'

'Mammy's right,' Barry said. 'It is the only thing to do. Put the ball in Betty's court. They must be the ones to tell David the truth since they were the ones that didn't tell him the truth in the first place and cut you out of the boy's life into the bargain.'

'I agree with Mammy and Barry too,' Angela said. 'And being as you can't see the solicitor till tomorrow I'd get the letter to Betty written straight away.'

'And the one for Daniel to leave with the solicitor,' Stan said. 'I'll see to them both this evening. Something else I have decided and that's to give up the tenancy on the house. I don't know when I'll have leave again and while I know the house is not much cop, it's better than nothing and a family could have the use of it. It's selfish to keep it on.'

'And if all else fails,' Barry said, 'you can always have the use of our settee.'

'Or floor,' Stan said. 'I'll be a seasoned soldier by then and able to sleep anywhere.'

So all was done by the time Mary and Angela, with Connie between them, assembled at New Street to see Stan off, as he was joining his company on the South Coast, and they all knew without much doubt that he would be off to France soon. Angela's insides trembled, and she held Connie's hand so tight the child complained.

Angela knew anyone watching them would think them a family and though Angela had grown to love Stan, she didn't love him as she loved Barry – that love was special. However, that morning she did embrace him and kiss his cheek and Mary followed suit for it just felt right. 'Look after yourself,' Mary said and then remarked ruefully, 'What a daft thing to say to a man off to war.'

Stan smiled. 'I promise I'll keep my head down,' he said as he lifted Connie into his arms. 'Will that do?'

'I suppose it will have to,' Mary said gruffly. 'Connie, give Uncle Stan a kiss. He has to be on the train shortly.'

Connie wound her podgy little arms around Stan's neck and kissed his cheek soundly. 'Bye Unky Tan.'

'Bye-bye my darling girl and I will be back to see you as soon as I can,' Stan said and he handed Connie into Angela's arms. 'You will write to me?' he said as he stepped into the train.

'Of course,' Angela said. 'Promise I will.'

The train doors were slammed, the whistle blew and billows of smoke filled the air as the train began to chug its way out of the station, leaving behind the acrid smell of coal dust. And Angela's eyes blurred with tears as she wondered if she would ever see Stan again.

Life continued as before as rumours of battles in strange places with foreign names filled the papers and now that Stan was probably embroiled in it, Angela read the papers as avidly as Barry, though previously she had only skimmed the headlines.

Stan wrote to them, but could tell them nothing of his location or any other war-related news, for the censor would cut it out if he tried. Instead they got little missives that gave them snapshots of army life, like the dugout assigned to the men when they had time to relax:

> *In the middle of a war our appearance still matters a great deal and I really can't see the point of being so particular . . .*

In early December Stan sent a clue that he was in France when he wrote:

> *Sometimes I really can't stomach the food in the Naafi and it would be nice to be able to go into town for a home-made pie and some of the pastries they are so famous for.*

'Got that through the censor,' Angela said.

'It doesn't say anything.'

'It says enough. 'The pastries they are so famous for" – that's France surely?'

'I'd say you're right, Angela,' Mary said. 'Anyway this has decided me. I will make him a small Christmas cake of his own and mince pies too and put them in the box I am making up.' She had already bought him gloves and a scarf and Angela added ten packets of cigarettes, a set of men's handkerchiefs and a big bag of the bull-seyes he was partial to.

'Good English food,' Mary said in approval. 'No need to eat the French stuff unless he wants to. And I'm sure pastries are all very well, but they would hardly fill a man. You need things that stick to your ribs a bit in cold weather like this.'

Angela thought Mary not far wrong because the days leading up to Christmas were raw ones. It didn't help that as December took hold there was little in the shops to buy and often the grocery shops' shelves were half empty. Everyone was talking about it. It was said that the wealthy were parking their cars or carriages in side streets and sending the drivers in with long lists of things. This left the poor, who couldn't afford to stock-pile, to manage the best way they could, although it was hard to feed families without even basic commodities.

'I've never actually seen this myself,' Angela said, 'though a lot of things I used to buy from the grocer aren't there any more and in the paper they said there's a lot of it going on and it must be true because the food I used to buy has got to go somewhere. Surely it's wrong.'

'Of course it's wrong,' Mary said. 'How can you mange without bread and milk and tea? And some of the butchers' slabs are near empty as well and the greengrocer's hadn't a potato in the shop the other day. Shopping takes all day because you go from shop to shop along Bristol Street to get a bit here and a bit there and still come back with your bag half empty. And,' she added, 'at least we have the money to do that. What of the poor devils who are tied to the one shop because they'll let them run up tick till pay day? What are they living on if there's nothing on the shelves?'

Angela thought about the number of people George Maitland gave tick to and knew Mary had made a valid point. 'It's a disgrace,' she said. 'The government should do something to stop it.'

'They won't care about the likes of us,' Mary said. 'They have a war to win. As long as the soldiers are adequately fed I would say, as far as the government are concerned, the rest of us can sink or swim. But I'll tell you what, the war can't go on for ever and people have long memories and they won't forget those shops who let down their loyal customers. They'll go somewhere else when the war's over.'

'We all have to live till then,' Angela said. 'Barry is working the long hours he has to just now and needs good solid food inside him, and Connie too, for she has a lot of growing to do.'

'Well if it comes to that we all need proper food,' Mary said. 'What would happen if you or I were to go down sick because we were so malnourished?'

'You're right,' Angela said. 'So let's start our boycott now. I'm going to start getting the groceries at Maitland's. It's a bit of a trek, but at least I will be able to get all I need.'

'How do you know he isn't into this selling to the toffs as well?' Mary asked.

'Because I know him,' Angela said, with assurance.

236

'He is an honest man with integrity and he would see this as wrong and have no part in it. And added to that he is no great lover of toffs. As for the greengrocery and the meat, we can buy all that from the Bull Ring because any toff or toff's lackey would get short shrift there.'

'Aye,' said Mary with a chuckle.

'And not a word to Barry,' Angela warned. 'He has enough on his plate just now.'

Angela was in fact quite worried about her young husband whose eyes often looked quite haunted and his face had a definite greyish tinge to it. The hours he put in at the factory were punishing, for the Government was pressing for greater production. Even more lines were set up and the employees had to work longer hours and much faster than before to make the products that were needed. Not many grumbled, for most had loved ones at the Front and wanted to do their bit too.

Barry always told Angela he was 'fine' when she asked him if he was all right, for he could never tell her what was really tormenting him, which were the pictures he had seen in the papers of the injured soldiers returning to Britain. He didn't want to be among them, of course he didn't, he just felt bad about the whole thing. And worse were the others who had made the ultimate sacrifice and whose bodies littered a foreign field some-where.

So Barry never knew of the women's journey to buy decent food in sufficient quantity to put on the table. George Maitland, when he heard why they were changing grocers, said he'd had toffs' drivers target him too, but he had sent them packing.

'This man I'd never seen before gave me this big order, like a roll of wallpaper it was,' George said. 'And I said that as I hadn't seen him before he must be a stanger to the area and if so, didn't he have a local grocer to deal with such a large order.

'He said that he didn't, so I asked him why he needed so much food and if he was buying it on someone else's behalf. 'Course he coloured up then and so I said, "If I fill your order it will nearly empty my shelves, so then what do the customers do who've been coming to me for years if I have nothing left for them to buy to feed their families?"

'"Can't you restock?" said the cocky young chap.

'"'Course I could," I told him,' George said to Angela and Mary. 'But then I said to him, "I couldn't do that immediately. It might be three or four days before stock was back in the shop. So you sling your hook and don't come back and tell your Mistress she'll have to tighten her belt like the rest of us are having to do.'

Angela shot Mary a smile of triumph for she'd known just how George would behave. And then George said, 'It might have been more difficult to do if Dorothy had been in the shop, though I would still have done it because I make the decisions, but Dorothy would tell Matilda and she would moan at me and Dorothy would put her oar in as well.'

'Oh dear,' Angela said. 'Is Dorothy your new assistant's name?'

George shook his head, 'No, worse luck. My assistant left to work in the munitions where the money is better and she didn't have to cope with Matilda. Dorothy is Matilda's sister. She's recently been widowed and Matilda wanted her here till she gets over it. Upshot is she's moved in lock, stock and barrel and Matilda suggested she works in the shop at busy times. I seem to spend a lot of time in the shop at the moment.' Both Mary and Angela could understand why and Mary said, 'You should take yourself to the pub a time or two and leave them to it.'

George smiled. 'That's never been my way.'

'Well maybe it should become your way,' Mary said. 'Make some friends of your own. All work and no play, you know?'

'I'll be all right,' George said, reaching into the lollipop jar to give one to Connie as he went on, 'And it will be lovely seeing you on a regular basis. I did so miss Angela when she left, but I bet you have your hands full now.'

'Oh yes,' Angela said. 'Connie takes some watching all right, but she is really the light of our lives.'

'Was he asking you to go back?' Mary asked as she pushed the pram back home.

Angela nodded. 'I think he was sounding me out.'

'Would you be tempted?'

Angela shook her head vehemently. 'I wouldn't want to leave Connie unless I had to and I definitely think Barry would be against it.'

'And he's bringing home plenty of money now too,' Mary said.

'That's all the overtime,' Angela said. 'And it can't go on at that rate for the hours are quite mad at the moment. I'll be glad when it's Christmas and he can have some time off, because he looks a little strained to me.'

'I've noticed he's quieter than usual,' Mary said. 'Let's

hope you're right. Thank God Christmas is no distance away.'

The McCluskys woke on Christmas morning to find it had snowed in the night and was still snowing, the snow turning to shimmering pools of gold beneath the lamps which gleamed in the night sky, for it would be a few hours yet till daylight. Connie had never seen snow and she was enchanted and straight away wanted to get dressed and go out in it despite the cold and the darkness.

Downstairs however, Santa had paid a visit and left Connie a jack-in-the-box that amused her immensely. And that wasn't all. She also had a new fleece-lined winter coat from her American Uncle Finbarr. It was royal blue and there was a matching bonnet and mittens. She looked as pretty as a picture in it. But more importantly Angela knew she would be as warm as toast in that coat and she intended to write and thank Finbarr heartily for he also sent ten dollars for them to treat themselves.

She wanted to congratulate Finbarr too for he wrote that he was getting married to a girl called Orla McCann who he had met at Mass. Mary gave a sigh of relief when Angela read that out because if he had met this Orla at Mass then she must be a Catholic. But it was even better than that for not only was she of Irish descent, but her family came from Donegal as the McCluskys did. She couldn't be more suitable and Mary was relieved that Finbarr's future at least looked set.

Colm hadn't any news like that himself but there was another ten dollars inside his letter and he said that

Mammy need have no worries because Orla was a great girl altogether and he was to continue to live with them after they married until he was ready to settle down himself. He hadn't forgotten his little niece either and for her there was a beautiful large book and Angela gave a gasp as she lifted it out because she had never owned anything so fine. It was called *The Treasury of Nursery Rhymes* and every nursery rhyme anyone could think of was written on the wonderfully illustrated pages. Angela stroked the book almost reverently and looked forward to hours of enjoyment for her and Connie as they shared the book together.

There was another parcel too that year and it was from Stan who explained in the letter that he had found himself billeted near a small French town as Christmas approached and so was able to buy them some authentic French presents, so both women had silk stockings and they were truly magnificent and felt delicious against the skin, but neither woman could think of an occasion when they would wear them for they were too ostentatious for Mass and they seldom went anywhere else. Barry on the other hand was very appreciative of the French Cognac.

'I think it's really lovely for Stan to remember us at all,' Angela said with a small sigh. 'And it seems horrible to seem ungrateful, but he seems not to have a clue what women like us would find useful.'

'Well how would he know?' Mary said. 'I think women are a great mystery for men, for Matt never had a clue what I might want or need either. There was no money ever for fripperies, but now and then I would have been grateful for a pair of stout boots, or warm slippers, but unless I gave out huge hints I usually went without.'

'Well we'll write and thank him anyway,' Angela said. 'And at least we won't have to pretend when we say Connie was delighted with her present, for she loved the kaleidoscope he sent when she had been shown how to twist it round.' And so Christmas went by and Barry tried to lift his despondent mood because it was Christmas after all. Angela wasn't fooled and she listened to her husband's restlessness in bed at night and worried about it, but she never shared her concerns even with Mary.

SEVENTEEN

The New Year was quiet and January was cold enough to numb fingers and feet, to form icicles on window ledges, to freeze the tap in the yard rock solid and for snow to fall from leaden skies, driven into drifts by the bone-chilling biting wind.

Getting about was hazardous, but groceries had to be fetched because there was little left to eat. Angela refused to let Mary come with her to Maitland's. 'It's too far for you. You might fall and break a leg.'

'So might you.'

'Yes, I might,' Angela conceded. 'So I'll be extra careful and if I should break something, I'll likely heal quicker than you. Look, it would be really helpful if you mind Connie for me and I'll take the pram. I can bring more back that way.'

Mary crossed to the window and gazed out. 'You'll never push the pram in this,' she declared. 'And it's still coming down thick and fast.'

'I'll be fine,' Angela said. 'Someone has to go and 'I've got that lovely warm coat from last year so I'll not freeze and if I can't push the pram I'll pull it. I did it a time or two before.'

However, despite her spirited words to Mary, Angela found the trek to Maitland's was challenging for the roads were thick with snow on top of impacted ice, the icy wind buffeted her from all sides and the pram she pulled behind seemed to get heavier and heavier, and that was when it was empty, so she didn't relish the journey home. She intended getting a full week's worth of food to keep them going longer so she wouldn't have to make this journey again in a hurry.

George, though glad to see her, expressed concern that she had ventured out on such a day.

'Needs must,' Angela said. 'The cupboards were nearly bare. I was waiting for a better day myself, but each one is worse than the one before and if we were going to eat I had to get supplies. I've left Connie with Mammy though, the day is not fit for either of them to go out.'

'Oh no it isn't,' George agreed. 'You did the right thing there. Now let's have that order and I'll fill it out for you as fast as I can, so you can be home warm and safe and dry as quickly as possible.'

And George lost no time in filling the order and as Angela was packing it all away in the pram, she marvelled that she could buy a full week's food. She knew many of her neighbours couldn't, even if their husbands were in full-time work, for wages were so low, many lived from hand to mouth.

The wages the men brought home were usually enough for the wives to pay the rent and any tick they had owing in the shops, get their husband's suit out of the pawn shop, buy food for the weekend and if there was any left at all, maybe buy a hundredweight of coal. On Monday morning they would pawn the husband's suit and use the money for foodstuffs and if there was more week left than money, they would run up tick at the grocery shop.

That had been the lot of many women. There was very little slack and anything could tip the balance, boots needing heeling, a harsh long winter meaning an extra hundredweight of coal, a sick child needing the services of a doctor, any of these could send them into rent arrears.

She had remarked on this just that morning to Mary. 'I can't help feeling a bit guilty,' she admitted. 'I served many women like that in the shop while we are sitting pretty because Barry is an indentured toolmaker, and a supervisor to boot, so he gets good money and even if there is a call-up he will not have to go and fight anyone, but these women's lives will just get worse.'

'Maybe not,' Mary said. 'Those women married to heavy drinkers or gamblers might fare better. I don't know what a soldier is paid but I imagine there is some system in place to pay something out to their wives and more especially if they have children. T'isn't as if they'll have a boozer on every corner of a French field, or a cosy betting shop set up in the trenches they say they're fighting in. Now if, as well as the Army pay, they were to get themselves a little job, which seems as easy as blinking these days, they might have more money than they have ever had in their lives without a husband tipping it down his throat, or putting it all on a horse. Tell you, Angela, while I can never agree with war and there will be a great many men killed

245

and terrible hardship, this war will be the making of some women.'

Angela had agreed with Mary and as she trudged home that day, lugging the overloaded pram after her, she thought of the women she'd served who'd had even less to spend than their neighbours because of their husbands' excesses. They were the fathers of the children hanging around the pub doors on a Friday night, each trying to get some money from their father before he blew it all. They were the fathers who gave their wives so little she could only afford to feed one person anything decent and that had to go to the husband because he was the breadwinner. The woman and children would usually live on bread and scrape and not much of that and the children were usually dressed in ragged clothes and were barefoot.

It always saddened Angela to see them so skinny, with their gaunt pasty faces. Oh yes, if the women married to such men could now get enough to feed themselves and the children properly and have boots on their feet and coats on their backs, it had to be a good thing. And as she reached home with an immense sigh of relief, she thanked God that she was married to such a good, kind and considerate man.

The big freeze went on through January, but soon people had more to worry about than the weather because on the night of 9th January two Zeppelins dropped bombs on King's Lynn and Great Yarmouth killing four, injuring many more and causing £7,000 worth of damage. The whole country was stunned and scared. They knew England was at war, but that was about soldiers and sailors and battles. The thought that innocent and unarmed civilians could be killed by bombs from the air was beyond their understanding. It was pulling everyone into the front line.

Barry felt sick to the pit of his stomach as he looked at the grainy photographs in the paper a couple of days later and saw the scale of the destruction and bemused people standing in the ruins of what had once been their houses and he wondered how Britain could hope to fight this airborne enemy.

Just days after this, Barry picked up the letter from the mat that had been pushed through the letter box and when he opened the envelope three white feathers fell out and he suddenly felt very cold and ashamed. Angela, coming into the room at that moment with Connie in her arms, saw his white face and the opened envelope beside him and fearing further bad news cried, 'What is it?'

Barry moved his arm so she could see the feathers as he said, 'Nothing much. Just what they send to all the cowards dodging war.'

'You're no coward.'

'Am I not?' Barry said sarcastically. 'Didn't I grasp Stan's get-out clause a little too eagerly?'

'It made sense, that's why,' Angela said. 'You have a wife and child.'

'D'you know, Angela, there are thousands of men at the Front,' Barry said. 'Don't you think some of them might be husbands and fathers too?'

Angela wasn't ready to face this yet, so instead of answering she said, 'I can't understand who would do this and upset us all so.'

'Oh you would be spoilt for choice as to who has done this,' Barry said. 'I can't meet the eyes of some I see at Mass knowing their sons will never come home again. And we're being snubbed by families we have known for years. I've noticed so I'm sure you have.'

Angela couldn't disagree with him and she nodded her head mutely.

'And that's another thing,' Barry said. 'One of the reasons Stan went to war was for Daniel. He said if he doesn't make it Daniel will get to read the letter he has left for him when he is twenty-one when he will also find out about the money. Knowing Stan as I do, when Daniel reads that letter he'll know straight away what a fine man his father was and be proud that he died doing something worthwhile.

'Stan said it would be totally different for Connie and how readily I believed him. He said she would understand that I couldn't go to war and leave everyone, but will she understand that when she's a little older and the other children are recounting what their dads did in the war? What will she say then? And there will be plenty about to tell her what a coward I was because they would overhear adults talking. I might never know who sent those feathers but whoever it was, they were only expressing what everyone else is thinking.'

Angela would have liked to refute what Barry said but she couldn't for she knew it was too true. She had been snubbed and had snide remarks directed at her, and she knew children were very cruel when they wanted to be. She had experienced bullying herself, but not for long because she had Barry and his four big brothers to protect her, but Connie might have no one and any

248

of the children who had lost a father, a favourite brother or an uncle might think taunting and mocking Connie might be a suitable distraction to help them cope with the pain of loss. And Connie would be considered fair game because her father was named as a coward.

Angela tried not very successfully to stem the flow of tears as she said, 'So you've decided to enlist?'

Barry nodded. 'I think it's time I did,' he said and his arms encircled his wife and the child she was still holding as he went on, 'What finally decided me were the bombs. They could be dropped from the sky to land anywhere and Britain has got nothing to counteract them and so we have to go over there and stop them now, for I don't think that attack will be the last by any means and I think the Army needs every man jack of us. No one should sit on the fence on this one because our loved ones here are in danger. I always said I would fight if my family were threatened and bombs dropping from the sky mean just that and I must try and protect you.'

He lifted his hand, suddenly releasing Angela as he said, 'Ssh, I hear Mammy stirring in the attic. Not a word to her now, I want to tell her when I have got time to explain it all, for it will be hard for her because she has already lost two sons, but I'll have to leave now really.'

'You've had no breakfast,' Angela said. 'Not even a sup of tea.'

'No matter,' Barry said. 'I can probably pick something up in the canteen.'

Angela heard Mary's ponderous tread on the lower steps and she quickly scrubbed the tears from her eyes and scooped the envelope and feathers into her cardigan pocket as Mary came into the room. But she had eyes only for her son. 'Are you still here?' she said for he was late leaving.

'I'm just away, Mammy,' he said, taking his coat from the hook at the back of the door as he spoke and with a kiss for Angela and Connie he was gone.

Barry told Mr Baxter of his decision immediately and could see how pleased he was and he got from behind his desk and shook him by the hand. 'I'm sure you're doing the right thing,' he said decidedly and Barry was glad of Mr Baxter's enthusiasm for it buoyed up his own, which had evaporated somewhat on the journey to work.

'Now,' Mr Baxter said. 'Have you anyone earmarked to take your place?'

'No, not really,' said Barry. 'Though I have been mulling through the idea of enlisting for some time, I only made the final decision when those bombs were dropped in Norfolk.'

'Yes, shocking wasn't it?'

'Yes and bombs from the air mean our loved ones aren't safe,' Barry said. 'Britain hasn't got anything like those Zeppelins, I don't think. So I thought the only thing to do was get over there as quick as possible and stop whoever is sending them. And I thought they would need every man they could get and what was I doing in a cushy number like the factory when I could be helping?

'As for who will take my place?' Barry went on. 'Sir, those women have shaped up better than I could ever have imagined and I could name half a dozen that could do the job quite as well as I can, but Pearl Mason will have a little bit of authority among the younger girls and she's well liked and also has a head on her shoulders.'

'Good, those are the qualities needed,' Mr Baxter said approvingly. 'Now I suggest you make your announcement to the girls on the shop floor immediately before the machines are started up, then you can make your way to Thorp Street Barracks. Send this young Pearl Mason to me.'

'You want me to go to Thorp Street Barracks today?' Barry cried incredulously.

'One thing I do know about war is that there is no place for shilly-shallying,' Mr Baxter said. 'You already said that you've thought about it for some time. Well waste no more of it thinking.'

'I haven't even told my mother yet, sir.'

'And is there anything your mother can do to turn you from this decision?' Mr Baxter asked.

'No, sir,' Barry said decisively.

'Well if I were you. I would get it all signed and sealed anyway,' Mr Baxter suggested. 'For in my experience a mother's tears can be very persuasive, but if it is all signed and sealed, whatever she says the die is cast.'

Barry could see the sense of that because he did find it hard to stand against his mother's tears and was well aware of his place in the family as her only son. First though, he had to tell the girls on the shop floor his intentions for he couldn't just disappear.

He could see the workforce were intrigued when they were asked to assemble by the steps that led up to the offices and when Barry appeared at the top of those steps and told them he was enlisting, there was a little ripple of applause.

But some were perplexed for Barry had often been the topic of speculation and many had assumed, since he wasn't in uniform like most young men his age were, he must have failed the medical. Now it appeared he hadn't even had a medical. Barry heard the murmurings and explained that as the factory was turning out a great deal for the war effort he was in a reserved occupation, but he thought now he would be more use in the army. He got a cheer of approval for this and those who were the loudest were those who already wore the widow's bonnet and the black armband on their overalls.

The recruitment room at Thorp Street Barracks was a long one. The wooden floor gleamed with polish and the tramp of Barry's work boots sounded very loud as he walked the length of it to stand before the desk at the back of the room, with his heart banging in his breast and his mouth unaccountably dry.

There was a little queue of people at the barracks facing two men in uniform behind a desk. The line of men shuffled forward slowly but at last it was Barry's turn and he saw that one of the men seemed much older than the other. The older one had a florid face and grey hair, not that Barry could see much of his face, for it was partially obscured by his large handlebar moustache. His eyes were not obscured though and they were steely blue, and he introduced himself as Colonel Sanders.

Barry was surprised at such a high-ranking officer

dealing with recruitment, till he remembered Stan said they had taken a lot of the military men out of retirement to do the routine desk jobs. The other man was younger and his face was more open. He was Corporal Withers and his eyes and hair were the same soft brown.

Barry had thought his mouth too dry for him to speak normally and if he made any sort of sound at all it would come out as a squeak. However, he was able to give all the details the two men asked for and explain himself when they expressed surprise at his age for most recruits were younger.

Barry explained about the factory where he had worked since he'd left school and the vast amount of war-related things the factory was churning out. 'I was in a reserved occupation,' he said. 'You see most of the workforce, who were men and boys, enlisted when war was declared, even the previous Gaffer, and someone had to teach the girls and women what to do, as none of them had done any sort of work like that before. But now the women in the workforce are up to speed as it were.' Barry went on, 'One of them is now quite able to take my place while I play a more active part in the war.'

'Good man,' Colonel Sanders said admiringly, so that even his large moustache seemed to bristle with approbation. 'A man choosing to join in this just war, is worth ten conscripts who have to be nearly dragged in to do their duty.'

'I didn't know you had started the call-up, sir.'

'We haven't yet,' Corporal Withers said. 'We are getting enough volunteers at present, but that might change before the war is won, so then we will have conscription and we'll have to try and turn reluctant young men into a fierce fighting force. But the next step for you now is for us to find out how healthy you are.'

Neither of the men were worried about Barry's fitness for he looked a fine, strapping chap, but he was sent to the male white-coated doctor who had a stethoscope hanging around his neck. The doctor had done this many many times and took Barry's temperature and checked his pulse rate before he weighed and measured him and sounded his chest and back. He asked him if he had any aches and pains and though Barry said he hadn't, he was still prodded and poked. The doctor looked into Barry's ears and his throat and examined his eyes and then, having told Barry to strip to his vest and pants, paid great attention to his legs and feet and finally he stood before the doctor who held his testicles in his hand and asked him to cough.

Barry had never been so embarrassed in his life, but for the doctor it was all in a day's work and part of the procedure and he asked Barry to dress and said he was A1 and well able to travel overseas after training.

Barry was joining the Royal Warwickshires and he asked how much he would be paid. It was Colonel Sanders who answered, 'You've heard of the King's shilling I suppose?'

Barry gave a brief nod.

'Well that's what you get, a shilling a day, seven shillings a week.'

It wasn't a lot but then Barry reasoned he didn't need a lot, as there wouldn't be that much to spend it on. 'I have a wife and a child,' he said.

'Yes, sixpence will be deducted from your allowance

for your wife and a penny for your child. The government will pay a weekly sum of one shilling and one penny a day to your wife together with the contributions from you and tuppence extra for your child from the government.' He made a swift calculation on a notepad and said, 'Altogether it comes to eight and fourpence a week.'

Eight and fourpence re-echoed in Barry's brain. It was not enough, not nearly enough. By signing on the dotted line he had reduced his family to penury. Almighty Christ, what had he done? How in God's name could they live on so little? But it was too late to think of that. His fate was sealed. 'Can I give my wife something from my pay?' Barry asked.

Corporal Withers nodded. 'You can indeed. Many men do that. To claim it your wife must take your marriage lines and the child's birth certificate and the child to the Town Hall. She must go herself, no one can go in her stead and as it may take some time to process it, she must do this without delay as soon as you start training. Have you to give notice to your present employer?'

'He said a week, that's all,' Barry said.

'Right, that will be a week today, Colonel Sanders. The 29th January, so how about you coming to the Barracks the following Monday, 1st February? Seven a.m. sharp. Don't be late. There's a truck leaving at a quarter past and I want you on it.' Barry knew he wouldn't be late, he was an early riser. That was the least of his problems and, unable to face Angela and his mother, he went back to work although Mr Baxter said he could go home after he was finished at Thorp

Street. He had no desire to go home and tell them what he had done for he had made their lives even harder.

Everyone seemed to think he had done the right thing and yet the thought of them all going hungry and Connie dressed in rags and running around barefoot would be his worst nightmare come true. He groaned aloud, glad he had the office to himself, for Mr Baxter had taken himself home and advised Barry to do the same.

EIGHTEEN

Afterwards, Barry was not sure how far he walked that night, but eventually he realized he couldn't walk all night and, even if he could, it would change nothing and he turned for home. He was mightily relieved that only Angela was in the room. She started when she saw him and her eyes he saw were full of concern and trepidation. He felt slight guilt that he had worried them so as he whispered, 'Where's Mammy?'

'Putting Connie to bed,' Angela said. 'And having a time of it because I kept her up to see you, only she got too tired to wait any longer, though she of course she didn't agree. Where on earth have you been till this time of night?'

Barry didn't answer that, but what he did say was, 'Shall I go up now?'

'What on earth for?' Angela asked. 'No, you may make matters worse. Connie's been quiet this long time so maybe Mammy's got her off at last. I've kept your dinner hot, though you scarce deserve it, scaring us so. Where did you go?'

Barry said nothing until his dinner was in front of

him and though he was hungry, for he had eaten nothing for hours, he felt slightly sick and he looked at Angela and said, 'I enlisted today.'

Angela gave a small gasp and yet she asked herself why she was so surprised because she knew that that was Barry's way. Once he'd made a decision he acted upon it. 'Is that what kept you?'

Barry shook his head. 'No, Mr Baxter gave me the time off for that. I thought I would enlist and be sent for the other formalities later, but they did it there and then. I think the mad dash for joining up has eased a bit though there were a fair few in front of me and as I left I saw a crowd of young fellows going in. As it was, I had my medical and everything.'

'When do you start?'

'I have to report on 1st February.'

'So soon?'

'For training just.'

'Even so,' Angela said, 'where will you train?'

Barry shrugged. 'Your guess is as good as mine,' he said. 'A couple of women on the shop floor said their chaps trained at a place called Cannock Chase. I don't know where that is and I don't much care, because it doesn't really matter where you train in the end as long as the training is done properly.'

'Oh, Barry, I am so going to miss you.'

'I won't be a million miles away,' Barry said. 'Not at first at any rate.'

'D'you realize we have never been apart?' Angela said. 'Not for one single day and night since I was just over eighteen months old. You have always been there for me and I thought you always would be.'

Barry knew Angela was very near to tears and he pushed his empty plate away and gathered her up in his arms, saying as he did so, 'Angela, I love you more than life itself, my absolute love for Connie often overwhelms me and I love Mammy too and feel responsible for her too. You are the three most important women in my life and I can't stay with you, because I must fight for you and try and make the world a safer place.'

Angela would have much rather Barry was staying here at home and keeping her safe where his strong hands would encircle her if ever she was afraid and she would feel protected and cherished. But what was the point in saying any of this now the decision had been made and so her sigh was imperceptible as she said, 'Is that why you didn't come home, because you haven't told Mammy what you've done?'

'Partly,' Barry admitted and then added, 'I didn't want to face you either because you don't know everything, but I suppose it's better to tell you together?'

'Here's your chance,' Angela said. 'I hear Mammy on the stairs. I was about to send out a search party for she's been upstairs ages. I'll make her a cup of tea, it's just a pity we haven't got a drop of something stronger. I have a feeling she might need it.'

Mary came into the room wiping her sleepy eyes with her apron. 'What d'you think?' she said. 'I have just woken up. I lay on your bed beside the cot to please Connie and I don't know whether I dropped off first or she did.' And then she looked at Barry and said, 'So you decided to come home in the end?'

'Yes, Mammy, as you see.'

'You been in some pub?'

'No, just walking, Mammy, trying to collect my thoughts.'

'Must have been some thoughts that took you so long.'

'They were, Mammy, and now I want to share them with you.' Angela gently pushed Mary down on the settee, and placed a cup of tea in her hands. 'You may have need of this,' she said and sat down beside her as Barry began to tell his mother what he had done and try to explain why he had done it. The tea was forgotten as Mary listened to the words spilling from her son's mouth. She couldn't believe she was hearing right. Stan had said he was safe and he needn't go to war for he could claim he was in a reserved occupation even if conscription was introduced, and he had done it anyway.

Oh dear Christ, her mind was screaming, how would they manage without Barry? How could she bear to see the only son she had left march off to a war he might not come back from? When shock caused her to shake, Angela took the tea from her and put it on the table and wrapped her arms around Mary and felt the abject despair and sorrow flowing through her that caused Angela to cry too, and the two women tightly embraced as their tears mingled together. And Barry, not able to bear to see the sadness he had inflicted on these two women that he loved dearly, fell on to his knees before the settee and held them both tight, and he too shed tears of guilt and shame.

A long time later when the crying eventually eased and they were all feeling a bit light-headed, Mary pulled herself from Barry's arms and sat up straighter in the chair and said as bravely as she could, though her voice wavered slightly, 'Well, Barry that was a shock for me all right, but crying never did any good at all. If you have enlisted then you have and there's nothing to be done. Angela, Connie and I will have to get along without you the best way we can, like so many more are doing.'

Barry, amazed at his mother's stoicism, took a deep breath and deciding he'd better tell the whole of it, went on to say, 'I haven't told either of you one of the worst aspects of my decision to join the army.'

Angela groaned, 'Oh God,' she said. 'Does it get worse?'

''Fraid so,' Barry said. 'I didn't know any of this from talking to Stan. 'Course he hadn't anyone else to consider. I know he cares about Daniel, but he hasn't got to provide for him. I really thought though that if you were prepared to put your life on the line your family would be looked after.'

Angela knew what Barry was getting at and she said sharply, 'Just tell me how much you will be getting,' and when he said how much it was, her mouth dropped open in disbelief. 'Eight and fourpence?' she repeated incredulously. 'What am I to do with eight and fourpence when the rent is three and six?'

'I will send you more,' Barry promised. 'I can't say how much because I don't know what expenses I might have, but it will be as much as I can afford.' And he went on to tell her how to claim the money and to do it the minute he left for training. 'By the time they process it, I will know how much I can send you and will get it set up straight away.'

'Barry,' Angela said, 'you'll have less than six and six with the money already taken out to give to me and Connie and you must keep some money for yourself, but even if you were able to give me the whole untouched seven shillings, it's not going to be enough.'

Barry nodded his head miserably.

'Well, I think it's a shabby way for a country to treat its army,' Mary said.

'I agree with you, Mammy.'

'And I'm a drain on you,' Mary said. 'Have been for years. I mean what am I but a useless old woman?'

'You're not that old,' Angela protested. 'And you better not be useless for I'm going to rely on you.'

'What d'you mean?'

'We don't know how long this war is going to go on for,' Angela said. 'If we're going to survive it at all, one of us needs to get a job and that's down to me and I can't do that without you. But,' she added with a twinkle in her eye, 'if you're too old and useless we'll have to tighten our belts and hope for the best.'

Barry marvelled at Angela's resilience She had been overcome with sadness and shed tears, but once she knew how bad the situation was she had a plan of action and one that involved Mary too for she said to Angela, 'You know I didn't mean that. Looking after Connie is a pleasure not a chore.'

'I think you're right about getting a job,' Barry said. 'What sort of work are you thinking of looking for?'

'Anything well paid,' Angela said.

'Not munitions,' Barry cautioned. 'They pay well because they are dangerous places. I don't want you working somewhere like that.'

Angela stared at him. 'I didn't particularly want you rushing into war,' she said. 'But you're going anyway, but you don't want me in any sort of danger.'

'Is that so wrong?'

'Well it's only that I don't want you in danger either. I mean when you're in France it's not to go to a vicar's tea party is it?'

Barry got Angela's point, he was leaving them in the lurch and they had to do the best they could. And so he said, 'All right. I'm sure you'd get something suitable and I really have no right to say anything about it.' And then he added, 'I could probably get you set on at our place. The work is heavy, but not dangerous.'

'I'd rather get something off my own bat,' Angela said and suddenly gave an enormous yawn. 'Let's go to bed,' she pleaded. 'I'm too tired to think straight and I want to wake early tomorrow and make the most of the short time we'll have together.'

Angela did fall into an exhausted sleep only to wake in the early hours, the time when everyday problems magnify, and found she was unable to sleep again as sorrow at what Barry had done that day overwhelmed her. She fought tears, as Mary had said they did not help and anyway they could disturb Barry and Connie too, but sorrow filled her brain and lodged in her heart and drove all thoughts of sleep from her.

She was almost pleased when she heard Connie begin to stir in the cot and she heaved herself out of bed and picked her up, though her eyes were gritty from lack of sleep and her whole body felt like a bit of chewed string.

However, mindful of her words the previous night,

she fought her fatigue to spend most of the afternoon at Calthorpe Park though the weather was squally and cold. And that night, much to Connie's surprise and delight it was her daddy who bathed her in the tin bath hanging from a hook on the back of the cellar door, which he filled with kettle upon kettle of water. And after he had bathed her and washed her hair, he carried her upstairs to where her Mammy had her pyjamas warming by the fire. Later it was Barry who carried her up the stairs to the cot Angela had warmed with fire-bricks wrapped in flannel and he tucked her up snug and warm and even read her a story before he left her to sleep. His heart ached as he descended the stairs. He had so wanted to see his child grow up and yet he knew that once his training was over and he set off for France he might not see her again for years and there was always the chance he wouldn't return from the war he had volunteered for and that thought made him feel very sad. But he could not load this on Angela for the situation was of his own making.

At Mass the next morning, the news filtered through the congregation that Barry McClusky had enlisted, for it was hard to keep things private in the cramped houses with paper-thin walls and anyway this was hardly a private matter. They would all know anyway when he disappeared for training.

Angela, looking around for a fairly vacant pew, spotted the three spinster women who always came to Mass together and then sat towards the front of the church behind the children. The three spinsters were regarding the whole family disapprovingly. They had snubbed the McCluskys when they heard that Barry was in a reserved occupation and Angela thought they were just the type of people to send white feathers out. She was more certain of this when a woman behind them leant forward and whispered something to one of them. A lot of whispering and nudging went on and then the three women swung round and the look on all their faces could only be described as a satisfied smirk.

Angela glanced at Barry, but he was dealing with Connie and had seen nothing untoward and neither had Mary. She was glad and knew there was no point in making them aware of it and so she contented herself with a baleful look at all three of them and then took her place beside Barry as people began shuffling to their feet for the first hymn.

Afterwards so many people wanted to shake Barry's hand and wish him 'all the best' that Angela, who'd had nothing to eat or drink because of taking communion, was beginning to think her throat had been cut. The priest hadn't been aware of what Barry had done until one of the altar boys mentioned it as they were changing in the sacristy after Mass and he too hurried out as soon as he could. 'God speed my boy,' he said. 'I will remember you in my prayers. Right is with you and will always prevail in the end.'

Barry wasn't so sure of that, but he wasn't going to argue with the priest at this juncture. Anyway now he had a hot line to God and he thought it good to have him on his side when he would be risking his life on a daily basis. As they walked home a little later he reflected that life was a funny thing. People who had snubbed him openly, even crossing the street to avoid meeting him, were breaking their neck to shake him by the hand that morning because he had done what they considered right and he wished he was so absolutely sure.

Many times that week, Angela wished she could stop time just there but never more poignantly than that last day. The following morning he would report to Thorp Street Barracks and life would never be the same again. So though it wasn't really the weather for it, after Mass they took the little steam train to Sutton Park from New Street Station. They left the pram behind and Barry lifted his small daughter onto his shoulders. She squealed with excitement swinging her little legs and beating Barry about the head with her podgy little hands as they walked into the town.

At New Street, Connie was fascinated by the noisy, bustling station where there was a sour smell and steam mixed with the coal dust wafting in the air. Sat atop her daddy's shoulders she wasn't afraid of the roaring monsters that seemed to hurl themselves into the station to stop with a clatter of wheels and hiss of steam. She didn't mind the man feeding the firebox at the front of the train with the orange and yellow flames licking around the coal he was shovelling. Sweat ran down the man's shining face, while smoke billowed out of the funnel above him into the already grey and sooty air.

A sudden shriek from another waiting train did make Connie jump, but before she could give voice to protest about it, Barry lifted her from his shoulders and put her in the train and got in beside her and so did her Mammy. Connie was so excited her tears were stopped before they'd properly begun. A train journey was a novel experience for Angela too, so she could perfectly understand why Connie was fizzing with the thrill of it all.

Industry, factories, houses and shops soon gave way to fields as they left the town behind. And this stirred a distant memory of a train journey undertaken through a similar landscape when Angela had travelled from Ireland to England years before.

There were fields of cows, some looking over five-barred gates to see the train pass with no sign of alarm and all chewing as if their lives depended upon it. Barry told the wide-eyed Connie that the creatures were called cows and the milk that she liked to drink came from a cow. Connie said nothing but she looked at her father rather oddly, not able to understand what those peculiar animals had in common with the man who ladled their milk into the milk pan they took out to him.

Angela laughed at the expression on her young daughter's face because she knew what she was thinking. 'You'll know what these are in the next field,' she said confidently.

'Hoss.'

'Horse, that's right,' Angela said.

She knew Connie would recognise horses, which were a common sight in Birmingham for many wagons were horse-drawn and not all omnibuses were petrol-driven either. Their own coalman used a horse to pull his cart and in the Bull Ring there were many horses carrying all sorts of things and the ones pulling the barrels of beer were usually the smartest and some had their manes and tails plaited and their coats were always shiny and smooth.

Some of the fields were cultivated and Angela remembered the little tufts of green that had been on top of many furrows when she had travelled from Ireland, but now the only thing on the top of these furrows was a dusting of frost. Angela pointed to another field further off, full of sheep relentlessly tugging at the grass.

'See their woolly coats, Connie,' she said. 'They're called fleeces and that's what many of your warm jumpers are made from.'

Connie looked suitably impressed by that and the train began slowing down to pull to a halt at a small station and Barry suddenly said, 'We've arrived.'

They stepped out onto the wooden platform and Barry said, 'This is it, the Royal Town of Sutton Coldfield.'

'Royal Town?'

'Yes, Henry the Eighth I think had something to do with the royal bit,' Barry said. 'He used to hunt here, it was all natural then, and he sort of bequeathed the park to the town, or that's what Stan said. He also said the people of Sutton are very proud of the royal title and the park and unless you live in Sutton Coldfield you have to pay to go in it.'

Angela shook her head, 'Surely not, Barry,' she said. 'Anyway how would you know such a thing because you told me you've never been here before?'

'Stan told me all about it,' Barry said as he put Connie back on his shoulders and led the way out of the small country station. 'He said he knew every inch of it because Kate's family lived in Erdington and he did all his courting in Sutton Park. They had to have Betty along as chaperone. She was quite a lot older than Kate and cross that her young sister had a boyfriend before she had and so she wasn't up to taking herself a little way off so they could have some privacy, or turning the other way so they could steal a kiss.'

'Be fair,' Angela said with a little laugh. 'If Betty was the eldest her parents would expect her to look after her sister. They didn't want their daughter ravished by some lusty young man if Betty took her eyes off her for a moment. Anyway, Betty has her own man now and Stan didn't have his beloved very long all told.'

'No, he didn't,' Barry agreed. 'And I think I can safely say that with Betty in charge there was precious little ravishing went on either.'

'Barry McClusky, you say that as if it's a bad thing,' Angela said. 'And you don't even know Betty.'

'I know of her,' Barry said as they left the station and set off down the slight incline and Angela realized that Barry must have taken great notice of what Stan told him because he seemed to know just where he was going.

'You mean you know this woman that you've never met because of what Stan told you?' Angela said.

'No, not really,' Barry said. 'You know Stan's not one for bad-mouthing people. Plenty of other people said things though. I was a kid, but I overheard a lot and she seemed to want to control everything. I bet that Roger's hen-pecked.'

'Oh how can you say that without a shred of evidence?'

'I just know that's all,' Barry said. 'People say she went after Roger for the house. He was one of the bosses in a place she worked at as a lowly filing clerk.

Roger's father had died a few years before and he had looked after his mother ever since. The old lady had become very infirm and I don't know how it all transpired but Betty ended up caring for her and she moved in completely in no time at all.'

'What's wrong with that?'

'Nothing,' Barry admitted. 'Only that Roger's parents probably had someone earmarked for him to marry, someone from his social circle which certainly would not have included Betty, or people like her in the general scheme of things. They were middle class, and Roger was their only child, went to university and all.'

'Well circumstances dictated differently that's all,' Angela said. 'Look at me and how differently my life turned out. Happens all the time and people make the best of it. Strikes me this Roger was very grateful to Betty for being kind to his mother. He might have seen a different side to her that no one else was that aware of.'

Barry shrugged. 'You could be right. Anyway, they were married and when the mother died a few years later they inherited the house and I admit it must have been a hard cross to bear not to be able to have their own child. In a way I can understand them spiriting Daniel away.'

'So can I,' Angela said. 'What I can't understand is their apparent desire to cut Stan out of his life altogether and for Stan to comply, thinking it's better for the boy. I'm sure this is all going to come out some day.'

'I agree with you,' Barry said. 'But Stan won't rock the boat unless he has to. Anyway,' he said as he came to a wooden gate, 'we're here now, so what d'you think of Sutton Park? Apparently, according to Stan, we have to come in the summer to see it in its glory.'

'Well what we can't change is the seasons,' Angela said. 'But as I haven't seen it before it looks quite impressive enough to me in the winter.'

They were in front of a hut and the man inside it took the money Barry offered and issued tickets and Angela was a bit surprised. 'Told you,' Barry said, holding up the tickets as they went through the gate.

'Well I've never heard of that before.'

'Nor me,' Barry admitted. 'But Stan said this is bigger than anything he had seen before. It has something like five lakes for a start. Anyway now we have paid hard-earned money to get in, let's at least have a look at the place.'

Angela had no problem with that and she looked out at the frost-filled meadow in front of them with a play-ground set to one side of it, which caused a cry of delight from Connie. The slide was too wet and crusty with frost but the swings were all right and the round-about and Barry was quite happy to push Connie as high and fast as she wanted to go.

In the end he called a halt though because he said Stan had told him about something and he wanted to see it for himself. 'What is it?' Angela asked.

'Something called the Crystal Palace,' Barry said. 'He said to follow the stream round and we'll come to it and if I'm not mistaken the stream runs by the edge of the meadow by that bank of trees.'

The stream was where Barry thought it was and they walked by the edge of it and Connie tripped over so many protruding tree roots that Barry lifted her on to his shoulders again. It was worth it though when they saw the palace for the first time, for it was truly magnificent. It was built on the edge of a lake and three floors high and on each floor were rows and rows of big tall windows looking down on to the large lawn in front of it. And stretching out to one side was a wondrous structure made completely of glass with a glass dome at the end. 'The conservatory,' Barry said.

Angela nodded. 'That must be the crystal bit,' she said. 'Love to see inside it.'

'Have to come back in the summer for that I'd say,' Barry said and added, 'It's built as sort of a replica of the Crystal Palace in London.'

'And is it a good likeness?'

'How would I know?' Barry said. 'I've never been to London. It was Stan told me that, but he hasn't been to London either.'

'So it might look nothing like the one in London and you'd not know the difference?'

'No,' Barry said. 'Nor care that much if you want the truth, but I'd like to come back when everything is open, play croquet on the lawn maybe and take a boat out on the lake.'

'That sounds nice,' Angela said. 'And what's that mass of stuff all covered over with something?' she asked, pointing to quite a massive pile of things at the edge of the gigantic lawn.

'That must be the fair Stan told me about,' Barry said. 'They've probably broken it down for the winter and I should say that's some sort of tarpaulin sheeting covering it to protect it from the winter weather.'

'A fair?' Angela repeated in surprise. 'A proper fair?'

'Oh yes, with all the rides and a little train that runs round the edge of it,' Barry said and grabbed Angela's hand suddenly as he said eagerly, 'We must come here one summer's day when this damned war is over. I want to see Connie enjoy the rides and hold her hand and let her paddle the stream or fish for tiddlers. I want her to be free and happy and untimately that's what we're fighting for.'

A sudden shudder ran through Angela and dread gripped her heart. A premonition of things to come? Surely not. Not able to share these thoughts, she said instead, 'I think this would be a good place to stop and eat the sandwiches. There's a shelter I spotted at the other side of the grass and it would be good to get out of the icy air while we eat.'

It was too cold for sitting long though and so they finished their sandwiches quickly. Even Connie didn't linger. No snow had fallen, but frost lay thick on the grass sparkling in the weak winter sun and crunching beneath their feet as they made their way to the woods.

The trees were bare, the branches stretching skywards like huge, glacial skeletons and they walked hand in hand kicking at the piles of frost-rimmed leaves, much to Connie's delight, and atop her father's shoulders she clapped her hands with glee. Then he delighted her still further when he put her down where she stood almost knee-deep in snow while he gently lifted a gilded spider's web from between two branches and even Angela, not a great lover of spiders in the general way of things, was slightly awed by the silver beauty of it.

However, the cold drew them back home in the end where Mary had soup heating over the fire. Angela was glad of it, but the cold stayed within her and she knew it was the kind of cold no soup could ease because from tomorrow Barry would start his training to be a soldier, to learn to use weapons he had only heard of, to learn to kill, a world she could not share where he would have to kill or be killed. She would lose part of Barry to the British Army and she must bear it as bravely as she could.

So when she said goodbye to Barry early the next morning, she did not cry though her eyes were very bright. She remembered their love-making of the previous night that had an energy and urgency to it though even then, Barry had been careful for he said he couldn't leave her with another mouth to feed, especially now.

Barry saw the smile playing around Angela's mouth and, knowing her well, guessed her thoughts and kissed her tenderly, proud of her control. He saw the tears brimming behind her eyelashes, but she didn't let them fall and even managed a watery smile for him.

His mother, on the other hand, sobbed copiously and Barry, even knowing her level of distress, was slightly impatient with her for crying wouldn't change the situation and he said, 'Give over, Mammy, for Christ's sake. You're upsetting Connie.'

It was true. Connie was in Angela's arms and her bottom lip had begun to tremble as she saw her Granny so upset. Mary made a valiant effort to control herself and Barry lifted Connie into his arms and kissed her. 'Don't cry, darling,' he said. 'There's nothing to cry for. I'll be back before you know it when I am a proper soldier.'

It was doubtful that Connie understood everything Barry said but she always felt safe held in her father's arms and so she sagged against his shoulder with a sigh. Barry's heart melted and his eyes met Angela's over the child's head and she knew what it was costing him to leave them. But it was something he had to do and so she lifted Connie from her father's arms gently and said, 'Daddy must go now, pet, and you must stay at home and look after Mammy and Granny. D'you think you can do that?'

Connie nodded her head sagely and Barry kissed his mother, wife and child on their cheeks, picked up his case and stepped into the street. They watched him stride away from the doorway, a shadowy figure illuminated now and again when he walked under a street lamp. The he turned down Bristol Passage and was lost to view entirely. Angela closed the door with a sigh and saw Mary was poking the fire with vigour and she smiled at Connie and said, 'Soon have some porridge made for you and I could do with a sup of tea. Puts new heart in a body that.'

The words were spoken in such a plaintive voice that Angela looked up and said to Mary, 'Are you all right?'

'Angela, I won't be all right till this war is over and done with and Barry is home where he belongs,' said Mary. 'But I'm not the only mother feels like this and I must bear it the same as them.'

'We will bear it together,' Angela said, reaching out and catching hold of Mary's hand. 'I feel exactly the same.'

'Oh Angela, you are such a lovely girl,' Mary said. 'I bless the day I took you in for you have never given me a day's worry and now we can be a comfort to one another.'

Just after breakfast, mindful of Barry's words about haste being needed in applying for a portion of his wages to be paid to her, Angela got together her marriage lines, Connie's birth certificate and her rent book for good measure and put them all at the bottom of the pram. 'Pity you got to take the wee one out in this,' Mary said. 'It's bitterly cold outside.'

'Mammy, the wind will hardly blow on Connie,' Angela said. 'I'm putting her in the coat Finbarr sent her for Christmas with the matching bonnet and mittens and she has fleecy leggings and the stout shoes Barry bought her. She'll have blankets over that will be tucked so well I don't think the cold weather will touch her. Anyway,' she added, 'there's no way around it, for if I want the money this is how it must be.'

'I suppose so,' Mary said. 'Stickler for rules, the army.'

'Have to be I should think,' Angela said. 'Oh and I might call in and see George on the way back. I've made a list of a few bits we could do with.'

'Are you going to sound him out about a job?' Mary asked.

'Not with him,' Angela said. 'He has Matilda's sister, Dorothy installed in there now, but he might know some shop that is losing their male assistant to the war or something like that. Anyway,' she added, 'Maitland's is the last place on earth I would work now. And if I ever allowed myself to be persuaded to, it wouldn't be long before I was arrested for assault.'

Mary laughed. 'That isn't like you, Angela,' she said. 'Who would you attack, Matilda?'

'Oh yes, her too for good measure,' Angela said grimly. 'But the biggest clout would be reserved for her sister Dorothy. She's supposed to "help" George at busy times, though I think she must do more to turn customers away than anything else. I made the mistake of going in once at a busy time and was served by her. She is a hard-faced, foul-mouthed harridan. She has a fat red face and two piggy eyes set into it like currants in a lump of dough, only they are bluey grey and as cold as steel, and added to that she has a bulbous nose and slack mouth.'

'Oh you took to her then,' commented Mary ironically. 'All right so she was at the back of the queue when the looks were given out, but it isn't like you to turn against someone because of the way they look.'

'Oh Mammy, if it were only that,' Angela said. 'Though if she cracked those features into a smile it might make her look better. She made it obvious she had no time for me, but then she seemed to have no time for any of the customers, goes on as if they were an intrusion. She was rude to each and every one of them one way or another. I got the full treatment and George couldn't really help because the shop was so busy.

'If it wasn't for George I would never go near the place, but because I worked there I know when the shop is busy and I avoid those times.'

'And are you sure that it will be a quiet time today?'

'By the time I get there it will be,' Angela said. 'There is a rush first thing but by the time we have walked to the Town Hall and back the rush will have gone.'

She sighed suddenly and said, 'When I worked there I would often wish he had married a softer and kinder woman . . . And now he has Dorothy too, and she's much worse than Matilda.'

'Oh,' Mary with a wry smile, 'Devil incarnate then?'

Angela answered in like manner. 'Good contender for it anyway. And you know I don't think George is coping with it at all well. Sometimes he reminds me of a whipped dog. Still,' she said, as she bounced the pram down the front step, 'there's nothing I can do about it and I best be on my way.'

But even as she made her way to town she thought of the life she imagined George had with the two women constantly badgering him about anything and nothing. She looked forward to seeing him though because she seemed able to cheer him up a bit.

Connie fell asleep on the way to the town and she was still slumbering nicely when they reached the Town Hall. The woman behind the desk dealing with the forms said they just had to see the child and there was no need to disturb her and Angela was grateful because Connie could be right grouchy if she was woken from a deep sleep.

All in all it hadn't taken very long in the Town Hall and the woman promised to process the claim as soon as possible and with a sprightly step, Angela set off for Maitland's shop.

NINETEEN

Angela turned the corner and stopped in shock for the shop was closed and shutters covered the windows. 'What happened to the shop?' she asked a boy playing in the street.

'It shut,' he said. 'After the man fell over.'

'What man?'

'The man what owned it,' the child said and added, 'Heard our Mom say as he'd had a heart attack and died.'

Normally such matters were not discussed in front of children, but this child seemed to be in the know and so Angela said, 'Are you talking about George?'

'Yeah that were his name, George.'

'And you're sure he had a heart attack?'

''Course I am,' the boy said. 'Our Mom was telling Beattie next door and I heard her and that's what she said.'

Angela felt suddenly sick as a wave of sadness almost overwhelmed her and she leant against the wall as her legs felt decidedly wobbly. She closed her eyes against the pain of the thought that she would never see George again.

'His posh wife's still here,' the boy said and Angela opened her eyes to see him still standing there looking at her in a concerned way.

'What?'

'That George's posh wife and the other one are in the flat 'cos I seen them through the window.'

Angela knew he could easily have done that for one of the windows did overlook the street. The flat could be accessed by going through to the back of the shop, but there was an entrance from the street, though Angela had never used it. She thanked the child, turned the corner and approached the front door with some trepidation, but she felt bound to at least say how sorry she was, for though the marriage was not what anyone could call happy, death is so final.

Anyway she would like details of the funeral and she pressed the bell and heard it jangle in the flat. And then there were footsteps on the stairs, the door opened and Matilda stood in the threshold and glared at Angela as she demanded, 'What are you doing here?'

'I . . . I've just heard about George and . . .'

'I hope you're not going to say that you'd like to express your condolences,' Matilda said. 'Not needed for I am far from sad. In fact it's what I wanted to happen for years.'

Angela gasped and was glad of the pram handles she held on to so tight for she could hardly believe what Matilda had just said.

'Shocked you have I?' Matilda said with a sneer.

'Yes, you've shocked me if that was your intention,' Angela said through gritted teeth. 'It's also the cruellest thing I have ever heard anyone say. I won't trouble you further if you would just give me the details of George's funeral . . .'

'Oh that's been and gone,' Matilda said, smiling at the evident disappointment in Angela's face. 'Died on Monday and was buried on Saturday. No point in hanging about. As for the shop I am selling it lock, stock and barrel and intend to buy a bigger and better house as far from here as possible so there's nothing here for you.' And with that she slammed the door in Angela's face.

Angela stared at it for a moment fighting the insane desire to beat on the door and tell Matilda and her sister what she really thought of them but she knew it would achieve nothing and she turned for home, glad that Connie had wakened. She propped her up so that she could see more and chatted to her all the way home and it kept her mind off the unpleasant scene she'd had with Matilda Maitland.

Mary had broth waiting for them both and as they sat and ate it Angela told her what had happened when she went to the shop. She was sorry at George's passing and just as shocked as Angela had been at the things Matilda had said. 'And I'm sorry that you knew nothing of the funeral as well,' she said. 'But you know you couldn't have gone to it anyway.'

'Why not?' Angela said. 'I mean I know the rules that Catholics can't go to services in other churches, but I thought funerals would be a bit different.'

Mary shook her head. 'Not in the eyes of the church I don't think,' she said. 'Mind you with the war raging people of all religions are being killed so that rule might have to be more relaxed.'

'Yes,' Angela said for the casualty figures made frightening reading and she thought of Barry soon to enter the fray and Stan already in it and no end in sight, and felt totally dispirited and her sigh was heartfelt.

Another nagging worry was that she had no job. She knew George would have helped her if he could and now that avenue was closed. She knew she had to find something though for if she didn't they'd never manage. The worry of that was etched on her face and Mary felt for Angela and the body-blow she had received that day.

'Tell you what,' she said suddenly. 'Let's have a Mass said for George. I know he's not a Catholic, but the good Lord won't mind and I don't think Father Brannigan will object either and it will settle your mind maybe.'

Angela thought it a very good idea. It seemed alien to her to be laid in the ground with no sort of ceremony at all and no people even asked if they would like to pay their respects.

'You don't know people weren't asked,' Mary pointed out.

'Oh I sort of do, Mammy, because this boy knew everything,' Angela said. 'You know the sort who does a lot of earwigging and very useful in this instance and if he'd known about the funeral he would have said so. Because he'd probably think it a bit unusual, you know, with no one asked and that.' She sighed and went on, 'You know I bet the only ones at George's funeral were Matilda and Dorothy. It's as if they couldn't wait to get rid of him, as if his life was of no account.'

'A Commemorative Mass will make all the difference, you'll see,' Mary said, giving Angela's hand a squeeze.

And strangely it did. The Mass was arranged for the following Monday and the priest announced it on Sunday so the church was fairly full of George's old customers on Monday. They greeted Angela like an old friend and afterwards they stood outside the church chatting.

The general consensus was that poor George had been nagged to death.

'Miserable cows, the pair of them, his wife and her sister.'

'Language,' admonished another. 'And you just outside the church.

'Only word to describe them,' the first woman said. 'See, she came round collecting all the tick owed.'

'Matilda did?'

'No the other one, Dorothy or whatever they call her. It were the same day George died. God, he'd be barely cold. Anyroad my Bert has only had three days' work the last few weeks so I'd run up a bit of tick. He'd had a full week that week though and I intended paying some of the arrears, but she demanded it all. Well I didn't have it and told her straight and she said she'd send for a constable. Well I couldn't have that so I had to pawn all the blankets in the house, and till I can get them out again Bert, me and the kids have to go to bed in our clothes with every coat we possess on top of us.'

'I was the same,' another put in. 'My old man's suit is so old and thin now that I don't get much for it. One of these days it will fall off his back and Christ knows what I'll do then if I can't pawn it. Anyroad there she was at the door, that Dorothy, all threatening like and saying she'd fetch the law out. I pawned my mother's old grandmother clock that she'd had as a wedding present years before. God she thought the world of that clock and it was beautiful and worth a bit you know, the only valuable thing I own and I just hope I can get it out of pawn before too long.'

And so it went on, a list of people hocking essential items because they were intimidated by Dorothy's threats of calling in the police. No one wanted to get mixed up with them. Some of the younger women had men in the forces, friendlier with Angela now her husband would soon be facing the same dangers as their own, and Angela noted with slight horror that two of the group wore the black bonnets of widowhood. They had five children between them and she wondered at their fortitude.

'Oh they're tough all right,' Mary said when Angela commented on this as they made their way home. 'And we must be tough too. I am ashamed of myself crying and carrying on so when Barry was only going for training.'

'Ah but . . .'

'Don't make excuses for me, Angela,' Mary said. 'I spoke to a lady back there with a black arm-band on. Her and her husband were married years with no sign of a child. In fact the women said to me she thought she was past the age of childbearing and when her periods stopped she thought she was in the change. But she wasn't and she gave birth to a son. They knew there could be no more and so this son was very precious to them both. He was the light of their lives, their reason for living and yet though they were proud of him as he marched off to war, they worried about him too.

They began to say the rosary every night, like making a pact with God to keep him safe, but maybe God wasn't listening for whatever way it was, he was killed in late November.'

Angela had tears in her eyes as she said, 'How do they go on after such devastating news?'

'I asked her that,' Mary said. 'And she said that they go on because it's what their son would want them to do. I hope we are never asked to make that sacrifice, but if we are we must be strong, as Barry would want us to be, and between us we have a child to rear and that child is special because she is part of Barry.'

Angela thought this wasn't the time to tell Mary she didn't just want part of Barry, she wanted all of him, hale and hearty to wrap his arms around her and hold her tight. And when the madness in Europe ended they could bring up their special child together.

Angela was to find anything could be borne if you have the right mind-set. She did miss Barry but his frequent letters sustained her. He couldn't tell her where he was, but he gave out enough hints for her to have a good idea that he was in Sutton Park. She remembered that last day often and it pleased her to think that she had seen the place where he would spend the weeks of training.

He could tell her little of what they were doing either, but she remembered what Stan had said about his training. Stan astoundingly was proving himself a first-rate soldier. She imagined it would be a surprise to him too. He could tell her little about it, but leading a company of men safely through enemy lines after their officer was killed earned him three stripes on his jacket.

Barry seemed to be enjoying the training, getting on fine with the other soldiers and as there was much he couldn't say his letters were full of fun instead as he described his fellow soldiers and the camaraderie between them all.

Angela wrote to him about the death of George but most of her letters were more cheerful, things Connie said or a skill she'd mastered, or places Angela had taken her. She said nothing about the money problems she had. His contribution, which was going to be five shillings a week, had not come through yet. Even Mary, used to letting one shilling do the work of two, was finding it hard to stretch the money and also pay the rent.

Part of that was because the shopkeepers on Bristol Street where she now had to take her custom had upped their prices since before the war. 'I think it grossly unfair,' Angela railed one day, surprised how little there was in her shopping bag considering the amount of money spent. 'And you know another thing, you can't ask for tick in many of the shops. There are notices to tell you not to bother asking because "refusal often offends".'

'Really,' said Mary. 'Oh that's bad. That's the only way some people have to manage the pittance they get.'

'Don't I know it,' Angela said. 'Anyway that means us as well. Though I have never had to ask for tick yet, I might be reduced to it now unless I do what I've been threatening to do and get a job. I've dithered because I don't want to work full-time, I would miss Connie so much and I think it's a lot for you too.'

'Don't you worry about me, Angela,' Mary said. 'I'm as strong as an ox and me and Connie can look after each other, can't we, pet?'

Connie didn't really know what they were on about, but she smiled anyway and said, 'Yeth' and Angela picked her up and hugged her. 'I'll have a word with Maggie when I see her tomorrow,' she said. 'She only gets eight shillings for a ten-hour shift five days a week packing meat pies and sausages and stuff and I know she's fed up.'

And Maggie was fed up. 'I've had enough,' she said almost as soon as they met the following morning. 'D'you know what the boss said yesterday morning?'

'No. What?'

'He said that we're doing important war work cos all the stuff we pack is for the troops. Anyway I said it was a shame it wasn't better paid then, when most war-related work was. All right so we're not making shell cases or bullets, but food is important to the troops too. After all they say an army marches on their stomachs.'

'Do they?'

'Yes. Haven't you ever heard that expression?'

'No.'

'It means . . . Oh it's obvious what it means,' Maggie said. 'Anyway this has decided me. I'm off to the munitions.'

'And I might be going with you.'

'You? I thought you said Barry didn't want you working there?'

'Maggie, given the choice I wouldn't work in those sort of places,' Angela said. 'But needs must. We really can't manage on the money. Even when Barry's extra five shillings filters through it will be little better.'

'Won't you miss this little one?' Maggie said indicating Connie. 'People tell me the hours are long.'

Maggie had brought Connie a game that one of her brothers had had that consisted of putting stiffened thickish cord through large wooden beads and Connie was concentrating so hard her little pink tongue was sticking out. Angela felt a rush of love for her and she answered fervently, 'I will miss her like mad, but the war can't last for ever.'

''Course it can't,' Maggie said assuredly. 'And we've got to deal with the here and now. Another reason I'm going is because of our Mom. See I'll be twenty soon and our Syd is just two years behind me and I reckon he will get called up sometime this year and our Mom will miss his money, so it will help if I am earning a bit more. Mind you,' she added fiercely, 'we wouldn't be sailing so close to the wind all the time if my father hadn't got such a thirst on him.'

Angela said nothing for it was well known Maggie's father liked his hooch and he was a regular down The Swan and they sometimes heard him sing his way home on Friday and Saturday nights.

'Anyway,' Maggie added, 'I will help while I am at home while I wait for my knight in shining armour astride a white horse to ride off with me into the sunset.'

'Oh yeah,' Angela said. 'Is this likely to happen sometime soon and is his name going to be Michael?'

'That would be telling,' Maggie said.

'Well he asked you to write to him.'

'Yeah and that's what I do, write to him,' Maggie said. 'And so far he hasn't said the magic words and proposed, but it's always best to be prepared.'

'You are a fool,' Angela said fondly.

'Takes one to know one,' retorted Maggie and their

eyes met and they both burst into laughter. Connie looked up in astonishment and for Maggie and Angela it was as if the years had rolled away and they were girls again at St Catherine's School. And Angela knew working in the munitions with Maggie would be much better than working without her, so when she said, 'Shall I make some enquiries then?' Maggie nodded her head. 'Do,' she said. 'It's no good putting it off.'

Mary was reluctantly relieved at Angela's decision for they couldn't survive on what they had coming in, but she was worried from a safety angle. 'It can't be that bad,' Angela said. 'There's plenty of people at it. Anyway no one seems to be really safe in this war. Look at those bombs that fell in London last week. They killed people and injured more and they were only going about their lives like everyone else when they were blown to bits.'

'Oh yes,' Mary said. 'That was really dreadful. I am really scared they might drop one of those horrible bombs in Birmingham.'

'I know,' Angela said. 'And I'm doing my bit to stop them because the soldiers can't fight if they have nothing to fight with. I will only be making munitions as long as the war lasts and it can't last for ever. And think of the money we can save during that time. So if Barry has a time finding a job after the war it won't be a disaster but if he goes straight back to his old job that money can be used for something else.'

'Like what?'

'Connie's education,' Angela said. 'If she is bright enough Barry wants her to matriculate and go on further than that if she can.'

'And what happens when you have a houseful of children?' Mary asked. 'Surely you're not intending bringing her up as an only child?'

Barry had said his mother must never know his views on limiting their family. It was against the Church's teaching and she would never understand and so Angela just said, 'We'll cross that bridge when we come to it. But more importantly for the moment, Mammy, is that you understand why I have to go for this job?'

'I do see that we've all got to do the best for our families and that's what you are trying to do. But I shouldn't tell Barry till you are actually working at the place. He didn't tell us about him enlisting till the deed was done so you can do the same.'

'And what of Stan or Barry's brothers who write regularly?'

Mary shook her head. 'They need to know nothing either,' she said. 'The time has come when women have to make their own minds up about their lives and not to look to their men's approval because most of them won't be around to give it or not. No, Angela, you take your job and we'll keep it to ourselves as long as we can.'

TWENTY

The Boss of the munitions factory, Mr Potter, had been clear about the rules when Angela was interviewed for the job. 'Everyone clocks in as soon as they arrive,' he'd said. 'And lateness is not tolerated. If a person is up to fifteen minutes late, they lose half a day's pay. The gates are closed at 6.15 and anyone arriving after that time will not get in and will not be paid for that day at all.' Then he fixed Angela with a beady eye and went on, 'In this industry we carry no passengers and can have no slackers or late-comers for it affects the output of the whole team. Now what you will do here is important work, for our troops cannot fight effectively without the means to do so. We expect our workers to realize the importance of what they do, arrive on time and work hard but carefully, for mistakes can mean accidents. Now are you up to that Mrs . . . Mrs . . .?'

'McClusky,' Angela finished for him. 'And yes I'm ready for it or I wouldn't be here.'

'I see you have a young child,' he said, scrutinizing the form she had filled in. 'Have you adequate care arranged?'

'Oh yes,' Angela assured him. 'I live with my mother-in-law. We have discussed it and she is quite willing to mind the child. My husband is training for the army and she knows as well as I how desperately the money is needed.'

'Well that seems all in order,' Mr Potter said. 'We'll see you bright and early on Monday morning.'

Angela never forgot her first day at the factory. She was always an early riser, but five o'clock was earlier than she usually rose, so Mary gave her the alarm clock that usually stood by her bed. When it shrilled out in the dark morning, she shut it off immediately, worried that it might have wakened Connie, but the child just murmured in her sleep, turned over with a sigh and slumbered on.

She had left her clothes ready on the chair beside the bed. She reached for them in the dark and carrying them and her boots in her arms she crept downstairs to dress. She also made a cup of tea and spread bread with marge and a smear of jam for she didn't know when she might eat again. Anyway it surely was not at all sensible to go to work hungry for she imagined you needed to keep your wits about you and a steady hand dealing with explosives.

As arranged, Maggie was waiting for Angela at the bottom of Grant Street and they greeted each other as they scurried down Bristol Passage to catch the half-five tram at the stop just around the corner on Bristol Street to take them to town. The ride was only a short one and usually they would walk such a distance easily, but once the tram reached the city centre they had to make their way to the Bull Ring and cross over it to Deritend where the factory was and they couldn't risk being late.

It was strange walking around the dark and almost silent town, the gas lamps throwing pools of light now and again and the only people they met were groups or pairs of women obviously, at that time in the morning, walking to a job of work the same as they were.

Strangest of all was to look down on the Bull Ring, usually a centre of bustle and busyness and often tumultuous noise. Then Angela realized it wasn't completely silent for though the shops were shut, the barrow boys were running up the cobbled hill. The rumble of the carts they pushed and their boots were the only sounds in the early morning as they parked their carts according to the dockets in their hands. Many of the costers shouted over to the two girls or gave them a cheery wave as they carried on down the hill. 'A barrow boy was telling me once a pitch by the Market Hall opposite Woolworth's is the best place,' Maggie said.

Angela nodded for she had heard the same. The Market Hall was an impressive building. A set of wide stone steps was in front of it with gothic pillars at the top of the steps and beautifully decorated arched windows all around and as they passed it Angela remarked, 'It's seems strange to see those steps without a scattering of people on them.'

'Ah, yes,' Maggie said because often men injured by this still-raging war would sell bootlaces and razor blades and the like from trays hung around their necks and sometimes groups of them fair littered the steps. 'Speaking of which,' Maggie said, 'I always feel sorry for them, poor souls.'

'You'd have to be real hard-hearted not to feel sorry

for them,' Angela said. 'But one thing I do miss is having the flower girls around Nelson's Column.'

'And they used to have some round St Martins too,' Maggie said pointing to the attractive church built of honey-coloured bricks at the bottom of the hill. It was a lovely church, all the windows were of stained glass, but the frames themselves were ornate too and the main window had an elaborate pattern of weaved stonework across the top of it. Added to that the main church had a series of small towers surrounding it and a magnificent steeple in the middle. Then in front of the church a line of trees and a fence where the flower sellers used to stand if the area around Nelson's Column was full as it often was.

'Precious few of them about now,' Maggie said with a sigh. 'I asked my dad why not and his answer was that we can't eat flowers.'

'Well he had a point,' Angela said. 'Things are bound to be different when we are at war.'

They were through the Bull Ring now and out the other end hurrying along narrow dark streets as Maggie said, 'Oh I'll say. Would we be going out at the crack of dawn to make weapons if we weren't at war?'

'I'd say not,' Angela said. 'If I ever thought of my future I would never have envisaged that one day I would be working in a factory making things for our chaps to kill others.'

'You nervous?'

'A bit,' Angela said, 'but more than nervous I'm sad.'

'Why?'

'Well because when you said the hours were long you were right. I mean six till six is bad enough, but Saturday

294

morning was supposed to be voluntary, but then I read in the paper that there is a crisis, a shortage of shells, and that's what we will be making, artillery shells, so I think Saturday morning will be semi-compulsory, like they'll make life difficult for you if you don't do it.'

Maggie nodded. 'You may well be right and not just to be awkward, but because they really are worried about this lack of shells. Mr Potter intimated as much to me when he interviewed me and said that most girls don't moan about it because they see it as a sort of duty to help their loved ones at the Front.'

'I do see that,' Angela said. 'Of course I do, only I feel sad for the hours I will be away from Connie. Mr Potter asked me about the care I have organized for her and that isn't an issue. What is an issue though is that I'd like to see something of her too.'

'Poor Angela,' Maggie said. 'I do see what you're saying and just at the moment I can see no way round it.'

'Nor me,' Angela said. 'But these long hours are going to be a strain on Mary too. I mean I know Connie is lovely, but they are a handful at this age. The point is though even when it's all over no one knows how hard life is going to be and if there will be enough jobs for all those returning soldiers, and that's why I thought it best to get a well-paying job and build a little nest egg for that rainy day that Barry was always so concerned about.'

'If it helps at all,' Maggie said, 'I think you are doing absolutely the right thing and Connie I'm sure will understand that when she is older.' There was no chance to say any more for they had reached the factory and as they went in through the gates, Maggie said, 'Remember we have to get that card and clock in straight away. I'm sure the other girls will put us right in what to do.'

And the girls might well have done, but their supervisor, who introduced herself as Mrs Paget, was waiting for them, and Angela looked at her slightly pinched features and her sharp eyes and knew that she would miss nothing and also stand no nonsense. She was welcoming enough to Angela and Maggie though and showed them how to get their card from the rack on the wall, which was in alphabetical order, and put it in the slot beneath the large clock and pull the handle, and the time recorded was seven minutes to six.

Then Mrs Paget took them to the changing rooms where they changed into boiler suits, rubber shoes and hats. Neither girl had ever worn any form of trousers in their lives for it would have been considered fast and Angela thought it felt very odd to have her legs enclosed but she was to find that they were the most practical and comfortable article of clothing she had ever worn.

The other girls, all togged up, had left now and Mrs Paget said to Angela and Maggie, 'Every bit of metal has to be removed and put in that steel box on the table.'

'Everything?' Angela questioned. 'Even my wedding ring?'

'Even that,' Mrs Paget said and went on in explanation, 'We can't risk anything generating a spark.'

Angela saw the sense of Mrs Paget's words but she still hated taking off the wedding ring that had never been off her finger since Barry had put it there and taking the locket from round her neck and even the take-out kirby grips that helped keep her bun in place. With a barely perceptible sigh she dropped the items in the metal box with all the others followed by a number of grips from Maggie which she used to try and tame her curly locks. 'Good girls,' Mrs Paget said, but she'd been watching their faces and added to Angela, 'I know that was hard for you, but we have to insist because we can't take any chances with explosives.'

'I do understand,' Angela said. 'It's just that those things . . . Well you know they're special to me. What happens to them now?'

'Don't worry,' Mrs Paget said. 'They will be quite safe. This box will be locked away in the safe till the end of the shift. Now,' she said to both of them, 'will you be all right for tomorrow? I mean you know what to do and everything?'

Both girls nodded and Mrs Paget said again, 'Good. Now all you need are masks and gloves which must be fitted before you go onto the shop floor.'

Angela thought the gloves weren't bad but it seemed very strange to have a mask around her face, but she told herself they probably know what they are doing and everyone would presumably be dressed the same. Even Mrs Paget had her mask and gloves on as she led the way out of the room and along a metal meshed floor to a padded door. Despite the padding they could hear the thump of machinery before Mrs Paget opened it.

But oh, when she did open it, the noise was such that it caused Angela to recoil from it. She had never heard noise like it for it was all-consuming, the roars and clanks and screeches and thumps filled her brain and hurt her ears, but a nudge from Maggie caused her to take a step forward. There was no way she wanted to go into that factory, but her feet seemed to move of their own volition until she stood beside Mrs Paget at the top of the steps looking down on the workforce.

As she descended the stairs behind Mrs Paget, she marvelled that the women didn't appear bothered by the noise, nor the acrid, sour smell that had lodged in Angela's nose, nor the yellowy-grey swirling dust that was everywhere.

Her eyes felt gritty and dribbles of water started running from them down her cheeks. Then it was as if something caught in her throat and she began to cough and cough and cough till it was difficult for her to draw breath. She couldn't work in that place she decided. She'd never even been inside a factory before and she didn't particularly want to do so now either. She would get some other form of war work. Maggie would understand and, catching sight of her panicky eyes above her mask, Angela thought there was a good chance she was feeling the same way, and if she did it would be even better and they could go together to some other place.

And then, she thought of Barry choosing to enlist as she chose to work in a munitions factory. How would it be for him if war wasn't quite what he expected so, when the order came to go over the top, he would ignore it and set off for home to choose something more suitable? The Army would take a very dim view of that and shoot him as a traitor.

Now she could walk away and do something else, but it was shells and more shells that were needed and someone had to make them, or the soldiers would be left unprotected. Was she the sort of person to do something else that suited her better although she knew what she was doing was not as vitally needed as making shells? The answer was obvious, of course she could not just walk away. She was no fragile flower and for better or worse she was sticking to making shells for the duration.

That evening Angela was so tired it was hard to put one foot in front of the other as they left the factory and crossed the almost empty Bull Ring, and Maggie admitted she was just as done in. 'I can't understand it,' Angela said. 'I used to work long hours in George's shop standing on my feet all day and I was often up and down the steps to fetch things down from the upper shelves so it's not that I'm unused to work.'

'Yes,' Maggie said. 'But Maitland's was a pleasant place to work, I'd say, and not a noisy one?'

'Well, no,' Angela said. 'But what's noise to do with it?'

'I think constant noise like that is hard to cope with,' Maggie said. 'It sort of drains you of energy. I mean did you still hear it through your dinner hour even though we were in the canteen?'

Angela nodded, but added, 'You might have a point and I think the heat doesn't help the tiredness either.'

She'd never felt heat like it when she had occasion to go near the furnaces. Not that you could go too close because they were heated white hot to soften the carbon sheets so that they could be made into a basic shell shape. They sizzled like mad when they were then placed in vast sinks of cold water and billows of steam rose in the air. And when the rudimentary shapes cooled they had be made smooth on the grinding machine before being filled with explosives and the detonators. But the heat from those furnaces permeated the whole factory, so by mid-morning, Angela could feel sweat running down her back.

'I suppose we'll get used to it,' Maggie said.

'Well all the others seem to,' Angela said.

'Yeah,' Maggie said. 'One of the women who's worked here since the beginning of the war asked me how I was doing in the dinner queue today. She said it's a culture shock to everyone at first because few women had worked in any sort of heavy industry before the war began. She assured me that we would get used to it and that we have to stick at it because our lads couldn't fight a war with no shells. Mind you, she said when she saw this place first she nearly turned tail and ran.'

Angela smiled ruefully. 'I nearly did just that,' she admitted. 'I couldn't believe I was going down those steps into my idea of Hell.'

'I thought there was something wrong,' Maggie said. 'I was pretty unnerved myself to tell you the truth, but you were like a coiled spring. What stopped you taking off?'

'What the lads are going through, to be honest,' Angela said. 'I got to thinking that however bad it is in France, Barry will have to deal with it. Anyway, I didn't know how you felt about any of it and I could hardly ask you anything over the noise of the factory and in front of Mrs Paget. Anyway, come on, our tram's in and will I be glad to get the weight off my feet, even for the relatively short journey home.'

Angela thought it hard being away from Connie all day and she told herself she would make it up to her when she got home in the evening, but she found she was weary enough to be thankful that Mary had a meal ready, and she only had to sit up to the table and eat it, and that Mary had washed Connie and she was all ready for bed in her pyjamas, and firebricks wrapped in flannel were warming the cot. All she had to do after they had eaten was carry Connie up to bed and read her a fairy tale from the book her Uncle Colm had sent from America before tucking her in.

Downstairs Mary was anxious to know how her first day at the factory had gone, for Angela had said nothing in front of Connie and even to Mary she played it down a little, though she mentioned the noise.

'Well that's no surprise for all factories are noisy places,' Mary said.

Angela nodded, 'I know, I just wasn't ready for the level of it. But almost as bad as the noise is the acrid stench. One of the women said when we stopped for lunch that the really awful smell was from the sulphur. She said it smells like rotten eggs and she was not wrong either and the yellow dust swirls in the air and gets everywhere. You should have seen my boiler suit before I changed to come home, it was covered and even stained my underclothes.'

'You wear boiler suits?' Mary said in amazement.

'It's the most practical thing,' Angela said with a slight

shrug. 'And we have rubber boots and hats that all our hair has to be covered with.'

'Goodness!'

'And that's not all,' Angela said. 'Every bit of metal has to be taken off, so from tomorrow I'm going to be leaving my wedding ring and locket at home.'

'Surely to God they don't expect you to take off your wedding ring?'

Angela nodded, 'Everything, even grips in your hair.'

'But why?'

'It's safer that way, Mammy,' Angela said. 'Remember we're working with explosives and anything metal could potentially raise a spark. They can't take the risk. Today I had to leave them in a metal box they put in the safe until we're ready for home so tomorrow and every day I'm at work I may as well leave them here.'

'I suppose so,' Mary said. 'I'll take good care of them, never you fear.'

'We have to wear a mask too,' Angela said. 'It's supposed to protect our mouths and noses, but the dust particles still get in and there's nothing to protect our eyes. Mine were streaming most of the day and the dust made me cough. Something else no doubt I will get used to. Oh and we wear gloves. I am glad of those because some of the carbon is quite rough when we get it first and also covering our hands means that we have fairly clean ones to eat our dinner.'

'Angela, it doesn't sound a safe or even healthy place to work,' Mary said. 'Could you not find something else? I'm sure that if you were to ask at Barry's works they would find a place for you. Maggie too most likely. I know the money won't be as good but . . .'

'It isn't the money alone, Mammy,' Angela said, 'though I admit it was the money attracted me first, but there is a shell shortage. Our soldiers are running out of shells. Making them isn't pleasant and I can't pretend it is, but fighting a war I shouldn't think is any picnic either. This way I feel I am really doing my bit for Barry and Stan and all the other chaps. It is important and essential work and we can't run away from it.'

'Do the other girls all feel the same way?'

'I would say the majority at least feel that way,' Angela said. 'I doubt the money alone would keep them there if they didn't feel they were making a difference.'

However it was tiring work because it was relentless and they were constantly under pressure to make more and more shells. Because of this she didn't keep late hours and Mary was never long after her seeking her bed either for she said Connie was the best early morning call in the world.

Angela had been at the munitions factory for five weeks when a letter arrived from Barry that chased all thoughts of tiredness and lethargy away, for he was coming home. The news was tinged with a little sadness for Angela knew it would be embarkation leave and yet she longed to see her beloved husband and hold him tight and feel his strong arms envelop her.

Barry was due to arrive on Thursday morning 25th March and he was returning the following Monday morning early and so as soon as Angela arrived at work that day she sought out Mrs Paget and asked for time off. She thought there would be no problem and so was stunned when Mrs Paget said she was very sorry but there was no time off allowed. Angela stared at her as if she couldn't believe her ears. 'It's my husband's embarkation leave,' she said.

'I understand that,' Mrs Paget said and added, 'I'm sorry.'

'It changes nothing that you are sorry,' Angela said angrily. 'This is about the husband I love, the father of my child that we haven't seen for weeks and when he returns to his regiment and they sail for France I might never see him again and you know that as well as I.'

'Of course I know,' Mrs Paget said. 'And you're not the only person who has asked this and the answer has been the same. It's company policy recommended by the government. None of the women working here has had a holiday of any sort. If the crisis about the lack of shells eases, some time in the future, then we may be able to be more flexible, but at the moment they are the rules I'm afraid.'

Well it might be company policy but Angela didn't think much of it and she said, 'I'd like to see Mr Potter please.'

She could see Mrs Paget was annoyed for Angela heard her sharp intake of breath and her nostrils pinched together as she said tight lipped, 'Mr Potter is a very busy man, but I'm sure he will agree to see you if you need further clarification. You will find however that he will say the same as me and you must go in the lunch hour as we have wasted enough time on this already this morning.'

Angela had no option but to follow Mrs Paget to the factory floor. Maggie looked up when she spotted her on the steps. She'd been as excited as Angela who had showed her Barry's letter on the way to work that morning. She had known too that she was going to ask for the time off. The noise prevented speech but above the mask her eyes lifted in a query and she was surprised at Angela's unhappy eyes and the shake of the head.

Standing in the dinner queue she was able to tell Maggie only the bare bones of what had happened between her and Mrs Paget so she hadn't really discussed it with anyone when she was summoned to the office to see Mr Potter and she went with a growling stomach and hoped they hadn't stopped serving by the time she returned.

And it did no good, for just as Mrs Paget had said, Mr Potter reiterated exactly what she had said and Angela used the same arguments to no avail. 'Look how many women we have in the workforce at any one time. What if many people wanted to spend time with loved ones bound for overseas? How would we go on if we allowed that and not fall badly down in the quota of shells we have to produce each week? We would be in trouble then, but that wouldn't worry me as much as the Army being short. You say your husband will probably be setting sail for France soon. Well it will be a short visit and an abortive one if he has no shells, because he cannot fight the enemy if he has nothing to fight with.'

Angela was still silent and so Mr Potter went on, 'Think of this from the other way round. Say you had a few days free and wrote and told him at the training camp, would you expect him to be able to go up to his Commanding Officer and be given time off to spend with you?'

305

'No of course not,' Angela said. 'But he's in the Army.'

'And so are you in a way,' Mr Potter said. 'The job you are doing is a very important one and one that carries responsibilities. Remember, the people who make the ammunition are just as important as the people who use it and they rely on us to produce the goods. Shortly your husband may rely on us and we cannot let our boys down. You do see that?'

Dumbly Angela nodded her head and Mr Potter said, 'Good girl. And I'll tell you what I'll do, I'll give you Saturday morning off so you can have two full days together.'

It wasn't enough, not nearly enough, but Angela knew it was all she was going to get and so she thanked him and went back to the canteen to find Maggie had saved her a beef pie. It was cold but Angela was too hungry to care and as she ate she told Maggie what Mr Potter had said.

Both Mary and Maggie were astounded by the factory's lack of understanding. Angela had not told Barry she was making shells, just said she was doing war-related work and was deliberately vague. In this letter she admitted the truth and then he could quite see why the factory had taken the stance it had because they had been warned about the lack of shells. In fact they had had a pep talk the same day that Angela's letter arrived. The Commanding Officer, knowing the men were heading off to start their embarkation leave the following day, had them all assembled in the drill hall and explained he wanted to talk about the womenfolk they had left behind back home.

* * *

'Many of you have been brought up to respect and protect women and in particular mothers, wives, sisters, girlfriends, but all that has been turned on its head with this war. You are no longer around to protect them and they have not only coped with that, but many are out at work and are running the country in our absence, doing jobs only men have done in the past. They are also making virtually all the weaponry we use. Make no mistake, without them we would be lucky to win this war. So when you go home, do not forbid them to work in these industries, tell them to take all reasonable precautions of course, but that's all. Support their efforts and tell them how valuable their work is and how proud you are of them, and you should be proud, for the women of this land have proved to be truly remarkable.'

With words like that ringing in his ears Barry thought he could do no other than be supportive of what his wife had chosen to do, just as he had chosen to fight, though the thought of his lovely Angela in a noisy, dirty, smelly factory secretly filled him with a horror that he knew he couldn't show for he had no right to do so.

The following morning Angela went to work reluctantly and then had to fight to keep her mind on the job for she kept thinking of Barry and wondering what he was doing. But she forced herself to focus for shoddy work could cause accidents and accidents in an explosives factory had to be avoided at all costs.

Barry in fact spent ages getting to know his daughter again who had changed so much in the weeks he had been away. Now going on for two, she was a little girl rather than a baby and knew a raft of words and sentences and used them constantly and was a regular little chatterbox and an amusing one. Her smile seemed to light up the whole room and sometimes she would sing the nursery rhymes or lullabies she had learnt from her mother or grandmother. Barry loved her so much he ached at the thought of saying goodbye to her on Monday morning.

He took her with him when he went to meet Angela from work that night, and as the two stood in the road the lamplighter came round because the dusk was beginning to tinge the day, and Connie was very excited for she was seldom out in the dark and she danced from one foot to the other. Despite the gloom they had been spotted by one of the first women surging towards the gate. One woman shouted back over her shoulder, 'Handsome soldier waiting for some lucky lady.'

The cry was taken up by the women following. 'I bet it's Angela's husband,' called another. 'She said he was coming home on leave today.'

There was a collective sigh of sympathy for every woman there knew what that leave signified.

But Angela had heard them and was battling her way through and they parted to let her go and when she saw Barry she gave a cry of unadulterated joy and dashed across to him and as his arms went around her, just as she imagined they would, she put her arms around his neck and burst into tears.

She wasn't the only one for the naked love between the young couple was emotional for the others as well and especially Maggie, and they all knew that soon they would be parted again and no one knew what the future held for any of them.

It was Connie broke the spell. Fed up with being ignored, she let out a cry and Barry's response was to lift her into his arms and plant a kiss on her cheek. Then he lifted her onto his shoulders and extending a hand to Angela said, 'Shall we go home?'

'Oh yes,' Angela agreed. 'But I usually go home with Maggie,' she added as Maggie came towards them to shake Barry by the hand. She had heard Angela's words though and she said, 'But these are not usual times are they? Your time together is limited and I'd say you need to make the most of every minute, so tonight I will go for the tram on my own.'

'Oh, but . . .'

'But nothing,' Maggie said. 'I'm off and I will see you in the morning.'

'Let her go,' Barry said, putting a restraining hand on Angela's hand when she would have called Maggie back. 'Maggie is a very wise girl and she knows that I need time with my wife and child before I share them even with Mammy. I had thought to walk, unless you are too tired?'

The shroud of weariness fell from Angela and the aches in her feet and legs ceased to matter because to walk would give them more time together and what was a little discomfort measured against that?

As they walked Barry told Angela a little of what his life had been like since he had left. He talked of the scratchy uniforms and the route marches in boots that gave him blister on top of blister till an old hand told him to wee in the boots to soften them.

'Ugh and did you?' Angela asked, the look of disgust plain on her face.

Barry laughed as he caught sight of her face as they passed under a street lamp. 'You wouldn't look like that if you had seen the state of my feet, believe me I would have tried anything, so I did as this old lag said and it worked a treat and the boots are more supple altogether and I wasn't the only one to take his advice either. Do you wear boots?'

Angela nodded. 'Um we do, but they're rubber ones,' and she went on to describe the care taken to ensure they were wearing nothing metal that might generate a spark. Barry was glad of the precautions for the girls' safety. 'I would say it's necessary,' he said. 'Shame about your wedding ring though.'

'It just seemed more sensible to leave it at home.'

'Oh yes I can see that. I'd love to see you in those boiler suits though.'

'What about your uniform?' Angela said. 'It's too dark to see it properly.'

'Oh wait till you see the shiny buckles and buttons that I have to polish every day. I don't see what point there is to it. T'isn't as if we are going to worry about such things in the heat of battle. The Sergeant said he wanted to see his face in our boots. For what purpose? They say the trenches are filled with mud and completely waterlogged a lot of the time, so it is a useless exercise unless we are going to have a quick polish of everything polishable before we go over the top.'

A mental image flashed through Angela's brain of Barry climbing out of the relative safety of the trench to meet a hail of bullets from the other side. She shut her eyes against the scene and felt tears stinging them as she said, 'Don't.'

'What?'

'Talk about going over the top.'

'Angela that's what will happen. It's what I'm training for.'

'I know that,' Angela said. 'And don't you think I'll have time enough to think of that when you are gone? Do we have to spoil the few days' leave you have discussing it now?'

Barry could see the level of Angela's distress and he said, 'You are right, no more war talk.'

Barry saw Angela's shoulders sag in relief and he was glad he hadn't told her how they were shown how to fix a bayonet to the barrel of a rifle and then charge at a straw-filled dummy bellowing and roaring like some sort of wild beast. 'And when you have the bayonet right in, give it a twist before you pull it out and you will have gutted him good and proper,' the Sergeant said.

It had made Barry feel quite sick and he said later back in the barracks, 'I don't think I could do that to another human being.'

'Haven't you learnt anything, McClusky?' a fellow soldier said. 'They are not human beings they're the enemy.'

'Yes, but . . .'

'There ain't a but, not in this,' said another soldier. 'Tell you straight, if it was him or me, I'd make sure it was him and if he touched my family, like they'd done in Belgium, I'd pull his guts clean out and lose no sleep over it.'

'Penny for them,' Angela said and jerked Barry out of his reverie.

'Sorry,' he said. 'And they're not worth a penny. Good job we're nearly home for Connie seems to be dropping off on my shoulders.'

Barry's words caused the drowsy Connie to jump and she said mulishly, 'Not tired.'

Barry's twinkling eyes met those of Angela and he said, 'Are you not, young Connie? Well in that case I think you can walk the last few yards home.'

When he let her down on the street though, she stumbled and would have fallen had Angela not caught up her hand. Barry caught up the other one and they swung her home and arrived through the door full of laughter and Angela stored such memories in her heart.

It was the first time that Angela had a real good look at Barry. In the light from the gas lamps she felt a thrill of pride run through her because he was so incredibly smart in his uniform. There was something about his manner too, he held himself straighter so he appeared taller. Even his walk was different, all those route marches Angela supposed, and if anything she loved him more than ever.

But if she thought Barry had changed Barry thought Angela had turned into a woman he hardly recognized. He had left behind a young girl and came back to a woman, and what's more a more self-assured and confi- dent woman, and where once she would have always deferred to him, he could guess that she would no longer do that for now she had to make decisions for herself. He was immensely glad the Commanding Officer had taken time to warn all those going home how life had changed for the families and particularly the women left behind, for in his heart of hearts he wasn't sure he liked the new Angela. He knew he could never say this to her, but he was used to being the master in his own house and he appeared to be that no longer.

On the other hand, he was immensely proud of Angela for the way she had coped and taken up the reins of the house and worked long and arduous hours to put food on the table and pay the rent, and though the job was dirty and exhausting she was glad to do it because it was essential to the war effort, and he knew whatever personal misgivings he might have, he would say nothing about them and only tell Angela how proud he was of her.

Angela was not used to being overly praised by her husband and was a little embarrassed, but even allowing for the fact she had changed considerably Barry was unprepared for what she said later as they sat before the fire with their last cup of tea before bed. Barry had asked her what she did in the factory and she had told him and then added, 'I can't ever say that I think war could possibly ever be a good thing and I know so many have died and we at home have tasted tragedy and suffered loss already and still it goes on. And yet this job, that I would never have done had the country not been at war, has opened up new horizons for me.'

'In what way?'

'Well I suppose like learning to drive the petrol-driven trucks.'

Barry stared at her with his mouth open. And then repeated, 'You're learning to drive petrol-driven trucks?'

Angela nodded. 'Not on the road yet,' she said. 'I started off in the warehouse just learning how all the controls on the truck work and how they control the engine.'

'Control the engine,' Barry repeated again. 'God I'm beginning to sound like Little Sir Echo, but this is mind-boggling. Do I take it that you actually know how a petrol engine works?'

'Basically yes,' Angela said. 'Sometimes mechanics are hard to find and if you are stuck miles from anywhere and your truck breaks down, you need to be able to get it going again as quickly as possible, especially if it's stacked with shells that are needed somewhere.'

'Oh I agree with that,' Barry said. 'But you don't ride on the roads you say?'

'No, I've had to practise in the yard till they were confident I'd got the hang of it,' Angela said. 'But they said last week that I'll be all right to go out soon, this week probably.'

'Well I think you're a marvel,' Barry said in admiration. 'What d'you think, Ma?'

'I'll tell you straight I wasn't for it at first,' Mary said. 'I thought it was too dangerous hauling those shells about the place, but Angela said that it was no more dangerous than what she was doing every day; shaping them and filling them with explosives and this way at least she gets out of that smelly, dirty factory.'

'I see what Mammy's saying,' Barry said. 'But you will take care won't you?'

'Of course I will,' Angela said. 'I have no wish to blow myself to Kingdom come. But just now I must seek my bed for the morning is not that far away.'

TWENTY-ONE

The next morning Angela just bit back a groan as the alarm went off. It had roused Barry too and he stretched out his hand and murmured, 'Morning, Mrs McClusky.'

'Hush,' whispered Angela. 'You'll wake Connie and she wakes up early enough without an alarm believe me.' And so saying she gave Barry a kiss on the cheek, slipped out of bed and gathering her clothes in her arms and went downstairs to dress as she did every morning.

She was just making a cup of tea when Barry entered the room and Angela turned in surprise, 'What are you doing up?'

'I wanted to say a proper goodbye to my wife, what's wrong with that?'

'Nothing,' Angela said. 'It's just so early.'

'Angela I'm a soldier,' Barry said. 'We can be up at any time and sleep on a clothes line, near enough. Come on and wet that tea and come and give me what I left my bed for.'

Angela melted into Barry's arms with a sigh of

contentment. 'I really wish they had given me the day off,' she said. 'I really don't want to go in today.'

'I know,' Barry said. 'I have the feeling it will be the hardest thing in the world to leave you on Monday. I must though or they would shoot me as a traitor and a coward.'

Angela sighed as she said, 'Mr Potter said our job making the shells was just as important as the soldier firing them.'

'He's right too,' Barry said. 'Now you give me that kiss I have been waiting for, and be on your way, and I will be at the factory gates when you finish.'

The kiss could have been their undoing, but for the thought that Maggie would be waiting on the road and Angela knew she had absolutely no right to risk her being late. Barry quite understood that but when he released her he was breathless and Angela moaned and her whole body yearned for more. 'Hold on to it until tonight,' he advised.

And Angela had a broad smile on her face as she lifted her coat from the peg for they had made love the previous night, although Barry had been hesitant, knowing how tired Angela was. Angela wouldn't hear of it, knowing they had to squeeze every last second from their brief time together.

'You all right?' Maggie said as the two girls met.

'Fine. Why?'

'You're just going round with a dirty great grin on your face that's all,' Maggie said as they hurried down Bristol Passage. 'I was expecting you to have a face on you that would sour cream, having to go in today.'

'No point being like that is there?' Angela said. 'I

mean I said it to Barry and he sort of said that lots of people have to do things they don't like when your country is at war. However hard it is for him to leave on Monday, if he didn't he'd be shot as a traitor, but a real rollicking is all we'd get. So having made the decision to come in, it's not fair to make everyone else's life a misery because of it.'

'Mighty glad to hear that,' Maggie said. 'Good, here's the tram. This March wind is a bit bleak at this hour of the morning.'

Maggie was right and Angela tucked her scarf well around her neck when they left the tram to walk across the town to the factory. She was glad to reach the shelter of it because as she'd walked across the Bull Ring she'd felt as if she had been blown to bits.

She wished the day to speed by, but never had she known a day to pass so slowly and many a time she felt her mind wandering, imagining what Barry was doing and yearning to be with him and she constantly forced herself to concentrate.

Eventually though the endless day drew to a close and at the gate Barry was waiting for her, but alone this time. 'Where's Connie?'

'At home,' Barry said. 'Mammy was getting her ready for bed when I left, though she said she will keep her up till we get in. She was exhausted, but then I've had her out most of the day.'

'Oh it's lovely to be spending so much time with her,' Angela said as she waved Maggie off towards the Bull Ring and took hold of Barry's arm.

'Well I have to make the most of every minute don't I,' Barry said. 'Anyway it's no hardship to spend time with Connie for the child is a joy to be with. But it suits me to have you to myself like this for I need to talk to you.'

'That sounds ominous.'

'No, it's nothing like that,' Barry said. 'It's just that I can't see a way round it. You know what they say about two heads being better than one?'

'What is it?'

'Well without putting too fine a point on it, Connie is getting too much for Mammy.'

'Has she said so?'

''Course not,' Barry said. 'Can you see Mammy admitting to that, especially when she knows how important it is?'

'Then I don't see what I am to do.'

'There aren't any part-time positions?'

Angela shook her head. 'No,' she said. 'All munitions jobs I have heard of are full-time. Some work shifts, I've heard. Any other than war work isn't so well paid and while the war lasts we do need the money. When the war is over and you are home again everything will be as it was before, but this is how it must be for now.'

No more was said about it though Angela did worry because she knew Mary was no spring chicken and as Connie grew she became more and more active and hard for Mary to keep an eye on.

When Angela arrived home she could see the lines of strain on Mary's face which was grey with fatigue and Angela's conscience smote her for not even noticing that until it was pointed out to her. Mary though was her usual self and greeted them warmly and bade them

318

sit up to the table for she had a delicious meal ready for them.

Angela slept badly that night. She was tired and they had spent a lovely evening together after both Barry and Angela put Connie to bed. And when they went to bed themselves a little while later, though Barry had loved her so tenderly, sleep still evaded her. She had been bothered at what Barry had said about his mother and annoyed that she hadn't spotted it herself and yet, if she had noticed, what could she have done? What could she do now?

However, she knew the sleeplessness was also caused by the thought that on Monday morning her husband would march off to war and she might never see him again. She couldn't stand it! It was too much to ask! The thought of losing Barry tore at her heart, and yet she knew she would have to stand it. He wouldn't be the only beloved husband and father at the Front and she knew she would have to cope as every other woman had to. But when he went away she knew one part of her heart would die.

Tired though Angela was, she was up early the following morning, not wishing to waste one minute of the short time they had left. After breakfast she made up a picnic for Barry and Connie and herself, and said Mary should have a day on her own to rest, and Barry said that they would bring in fish and chips for dinner and so she had nothing to worry herself about. His mother protested and said it was nonsense spending their money that way. But they both expected her to react like that so they paid no heed.

319

The morning was mild though a slight breeze was riffling through the trees as they made for Cannon Hill Park with Connie in the pram for it was a long trek for little legs. The day was a magical one and though poignantly sad for the adults, Connie felt no constraint and when she was tired out from running around the grass with her daddy he took her to the playground. Barry helped his small daughter climb the steps of the high slide and come down in a whoosh, or pushed her as high as high on the swings or spun her so fast on the roundabout she was dizzy when she came off.

They had their picnic on a grassy incline overlooking the lake; Angela spread the blanket while Barry got out the sandwiches and as Angela sat she thought everywhere looked fresh and clean, the grass verdant green and the daffodils bright yellow in the borders. The sky was Wedgewood blue and the wind sent white fluffy clouds scudding across it and rippled the water, the low sun glinting on the waves. It was so beautiful, so peaceful and it was hard to believe that just across another small stretch of water, men were holed up in trenches shooting at one another. Barry was thinking the same thing and he said, 'Hard to believe we're at war isn't it?'

Angela nodded and said, 'It is indeed.'

'This is what we're fighting for really, so that we keep England like this, a green and pleasant land.'

'I know.'

'Some things are worth fighting for.'

Angela swallowed hard before saying, 'I know that too. I just wish that it wasn't you doing the fighting. But as it is, I wish we could stop time now here, just for a wee while.'

'I wish that too,' Barry said urgently. 'But as that won't happen at least I will take another memory to sustain me when I am away.'

Angela sighed and lay back on the grass and closed her eyes.

'Connie and I are going to feed the crusts to the ducks,' Barry said. His words jerked Angela from her little doze and she said, 'Hold on to her then.'

She sat up and watched the two walk down to the water hand in hand, with their bag of crusts, and her heart constricted with love for them both.

Ducks fed, Connie seemed sleepy and so Angela lay her down in the pram and as they walked around the park, she dozed and Angela gave a sigh. It could have been contentment, but Monday morning was looming ever closer. 'Where are we going tomorrow?' she asked Barry and went on, 'Sutton Park might be nice now the weather is a wee bit warmer.'

Barry shook his head. 'Not any more,' he said. 'Not with the Army commandeering so much of it. I heard tell they were building a prisoner-of-war camp there too. Anyway I did most of my training there, so I saw plenty of it. The next time I want to go there is in peacetime, when I am home again for good.'

'Fair enough,' Angela said.

'There's something else as well,' Barry said. 'I know we have been trying to take the burden off Mammy by taking Connie out and about, not that that has been in any way a chore, but she might feel a bit neglected if we take off for the whole day on my last day home.'

Angela could see that, for trying to spend most of his precious leave with his wife and daughter meant

321

that he hadn't spent a great deal of time with his mother. 'We haven't worked up any sort of solution to Connie's care while I work,' Angela said.

'No,' Barry agreed. 'I suppose we'll have to leave things as they are for the time being.'

'Well let's not spend any more time worrying about a problem we can see no way of fixing,' Barry said. 'I'm looking forward to feeding the inner man at the moment, so shall we head home via the chip shop?'

'Oh I should say so,' Angela said with a smile as she turned the pram around.

Next morning before Mass Angela saw Maggie in the porch. 'No point asking how you are,' Maggie said to Angela. 'You're like a cat that's got the cream.'

'Ooh it's been lovely,' Angela said. 'But it's Barry's last day and tomorrow he will be gone and I will be back at work and worrying about Mary.'

'What about Mary?'

'Barry thought she looked tired. I felt bad I hadn't noticed it myself because when I really studied her myself, he was right. It's no good asking her because she always claims she's fine, but really she's not. Barry thinks she might be finding Connie a bit of a handful.'

'Well she is a bundle of energy that child,' Maggie said with a chuckle. 'My own mother said just the other day that Mary was getting very tired looking. Why don't you put Connie in the nursery?'

'What nursery?' Angela asked.

'The one set up for mothers engaged in war work,' Maggie explained. 'Think there's one on Bristol Street.'

Angela would have asked more but the strains of the

organ were heard and she had to join her husband and child for Mass was about to start, so it was after Mass she learned more. The nursery was free to mothers who were engaged in war work and they took babies from six months. 'How d'you know so much about it?' she said.

'From Sonia,' Maggie said. 'I was working with her when you were learning to drive in the yard.'

'Isn't she a widow?'

'Yeah and left with two nippers, three and just eighteen months,' Maggie said. 'She told me straight she couldn't feed and clothe them adequately if she didn't have the nursery and the kids love it. Sonia said they have three meals a day too.'

Barry joined them then with Connie in his arms and Angela and Maggie filled him in about the nursery and he was impressed. 'Sounds just the job,' he said and turning to his daughter he asked, 'Would you like to go to nursery, Connie?'

Connie didn't answer her Daddy but her eyes were perplexed for she didn't know the word.

'Nursery is a place where you will have lots of toys and children to play with.'

Connie's face was a beam of happiness. 'Yes,' she said. 'Me go.'

'Well she's easily persuaded,' Barry said.

'Barry, she is not yet two years old,' Angela said. 'Your mother will be a different kettle of fish altogether.'

And Mary wasn't at all keen on the idea. They didn't attempt to tell her anything until she had eaten a good Sunday roast dinner when she might be feeling a little more compliant. Angela put Connie to bed for a rest so that Mary could have their undivided attention but the strategy didn't work all that well for they had barely begun to explain when Mary snapped, 'I am not in my dotage totally you know.'

'We know you're not,' Angela said soothingly, 'and no one is suggesting you are, and it isn't as if you are not doing a good job, because you are. But I don't want you to make yourself ill with exhaustion.'

'Well I won't, will I, looking after one small grand-daughter?'

'Mammy they're very tiring at this age,' Barry put in.

'D'you think I don't know this when I've had a fine big family of my own?'

'Mammy things were different then,' Barry said.

'All I ask is that you let her try it?' Angela said. 'If she is unhappy she needn't stay.'

'And what will I do all day when she is away at this nursery place?' Mary demanded.

'You could always rest more, take it easy you know?' Barry said.

'I'll have rest enough in my box,' Mary growled and then looked at Angela accusingly. 'You said you needed me, that you couldn't do this job without me.'

'Mammy I swear to you I had never heard of this nursery until today,' Angela said. 'But I will probably still need you because it's unlikely they will open to cover the hours I work or Saturday mornings. I will have to find that out, but I think I will still need you to take her there in the morning and fetch her home in the evening.'

'And how will you be able to find anything out about this nursery when you are working all day every day?'

'I'll take the day off.'

Barry gasped. 'I thought you couldn't have days off just like that?'

'You can't,' Angela said. 'And I'll likely get into trouble for it, but I don't care. What's the alternative anyway?'

Barry had so wanted Angela to come and see him off at the station, but knowing the situation he hadn't asked. And now, because she had to check out the nursery, she would be able to see him off properly first.

But then Angela said, 'Even before this business with the nursery, I had a mind to defy Mr Potter. I think it is unreasonable to expect us to just carry on as if something momentous isn't happening in our own lives. And I can think of nothing that will change my life more than when my husband steps on that train on his way to fight in a war. I will try hard to hold the tears back, but I will be upset and sometimes that makes me all jittery inside, and for the job I do you need a steady hand, and I doubt my mind will be on the job either and it would be easy make a mistake, and a mistake in a munitions factory can be fatal. I think it will be far better and safer for me to stay away from the place the day you leave.'

'I think you do right,' Mary said. 'It shows a lack of compassion in your employers to not understand that.'

Barry said nothing, too choked by Angela's words, but when his arms went around her and his lips met hers words weren't necessary.

Connie was shouting and Barry went to fetch her and as he came down, he said to Angela, 'Let's see if we can find this nursery and not have you searching for it tomorrow and take Connie down to the canal later to see the barges.'

Angela was agreeable to this and they set off with Connie in her preferred place on her father's shoulders.

The nursery, called The Acorns, was the other side of Bristol Street over Pershore Road which was where Angela always turned down the other way on her way to Calthorpe Park, which was why she hadn't noticed it, especially as Maggie intimated that it was fairly new. It was a long low building and it had quite a large playground at the front and the windows Angela could see were decorated in some way. 'This is your nursery, Connie,' Barry said. 'What do you think?'

Connie gazed at it and then looked at her father who had told her about the children and toys at the nursery, but her tongue couldn't quite master the word children. 'Toys,' she said.

Angela knew what her daughter was getting at and she said with a smile, 'All the toys are inside.'

'That's because it's closed,' said Barry. 'Locked see,' he went on, lifting Connie and showing her the lock fastening the large metal gates together. 'When Mammy brings you tomorrow, it will be open and you can see it for yourself. Now we're off to look at the canal.'

Connie was quite interested in the water though it was slightly brown and oil-slicked and had a pungent smell, but she was fascinated by the boats that her Daddy called barges. They were pretty and painted on the sides and moored to the rings on the towpath.

'Elephants and castles,' Barry said when Connie pointed out the painted barges. 'They always paint elephants and castles and don't ask me why because no one seems to know.'

'They are pretty though,' Angela said. 'Imagine having

our house painted like that, Connie, because those barges are like people's floating houses where they live.'

'Tell you what,' Barry said. 'A few elephants and castles or any other damned design might cheer our back-to-backs a treat.'

Angela laughed. 'Barry, I don't think there is anything anyone could do to make those houses a bit cheerier. That would be a lost cause altogether.'

They walked along the towpath with Angela holding tight to Connie's hand and all was quiet and still. 'Because it's Sunday,' Barry said in a low voice. 'They're all resting up. I was hoping to see a barge going through the locks, but we're out of luck today. Shall we make our way home and give Connie a turn in the playground in Calthorpe Park on the way.'

Angela nodded. 'Well we are nearly at the entrance to it.'

However when they left the park there was a hurdy-gurdy man at the entrance with his barrel organ and monkey. He had a weather-beaten face with two twinkling black eyes and he had on a well-worn dark-red jacket and black corduroy trousers tucked into well-cobbled boots. Angela was delighted to see the monkey was dressed too and more flamboyantly in black and white striped trousers, a red shirt and a black waistcoat with a felt hat on his head.

Connie's eyes opened wider still when she spied the monkey, and then the barrel organ started to play and the monkey danced up and down on top of it as Connie clapped her hands in excitement. The music brought a fair crowd. Other children playing in the street left their games and others came out of their houses and some adults too, all clustered around the hurdy-gurdy man listening, tapping their feet to the music, some humming along and some clapping the beat and everyone laughed at the antics of the lively monkey.

The music drew to a close and there was a ripple of applause and then further laughter as the monkey took off his hat and proffered it to collect donations. Many then turned regretfully away, but Barry dropped three pennies into the hat before they too left the hurdy-gurdy man and turned for home.

Seeing the hurdy-gurdy man was the high spot in Connie's life and when they arrived home, she tried with her limited vocabulary to explain to her grand-mother, her obvious delight keeping them all entertained especially when she tried to copy the dances the monkey did.

Much later and with Connie in bed, closely followed by Mary, Angela was putting the last few bits in Barry's kitbag when she said, 'D'you think you'll see much of Stan when you're over there?'

She had so hoped this was the case because Stan was a Sergeant now and so might be more protected than the ordinary privates, and with Stan a friend of the whole family and with him not wanting Barry to go in the first place, maybe he could see a way of keeping him safer.

However, Barry dashed those hopes straight away. 'The Western Front goes for miles and miles,' he said. 'Involving thousands of soldiers. Unless we had joined together into the same Pals Regiment I think the chance of finding an individual soldier a very slim one.'

'But he's a Sergeant now.'

'And so are countless others,' Barry said. 'And my time is not my own don't forget. I doubt I can wander around on my own asking questions, which is not a very safe thing to do in wartime anyway, and it would be frowned on for a private to be too friendly with a superior. Whatever you were in civvy street has to be left in civvy street. My fellow soldiers would probably see it as toadying up in the hope of getting special privileges. And it wouldn't do Stan any good either, the others might easily think he was the other way, you know?' Barry finished with a wink and a jerk of his head.

'No I don't know,' Angela said, completely perplexed. 'What are you on about? Other way from what?'

Barry sighed, 'If an older soldier took too much interest in a young private, they might think he was the sort of man who likes men the same way that most men like women.'

Angela was totally shocked for she hadn't known there were any men like that and at the thought of it she felt the heat flood her face and knew her cheeks would be crimson with embarrassment as she said, 'Oh surely not?'

'Oh it's a distinct possibility,' Barry said. 'And proof isn't needed. Just a hint of scandal like that and Stan's life would be ruined. So you see it's better that we don't meet at all.'

'I do indeed,' Angela said.

'And now we have talked enough,' Barry said. 'I want a special memory to take with me when I march out tomorrow.' He took Angela by the hand as he spoke, but she made no protest as he led her to the stairs and they went up hand in hand.

TWENTY-TWO

The smoky steam-filled station was full even at that hour and Angela saw she wasn't the only one saying goodbye to her husband or sweetheart. Some had brought children, as she had brought Connie because Barry had wanted her there. And all the men were in uniform and some of the women were crying. Angela didn't blame them for she felt like doing the same, but iron resolve prevented the tears from trickling down her cheeks, lest they upset Connie.

Barry felt as if his heart was breaking for he was leaving behind the two people he loved best in all the world, and yet he couldn't in all honesty say he regretted his decision because it was not right for him to sit pretty at home while others risked their lives daily. 'This is it then,' he said as they walked towards the waiting train.

'Yes,' Angela said, her husky voice barely above a whisper.

Barry knew Angela was perilously near to tears and so to help her compose herself he picked Connie up into his arms. 'Now Connie,' he said, 'I want you to be a big brave girl for Daddy. Can you do that?'

Connie nodded her head and Barry went on, 'I must go away and I want you to be a big brave girl and look after Mammy.' Connie's eyes opened wide for she had never seen her father so serious before, but when he went on, 'Will you do that?' she nodded her head again and he placed her in Angela's arms and put his arms around them both and said, 'And Mammy will look after you too, until I come home again.'

Angela thought her heart was breaking into pieces as Barry said, 'That is the picture I want to take to France and the one I want to see when I come back, though you might not be in your Mammy's arms then, Connie, for you are a big girl now and it takes time to win a war.'

Angela gave Barry a watery smile but she did not speak for if she'd tried she'd have burst into floods of tears as many women were doing all around them. Barry knew there was no point in prolonging the parting any longer for it didn't help. And so with a sigh, he kissed his wife and young daughter and boarded the train. He closed the door, for the guard was slamming the others, but slid the window down.

'I will say the rosary every night,' Angela promised, 'and God will protect you.'

'Aye,' Barry said with a wry smile, 'the bullets will bounce off me, or I may catch them in my teeth and spit them back.'

It was too much and Angela could no longer hold her tears in her brimming eyes and Barry leaned forward and kissed them as they trickled silently down her cheeks.

'All aboard.'

The last few stragglers got onto the train, the guard

slammed the last few doors shut, there was an ear-splitting shriek and the engines began to throb. The guard then blew his whistle and stepped onto the footplate as the train began to chug its way out of the station and Connie and Angela waved until they could see Barry no more.

As she turned to leave the station Angela felt a sadness so deep it was as if she had lead weights attached to what was left of her heart. Connie noticed her tears and touched them gently with her finger. 'Cry?' she asked.

Angela swallowed the lump in her throat and said, 'No, it was just the smoke in the station making my eyes water. Now shall we go and see about this nursery for you?'

'Ooh yes,' Connie said, and Angela was glad she was distracted so easily and was too young to feel the loss of her father, for she imagined Mary's sorrow would be enough for her to cope with.

However that would be later because she had told Mary she would go straight to the nursery after seeing Barry off. 'I only have this one day and I want to see around the place and talk to them and possibly put Connie's name down for they might not have a place right now.'

'Would they be open so early?'

'They're sure to be,' Angela said. 'They're for mothers doing war work.'

Angela was in fact pleased to have something to do after seeing her husband set off to join his regiment and presumably sail over to France in the very near future. She knew she couldn't break down, but must be strong for Mary and Connie as well as herself for she knew they must bear it the same as everyone else.

So she turned her energies to checking out the place where she hoped her daughter would be spending many hours of the day. She was delighted with the light airy rooms, and the staff who seemed to really care about the children, and the array of toys sent Connie into raptures.

The nursery was open from 7.30 to 6.30 so Angela would not to able to bring her or pick her up, but Mary wouldn't mind that so it wasn't a problem. Because many children came early and stayed till late they had breakfast at eight o'clock, a full dinner and pudding at twelve o'clock and a tea at four thirty, Mrs Cassidy the superintendent of the nursery said, 'And children of Constance's age will be put down for a nap after dinner.'

'That sounds wonderful, and the charges?'

'For women engaged in war work it's free, paid for by the government. You are doing valuable work and we are looking after your child so you can continue to do that. I don't think I could ever work in a factory, but I am doing my bit this way.'

'And just as valuable work as mine I'd say,' Angela said. 'When could she start?'

'Well,' Mrs Cassidy said. 'The question is, is your daughter used to being left?'

'I don't know,' Angela admitted. 'I have only ever left her with my mother-in-law and that was all right until she got more active. My husband was on leave and he said it was getting too much for his mother.'

'Did she agree?' Mrs Cassidy asked with a smile.

'Not straight away no,' Angela said. 'My husband persuaded her and she listens to him. She will be the one bringing Connie and taking her back at the end of the day, because I work from 6.30 to 6.30, and when she sees this place I'm sure all doubts will leave her.'

'It's nice of you to say that,' Mrs Cassidy said. 'I was going to suggest that your mother-in-law brings her next Monday, just for the morning and stays with her. And then on Tuesday leave her to go shopping or whatever for a few hours, and gradually extend it so that she is ready to start full-time the following week. Not all mothers can do this but for those who can, we find the children settle quicker.'

'I don't think Mammy will have any problems with that,' Angela said.

And Mary didn't of course and was looking forward to seeing the place herself. But that was for the future; when Angela rose from bed on Tuesday morning she knew she was in for a telling off at the very least. 'And I have my answer ready too,' she said when Maggie asked if she was nervous. 'Because for a start Mr Potter shouldn't be able to run our lives and tell us what to do.'

'He has the power to sack you.'

'Yes,' Angela said. 'And if he does how long do you think I would be out of work as an experienced munitions worker who can also drive?'

'I'd hate you to leave.'

'I've no intention of it,' Angela said. 'But I won't be treated as if I am Connie's age.'

So Angela wasn't surprised when Mrs Paget asked her to see Mr Potter before she began work and moments later she was standing facing him across the desk. 'I am very disappointed with you, Mrs McClusky,' he said.

'Oh,' said Angela. 'Why is that exactly?'

'I think you know why,' Mr Potter said testily. 'I explained how important the work we do is and that was the reason you could have no time off even though your husband was on leave, and you defied me.'

'Yes,' Angela said. 'I did.'

Mr Potter was a little taken aback by Angela's directness. 'And why is that?' he asked.

'Mr Potter,' Angela said, 'I am not claiming to be a special case, for many here love their husbands, but I have known mine since I was eighteen months old, as his parents took me in and brought me up when my parents and siblings died. I loved Barry as a brother before I loved him as a husband. He has been a big part of my life always and it was an inhumane request for me not to go to the station and kiss my man goodbye, knowing that I might never see him again. In fact if I had come in I would have felt a failure as a wife, and just as importantly a hazard to myself and my fellow workers because I would be upset and my mind definitely not on the job in hand, and lacking in concentration can lead to accidents. I would say your directive is dangerous.'

Mr Potter was affronted. 'You, Mrs McClusky, are being presumptuous.'

'No. I'm not,' Angela retorted. 'I am talking sense. But I was off for another reason. When I began here my mother-in-law took on looking after my daughter, but she's not a young women and it was getting too much for her and I had to find a nursery place for my daughter, or I would be standing before you now giving notice because my child-care arrangements had fallen through. Would you have preferred that?'

336

Mr Potter could find nothing to say to Angela because what she said made eminent sense, but the way she spoke to him was not exactly respectful. So he contented himself with saying curtly, 'You will of course lose a day's pay.'

'I expected no less,' Angela said. And then because Mr Potter's pompous attitude annoyed her she added, 'You're all heart.'

Mr Potter glared at her and Angela knew he would have liked to have given her the sack there and then, but he couldn't because she was needed. 'Will that be all?' she asked and he growled, 'Yes get back to work. You've wasted enough time already.'

'You've made an enemy there I'd say,' Maggie said when Angela told her what had transpired as they made their way home.

'Well that won't give me sleepless nights,' Angela said. 'It's the constant worry about Barry that's going to do that.'

Mr Potter had assumed that when confronted and accused of defiance Angela McClusky would have been apologetic, cowed even, and her assertive attitude had stunned him. After she had gone though, he had to concede that much of what she said made sense with regard to saying goodbye to loved ones and he vowed to be a bit more understanding in the future.

Angela was unaware of this and as far as she was concerned nothing had changed but she was far too busy to let it concern her unduly. On the homefront there were no problems. Mary had been very impressed with the nursery at the first session when she had stayed

337

with Connie. 'Not that she cared whether I was there or not,' she said to Angela that evening.

Mary was right and Connie who'd never before had so many friends to play with nor so many toys and she was in her element and settled to nursery as if she had been going to it every day of her life.

Angela wrote and told Barry all about it because he said he wanted to know all the news from home, however trivial, and everything concerning Connie. In his reply he included a copy of the photograph the army had taken for their records. Angela had already received a similar photograph from Stan who asked her to give it to Daniel if he didn't survive. Angela promised she would and put it away in the box where she kept the letters.

However, when Barry's came she took it to a photographer in the town the first Saturday afternoon and had it enlarged and bought a silver frame to put it in and it had pride of place in the bedroom. She was so glad to have it, not only for her own sake but also to show Connie the fine man her father was, lest as time passed, she might forget him. Every night Connie asked God to bless her Daddy and kissed his picture before settling down to sleep. And Angela had his picture before her each night as she knelt to say the rosary for she had made a bargain with God, a decade of the rosary every day in exchange for Barry's safety.

Mary too was glad to get a photo of her son for Angela had given her the original. And she too began praying for his survival and safe return. Time hung heavy on her hands to begin with and she missed Connie sorely though she owned caring for her full-time had

338

been a strain and yet without her she didn't know what to do with herself.

Angela encouraged her to rest, but Mary said resting had never been a major part of her life and anyway a person can have too much of a good thing and she was done resting now. However, few people need to be idle in wartime and she was soon engaged in knitting for the troops. It was a social event, arranged by the church and all the wool was donated and they knitted gloves, socks and a strange thing called a balaclava. Another day she rolled bandages for the military hospitals and on another she helped out at the canteen at the Brracks. That together with the shopping, cooking, cleaning and taking Connie to nursery and bringing her home again kept her happily busy and made her feel she was doing something useful.

So life settled down to as even a keel as it could in wartime. Worry about Barry was always there like a nagging toothache and Angela was concerned for Stan too. Barry had written that he had seen no sign of Stan and as he had said it was highly unlikely they would meet up, Angela wasn't surprised. But she lived for Barry's letters for they at least showed he was alive.

Angela didn't know where he was, but by that time there was talk of a campaign at a place called Gallipoli and some other place called the Dardanelles and she supposed he could be involved there. But in the *Evening Mail* one night was a map showing the whole of the Western Front and she studied it for a long time trying to take in the vastness of it and could quite see why it was highly unlikely that Stan and Barry would ever catch sight of one another.

Connie continued to love her nursery and would have gone Saturdays and Sundays if it had been open and in just a few short weeks she was more independent and her speech had improved tremendously, so when her second birthday loomed, 24th May, Angela decided to have a little tea party for her birthday and invite some of her special friends from the nursery too. Her birthday was on Monday that year so Angela decided to have the party the day before. Mary threw herself into cooking for this special party and the centrepiece was a beautiful chocolate sponge cake. 'I don't know where you got all the stuff,' Angela said, surveying the table, for around the cake there were iced biscuits, fairy cakes, ginger loaf, sausage rolls and scones, small sandwiches cut into quarters and a jug of homemade lemonade.

'It wasn't easy,' Mary said. 'It wasn't like before the war when you could just go to any shop and get everything you would need, now you have to pop from one shop to another and buy up what they have on the shelves.'

'Oh don't you miss George at times like this?'

'Yes I do,' Mary said. 'I would have probably got everything in Maitland's shop because, like you always said, he was a man of integrity and didn't sell to the nobs and leave his regular customers in the lurch like so many are doing.'

'I do miss him still,' Angela said. 'He was always so good to us and I wish he hadn't had to die like that.'

Mary nodded. 'Me too. Nagged to death, poor soul. Still they got their come-uppance. What goes around comes around they say.'

'Mammy what are you on about?' Angela said, perplexed.

'Oh I forgot to tell you,' Mary said. 'Some woman at the Knitting Club was telling me that Matilda and that sister of hers Dorothy bought a house in Pershore Road, near to this woman, and she said that Dorothy had a stroke not long after they moved in and she is completely helpless and Matilda has to do everything for her.'

'No!' Angela exclaimed, a bit ashamed of the smile on her face.

Mary nodded. 'It's true enough,' she said. 'See, Matilda wanted to get Dorothy taken to the hospital, but they told her straight they hadn't the space, or beds, or doctors. She was telling this woman all about it. Doesn't do to be sick now because most common wards are earmarked for casualities from the war and many doctors have joined the Medical Corps and are serving overseas and nurses the same.'

'You know I never thought of that.'

'Apparently they have these women called VADs in some places, it's the Voluntary Aided Detachment and these are girls and women over the age of twenty-three from posh homes who don't need to be paid and they're there to help the nurses. But I heard lots of those have gone to the Western Front as well.'

Angela nodded. 'I read about that in the paper. A lot of these posh folk were in the suffragette movement before the war and they stopped all campaigning once war was declared to help in the war effort.'

'Well since war was declared women have done so much they are virtually running the country, which I

341

would say has done more to advance their cause than all the protests and demonstrations they made before it.'

'You could be right,' Angela said. 'And they're game enough. The nurses say they couldn't run the hospitals without them and it's pretty stalwart of them to travel to France to work in the field hospitals. They must see some horrific sights and it's not exactly safe and yet I can't help wondering if they see it as a bit of an adventure too.'

'D'you think so?'

'Yes I do,' Angela said. 'I think I'd feel that way for these girls were very constrained before, they had to be chaperoned everywhere and there were so many things they weren't allowed to do. Even now they can't be paid.'

'Oh that's because if they were paid, it would bring shame on their fathers because people would say their fathers couldn't afford to keep them.'

'That's exactly what I mean,' Angela said. 'But really whatever reasons they have for doing it matter less than the good job they are doing as general nursing aides freeing the trained medical staff to attend where the injuries are more severe. I mean, I'd like the best doctors and nurses out there treating Barry if he was injured, and Stan as well.'

'I agree,' Mary said. 'And it means that Matilda has to care for her own sister.'

'And with anyone else I would feel sorry for them having to do that,' Angela said. 'But with those two horrible people I can't help feeling it serves them right.'

'Don't blame you, girl,' Mary said. 'Cos I felt a bit

the same. Anyway without Maitland's I did get all the stuff I needed for the party in the end and Connie's delight made it all worthwhile.'

And Connie was in a fever of excitement and so were the four little girls she had invited from the Nursery. Two of the mothers worked making shells at the same place as Angela and Maggie, and Maggie popped in too and so it was a merry little party. And when Angela watched the children sing Happy Birthday to Connie she felt a surge of happiness and stored it all in her head and her heart to tell Barry in her next letter.

TWENTY-THREE

Both the spring and summer of 1915 were in the main warm and sunny and it was even warmer in the factory and although Angela like all the rest stripped down to her underwear under her boiler suit, after just a short time in the factory her face would be red and glistening and she would feel beads of sweat running down her back and by the time she had finished her shift her clothes were usually sticking to her.

She knew she was luckier than many because sometimes she had the opportunity to get out of the factory and drive the lorries which was a lot more pleasant. But she was always grateful for the bowl of warm water Mary had ready for her at home as well so she could wash herself all over before she ate. She knew she owed Mary a lot for though she worked long hours, life would be much harder for her if she had to cook a meal when she got in every evening and somehow manage to shop and clean as well.

The nice weather did mean though that almost every Sunday and sometimes Saturday afternoon too she could go somewhere nice with Connie. She valued the time spent with her a great deal as she saw so little of her generally.

But the summer passed and by the time Christmas was approaching the summer was just a memory. She was driving more now which she thought far more interesting than making shells ad infinitum. She had tried to get Maggie to take a driving course but she said she was too scared and she tried to encourage her again one day as they travelled into work in mid December. 'I'd crash into something,' Maggie said.

''Course you wouldn't,' Angela said. 'Why would you do that? You steer with the wheel and there is a brake if you feel you are too close and you can go as slow as you like to start with.'

Maggie shook her head. 'It's never been something I've ever wanted to do.'

Angela laughed. 'Well I bet making shells wasn't on your list of things to do either.'

'Well no, 'course it wasn't, but the money's good.'

'But this is an opportunity that we wouldn't have any other time,' Angela said. 'This is a dreadful war, the casualty figures are scary and I wish Barry and Stan were not involved at all and I wish the country had not emptied itself of men, but it has and we couldn't stop it. And because that has happened women have had the opportunity to do things we have never done before and driving to me was just one more thing. I never in my wildest dreams thought I would get behind the wheel of a truck and drive it to factories and distribution depots all over the place. I couldn't pass up the chance and I'm glad I didn't because I love it.'

'I know you do,' Maggie said. 'But it really isn't for me so stop bullying me about it.'

Angela grinned. 'All right,' she said. 'You have got a point. I have been badgering you and it isn't fair. If you really don't want to learn to drive that should be your choice.'

Maggie sighed with relief and to change the subject a little asked Angela if she'd finished the Christmas Boxes for Barry and Stan. 'More or less,' Angela said. 'Still it will be a funny old Christmas with just Mammy and myself. If it wasn't for Connie I wouldn't be bothered putting up decorations or anything.'

'Well it doesn't give a person much heart when they just have the one day off.'

'I know. Stingy lot,' Angela said. 'Mammy couldn't believe we just had Christmas Day.'

'Mmm,' Maggie said. 'I suppose what you have got to tell yourself is that fighting men don't even get that and me and our Mom will be filling our own Christmas Box next year.'

'Syd?' Angela said for that was the name of Maggie's eldest brother.

Maggie nodded her head. 'Only turned eighteen a few weeks ago. Mom's cut up about it but there's nothing to be done. He must go like the rest.'

'Does he mind?'

'I'll say not. He can't wait, silly fool,' Maggie said. 'He thinks it's like some Boy Scouts' Jamboree. He's trying to hide it from Mom but I know our Syd.'

'I suppose it's better that he's keen rather than the other way round when he has to go anyway,' Angela said.

'Maybe you're right,' Maggie said. 'They don't hang

347

about. Provided he passes his medical, he will be in before Christmas.'

'That's not that far away now,' Angela said. 'And then the turn of the year. I wonder what 1916 will bring, the end of the war perhaps?'

'Not a chance,' Maggie said. 'I stopped believing in fairy tales years ago.'

In the Eastertide of 1916 there was an insurrection in Dublin when rebel forces known at the time as The Brotherhood took over the General Post Office and various other strategic places in Dublin. 'I suppose they imagined with England fighting Germany the government had their hands too full to worry about them,' Mary said.

'Can't see it myself. Can you?' Angela asked.

Mary shook her head. 'No,' she said. 'And I dread to think of England's response to this. I don't think it will achieve anything. I mean I'm angry like we all are, England promised us independence if we helped them in the war but since then they have done nothing about it. All those young men, 125,000 of them, joined up in all good faith and many have been badly injured or have not returned at all and England is still silent about the promise it made. Well to be honest I expected nothing else, in my heart of hearts, but violence is not the way to protest and it is affecting their own. It tells you in the paper about the ordinary Dubliners unable to walk the streets for fear of being shot at. In fact it says many shops have put up their shutters and ceased trading to try and prevent looting.'

'Well soon there'll be nothing to put in the shops,'

Angela said, 'for they have hold of the railway station and they are letting nothing out.'

'I know,' Mary said. 'And the poor people have had their cars and carts and all else purloined to form the barricade in a place called St Stephen's Green. It's supposed to be a beautiful place and they have dug trenches all through it.'

'It can't be let go on,' Angela said. 'Germany or no Germany, England won't stand for this much longer.'

And it didn't for the next day a field gun was placed on the roof of the Sherbourne Hotel, which stood facing one corner of St Stephen's Green, and began shelling and shooting the rebels and they fled to the Royal College of Surgeons. There was another rebel contingent set to guard Mountford Bridge, which was the bridge leading from the Kingstown Docks where British ships off-loaded 10,000 extra soldiers. Another field gun was installed in a place called Merrion Square and it routed those guarding the bridge, and on Wednesday of that week the gunship *Helga* sailed up the Liffey pounding those occupying Liberty Hall.

Surrender was a foregone conclusion and it came on Saturday 29th April. The rebellion had lasted six days and left 450 dead and 2,000 injured. 'It will take a sight longer than six days for Dublin and the Dubliners to get over this,' Mary said grimly. 'Dublin has been burnt, battered and bruised, there is little food to be had, people's businesses have been looted and other lives destroyed with the loss of those cars and carts, and I feel sorry for the families of those men who have lost their means of making a living, not to mention the maimed and the dead.'

'Will they all be shot d'you think?'

'I can't see what other outcome there could be for whatever they choose to call themselves, the English will only have one word for them and that is traitors and they shoot traitors.'

Mary was right. Three hundred people were arrested and one hundred and eighty of those were sent to England and held without trial, including a man called Roger Casement and another called Eamon de Valera who had his execution changed to a life sentence because he had an American passport. Over the next fortnight ninety people were condemned to death. Later it became known that fourteen leaders had been killed in the stone breaker's yard in Kilmainham Jail, just days after the uprising.

Upsetting though this news was, war news took precedence and also worry about their loved ones fighting a bloody war somewhere in France. Angela was delighted when she heard that the private soldier's wages were raised from a shilling a day to two shillings. Barry said he was sending the extra seven shillings to her together with the five shillings he was already sending. Angela said she didn't need it with her wages but he insisted.

I know you to be no spendthrift, he wrote. *Any money left put in the savings account.*

He had no need to write that really for Mary looked for bargains to make her good nutritious meals with, and with Connie having her dinner at the nursery and Angela having hers at the subsidized canteen, money went further anyway and any surplus went straight into the Post Office.

*   *   *

350

Throughout the spring there had been talk of a new Front opening in France which might shorten the war. No one really knew a great deal but rumours were rife. The Front was going to stretch for fifteen miles to the north of the river Somme, and soon the river would give its name to the bloodiest battle in the war so far, the Battle of the Somme. The earth was chalk and so the trenches criss-crossing the area were white and crumbly.

Some of the men assembled that early summer's day were new recruits held back for this campaign to fight next to seasoned soldiers now battle hardened, all part of Kitchener's New Army. As usual the British had been bombarding the enemy. It had been going on for a week and so the men were told opposition would be minimal.

Unbeknownst to the British, the Germans, used to this pre-battle bombardment, had moved their lines back, digging deep down into the crumbly chalk to make shell-proof bunkers, so when the British bombardment was over and the British began to advance, expecting little opposition, the Germans crawled out of the bunkers ready to face the enemy. Certain of victory, the British Army invited the newsreels in for the first time.

And so there were banks of reporters and camera-men everywhere and the newsreels rolled and captured the men leaving the trenches in waves, some not making it over the top as a bullet found its mark, and the soldier would jerk and fall back into the trench he had just left. Others were hit as they ran towards the coils of barbed wire. The cameras could not go further into No Man's Land but the press could hear all right, the barking of the guns and the whine of shells, mixed with the screams and cries of men that went on and on.

Towards evening, with the Germans eventually in retreat, quietness descended. One or two intrepid cameramen took their cameras from their tripods and, carrying them, slithered under the wire as they had seen the soldiers do, though some hadn't made it and were impaled on the wire, and then they were through and stood and surveyed No Man's Land, shocked to the core. So the cameras recorded the ground littered with bodies and parts and pieces of bodies and the men with half a skull or limbs missing often lying in a pool of their lifeblood which was soaking into the chalky soil. Some were still alive, twitching or lying still with bleak deadened eyes in too much pain to even cry.

The orderlies were using the cover of the gathering dusk to move the bodies and the cameramen helped them with tears in their own eyes. And later when they found out it was estimated that 2,000 men died in the first hour of the conflict they weren't surprised. On that first day alone there were 60,000 casualties. They knew that many in England would scarcely believe that things were as bad as they had seen for themselves because the soldiers' letters were censored and the reporters and cameramen all thought it was about time the general public knew the truth, because what they had witnessed was more like a massacre than a battle.

And so no punches were pulled when the newsreel was published and it was shown at cinemas. Angela never visited the cinema, but many of her workmates had been and so had seen the newsreel and shared the full horror of it with the rest of them the next day. The girls listened in horrified silence as they spoke about the absolute slaughter of British soldiers that day and the words they spoke caused the blood to run like ice in Angela's veins. She could scarcely believe what they were hearing and Maggie too was shocked to the core and before they caught the tram home that night, they bought a selection of papers each and Angela noted that the fiasco of the Somme was on the front page of every one.

Later, with Connie safely tucked up in bed, she studied them with Mary that night. There was no guarantee that Barry or Stan were anywhere near the Somme that day and yet she felt in her bones that they had been. 60,000 casualty in 24 hours, the numbers revererated in her head and the harrowing pictures showing the scenes captured on the cameras hours after the virtual bloodbath she knew would haunt her forever.

Before that day while everyone at home knew war wasn't a great experience and men were maimed and killed and that was awful and dreadful, it was the newsreels and the newspaper articles that brought what had happened in the Battle of the Somme into into their own living rooms.

'My God,' Angela said. 'The death toll's colossal.'

Mary sighed. 'I know, they must have just been mown down. Some never even got out of the trenches and others were impaled on the barbed wire as they reached No Man's Land.'

'And how the injured suffered,' Angela said with feeling. 'They had lost limbs . . . oh many had perfectly dreadful injuries and the battle was so fierce they had to wait all day in the hot sun to be tended.'

She was affected even by the grainy pictures from the newspaper, they were quite graphic enough, capturing the savagery of it so well. She was glad that they were just black and white and didn't think she could bear to see the film. 'And Barry could be part of this,' Angela said. 'And Stan could.'

'We would have heard if anything had happened to them,' Mary said. 'They would send a telegram.'

Angela knew that that was how many learned the bad news of their loved ones, but thought it might take some time to work out just who was killed, or badly injured and send the relevant telegrams, especially as the Battle of the Somme was still going on, and the loss of life was still high though it was not as high as on that first day.

However Angela saw no purpose in telling Mary her inner thoughts, time enough for her to worry when there was something to worry about and so she contented herself by saying, 'The point is, Mammy, every man killed was someone's father or son, husband, sweetheart or brother and they will all be missed and I'm thinking there will be many grieving people throughout the land just now.'

Mary sighed. 'I know and I know too I'm being selfish, but it isn't totally wrong to be glad that your lad is still living even though another person's might be dead, is it?'

Angela gave Mary's shoulder a squeeze as she said, 'No of course it isn't and you haven't a selfish bone in your body.' And then she added, 'This was supposed to shorten the war, according to the Government. Huh! If it means carnage on this scale I would say it's too high a price to pay.'

Angela waited daily for the buff telegram to be delivered to their door. It affected her nerves and disturbed her sleep but she could do nothing about it. The only good thing was that after such a tremendous loss of life, at a stroke many areas in cities, as well as small towns and villages, had lost all their young men. The Pals Regiment idea was dropped.

Barry used to write once a week, but when he had been in the army a while sometimes a fortnight would pass and then two or three letters would arrive together. But when it had been over three weeks since a letter from Barry came through the door, Angela was coming to terms with the fact that Barry was not ever coming home again. So when a letter was waiting for her as she came home from work one evening in early August and it was in a hand she didn't recognize, she assumed it was from some Department of the War Office to formally announce Barry's death and with a heavy heart she opened the envelope and withdrew the letter and then cried out with joy.

Mary had had her head down, trying to prepare herself for the bad news she was sure the letter contained and now her head shot up and she noted the light shining in Angela's face, and the tears glistening in her eyes and she cried, 'What is it?'

'Barry.'

'Barry,' repeated Mary incredulously. 'He isn't dead?'

Angela knew that despite Mary saying they would hear officially if anything happened to Barry, she had begun to lose heart that she would ever see her son again.

Angela threw down the letter and caught Mary's hands up in her own and said, 'No, he's not dead, but very much alive. He has been injured though and still can't write because his arms are in plaster and so a VAD is writing this on his behalf.'

Barry had found that he was unable to express himself as he normally would when telling a third party rather than committing the words to paper himself, which meant he was unable to say many things due to embarrassment. He also had no intention of telling Angela of the fever that nearly killed him, nor of the very real fear that he might lose his arm, peppered as it was with shrapnel. Angela didn't have to know, but it meant that he had very little he could tell her as he was not allowed to mention that hell-hole at the Somme either.

But Angela didn't care how brief the stiff little missive was because it told her all that she needed to know and that her Barry was alive and as well as could be expected when fighting a war. 'He did catch sight of Stan too,' Angela said to Mary scanning the letter again. 'He calls him just S but that's who he means, but he said he was too far away to speak or anything and he doesn't know what happened to him afterwards. Who would be informed if anything happened to Stan?' Angela asked.

'Betty I suppose.'

'Doubt she'd welcome telegrams or whatever arriving if she hasn't told Daniel the truth about his father.'

'She might have no say in it.'

'Well I hope she'll tell us if she does hear bad news,' Angela said. 'Or anything could happen to him and we'd know nothing. It could have already happened because we usually hear from him every fortnight or so and it has been a month now. I mean he might not have made it.'

'Write to her, why don't you?' Mary said. 'Ask her straight.'

'I will,' Angela said. 'But I will write a reply to Barry first. Have to get my priorities right.'

TWENTY-FOUR

Before Angela had a chance to write to Betty she received a letter from Stan explaining that he had been unable to write before because he had been injured. He didn't explain his injuries, seeing no purpose in telling her that he had been in a coma for a week, or that when he came round he had been raving. The savage butchery he'd witnessed, and contributed to, was too much for his brain to cope with.

No need telling Angela any of that but he did want news of Barry and was immensely relieved to hear that he had survived too. So was Angela, knowing that in hospital they were safe. The Military Hospital was on the South Coast and with the job she had, she knew she wouldn't be given time off to visit either of them, but she was able to write.

'I suppose we must just be grateful that they have been shipped to Britain,' Angela said. 'In his letter Barry said many were being treated in Field Hospitals. I mean a proper hospital is bound to have better facilities.'

'I should hope so,' Mary said. 'So probably the severity

of illness or injury determines who will be sent back to Britain.'

'D'you think they will have leave after, you know when they've recovered a bit?'

Mary shook her head. 'I would like to say yes,' she said. 'But I doubt it. That battle that started with that terrible loss of life on the first day is still raging.'

And it was, day after day with no side gaining much ground, for Angela avidly read the news in the papers. 'I would say that losing so many soldiers would mean that they want these patched up and back on the battlefield in short order.'

Angela thought Mary was right. Everywhere she went now she saw more and more widows' bonnets, more people with black arm-bands which signified how bad the losses were on a daily basis and she knew if they were to have any chance of winning this brutal, savage war they couldn't really do without all those trained soldiers. So many had died, those who could recover would be needed again.

The long summer was a good one and most days the sun shone from a sky of cornflower blue and Angela was glad to be out of the hot stuffy factory, for most of her time now was spent delivering the shells. Mr Potter was pleased with Angela, despite their disagreement about her taking time off to say goodbye to her husband. In fact it had made him rethink his rigid stance and relax it a little and so it was common now for any woman in a similar position to be given time off. Mr Potter knew Angela was no shirker and a natural driver and she had been sent to areas of that teeming city she didn't know existed and she loved the freedom of the roads.

In late August Barry wrote the weekly letter on his own and said his arms were nearly as good as new, he just needed a bit of physio. He was then going back to the fray and Stan too wrote that he was improving daily. Angela was relieved they were both getting better but she knew when they left the safety of their hospital beds the dread would settle in her heart again.

Part of her thought that because they had both survived that ferocious first day of the Battle of the Somme, and so had Maggie's Michael, when so many hadn't, it could be seen as a sort of talisman for them both surviving the war. It wasn't as if they had got away unscathed.

In her heart of hearts though, she knew the fight was far from over. Those who had said the Somme would be the deciding battle in the war were proved wrong and, as for shortening the war, it had done the opposite and had been an abject failure and she had to face the fact that they might lose the war altogether, or they might win after all but the cost would be the body of her darling husband and the father of her child left in a French field, and that would destroy her totally. She wanted nothing bad to happen to Stan either for he was very dear to them all and when they returned to the melee in France, worry could have overwhelmed her if she'd let it. During the day though, especially if she was driving, she had to push these worries to the back of her mind and concentrate on the road.

There was torrential rain in October putting an end to the lovely summer, but while no one enjoyed it much it was much worse for the troops trying to advance across battlegrounds turned into muddy quagmires.

Because the war had been brought into homes via the newspapers illustrating the first day of the Battle of the Somme, Angela and Mary knew how much the soldiers must be suffering.

They knew more about this battle now, though it wasn't one battle but comprised many battles and they didn't seem to be going forward very quickly. As Mary said, it was like them taking one step forward and two back, and it did seem a bit like that and it was hard to remain hopeful.

Halfway through November though the battles on the Somme were over. In one of the bloodiest battles in history the British had suffered 420,000 casualties, the French nearly as many, and they had gained just 8 kilometres, about 5 miles of enemy ground.

The figures were staggering. It was hard even to imagine so many people. It was as if the world had gone mad. There would be no young men left, because those casualty figures were only for the battles fought around the river Somme. Soldiers had been killed before 1916 and were still being killed in battles being fought elsewhere.

Angela's eyes were full of pain when she lifted them from the paper and met Mary's, and she imagined all the families getting the telegrams to tell them their father, son, husband, brother or uncle was never coming home again. He was littering a foreign field in France with comrades who were killed alongside him. 'This is not a war,' Angela said to Mary. 'This is carnage on a massive scale.'

* * *

Neither woman had much heart for Christmas, but Connie was only a child so for her sake Angela got down the tree and the decorations from the attic and put them all around the room and Santa visited with books to read, colouring books and a paintbox, and a whip and top. So for her it was a good Christmas.

Connie had stopped asking about her father and though she kissed his picture at night he was really a stranger to her and that bothered Angela. She was not the only one, many other children's daddies were soldiers as well and most of them hadn't a clue what daddies did. 'Why worry about it?' Mary said. 'Barry can't fix that till he's home again.'

'I know,' Angela said. 'It's just sad that's all. Not just for Connie. I mean for all the children.'

'War is sad,' Mary said. 'There is no better word for it.'

The year turned 1917 and peace seemed as far way as ever. The winter was bleak and snowy, gusty winds driving the snow into drifts. It was hard for people to get around, Angela had to take great care driving the trucks on the wet, slippery roads, and even basic things were in short supply in the shops, which was also blamed on the weather.

March was drier, but blustery. 'Well it is supposed to come in like a lion and go out like a lamb,' Angela remarked to Maggie, both holding on to their hats for grim death as they crossed the Bull Ring after leaving the tram.

'We're a third of the way through the month,' Maggie complained. 'Anyway I wish that wretched lion didn't have such a roar. These winds could take a person off their feet.'

'You're right,' Angela said. 'Hold your hat with one hand and link arms with the other and we might get to work in one piece.'

They did, though even linked they were blown from side to side and everyone was talking about it as they clocked in.

'I never thought I would be so pleased to see the factory as I was today,' said one girl and there was a ripple of laughter at that.

'I know what you mean,' said another. 'It's blooming hard going and it takes your breath away.'

'Hope it dies down a bit before home time,' Maggie said. 'Pity you, driving in this, Angela.'

'Maybe I'll not have to do much today,' Angela said. But barely had the words left her mouth than Mrs Paget entered the room as they were changing into their overalls and said that Mr Potter wanted to see her.

Immediately one of the girls said teasingly, 'Oh what you done, Ange?'

'Been a naughty girl I reckon,' said another.

'That will do girls,' Mrs Paget said. 'On to the shop floor if you're changed and stop wasting time teasing Angela.'

Grumbling good-naturedly they made their way down to the factory and, slightly intrigued, Angela went down to Mr Potter's office and was astounded by what he asked her to do. 'The coast, Mr Potter? I've never driven anywhere near a distance like that.'

'I know but really you're the only one I can send,' Mr Potter said. 'You are the best driver and one who can read maps.'

'Yes, but . . .'

'Angela there is a container ship leaving on the afternoon tide and there is room on it for more shells and you know how important those shells are. We have them made but they are doing no good here. They are loading the big truck as we speak.'

'I've never taken the big truck out,' Angela protested. 'Bert always drove that. He'd not like anyone touching his truck, you know that.'

'He hasn't got to like it,' Mr Potter said. 'The fact is, Bert came out of retirement when the war began and he had a heart attack last night. He's not dead, but the doctor has said he is no longer fit for work.'

'Sorry to hear that,' Angela said. 'He was a nice old fellow.'

'He was,' Mr Potter said. 'Still is, but it is too much for him. He often looked strained. His wife is pleased because she's been worried about him for ages. I've been a bit concerned myself just lately. Even if he had been at work today I would have hesitated to send him on such a journey.'

'Oh that would really have set the cat among the pigeons,' Angela said. 'You know how possessive he always was about that truck.'

'I do indeed,' Mr Potter said. 'But it's time now for Bert to take life a little easier and as it is, at the moment there is only you.'

'I think I'd be nervous driving that.'

'It's not that much different to driving the smaller one,' Mr Potter said. 'And a sight safer in the wind today. Now, after you're done, get something to eat in the town before heading back,' Mr Potter went on giving her a ten-shilling note along with the paperwork needed to give access to the docks. 'You might be later back than usual, is that a problem?'

Angela shook her head. 'No. Maggie will call in and tell Mammy if I'm late back.'

'Good,' Mr Potter said. 'And I will be still here whatever time you arrive. I want to see that you are in one piece and make the truck secure for the weekend.'

'Righto.'

'You're all set then,' Mr Potter said. 'The truck should be ready for you now.'

The truck was ready, filled with as many shells as it could carry with tarpaulin sheeting roped on top of it and it looked very big, enormous in fact. 'Are you ready?' Mr Potter asked.

'As ready as I ever will be I suppose,' Angela said as she climbed into the cab. She seemed very high up and that gave her good visibility. The engine growled into life and Angela found it was surprisingly easy to manoeuvre and though she edged her way a little cautiously out of the yard, once on the open road she felt more confident. The sky was just beginning to lighten and she set off at a steady lick for Plymouth was some distance away and if the ship was sailing on the afternoon tide she had to be there in time to have the shells unloaded to catch that tide.

Mr Potter had drawn Angela a very detailed map and she followed it meticulously and found the docks easily. All her paperwork seemed to be in order and she was waved through. She was in a queue of trucks on the same errand and she saw only two of the drivers were men. The queue was moving slowly as they were offloading the shells straight from the trucks to the cargo holds of the ship and Angela was very glad she had made good time, there being many trucks trailing along the road behind her. She was suddenly aware of how stiff she was and as the trucks before her were stationary she got out to stretch her legs. The girl from the truck behind her got out too. 'God,' she said to Angela, 'I'm as stiff as a board.'

'Me too.'

'Come far?'

'Birmingham. What about you?'

'Exeter. You've come a fair distance.'

Angela shrugged. 'They need the shells don't they?'

'Oh I'll say they do,' the girl said. 'After the battle of the Somme I'm surprised they had any left. Did you see the newsreel?'

Angela shook her head. 'Couldn't bring myself to watch it.'

'You got a chap in the forces?'

Angela nodded. 'A husband. He was injured at the Somme, but it wasn't life-threatening. He was one of the lucky ones.'

'He was certainly.'

'How about you?'

The girl shook her head vehemently. 'Not getting involved with anyone till this little lot's over. I have two sisters, my eldest sister's husband was killed and our middle sister's fiancé too. It's not worth the heartache, but I sometimes wonder if there will be anyone left for us when it grinds to a halt. Seems to me the whole world is being stripped of young men. Oh looks like we're moving again.'

The girl was right and Angela climbed back in the truck, but as she moved forward the girl's words reverberated in her head, 'a world stripped of young men'. A whole generation lost. It was a sobering thought.

Angela's truck was unloaded shortly after this and she set off for the town for something to eat. It was a rare occurrence for Angela to eat out, but she avoided anywhere that looked any way posh, for she was in her work clothes, eventually settling for a small cafe where she had fish and chips with two slices of bread and butter and two mugs of very strong tea and felt in great shape for the journey back.

It was slower going home though, because she encountered more traffic as she neared the cities and then had to negotiate her way through them. The dusk deepened as she approached Birmingham and that meant that she had to cut her speed because the lamps were not very effective.

She gave a sigh of relief as the factory loomed before her. Mr Potter must have heard her coming because he had the gates open and she was able to drive straight into the yard, where she stopped, turned the engine off and jumped down with a sigh of relief. 'All right?' Mr Potter asked anxiously.

'Fine, just a bit stiff sitting in one position so long,' Angela said. 'I'm more tired than I imagined I'd be as well.'

'All that concentrating would tire anyone,' Mr Potter said. 'And it has been a long day for you. It's half past seven now.'

'Yes, I'll just take my boiler suit off and get my coat

and be on my way,' Angela said. 'I'll be glad to reach home tonight.'

As she got out of her boiler suit though she heard the jingle of coins in her pocket and so before she left she sought out Mr Potter who had returned to his office. 'These are yours,' she said, placing the coins on the desk. 'The meal was only two shillings.'

'Keep it,' Mr Potter said. 'You earned double that by what you have done today.'

Angela was quite surprised. Mr Potter was not known for gestures like that, though he was usually fair and she hadn't expected extra cash for doing what she had today. It was all part of doing her bit. 'Thank you Mr Potter,' she said. 'It's very generous of you.'

'Not at all my dear, not at all,' Mr Potter said. 'Least I could do. Now do you want me to call a taxi for you?'

Angela had never been in a taxi and she imagined the hoo-hah in the street if she arrived home in one and so she said, 'There's no need, Mr Potter, I only live a step away.'

'If you're sure?'

'Positive,' Angela said. 'I'm just glad the wind has died down. Maggie and I were nearly blown here this morning and I hadn't a great desire to be blown back home again this evening.'

'See you tomorrow then.'

'Yes see you tomorrow,' Angela said and reflected as she walked across the Bull Ring that she would rather Mr Potter had given her the morning off than let her keep the eight shillings change. But he hadn't and that was that and she was sure when she had eaten the meal

Mary would have kept warm for her and had a good sleep she would feel as right as rain.

She alighted from the tram and went up Bristol Passage, only yards from home now, when she suddenly found her way blocked by three soldiers. Even in the dimness of the passage it was apparent that all three were very drunk and she gave a sigh of impatience as she said, 'Can you let me pass please?'

'Oh hoity toity,' said one of the men. 'What if we don't want to?'

Another said, 'What are you doing abroad this time of night anyway?'

'Oh let me pass,' said Angela. 'I'm just coming from work.'

'And what manner of work is it that you do at near eight o'clock at night?' the first man asked.

'You're a street woman aint ya?' the second man said accusingly.

'Don't be ridiculous,' Angela snapped. 'I am a respectable married woman.'

The man nearest to her lifted up her left hand. 'No ring,' he said. 'Who you trying to kid?'

He threw her hand down and it brushed against her coat pocket where she had put the coins Mr Potter told her she could keep and they jingled together. The soldier heard it too and his hand dived into her pocket though she tried to stop him and withdrew the coins with a cry of triumph. 'And these are her earnings for this night's work.'

All of a sudden Angela was blisteringly angry. 'How dare you harass and assault me this way. That money was earned honestly so please return it to me and move

370

out of my way and let me pass. What if I was to scream?'

'I wouldn't suggest you do that, lady,' said the first man. 'See we're professional soldiers and we know how to silence people.'

'Are you threatening me?' Angela asked as a sense of unease flowed through her.

'Take it how you like, but you be nice to us and no one gets hurt,' the first one said. 'All we want is only what you've been doing all night anyway for mugs what pay. We're taking it for free, that's all, cos we don't pay for sex.'

'You've got it all wrong,' Angela protested, but got no further. One of them pulled a dirty hanky out of his pocket and tied it so tight around her mouth it cut into the sides and as she protested, he growled, 'Too much talking, lady. We want action.'

Another tied her hands behind her back with a bit of string and she was dragged struggling into a nearby entry, hearing buttons pop off her coat and the tear of her dress as she fought like a tiger, throwing her head from side to side, kicking out and suddenly the string tying her wrists loosened and she began wriggling one hand free.

The man who had spoken to her initially was the one to take his turn with her first and she felt nausea rise in her, for apart from the shame and degradation, the man stank and his putrid breath smelled of stale beer and cigarettes and possibly rotting teeth and even in the dimness she could see the vivid red scar that ran the length of his creased cheek. And then one hand was free and she attacked him with her nails, scoring deep scratch lines down his face.

371

With a howl of rage he turned her round and pushed her face against the bricks and re-tied her hands so tight the string cut into her skin and she moaned with the pain of it. 'Shut up, you stupid bitch,' the man said. 'I haven't started yet. I warned you, I said to be nice to us and what you did was not nice at all.'

Angela began to tremble as the man grasped her by the shoulders and swung her round, throwing her against the wall, her head hitting it with such force she almost lost consciousness. And before she had time to recover from that he aimed a punch at her face and she felt her nose spurt with blood and the second punch closed one eye completely. She wasn't aware of much after that. Her coat was open because it had lost so many buttons and the man took hold of her dress and ripped it straight down the middle and the petticoat the same and then pulled at her knickers till they fell to the floor. 'Now spread your legs, bitch,' he snarled but Angela seemed incapable of even understanding what he was saying so he kicked them open. 'Oh I'm going to enjoy this,' he cried.

Angela only felt the pain of it though she was drifting in and out of consciousness as one after the other had their way with her. When the last one finished she sank to the ground. She was in agony, her body was on fire and the first man aimed a kick and when his army boot powered into her abdomen she curled into a ball groaning with pain so intense she wanted to die.

She wasn't sure how long she lay there in too much pain and too frightened to move, but she knew she had to move or Mary would be worried enough to send out a search party. Getting up was a major undertaking but after several attempts, eventually, she was on her feet, bent over because of the kick and staggering despite balancing herself on the wall.

Her home was only yards away, but it took a long, long time to get there and she stumbled and nearly lost her footing often. She almost fell through the door and Mary who was tending the fire looked up. Her mouth dropped open. 'Almighty Christ!' she cried, throwing down the poker and darting to Angela who was sagging on the doorstep. 'What in God's name happened to you?' she asked again as she helped her to the settee.

Angela told the astounded Mary what had happened to her when she had nearly reached home and safety and Mary was shocked to the core and said it was a dreadful thing to have happened, absolutely dreadful and she wanted to inform the police, immediately. 'No men should get away with this,' she declared.

'I agree,' Angela said speaking with difficulty because of her smashed nose and a split lip. 'Yet they will, because I don't want to tell the police. It would be all round the neighbourhood in no time at all and what if someone thought Barry should know? Can you imagine how he would feel to hear about me violated like that and him not here to protect me? Don't you think he has enough to deal with without this worry on his mind?'

And the devil of it was that Angela was absolutely right and her abusers would walk the streets to do it again to some other young woman. Mary got a bowl of warm water and began to tend Angela's face. 'We must put it behind us,' she said. 'For if we cannot do that they will have won.'

'Huh, haven't they done that already?'

'No I don't think so,' Mary said. 'They abused your body. Don't let them have your mind as well.'

Angela sighed and said, 'I do see what you're saying and I will do my best, but I can't promise not to be nervous walking home on my own in the dark now, though that has never bothered me before. The best of it is Mr Potter offered me a taxi home and I refused it. I think I'll say a resounding "yes" next time.'

When Mary had done what she could for Angela's face she left her eating a bowl of stew she had warmed up for her and went to tell Maggie that she wouldn't be at work. 'What excuse shall I give?'

'If you can get Maggie on her own, you can tell her the truth,' Angela said.

Mary did get Maggie on her own and she came back to the house with her. She was as appalled as Mary had been when Angela told her the whole tale and quite understood why she didn't want the authorities alerted. 'The point is they have made quite a mess of your face and you will need a few days off till your face is more or less back to normal. You can't come to work like that.'

'What will you say is wrong with me?'

'That you've had a bad fall down the cellar steps,' Maggie said. There was a pause and then Maggie added quietly, 'Angela have you had any thoughts on what you will do if there are consequences?'

'Dear God, don't wish that on me,' Angela cried.

'Dealing with the memory of the whole thing is enough for me just now.'

'Sorry, Angela,' Maggie said. 'You are right. And should the worst happen we will cross that bridge when we come to it.'

TWENTY-FIVE

The following morning when Angela opened her eyes she groaned for her whole face throbbed, and between her legs, which she was to find out had bled, and her stomach felt as if she had been kicked by a mule. When she struggled from her bed she found it difficult to stand up straight. As she stood holding on to the wall for support, waiting for the room to stop spinning, she heard Mary and Connie go past her door on their way downstairs. Connie had moved into the attic to share a bed with her grandmother because Angela had to get up so early, but not today.

Gingerly and very slowly she followed them after a minute or two. When she opened the door into the room it was to see Connie with her warm dressing gown and slippers on sitting up to the table eating a bowl of porridge. Connie hadn't been aware her mother was home because normally she wasn't on Saturday morning so she was pleased to see her but could see there was something wrong. 'Your face,' she said.

'Yes I fell down the cellar steps yesterday,' Angela said.

Connie nodded gravely. She knew all about falls, they happened to her all the time. 'Poor Mammy.'

'Yes indeed poor Mammy,' Mary said. 'And one that should still be in her bed. Here,' she said holding out a bowl of porridge, 'get that down you and I'll make us both a cup of tea and then you get back to bed. And don't even bother protesting,' she said as Angela opened her mouth.

Mary sat down with her own porridge and said, 'When we've finished this me and Connie will get dressed and go shopping like we do every Saturday morning and you sleep if you can, for it's just turned half past seven.'

It was two full hours after Angela's usual time of rising and yet she felt more tired than she'd ever felt in her life and as Mary seemed to have everything in hand she decided to do as she was told for once and returned to bed. It was such a relief to lie down and ease her aching body and she closed her throbbing eyes and when Mary looked in later just before she went shopping Angela was in a deep sleep.

She woke with a shriek and a yell two hours later and this became the pattern over the next few days. Angela was constantly tired, but wary of closing her eyes because memories of the abuse would crowd into her mind. She knew she would be better off back at work with less time to think, but Mary was worried about her emotional health as well as physical and thought a good rest was needed because she wasn't the same girl she'd known and loved all these years.

Angela knew she wasn't the same person and couldn't seem to do anything about lifting her spirits. Anyway her face took time to heal and in the end Angela had the entire week off work. She was glad to return and Mr Potter was very glad to see her and she was busier than ever now Bert was in full retirement.

But as the days passed, from when she opened her eyes in the morning till she closed them at night she was filled with the dreadful thought and fear that one of those monsters who had raped her might have made her pregnant. Mary knew and shared that fear and when eight weeks after the attack there had been no sign of any of the cotton pads soaking in the bucket she mentioned it to Angela one night after she had eaten and Angela said she had had no sign of her monthlies. 'It could be just the shock of it all,' Mary said. 'You know shock can do that sometimes.'

'And what if it isn't shock?' Angela said. 'What if the unthinkable has happened and I am carrying a child, then what the Hell am I going to do?'

Mary shook her head helplessly and then she said resignedly, 'Bring it up I suppose.'

'Bring it up!' Angela repeated. 'Are you mad? I must get rid of it.'

'Ah no!'

'What's the alternative?' Angela said. 'You know the life we'd live here if they knew I was pregnant by someone else, with my husband away fighting. I would be shunned and castigated in public and by association so would you and can you imagine the life the child would have? He or she would be vilified, he or she would be taunted and bullied and guess what, Mammy, and this will shock you, but I shan't care what happens to this child. It will have no love from me because I don't want it and never shall.'

'You may feel differently when it's born.'

'How would I, Mammy?' Angela asked. 'The father of this child is not my beloved Barry, the father of the child I might be carrying is a cruel, beer-sodden rapist. I don't know which one of the those three drunken soldiers is responsible for putting me in this postion, but it doesn't really matter for one was as bad as the other. Yet you want me to love this child, and Barry to return from war and bring up another's bastard? You ask too much, Mammy.'

Mary was in tears as she answered, 'I do my darling girl, but there isn't any other solution.'

Angela decided she needed to see Maggie, she might have some other ideas. However, getting rid of an unwanted pregnancy was not something she could talk about when anyone might overhear because it was illegal to abort a pregnancy. And so on the tram that morning she asked Maggie if she would call round that evening as she had something she needed to ask her.

And Maggie, looking at Angela's face and her anxious eyes, had a good idea what it would be about, but also knew she couldn't speak about it in public, she had to wait until they were alone. And so that evening Maggie sat opposite Angela and Mary and said to Angela quite bluntly, 'I'm telling you straight there is no easy way of stopping a pregnancy once it has begun because it means aborting the baby.'

'Is there anything?'

Maggie nodded and added, 'There are a few back-street abortionists but they are hard to find 'cos asking around is risky and they keep changing addresses to keep ahead of the police. But these places cost and sometimes it doesn't always work and that can mean that the baby is damaged in some way, but I can try and find out if you like.'

'Yes. Yes please.'

'No,' Mary said. 'Thank you, Maggie, but the answer is no.'

Angela shot round annoyed at Mary's interference and Mary said, 'Hear me out, Angela. I don't know where these people are and neither does Maggie and the minute she begins asking questions others would wonder why, because you don't enquire about the whereabouts of a back-street abortionist to take afternoon tea together.

'Then there's the safety element because these people are not qualified. Some know bugger all, others are dirty devils that leave a woman with an infection that means she can never conceive again. I said I know no abortionists and that's true, but over the years I have seen their handiwork enough times and it's not pretty, like the young lass who bled to death, too scared of going to prison to summon an ambulance. You can't put your life at risk in the hands of these butchers for you have Connie to think about.'

'I agree really,' said Maggie.

'Right,' Angela said testily, 'both of you are busy telling me what not to do, so I'm sure you must have a great plan of what I must do instead.'

'Have the baby and put it up for adoption,' Mary suggested.

'And have someone write and tell Barry that I was carrying on with another man and had given birth to his child.'

'Barry would never believe you had found someone else.'

'No, not if he was home he wouldn't, where he saw me every day, but being over there it's different and they have been away a long time, and some women do play away. Barry's mate received a Dear John letter from his sweetheart a few days ago. Barry might well believe malicious gossip and that would destroy me.'

'You could write and tell him first,' Maggie said.

'We thought of that,' Angela said. 'But it would mean telling him about the attack and . . . Well we're told not to worry them unduly.'

'You can see why,' Maggie said.

'Absolutely,' Angela said. 'But it means we're right out of options, not that we had a great bundle of them to start with.'

There was silence for a moment and then Maggie said, 'Can I tell Mammy about you?'

'Why?' Angela said. 'The fewer people that know the better just at the moment.'

'I know, I'll pick my time don't worry. No one else will hear the news, but I have a special reason for Mammy to know about this attack, but I must have your absolute promise you won't tell anyone else what I'm going to tell you.'

'You have it,' Angela said.

'Aye I promise,' Mary said, wondering what secret Maggie was about to reveal.

'This happened to my mother,' Maggie said. 'No one knows, not even my father but she told me I suppose to try and keep me a bit aware. She was in service and raped by the son of the house. He put the blame on to her, said she was gagging for it and . . . well you know the sort of thing?'

Both women nodded and Maggie went on, 'He was believed of course and she was dismissed without a reference and when she went home her mother wouldn't let her in.'

'Didn't she believe her either?' Angela asked, slightly incredulously for she could never envisage a time when Mary would turn her back on her.

'I don't know if she did or she didn't,' Maggie said. 'Maybe she thought it was probably true but couldn't take the stigma, you know?'

Again Mary and Angela nodded. 'What happened?' Angela asked because for poor destitute women there was only the workhouse.

'Auntie Phyllis happened,' Maggie said, 'and she was the sister of Mammy's mother. So Mammy wrote to her Aunt Phyllis telling her what had happened, and Phyllis went to the workhouse and got Mammy out. She looked after her until the baby, a boy, was born and took it to the Sisters of Mercy at the Catholic Orphanage and told the tale of a young, single Catholic girl who had lost her life giving birth. They took the child and Mammy recovered and she went on with her life and no one is any the wiser. Point is, Phyllis is older now and I don't know if she would be up for doing this again, but if she is you could bide with her, moving in just before you begin to show, have the child and put it up for adoption.'

'I think that is the best plan all around,' Mary said.

'So do I if Phyllis is willing to do it, but what about work?'

'You leave that to me,' Mary said. 'Don't give notice or anything and I will tell them you have been called over to Ireland for a family crisis.'

'They know I haven't parents or siblings.'

'But they don't know that you haven't grandparents, or aunts, uncles or cousins,' Mary said. 'Don't worry. I will be deliberately vague, but stress it was unavoidable.'

'I will talk to Mammy tonight,' Maggie promised. 'She will believe what I will tell her, shocked by it I imagine, for she knows you to be a respectable girl from a good family and she'll tell Phyllis that too.'

'Thank you,' Angela said. 'I suppose it's as well to have a plan in place sooner rather than later.'

Phyllis Crabtree (Auntie Phyllis) lived in a fine brick house in Albert Road, Aston, and a fortnight after the talk with Maggie, Phyllis had asked to meet Angela on her own on Sunday afternoon so she could see for herself the type of girl she was.

Angela had felt rather nervous meeting this stranger who could change the course of her life or not, and when she saw the house she was more nervous still, for it had large bay windows overlooking a small garden behind an ornate fence, and a cobbled path and a white scrubbed step led to a good solid wooden door with a half moon of stained glass set in the top of it. Angela nearly turned tail and headed back home but she reminded herself what was at stake and rang the bell.

Phyllis was very friendly though. She was a tall woman, Angela noted, and her brown hair, which was liberally streaked with grey, was caught up in a round bun on top of her head, making her look even taller.

She was very smartly dressed in a navy skirt that reached almost to the floor, just showing soft leather shoes from underneath, and a pink long-sleeved silk blouse fastened at the neck with a cameo brooch.

'Come in do,' she said as she opened the door, 'you're very welcome,' and as she led Angela down the black-and-white-tiled hall she pointed out the parlour and the sitting room before they came to the cloakroom where Phyllis said Angela could leave her coat. As she hung it up Angela thought how wonderful it would be to have a room just to hang coats in. And that wasn't all, for there was another room Phyllis referred to as a breakfast room plus a kitchen Mary would die for.

On the stove in the kitchen a kettle bubbled away and beside it was a tray laid for tea with two cups and saucers, milk and sugar and a plate of delicious-looking cakes. Phyllis poured the boiling water into the teapot and said to Angela, 'Can you bring the tray?'

Nervously Angela lifted it and followed Phyllis as she made for the very finely furnished parlour. 'Put the tray on the small table,' Phyllis said. 'And please take a seat.'

Angela did as she was bid and sat a little tentatively on the cream brocade settee as Phyllis poured tea for the two of them. Angela studied the woman she might spend some time living with. She had quite a long face, with high cheekbones and quite a large mouth, but her eyes were kindly and full of concern. And now those eyes were turned on Angela as Phyllis handed her a cup of tea and said, 'Now tell me about yourself.'

So Angela told Phyllis about growing up in the McClusky household after her entire family were wiped out. She told about the older two boys she considered brothers travelling to America for they could find no work in England.

'They prospered though,' she said. 'And so when Sean and Gerry, the two younger boys were struggling to find work they said to join them in America, but they travelled on the *Titanic* and so drowned at sea. Barry and I no longer felt for each other as brother and sister but as lovers and we decided to marry young to give Barry's mother in particular something to look forward to. Good job we did too,' she went on, 'because Barry's father became very ill shortly afterwards. You see, I'm the daughter he never had and he did so want to walk me down the aisle and he got to do it.'

'What a mercy that you got married when you did then,' Phyllis said. 'Is your husband in the army now?'

Angela nodded. 'And we have a little girl of four who has a nursery place because I do war work, but we also live with my mother-in-law, which isn't difficult as she is the one who brought me up from when I was a baby.'

'Have you been able to tell her what happened to you?'

'Oh yes,' Angela said. 'She saw the state of me when I arrived home. I was attacked you see and the men made quite a mess of my face.'

'I see,' Phyllis said. 'So tell me exactly what happened to get you into this situation?'

'Well,' Angela said, 'usually Maggie, your niece, and I come home from work together, but that day I was asked to take an urgent consignment of shells to the docks.'

'That's some distance,' Phyllis said. 'How did you do that?'

'I drove the lorry.'

'You mean you can drive?'

'Yes and that day it was a big truck too,' Angela said. 'I'd never before driven one as big as that, though I have driven it a lot since. We had an old man used to do the big runs like to the docks, brought out of retirement specially, but he'd had a heart attack the night before and though he didn't die the doctor said he couldn't do it any more.'

'You know,' said Phyllis, 'sorry for butting in, but I have to say that while this war should never have been fought and it is a tragedy that so many young lives have been lost, yet, in another way it has opened up new lives for many young women, like you driving for example. Won't be able to deny us the vote when this little lot is over.'

'I'm not that interested in politics,' Angela said, 'though I know all about the Suffragettes. But I do know what you mean about the war, though personally I would rather have Barry by my side and had never learned to drive, but now I can, I must use that skill to help in any way possible, including driving down to the docks. But that day I was late getting back to the factory and Maggie had gone. The Boss offered to call me a taxi, but I thought the people in the street might take the mickey and think I was getting above myself. Anyway my house was not far from the town and I had made the journey every day for months and wasn't the slightest bit nervous and so stupidly I refused his offer. I was assaulted by three drink-sodden soldiers just yards from my home.'

As Angela began to relate her ordeal, Phyllis felt

enormous sympathy for the young woman for she wasn't just telling the tale, but reliving it again and she heard the shame in her low voice, saw the crimson flush redden her cheeks and watched her face contort as if remembering the pain and her eyes fill with anguish. As the tale drew to a close she was enraged that the brutal thugs who assaulted her so were allowed to walk free to do it to someone else.

The result of this was that Phyllis was very impressed with Angela and was quite prepared to help her. 'I will leave it up to you to decide when to come,' she said. 'Just don't leave it too late.'

'No I won't,' Angela assured Phyllis. 'But with my little girl I wasn't showing until about seven months or so.'

'It may be the case again,' Phyllis said. 'And then it may not be. Every pregnancy is different.'

Angela knew this, but sincerely hoped it was later rather than sooner for when she went to live with Phyllis she would have to leave Connie with Mary for secrecy was everything and four-year-olds weren't that good at keeping secrets. Anyway, she was settled in the nursery and might lose her place if she left and Angela fully intended to return to work when this was all over. It broke her heart to have to leave Connie for so long, though she knew it was the only thing to do.

She blessed the shapeless all-enveloping boiler suit they had to wear that would conceal a number of sins, including an expanding waistline. It also helped that she wasn't with the girls much as she had taken on Bert's driving duties as well so was on her own in one of the trucks most of the time.

Mass at St Catherine's was the point where her pregnancy was in danger of being spotted. Angela would rather have popped along to St Chad's where no one knew her, but that would have been remarked upon and even worse, if Father Brannigan didn't see her at Mass he might come to the house to find out why not and that would never do. So as summer ended and an autumn nip was in the air she took herself off to the Rag Market one Saturday afternoon and came home with a baggy winter coat and a tight corset and every Sunday morning she would lace herself into the corset in an effort to pull in her stomach.

She felt so differently about this pregnancy. She had so looked forward to Connie's birth. She'd longed to see what she looked like and hold her in her arms, but this pregnancy she viewed dispassionately, as an unwelcome intrusion into her life. Even when she felt the baby quicken she couldn't think of it as a human child, but as a bit of rubbish she had to get rid of.

The baby was due mid December and so in mid September Angela wrote to Phyllis and suggested moving in with her on Monday 8th October. Phyllis wrote back by return and said she was looking forward to seeing her again and asked if she could come after dark so the neighbours wouldn't see her arriving.

Angela was just glad she had another evening with Connie and that night she gave her a piggy-back up the stairs and Connie was giggling as she slid off her mother's back on to the bed. She supervised Connie's prayers when she blessed everyone and for a moment Angela considered telling Connie she was going away for a few days. But she knew she would probably be upset and would certainly ask twenty questions and might be difficult to settle and Phyllis was expecting Angela that night and she didn't want to arrive too late. So as she tucked her into bed she gave her a kiss and looked at that dear little face she wouldn't see for some time and she gave a sigh as she said, 'I love you my darling girl.'

Connie sat up in bed and wound her arms around her mother's neck and said, 'Don't be sad, Mammy. I love you too. Lots and lots I do.' She kissed Angela's cheek and then snuggled down in bed looking absolutely angelic.

Angela almost stumbled from the room blinded by tears. Mary knew she would be upset when the time came to leave and she said, 'Don't fret about the child for don't I love the very bones of her? And I will look after her as well as I can.'

'Oh Mary, I know that,' Angela said. 'It's not that that I'm worried about.'

Mary had hold of Angela's hands and was looking directly into her eyes as she said, 'Darling girl, you are doing the only thing you could do that's better for everyone. As for Connie she will undoubtedly miss you, but I am at least familiar and her routine will not be disrupted and the time will soon pass.'

Angela knew that for Connie a week was a long time, but there was nothing else she could have done and she knew it wouldn't help to delay any more. She remembered to take her wedding ring for she would need to wear it at Phyllis's and now she was no longer at work she put the locket around her neck and then she kissed Mary, and stepped out into the night.

*　*　*

Phyllis was really pleased to see Angela and so positive it soothed Angela's soul a great deal and dispelled any lingering doubts she had by her very attitude. She said she had a plan, but didn't elaborate further on what that was until they were sitting down with a cup of tea.

'Now I will have to say something to explain your presence here,' Phyllis said to Angela. 'So from now your name will be Amy Bradley, for Angela is too unusual a name for this area, and you are my niece and also a pregnant war widow. You have come to stay till the baby is born because my house is more suitable than the cramped back-to-back you live in and share with your husband's family, but you intend returning home for Christmas.'

'Goodness you have thought of everything.'

'Yes I have even bought you this to wear to Mass,' Phyllis said and produced a black widow's bonnet from the shopping bag.

The blood drained from Angela's face and she said, 'I . . . I can't wear that. Thank you but no. It's like . . . like.'

'It's like nothing,' Phyllis said sharply. 'You are not bringing bad luck on your husband by wearing a bonnet to make our story more authentic and believable. You explained to me that you were doing this for him too, to prevent any malicious gossip by someone not in possession of all the facts contacting your husband and saying you'd been carrying on with someone and were having your fancy man's baby. That could happen. It's been done many times before. Some people's life's work is to make trouble for others. How much would such

391

news upset him as he goes to face the German machine guns and shells and sniper fire?'

Angela gave a gasp. 'I couldn't endure that,' she cried. 'Oh, it would hurt him tremendously, desperately,' Angela said and she took the bonnet from Phyllis and said, 'Thank you once again and I will wear it. I was being silly.'

Angela had never lived in such luxury. She had a large, comfortable bed all to herself with a matching wardrobe and a chest of drawers and a bathroom just down the corridor and she told herself not to get too used to it because she'd be back in Bell Barn Road before that long.

Phyllis was right too about the widow's bonnet. It evoked compassion from everyone when she wore it to church that first Sunday morning. They gathered around the church door after the Mass. There again Phyllis had her tale ready. 'Only married five minutes,' she said. 'Married quick because of the call-up and he never even knew he was going to be a father when he was killed.'

Many had similar heart-wrenching stories and the women spoke comforting words of empathy and understanding, but though Angela wasn't the only one wearing such a bonnet, she was so young and she played her part so well as the sorrowful widow that none disbelieved her. It was also quite conceivable too that she came to give birth in her aunt's comfortable home. They all knew how cramped the back-to-back houses were at the best of times and hospitals were bursting at the seams with the war wounded.

Angela was always glad to see Maggie who came every Sunday afternoon. She brought all the gossip from the factory and the streets around, news of Mary and Connie, and brought any letters that had arrived and she would wait while Angela wrote replies and in this way convinced Barry that life was going on as it always had done and nothing untoward had happened.

Despite Maggie's visits the days passed slowly but it was December at last with squally wind and snow and bone-chilling cold and the baby's due date, the fifteenth, slipped past with no sign. Phyllis had asked a friend of hers, Sally Metcalfe, who was a retired nurse, and also discreet and non-judgemental, to help at the birth. She had put her in the picture about what had happened to Angela and Sally agreed that in the circumstances adoption was the only answer. She was not a jot concerned that the birth was delayed. 'Babies come when they are ready and that's all there is to it,' she said complacently.

That was all very well, but Angela had wanted to be home for Christmas. It would be hard for her not to be at home to share Christmas Day with her child, and she imagined harder still for her child to understand, and also she thought Mary had held the fort on her own for long enough.

She was in an agony of impatience and then eventually in the early morning of the twenty-first, Angela awoke to water gushing out from her and realized her waters had broken. She felt a leap of excitement knowing that soon the foreign unwelcome baby would be expelled from her and she would be free again and could go home.

At first Angela welcomed every contraction knowing each one was bringing the birth closer and she thought it far too early to wake Phyllis, but was very glad to see her when she did pop her head around the door at half past seven to see how she was. By then Angela was in extreme discomfort and Phyllis went straight down for Sally and her calm presence in the room immediately reassured Angela, though the pains were getting stronger.

Angela found labour progressed much quicker than when she was giving birth to Connie and she soon had the urge to push and Sally had only been there a couple of hours when Angela gave birth to a baby girl, and she gazed at Sally who had caught the child up in her arms as newborn wails filled the air, and felt nothing. When she said this however neither Phyllis nor Sally were shocked. 'I think that's quite understandable after the way you were raped,' Sally said. 'And it's far better that you feel nothing for the wee mite if she's going for adoption.'

Angela sighed. 'I suppose and in the circumstances it's all I can do, but I feel sorry for her, being denied her mother's love.'

'You can't pretend what isn't there,' Phyllis said. 'And why should you feel love for a child conceived in such a savage way? Every time you looked at her, you would be reminded of that ordeal.'

'I know,' Angela said. 'And even if I could learn to love her, I couldn't expect my husband to feel the same. And the neighbours would draw their own conclusions. I didn't report the rape, you see, because I didn't want Barry to know of it, so they would have no idea I was attacked.'

'Don't feel bad about this,' Sally said for she had seen the tears in Angela's eyes and heard the catch in her voice. 'Your baby will be taken by some couple who cannot have children of their own and I'm sure they will love her dearly.'

Angela remembered Stan staying something similar about Betty. At the time she had said she would never give a child of hers away and could never envisage anything that would change that. But here she was, going through with it. And although Stan had relinquished all rights to Daniel, he knew who his son was going to and knew they would love and care for him, whereas she was abandoning her baby to the unknown.

'Why don't you lie down and have a wee rest while the child sleeps,' Sally suggested and though Angela obediently lay down she knew she wouldn't sleep.

But she was more tired than she realized because though she did toss and turn for quite a while eventually her eyes closed. She slept for three whole hours and when she awoke she was hungry but less emotional about the decision made about the baby's future. Both Phyllis and Sally kept the child away from her as much as possible. 'You mustn't feed her,' Sally said. 'We have that all in hand and will feed her from the bottle for the short time we have her, for Phyllis will take her in tomorrow.'

'I would like to send a letter with the baby,' Angela said.

'I don't think it would be appropriate to say what happened to you.'

'No I wouldn't do that,' Angela said. 'I just wanted to tell the child that I love her and though I actually feel nothing for her, that isn't her fault and it might help her a little if I write that I love her, but am unable to care for her properly.'

'I think that's a nice thing to do and it may well be a comfort to her when she's older,' Sally said. 'I'd get that written in plenty of time for Phyllis will take the child early tomorrow morning and have her installed by Christmas.'

'And I can go home.' Angela didn't say it, but that suited her down to the ground.

The next morning, Phyllis set off with the baby wrapped up warm against the winter chill in the basket bought for the purpose. 'You will be all right won't you?' she asked Angela because Sally had returned home.

'I will be perfectly fine,' Angela said. 'But you had better be on your way. Yesterday Sally said something about the children taken to early Mass.'

'Yes,' Phyllis said, 'it would be better to get there before that happens.'

As soon as Phyllis had gone Angela went upstairs and pulled her case from the top of the wardrobe in the room she had been using and began to fill it with all the things she had brought with her all those weeks ago. She hadn't quite finished when she heard Phyllis returning and she went out to greet her and was astounded to find she had brought the baby back with her.

'What happened?'

'They were full,' Phyllis said. 'Chock-a-block they said they were. Apparently with the war and everything, adoptions have dropped off quite a lot and they couldn't squeeze in another child and certainly not a baby at the moment.'

Angela glanced at the baby still slumbering peacefully in the basket and she looked so small and vulnerable and she had a sudden longing to hold her in her arms. She clenched her fists and held her arms stiffly at her sides to prevent herself from doing that and said, 'Did they suggest anywhere else?'

'The only place left,' Phyllis said flatly. 'The workhouse.'

Angela gave a shiver for just the thought of that place struck terror into the hearts of all working-class people. 'What if they are also full?'

'They're never full,' Phyllis said. 'I mean do you ever see any queue of people waiting to go inside?'

'No,' Angela said. 'And the thought of leaving her in an orphanage is bad enough, though I know they do everything they can to find good, Catholic couples to adopt the babies and young children, but some people never come out of the workhouse. It's rare for anyone to adopt a child from the workhouse. I've never heard of it happening. They might on the other hand send a girl of twelve or thirteen into service to labour from dawn to dusk twelve hours or more each and every day. You see the poor scrawny and exhausted young girls at the shops sometimes and they look as if they've never had a decent meal in the whole of their lives. How could I subject this poor little helpless baby to that?'

'Everything you say is right,' Phyllis said. 'The baby stands little chance of being adopted from the workhouse. People have to be on their uppers before they seek help from the parish. Most children in the workhouse are not available for adoption anyway because they are not officially orphans. They are looked after so their mothers can work and not be too much of a drain on the parish coffers. And even though we know this and recognize it is not ideal, we are still not burdened with options or alternatives.'

Angela knew that only too well and she nodded mutely and Phyllis, catching sight of her sorrowful face, felt very sorry for her. 'Look,' she said, 'I must get ready for eleven o'clock Mass. I'll see to the baby first and she should sleep till I'm back.'

Again Angela nodded and watched as Phyllis fed and changed the baby and laid her in the cradle by the fire where she would be nice and warm.

'You should be all right now,' she said as she prepared to leave herself. 'I'll be straight back. And after dinner when Maggie comes she might be able to think of something that hasn't occurred to either of us.' She didn't believe it for a moment, but she wanted to take a little of that intense sadness from Angela's face, let her hope a little longer. Angela grasped that thought like a life-line though, knowing how resourceful Maggie was.

However soon she had more to think about, because Phyllis wouldn't have got right to the end of the road when the baby began fidgeting and making the little mewling noises many babies make before waking up properly.

Angela tried rocking the cradle with her foot, but the baby continued to whimper and then to wail. Angela's breasts began to ache and she felt milk seep from her nipples in response to the baby's distress and this was despite the tight binding cloth Sally had bound round Angela's breasts to give her some ease until the milk had dried up.

Angela had a sudden longing to put the baby to her breast, feel her tug at those swollen nipples and swallow the milk that should have been her birthright. But she resisted the temptation and anyway knew the child could not be hungry for she had just been fed and it must be wind causing her pain, and almost gingerly she picked her up, laid her against her shoulder and began to rock her gently while she rubbed her back.

And as she did so, she felt the shell she'd put around her heart to try and prevent her from loving this child, shatter and break apart and she knew her love for this child, regardless of her conception, was as deep as the love she had for Connie and, had the circumstances been different, she would take her home without hesitation.

However, the circumstances weren't different and privately admitting her love for the baby did not change the situation one bit, except feeling as she did now, it would cause further heartache to walk away from her.

When Phyllis returned from Mass she saw at once that Angela's attitude towards the child had changed. She was still holding her for Angela hadn't wanted to put her down, though any pain she'd had was eased and she had fallen into a deep sleep. Phyllis felt her heart constrict with pity for Angela. She had planned to get the child away to the orphanage before any bond was formed between them like she had done with Maggie's mother all those years ago, but in this case it looked very much as if she was too late. 'Oh, Angela,' she cried. 'You shouldn't have touched her.'

'I had to,' Angela said in her own defence, 'she was crying.'

'And now you feel differently about her?'

'Yes I do,' Angela said. 'And I can't help how I feel, but I know it changes nothing.'

'No,' said Phyllis, 'it doesn't and we can't let it and that's the pity of it.'

When Maggie arrived, she was enchanted by the baby but she was careful not to go overboard, as she would usually, for these were not usual times and the future for the child was very uncertain. She was quite shocked that the orphanage was full and though she thought hard she could come up with no solution but the workhouse. 'The only thing is,' Maggie said, 'I think if you just turn up with the baby in your arms they'd insist on taking you in as well.'

'They couldn't do that,' Angela said. 'Anyway I wouldn't go.'

'I don't think you would have much of a choice,' Phyllis said. 'Maggie is right, they look after the child and put the woman to work to pay for their keep because you are living off the parish.'

Angela glanced from one woman to the other in panic. 'What shall I do then because I can't do that?'

'There is only one thing to be done,' Phyllis said. 'It is a terrible thing to do and I never ever thought I would be advocating it, but in the circumstances it is all I can think of and that is to leave her on the steps of the workhouse.'

Both Angela and Maggie gasped and Angela said in horrified tones, 'What a dreadful thing to even contemplate.'

'Agreed,' said Phyllis. 'Give me an alternative and I will gladly take it.'

Angela could think of nothing, but she did say, 'Are you sure they'd want me to go into that dreadful place as well?'

'They might not if you tell them everything and I mean everything,' Phyllis said. 'And they may not believe you were attacked at all, as you didn't report it to the police. What I'm saying is there would be a hue and cry and there would be no way to keep it secret and it's almost certain one of your neighbours will get to hear of it and then you cannot really protect your husband from hearing about it either.'

'Oh what am I to do?' Angela cried. 'Maggie what would you do if you were me?'

Maggie took a deep breath and said, 'Though it goes against my conscience and tears the heart out of me to say it, I believe to leave her on the workhouse steps is the only thing to do.'

Phyllis gave a gasp at the anguish in Angela's beautiful eyes. There were tear trails on her face too and Angela felt as if her heart was breaking as she said in a voice husky with distress, 'That's what must be done then.'

'Not you,' Phyllis said. 'If you're sure, I will take her.'

'No,' Angela said. 'I will take her.'

'You are not fit,' Phyllis protested. 'You are just days from giving birth. By rights you should still be in your bed, never mind gallivanting all over the place.'

'If this heinous thing has to be done, it must be me that does it,' Angela said. 'She is my daughter and this is the last service I can do for her. I will be able for it, don't worry.'

There was nothing further Phyllis could say, but she thought Angela looked very white and strained. She owned that the worry about what would happen to the child would undoubtedly have contributed to that strain and yet still Phyllis thought that she was doing too much and too soon.

She knew Angela wanted to be back home as soon as possible for the sake of the young daughter she had been separated from for many weeks. She could quite understand her impatience to be back with her, especially as the child was only four and a firm believer in the powers of Santa, and when Maggie had asked her what she wanted Santa to bring her she said she was going to ask Santa to bring her Mammy back home, that was all she wanted.

Such earnest and heartfelt words from such a young child brought tears to Phyllis's eyes and Angela had been broken up completely, so Phyllis knew, come what may, Angela intended to make it home by Christmas Day.

'It's how to do it bothers me,' Maggie said.

'What d'you mean?'

'Well you can't just walk up to the main gates if you're trying to get in unseen. Chances are they'd be locked anyway and there's a high wall around the rest of it.'

'Then how am I going to do it?'

'It's a problem all right,' said Phyllis. 'They have very high walls at the front, but maybe they are not as high all around. Only thing to do is reccy in daylight. I'll go into the town tomorrow and take a look.'

'Tomorrow is Christmas Eve,' Angela said quietly.

'I know.'

'Well what if I can't find a way in tomorrow?'

'Angela, let's cross that bridge when we come to it,' Phyllis advised. 'And in the meantime, pray hard tonight before you sleep.'

TWENTY-SIX

Phyllis was in a more positive mood when she arrived home from town the following morning. She was a little disconcerted though to see the baby in Angela's arms, especially as she had said to Angela before she went that she had already changed her and given her a bottle of milk as well.

'Angela,' Phyllis said warningly, 'you are only making it harder for yourself.'

Angela tossed her head and said, 'D'you know, I don't much care how hard it is for me, because I deserve it to be hard. I can see from your face you have good news as regards getting into the workhouse grounds so these memories will have to last a lifetime.'

'Oh Angela, I feel sorry for you and I wish there was a better outcome for both you and the child, but it isn't your fault.'

'Up until now it hasn't been my fault, I agree,' Angela said. 'But getting rid of my child will be my fault, because it will be my decision and it's wrong and quite possibly a sin.'

'And the alternative is?'

'That's the devil of it, Phyllis,' Angela admitted. 'There isn't one, but I'll never forgive myself for what I am forced to do this night, not till the end of my days.' She glanced at Phyllis and said, 'You've found a way in haven't you?'

Phyllis nodded. 'In Whittal Street,' she said, 'the road that runs alongside the workhouse down to St Chad's.' Angela nodded and Phyllis went on, 'Part of the way down that road there's an entry and at the bottom of the entry is a gate. It was fastened in some way though I couldn't take too much of a look at it in case I was spotted. But even if you couldn't open it, you could climb over it and lift the basket over because it isn't a big gate. From what I could see it leads on to the place where a load of bins are stored at the side of the house. If you go after dark, and that's four o'clock these winter days, you should get in without being seen. It's important that you get away as soon as the door is opened because they might search for you and might work out how you got in, so get out as soon as you can and make for St Chad's, for it's unlikely that they'll think of you making for a church, so you'll probably be safe there. And if there is a hue and cry, and there might well be, wait until it has died down before you make your way home.'

Angela knew that Phyllis spoke sense. The workhouse, she imagined, would take a very dim view of people dumping children on their steps and if she lingered in the yard and they gave chase she could be caught and that would never do.

Never had a day seemed to drag like that one and while one part of her wanted to get the dreadful thing she had to do over and done with, another part of her wanted to hold back time, for after that day she would never again see the child she had given birth to, who was already entwined into her heart.

Eventually the sky began to darken and Angela gave the last bottle she would ever give to the child and then changed her. They had planned this with care for the December day was raw. The basket was padded out with a soft, woollen blanket and she was dressed in a little vest and a winceyette nightdress and a thick woollen matinee jacket. She had bootees on her feet and mittens on her hands and a bonnet covering the black down on her head. More blankets covered her and Phyllis had even cut a piece of thin rubber that she had bought at the Bull Ring to go on top because she said, 'Even if it isn't actually raining the nights could very damp.'

Then Angela was ready in the hall with her small case in one hand and the basket with its precious load in the other. She was very pale and her stomach growled for she hadn't been able to eat all day through nerves and she was feeling light-headed. But when Phyllis said, 'Are you sure you are well enough to do this?' she answered her heartily enough, that she was.

And then she said to Phyllis, 'There are no words to thank you enough for what you have done for me. I don't know what I would have done if you hadn't agreed to help me. I know the outcome would have been totally different.'

Phyllis shrugged. 'You have been dealt one bad hand in life and yours might have been ruined, though you had done nothing wrong. So bless you my dear. Let's hope and pray your young man comes home safe from this unholy war and you are able to settle down in peace and raise your daughter.'

'Oh, yes,' Angela cried. 'Please God.'

'Please God indeed,' Phyllis said and though she wasn't a demonstrative woman generally, she put her arms around Angela and held her tight for a few moments. She knew she would miss Angela because she was good company and she was glad she had been able to help her and she said, 'I do hope it goes all right for you this evening. Will you let me know?'

'Of course,' Angela said. 'I intended doing that anyway. I'm not going straight back to work. I want to spend a few days with Connie and Mary.'

'I should think you won't be rushing back to work,' Phyllis said. 'You have just had a baby. You should be resting.'

'Well it's true, not much rest is to be had in a munition works,' Angela said. 'So I'm having a break, so I'll come up and see you the day after Boxing Day. Connie's nursery opens then and we'll be able to talk more freely.'

'Oh I shall look forward to that.'

Suddenly at the door, Angela leant forward and kissed Phyllis's cheek. Phyllis gave a little gasp and put a hand to her cheek which was reddening into a blush. Angela went into the night carrying a case in one hand and the basket over the other arm. She knew both would get heavier with every step she took, but she couldn't risk taking a tram for no one must see her abroad with a newborn baby on a bleak December night.

If there was a bit of commotion about a child left on the workhouse steps and made the news, they might put two and two together.

She continued to put one foot before the other while her aching arms began to throb with pain. She was taking the side roads to avoid meeting people and they were not that well lit, but now and again she would pass a hissing gaslight and the pool of light showed her the sleeping baby and her heart would constrict with love for the child she had to give away. She was immensely relieved that she didn't have to go far because the workhouse was this side of town.

It was on a road called Steelhouse Lane, the road named because of the large police station across the road from the workhouse and Angela imagined there would be few people about in that area at night.

She was right, there wasn't a soul about. She passed the front of the workhouse and thought what a grim and forbidding building it was. It was large with many floors, built of pale brick but looking dark, unwelcoming.

A high brick wall surrounded it apart from the firmly locked gates in the centre which led to a short gravel path and then three steps to the heavy solid studded door. It almost broke Angela's heart to think of her daughter spending her first Christmas in that miserable place, especially as she knew it was just one of many Christmases she would spend there.

Angela averted her eyes from the edifice and made her way to Whittal Street which ran down to the right side of the workhouse. At the end of that short road was St Chad's, which was Birmingham's Roman

Catholic Cathedral, where she might run for sanctuary if she was pursued. The nearer she got to the place where she must relinquish her child the worse Angela felt. Her whole body felt heavy and cumbersome and there was an agonising pain in her heart and it was only the thought of soon seeing Connie that sustained her.

She found the entry easily enough, but it was like a big black hole for there was no light at all and the darkness was intense. But she couldn't dither on the pavement and so she went in, shuffling along uneven cobbles cautiously, hearing her heart thumping in her breast and her mouth suddenly so dry she had trouble swallowing.

When she came to the gate she laid down the case in order to have one hand free to feel all over the gate and try and work out how it was fastened and eventually on the other side of the gate she felt bolts, one at the top and one further down and they didn't seem to be held fast in any way, but they were stiff.

She put the basket on the ground beside her and tried to ease the first bolt out slowly, worried that it might suddenly shoot out with a bang if she was too firm, or open with a penetrating screech.

And then the baby began to whimper. She had slumbered beautifully while she had been carried, but now she was registering her discontent.

It was the very worst time for her to cry, or make any noise at all, and Angela had slid open the first bolt, and as she reached for the second the baby's whimpers became louder, and she threw caution to the wind and drew the bolt free with haste. The gate opened without a creak of any sort and as soon as she picked up the basket again the baby stopped crying.

The way was open for Angela to do what she had come to do and yet suddenly she couldn't move, it was as if she was rooted to the spot.

She couldn't do it, she decided. It was inhuman to expect her to put the child she had just given birth to on the steps of that vile-looking place and never ever know what happened to her. It was too cruel to ask a mother to do that and hot scalding tears fell from her eyes at the thought of it.

And even while the tears rained down her face she thought of the practicalities of keeping the child, as she had done before. She thought she could just about stand the condemnation and disdain she knew would be shown by many of the neighbours if she brought home a newborn baby when her husband had been away two years.

It would be harder to bear if their contempt impinged on Mary and even little Connie as she knew it might well. But how could she risk word getting to Barry and what if he was so upset he failed to keep his wits about him and was killed because of it? Could she ever live with herself if that happened? She knew she couldn't.

And how would they live if she couldn't work? Mary wasn't up to the care of a newborn baby and the nursery only took children from six months and might not take her at all if they knew the circumstances of her birth. In fact Connie might lose her place too. That would be disastrous for them all for the savings she had accrued wouldn't last for ever. And what would happen when

Barry came home and said he wasn't prepared to care for a child forced on his wife in that violent way. He might even think the child had bad blood.

She couldn't blame Barry for feeling that way if he did, nor could she disobey him and so she would lose the child anyway, which would upset them both more than if she left her now.

She faced the fact that that small child's life was going to be sacrificed for the good of everyone else and that thought was hard to bear. If only she had something to give her to show how much she was loved. The letter was stowed in the basket where it would be found, but she would have liked to have given her something of her own, something she valued. And then she remembered the locket, her most treasured possession.

It should have gone to Connie on her wedding day, but all her life she would have the love of a mother and this little mite would have nothing. She took the locket from around her neck and eased one of the baby's hands from the covers and took off the mitten. When she touched the baby's palm with the locket her little fingers folded over it and Angela replaced the mitten and put the little hand under the covers again.

She went through the gate for it was no good delaying this any longer and she crossed the small yard and walked against the wall so she wouldn't be seen by anyone looking out of the windows, which was highly unlikely because the yard was as dark as the entry. When she reached the corner of the house she peeped around furtively to check there was no one about and then before she could lose her nerve altogether she placed the basket on the top step, pulled the bell rope on the wall and heard it jangle in the house.

They took a long time to answer the door and Angela was getting so chilled, her teeth had begun to chatter. And yet she kept her eyes focused on that door and when it began to open, she was off like a hare. The person who had opened the door gave a bellow, probably on realizing that there was a baby in the basket, and as Angela raced across the yard she heard the sound of many boots pounding through the house towards the door.

Then she was in the entry, showing no caution now nor panic, remembering to pick up her case, and with it bumping against the side of her legs, she was out and tearing down Whittal Street towards St Chad's.

She barely took time to get her breath back in the porch, but in the church she saw there were a good few people praying already and lighting candles and so she made sure to dip her hand in the font as she entered the church and genuflect before the altar because people would think it odd if she didn't. She didn't skulk at the back of the church either, but made her way into the main body of the church and entered a pew beside two other women for she thought that was safer if she was pursued. She stowed her case under the pew and she knelt with head in her hands and tried to still her pounding heart as she prayed for the child she had just abandoned and Barry and Stan and all the fighting soldiers and their families.

Phyllis had said that even if she were chased they wouldn't think of St Chad's and she would be safe in there. But people did come from the House looking for her. She heard the commotion at the back of the church and though many looked round, she kept her eyes firmly on the altar. The priest was a man called John Hennessy who people said was a kindly soul. He had not seen Angela come in but he had attended Catholics at the House and it always upset him to see how many were treated, especially the ones they called fallen women. A fair few were mere girls and forced into the sex that resulted in a child. So he had little time for those working at the House and he frowned as he asked the two men what they wanted.

They said they were looking for a girl who had left a baby on the workhouse steps and run away.

'And did you see her come in here?'

'Well, no, Father. Not exactly,' one of the men said. 'Fact is we don't know where she went. She like disappeared into thin air. We thought we'd try here on the off chance.'

'Well as you can see,' the priest said, 'there are no runaway girls here, just respectable men and women saying a few prayers before the greatest event in the Christian Calendar, the birth of our Lord Jesus Christ and I'm sure they do not welcome this intrusion.'

The priest said this with such authority that the men from the House were apologetic. 'Sorry, Father.'

'Yes, well, I suggest you look for that unfortunate young woman some other place for she is not here.'

They went on their way and Angela breathed a sigh of relief and Father Hennessy made a mental note to pray for the poor girl they were searching for. She must have been desperate altogether to leave her baby in the indifferent care of the workhouse and he was sorry for her, whoever she was.

Angela had the urge to leap up and follow the men out but she controlled that urge and waited till half an hour had passed and then she set off for the Bull Ring and home.

Anxious now to be home as soon as possible, she took a tram along Bristol Street. As she alighted and went up Bristol Passage she gave a shudder remembering her ordeal at the hands of three drunken soldiers who weren't worthy to wear their uniform. She had never walked this way in the dark and alone since that night because she was usually with Maggie and if she had to work late, she took up Mr Potter's offer of a taxi home. It always caused a bit of a stir in the street but better that, Angela thought, than risk being violated.

She mustn't think of it again, she told herself firmly. All sad thoughts must be shelved. She hadn't seen Connie for two long months and the last thing the child wanted was a Mammy with a doleful face, especially with it being Christmas Eve too.

Maggie had told Mary Angela was making for home Christmas Eve if everything went to plan and so Mary was half expecting her, but said nothing to Connie just in case she didn't make it.

Angela opened the door with a smile nailed to her face to see Mary and Connie at the table eating a meal. She set the case down as Connie turned her head. When she saw her mother framed in the doorway, her mouth dropped open and the blood drained from her face.

Angela shut the door with her foot and said, 'Hello Connie.'

Her words seemed to galvanize the child, who leapt from her chair into her mother's waiting arms, and then she burrowed her face into her mother's neck and burst into tears.

TWENTY-SEVEN

Connie had longed for her mother's return and asked Santa to bring her home for Christmas, and he had, and she was very happy about it. But, the Mammy who came home was not the same as the one who left. She looked the same and sounded the same, more or less, but . . .

Connie hadn't the words to say to show how she felt and she didn't understand the innate sadness and guilt that clung to her mother. However she knew something wasn't quite right and that unnerved her and so she didn't want to let her mother out of her sight. So when she learned her mother didn't intend going straight back to work after Christmas, she refused to go back to the nursery when it opened the day after Boxing Day.

Angela didn't mind spending some time with the child she had missed so much but when she refused to go to nursery she thought she might leave her with Mary while she returned to Phyllis's to tell her how things had gone. However, Connie became so distressed when she suggested this, she knew she had to take her. 'You

417

must come too, Mammy,' she said to Mary as they washed up the breakfast things. 'You know Connie has ears on her like a donkey and there are things to be said that I definitely don't want her to hear.'

Mary could quite see that and anyway she had a great desire herself to see this lady who had looked after Angela so well when they had no idea where to turn and thought all was lost.

Phyllis was delighted to see them and be introduced to Mary whom Angela had always spoken of so warmly and she had a special smile for Connie. 'Did Santa come and bring you nice things?' she asked.

Connie nodded, thinking of the paint box and a pad with lots of paper to paint on, a beautiful white teddy from one uncle and soft leather boots from the other and a jigsaw from her Auntie Maggie.

'And what was your favourite present?' Phyllis asked.

'Mammy,' Connie said without hesitation and then went on, 'I asked Santa to bring her and he did, before the other presents because she's special.'

Angela felt a lump form in her thoat as she realized Connie was deadly serious. She had no idea that was what she thought but Phyllis didn't turn a hair. She just nodded sagely and said, 'That must have been the way of it all right.'

'Yes,' Connie agreed happily.

'And do you think you could eat some biscuits with a glass of milk?'

Connie decided she liked this lady, whoever she was, and she nodded her head eagerly. 'Yes please.'

'I have the kettle on for us too,' Phyllis said. 'It won't take me a jiffy.'

'And I have some Christmas cake and a few mince pies,' Mary said.

'Oh we'll have ourselves a little feast,' Phyllis said as she got to her feet.

'I'll give you a hand,' Angela said and immediately Connie slid off the seat beside her. 'I'm only going as far as the kitchen. Stay here and I'll be back in a moment.'

Connie had her mutinous face on and for a moment Angela thought she was going to argue with her. Mary knew that too and said, 'Bold girls who don't do as they're told don't deserve milk and biscuits in my book.'

Connie looked at her Granny who could be stern when she chose and she decided to not risk her getting angry and so she sat back down on the chair.

'You see how she is,' Angela said to Phyllis as she reached the relative safety of the kitchen.

'I see a very unhappy girl,' Phyllis said.

'She won't let me out of her sight,' Angela said. 'When she realized I wasn't going to work straight away she refused to go to nursery and then when I suggested coming here without her she got really upset. I had to bring her.'

'Of course you did,' Phyllis said. 'She is a confused girl at present and there is a shadow behind her eyes and that's distrust. She loves you very much and she doesn't want you to disappear again. You must be very gentle with her. Shall we go back now? I think we have it all organized.'

As Angela followed Phyllis down the corridor she thought that though she had had no children herself she had seen straight away what ailed Connie. And she was so right, making Angela feel ashamed that her actions had caused Connie's unhappiness.

When Phyllis handed Connie the plate with the biscuits on she looked at her mother straight away because there were four of the most delicious-looking biscuits on that plate. They didn't have that many biscuits and even then she was never allowed four straight off. Mammy always said that was greedy, but she didn't seem to see and so Connie polished them off quickly in case she should suddenly take notice.

They tasted as good as they looked and she sighed in contentment and took a gulp of milk before saying to Phyllis, 'Did Santa come to you?'

'Sadly no,' Phyllis said with a smile. 'It wasn't that I was a naughty girl or anything, Santa just doesn't come to adults.'

Connie looked a little sad about that and so Phyllis said, 'I have got toys here in my house, just in case I might want to play with them.'

Connie wrinkled her forehead. She didn't think adults played with toys but this lady might for all she knew so she just said, 'Where?'

Phyllis said, 'They're right here in the cupboard.' Then she went on to ask Connie, 'You know Maggie don't you?'

'Auntie Maggie,' Connie confirmed.

'Well she has lots of young brothers and when they were small they would come for a visit and they would get very loud and unruly if they got bored.'

Connie didn't know the word unruly, but she knew the word loud very well, especially when referring to boys. There were plenty of loud boys at her nursery and they didn't have to be bored or anything, it was just the way they were and so she nodded and said, 'I know.'

'So I bought some toys and stored them in this cupboard by the fireplace. There's a Noah's Ark they seemed to play with a lot and a spinning top they all liked. There's a box of lead soldiers somewhere and some books. Would you like to play with them now?'

'Ooh yes please.'

Phyllis opened the cupboard and Connie dived happily into it pulling out one thing after the other. She thought it an unexpected treasure trove for toys weren't that plentiful in her house either. Mary took the seat nearby and Angela and Phyllis sat on the other side of the room so that as long as they kept their voices low they could talk with ease and Angela told Phyllis how dreadful she felt about actually leaving her child on the steps of the workhouse. 'I gave her my locket,' she said quietly.

Mary's head shot up at that, though they were speaking quietly, and she walked across to Angela. 'I thought that was going to be given to her ladyship,' she almost hissed indicating the child playing on the floor.

Angela sensed that Mary wasn't happy with her doing that. She understood, for the locket was given into her keeping by her mother, and she would want it to go to Barry's child and she attempted to explain: 'Mammy, through all her growing up Connie will have every ounce of my devotion and attention. I love her far far more than words can say and she is special, because she is part of Barry.

'But the child I gave birth to is still my daughter however she was conceived. She is a child I can never

421

acknowledge and even worse than that, I will never see her again nor know what happens to her, but I am certain she will have a miserable childhood in that place. I wanted to show her that somewhere there was once a mother who loved her and I had nothing to show that but the locket. It was the only thing of value I ever owned and it seemed right I give it to her. It is the only part of me she will ever have.'

Phyllis took Angela's trembling hands. She seemed unaware of the tears coursing down her face and said, 'I fully understand why you gave the little one the locket, but can you be traced by it?' She knew that if they could find out who she was by the locket, she might be in trouble and Phyllis too, for she was sure it was a crime to abandon a child.

It was Mary who answered because she had followed Phyllis's train of thought, but Angela was struggling to control her emotions before the eagle-eyed Connie noticed her mother was upset. 'No,' she assured Phyllis. 'All the locket contains is a miniature of Angela's parents on their wedding day and the other side held two or three of the many white-gold ringlets Angela had as a young child. There is no writing anywhere, not even dates. And Angela,' she went on, turning to face the girl, 'I spoke out of turn. This I know was hardest thing you have ever had to do and I understand the dilemma you were in and you were right to give the child the locket. In that place it's probably the only thing she'll ever own.'

'I know it was very hard for Angela too,' Phyllis said. 'Believe me, if there had been any alternative we would have taken it.'

'I know you would,' Mary said. 'I'm not criticizing you in any way. I think the whole thing is unbelievably tragic and I can only thank you again for what you have done for Angela.'

When they were leaving shortly afterwards Phyllis said, 'If you will be able to carry it you could take the ark home if you like. Connie was very taken with it.'

'Oh I couldn't.'

''Course you could,' Phyllis said firmly.

Angela shook her head, 'No, it's made of wood and painted and everything. It must have been very expensive.'

Phyllis shrugged. 'I really can't remember. I bought it years ago and it isn't as if it's new. It's been well played with over the years. Look,' she went on as Angela still hesitated, 'I don't have small visitors any more. Maggie's brothers are all grown up. And it's unlikely you and I will ever see each other again, for how would the friendship be explained? You were supposed to be my war-widowed pregnant niece. This is the end of the road for us so let your daughter have this as a sort of late Christmas present. I would like to think of her playing with it.'

Angela could no longer refuse, she was too choked up because she knew that Phyllis was right, they would never see each other again and she realized the sacrifice she made for a perfect stranger. It was different for Maggie's mother because she was Phyllis's niece and part of their family.

It was hard for both of them to say a final goodbye because they had become close, but she had to face the truth that Phyllis was someone she had needed at a certain point in her life, but now that period was over and she had to go back to her old life and Phyllis had to do the same.

With the ark packed away in various bags Phyllis had pressed on them, and Connie in a state of extreme excitement at being allowed to take the ark home with them, it was hard to hold back the tears as Phyllis and Angela hugged for the last time. But it had to be done and as they set off down the road, Angela wiped her eyes surreptitiously lest Connie see that she had been crying.

'You all right?' Mary asked.

Angela nodded. 'Have to be I suppose.'

'And that's the truth right enough,' Mary said. 'Mind you I am surprised you wanted to come home after living in that house for a couple of months with all mod cons.'

'Home is where the heart is, you know that,' Angela said. 'My heart is with you and Connie and Barry in the back-to-back we all live in.'

That night Connie played up about going to bed in the attic on her own. She had always been so good before, but now she said she was frightened. She couldn't explain why she was frightened but Angela, catching sight of her child's ravaged panic-stricken face, knew she was gripped by a real and genuine fear that if she went to bed her mother might disappear again. It tore at Angela's heart strings because it was her fault. She shouldn't have sneaked away without a word to Phyllis's after Connie had gone to bed at night. She should have tried to explain to her.

Realising this, she was gentle and understanding with

424

Connie who ended up sharing her mother's bed. 'There was nothing else I could do,' she said to Mary when Connie had eventually settled down for the night. 'All this all stems from disappearing without a word and then staying away for over two months. That's half a lifetime for a child.'

'This whole business has certainly upset her,' Mary agreed. 'I have never known her like this.'

'I'll have to regain her trust,' Angela said. 'All the time I was away, though I missed Connie, I never knew what it was doing to her. All my energies were on the child I would be abandoning, because you were right, I couldn't help myself, I did learn to love the child after the birth and of course it was even harder to leave her then, unbearably hard. But I can't help her now and so must put any worries about her out of my mind as much as I can and concentrate on Connie, who I can do something about, and do all I can to help her recover her love and trust in me. Connie is my first priority and I owe it to her to be the best mother I can be.'

Angela tried to do that in the next few days as she allowed herself to really recover from the birth and she spent that time with Connie. The weather wasn't kind to them but Connie just enjoyed being with her mother. Despite what she had said to Mary, though, thoughts of the child she had left behind did creep into her mind more often than she would have liked, but she pushed them away and didn't let them spoil her times with her young daughter.

Those thoughts did return at night, very often invading her sleep, and left her lying awake worrying that leaving the child in the way she had done was a sin. She knew she would never be able to admit what she had done to a priest, not even in the partial anonymity of the confessional box. That meant she had done no penance of any sort nor received absolution and she shouldn't receive communion with such a sin staining her soul, but if she didn't go people would think it odd and might even remark on it.

This bothered her so much at the first Sunday home that she prayed more devoutly at Mass than she had done in a long time. She said how sorry she was for what she had been forced to do and asked God to show her some sacrifice she could make in atonement for what she had done. There was no blinding flash of light, nor did God's angry thunderous voice re-echo in her head, but she was confident that he would show her some way that she could make it up to Him without involving the priests at all.

Despite the fact that Maggie had said that Mr Potter would welcome her back with open arms, Angela hadn't been convinced and wrote to him after they returned from seeing Phyllis and he wrote by return saying he was looking forward to seeing her again and suggesting her starting the following Monday.

TWENTY-EIGHT

Mr Potter was pleased to see Angela again and told her as soon as she was changed to go down to the delivery yard. Angela had thought that someone else would have taken on the driving in her absence and she would be back in the factory, but Sylvia, the woman who had covered for her, was quite willing to relinquish the role back to Angela. 'I don't really like driving,' she said. 'I learnt to drive because I thought I should, but I don't enjoy it and some of those trucks are heavy and difficult to manoeuvre, so I'm glad you're back. I will be better in the factory.'

Angela was sorry Sylvia felt that way, but very glad to get her old job back. She just loved the freedom of the open road.

However when she arrived home she found a letter had arrived from a solicitor to discuss 'matters to her advantage'.

'I wonder what it's all about,' Angela said. 'I've never had anything to do with a solicitor. Anyway there is no way I can take time from work after just having three months away. I'll have to write and say so.'

427

Towards the second week in January the Bank Manager, Mr Higgins, called to see Angela one evening and said that in view of the vital work Angela was engaged in he would open the bank the following Saturday afternoon so that she could view her inheritance and give instructions as to what to do with it.

'There must be some mistake,' Angela said. 'I have no inheritance.'

'This is from Mr Maitland's estate,' Mr Higgins said. 'He left you some jewellery that had belonged to his mother.'

'Jewellery?'

'Yes indeed,' Mr Higgins said. 'Some nice pieces amongst them. And I apologize for the delay in contacting you. These were not part of the will he left with Geoff Rogers and Co. but some private arrangement between him and Geoff Rogers. It's all legal and above board and they were lodged in the bank for safety's sake. Apparently he was adamant his wife should not have any knowledge of them.

'I didn't know George had died, nor that just days later Geoff Rogers heard of the death of three of his four sons, and that the surviving son was critically injured in a hospital on the South Coast, and he went to see him and completely forgot about the jewellery until he returned, which is when I contacted you.'

Angela remembered how Mary and Matt had suffered over the death of two of their sons and could quite understand the man's distraction. She said this to the bank manager and went on to say, 'I didn't know anything about this, nor was I expecting anything.'

'I believe he thought a lot of you.'

'I thought the world of him,' Angela said sincerely. 'He was a lovely and kind man, but I only helped him in the shop and never in the world would I have expected him to leave me anything. I am just so sorry he is dead.'

'If you come to the bank on Saturday afternoon you can see the items for yourself,' said Mr Higgins.

'Yes I will be there,' Angela said. 'Thank you making special arrangements for me.'

She went with Mary as Maggie offered to look after Connie and she was nervous and bewildered and so was Mary. Angela had never been into a bank before, the same as most working-class people in those days. Banks were not for the likes of them. If they should manage to save anything at all, a very rare occurrence with a great many, money went into a box under the bed or sometimes the Post Office.

Knowing how awkward she was probably feeling, Mr Higgins was kindness itself to both women and Angela was grateful for his understanding and then was overcome with the kindness and generosity of George when she saw the array of beautiful things that now belonged to her: a pendant on a gold chain, a pearl necklace and a diamond one, an array of bracelets and brooches and a diamond ring. Angela was completely overawed and knew that never in a million years would she have an occasion to wear any of it and she said, 'Mr Higgins, I know nothing about jewellery, but is any of this valuable?'

'Oh yes, there are some lovely pieces here,' Mr Higgins said. 'But I couldn't give an accurate value, not being a jeweller. That could be arranged though?'

'That won't be necessary yet,' Angela said. 'For now

I want everything to stay in the bank where it's safe. I don't want to make any decisions until I can speak to my husband and I won't see him until this blessed war is over.'

But she already knew what she wanted to talk to Barry about and that was selling some of the pieces to fund a secondary education for Connie and the rest of the pieces would be given to her on her wedding day in place of the locket.

'As you wish,' Higgins said. 'It is no problem to us to store them for you.'

And so life continued as it always had. Connie got over her fear that her mother might disappear again and returned to the nursery, but not for much longer because she would be starting at St Catherine's School after Easter and Angela was glad because Connie was outgrowing the nursery. Barry wrote that he could scarce believe that the toddler he left behind would soon be at school and it brought it home to him more forcibly how much of her childhood he was missing.

However, just before Easter the Germans launched a Spring Offensive. Angela couldn't believe it. After an icy, blustery winter, she had been looking forward to spring, when the sun might warm her body and heal her soul because she still felt a little battered and bruised. Added to that she was war weary, everyone was war weary and looking forward to a lessening of hostilities and now the Germans seemed to be starting again. So many had already died and the fields of France ran with blood. But the soldiers were tired, both Stan and Barry had mentioned it, and now they must raise their game to counter the German advance. Angela prayed, imploring God to keep her husband safe a little longer.

The German assault began on 21st March and it was called St Michael's Offensive. 'Funny nation the Germans,' Angela remarked when she read this in the papers they scrutinized every evening. 'Fancy calling an Offensive after a Saint.'

'Does seem odd,' Mary said. 'And yet a woman I met shopping was telling me that it's a very Catholic country.'

'Germany is?'

'That's what she said.'

'I never thought that of Germany,' Angela said. 'France certainly, but not Germany.'

'No I have to admit I don't know much about these people our boys are fighting. But this woman seemed to know a lot and she says that the Kaiser is pinning great hope on this new offensive. He's looking for a speedy end to the war, with Germany the victors.'

'Surely she shouldn't be talking that way?'

'Maybe not, but there was only the two of us in the shop,' Mary said, 'and she didn't say that's what she wanted. She had two sons and both enlisted. The eldest was killed last year and she worries greatly for the other one.'

'Oh I bet,' Angela said. 'I worry about Barry as soon as I open my eyes in the morning and when I sleep I dream about him.'

'I know,' Mary said, 'and yet there's no saying Barry is even involved in this.'

'That's true,' Angela said. 'But he must be involved

in something for no letters have come this week, nor from Stan either.'

'Yes,' Mary said. 'But that has happened before.'

It had and the first time there had been no letters Angela had been a nervous wreck and then, three weeks later, a bunch of letters came together. She accepted the fact that if Barry was actually fighting, he would have little time and less inclination to write her an epistle. And even letters written might be difficult to post, but letters were literally her lifeline, letting her know her beloved Barry was alive and well.

'And,' said Angela, 'if that woman you met shopping is even a bit right they may need every man jack over there deployed to fight this Offensive for it's inconceivable that Germany might win. Too many of our boys' bodies litter the fields of France, or arrive home maimed and damaged, to let the Germans win now, or they will have given their lives in vain. If this is the final push they need to give it all we have to repel the German Army. And I am saying that knowing that Barry and Stan may be in the thick of it.'

And they were in the thick of it. They had been told very little but veterans like Barry knew the German surge had to be overcome at all costs and the Germans beaten back, that the outcome of the war might depend on it. The fighting was as fierce as ever, but Barry was an experienced soldier now.

He had often worried for Stan but Angela always assured him that she was still receiving letters from him so he was bound to be all right. But Barry often wondered if she would tell him if anything had happened to Stan for the women were told not to worry the men at the Front. He had never caught sight of him before now, but he saw him that day because Stan had come looking for him.

He knew the next day Barry was preparing to go into the front trench to lead the second attack and Stan, who'd seen neither hide nor hair of Barry through all the years of war, decided to seek him out and wish him luck. The day was a cold one and Stan squelched through the muddy ground, the smell of cordite hung in the mist of the early morning and the sounds of fierce fighting could be heard, the crack of rifles, the thumping boom of the big guns, the incessant clatter of machine guns and the whistle and whine of shells.

Barry was standing talking to some of the men that he would be sending over first the following day and Michael Malone was amongst them and he was ridiculously pleased to see Stan in the distance. He had lost many friends and comrades and for Stan to have got through so far virtually unscathed was amazing. Barry's face split into a huge grin and he gave Stan a wave. It was as he started to walk towards him that he saw the arc of a shell in the air, but Stan had his back to it. Barry started to run, shouting a warning, but Stan couldn't hear, so Barry launched himself in the air and threw himself on top of Stan as the shell hit the ground and exploded, killing Barry outright and the two soldiers beside Michael and blowing Michael's left leg clean off.

When there had been no letters for five weeks, Angela was frantic. Each day she woke with a dead feeling inside her and was glad of the job that gave her no time to think and worried about Mary spending hours alone in the house. 'It must be awful not knowing anything,' Maggie said to Angela one morning. Michael's mother had been to see Maggie and told her of Michael's injuries and she had been shocked and saddened and yet glad to know he was alive, but for Angela there was just silence. There was no way of finding out what had happened to him.

'It is awful,' Angela said. 'See, this has happened before, this lack of letters and then two or three come together. But it's never gone on this long and for Stan's letters to stop as well . . . ' Her voice trailed away and her eyes looked very bleak as she said, 'I hope to God nothing has happened to him Maggie. I don't think I could bear it.'

Maggie was very much afraid the unthinkable had happened and Barry was already dead, but if she was right she didn't want her friend to go under and so she spoke quite briskly, ''Course you'll be able to bear it. You'll have to cope because you have a child to see to and she is part of Barry and you owe it to him to bring her up the best way you know.'

'You are right, Maggie, so right,' Angela said. 'And the first thing I must do is try and find out what's happened to Barry. I won't be in tomorrow, at least for the morning and Sylvia can do any deliveries needed.'

'Well I won't blame you,' Maggie said. 'And neither will anyone else, but I don't know what Mr Potter will make of it.'

'Well if he doesn't like it he'll have to lump it,' Angela said almost fiercely. 'To me this is more important than making shells.'

She didn't say that to Mr Potter, but she did say she was fed up living with uncertainty. 'Barry wrote to me two days before the Germans started their Spring Offensive and that's over five weeks ago. Since then I have heard nothing, I don't know whether he is alive or dead and I need to try and find out and I intend to have tomorrow off to do that.'

Mr Potter realized Angela was coiled tight as a spring, her voice too betrayed just how anxious she was and he knew he was looking at a young woman at the end of her tether. So all he said was, 'Are you going to the Barracks at Thorp Street?'

Angela nodded. 'I wouldn't know anywhere else to try.'

'Nor I,' Mr Potter said. 'Take tomorrow off and find out all you can about that young husband of yours and I really hope the news is good.'

'So do I Mr Potter,' Angela said. 'Oh so do I.'

Mary approved of what Angela was doing but all Connie heard was that her mother wasn't going to work the following day and she was ecstatic because Mammy promised her that they would have breakfast together and then she would take her to school and meet her teacher Mrs Cleary.

Connie had begun at St Catherine's School just over a fortnight ago when it re-opened after the Easter holidays and according to Mary, possibly helped by going to nursery, she had settled to it as if she had been going all the days of her life.

The next morning Angela woke with knots of apprehension in her stomach while Connie was still fizzing with excitement. She had no appetite, she hadn't had any for days, but having breakfast together mattered to Connie so she forced herself to eat the bowl of porridge Mary insisted on before school and they walked hand in hand along Bristol Street and Angela remembered going the same route hand in hand with eight-year-old Barry when she was Connie's age, for all the McCluskys had gone to St Catherine's.

She stood in the playground and let the memories flow, her and Maggie skipping or throwing a ball up the wall or joining with others to play cops and robbers or tag. The bell was rung by an older child as it had been in her day and when the teachers came into the playground the children lined up in front of them and Connie went up to the teacher who was obviously Mrs Cleary and pointed her mother out and the teacher approached her smiling. 'Connie didn't really need to point you out for she is the image of you,' she said to Angela.

'I know, but she's excited I'm here. I don't usually make it because I work long hours in a shell factory. I'm playing hookey today.'

'She told me what you do. You have a bright girl there, Mrs McClusky. She says her father is a soldier.'

'He is,' Angela said. She bit her lip anxiously and then because the teacher was so approachable, she went on, 'He's missing, not officially, but we have heard nothing for more than five weeks. I've had the day off to see if I can find out more.'

'Oh good luck,' Mrs Cleary said. 'I must get the children back to the classroom before they break ranks and run amok in the playground, but I do hope you find all is well.'

'Thank you,' said Angela and watched Mrs Cleary leading her class in, with Connie giving her a surreptitious little wave as she turned the corner, which caused a smile to tug at Angela's mouth.

The women in the office at Thorp Street Barracks couldn't really help. 'I thought you might have casualty lists or something,' Angela said.

'We will have,' said the young woman behind the desk. 'You must understand they are difficult to compile when the conflict is still going on.'

'And you must understand that Barry is my husband, the father of our daughter, and I am desperate to know what has happened to him.'

'I know,' the girl said more sympathetically. 'You're not the first to ask, believe me.'

'Maybe that's because we are told nothing,' Angela said ironically. 'See, these are not numbers on a page, or percentages, they are people, sons, fathers, sweethearts and uncles and these people need to know and as soon as possible what has happened to their loved ones. Has anyone even made an educated guess how many have died in this Offensive to date?'

The girl shook her head. 'They may have done that, but I have no figures given to me.'

Angela felt suddenly so helpless and downhearted. She felt her shoulders sag and she had the desire to lie on the floor and weep.

'Look,' the girl said. 'All I can advise is to try to be patient for if anything has happened to your husband you will be informed in due course.'

'And that's all the help you can give me?'

'Yes I'm afraid it is.'

'Thank you,' said Angela, wondering what she was thanking her for.

She thought of going back to work, but she was too dispirited. They had all known in the factory why she'd had the time off and would be asking questions she couldn't answer and it would make her feel worse than ever.

On the other hand, going home to Mary to tell her she knew no more than when she had set out that morning was not a great prospect either. But she could hardly walk the streets all day and she supposed Mary had to know how it went regardless and so she turned for home and arrived in tears.

Mary cried too when Angela told her what had happened at the Barracks with the girl in the office. Later, when she was calmer she said, 'I was so cross with the girl behind the desk and it really wasn't her fault. She was only young and if she hasn't been given the information there is nothing she can do about it.'

'I suppose not,' Mary said. 'We just have to wait then?'

'Fraid so.'

'Bloody hard isn't it?'

'It is bloody hard. I think it's the hardest thing in the world.'

Angela was glad when it was time to collect Connie. Connie had not known whether she would or not, so she was delighted to see her mother and all the way home she chuntered on about her day and how good it had been. They were going to go in the front door, but there was something stopping it from opening so they went in the entry door. They found the body of

Mary slumped against the front door, blocking it, and there was a crumpled telegram in her hand.

With a cry Angela was on her knees beside her. Mary wasn't dead, as she had feared, but she needed help and Angela went out of the entry where the children were playing and sent Freddie Webster for the doctor for she knew him to be a sensible boy who lived down the yard. The doctor had a surgery on Bristol Street, which was no distance, and Angela watched Freddie's legs pounding as he tore down the street and knew he would be there in no time and gave a sigh of relief.

Connie was sitting on the floor patting Mary's face gently and as her mother came in the entry door she turned with troubled eyes and said, 'Why won't Granny wake up?'

Angela got down on the floor beside her daughter and held her close as she said, 'Granny is very tired and needs the doctor to help her wake up.'

'Oh. Is he coming then?'

'Yes he's on his way,' Angela said. 'So soon Granny will be as right as rain again.'

'Yes,' said Connie, happier now for she knew doctors were very clever people, not that she ever went to the doctor's because they cost money and anyway she was never sick, not that sick to need a doctor. But if there was something wrong with Granny that needed a doctor he would fix her in no time, she was sure.

'Now we need to make Granny more comfortable,' Angela said. 'We need a pillow and a blanket.'

'I'll get them, Mammy.'

'You get the pillow from my bed,' Angela suggested,

getting to her feet. 'I'll fetch the blanket, it's too big for you and you might fall down the stairs.'

When they returned to the room Angela moved Mary a little away from the door and placed the pillow beneath her head and tucked the blanket around her as Freddie's mother, Nancy put her head around the entry door and said, 'Our Freddie's just come in and said you sent him for the doctor.' She came into the room as she spoke and saw Mary comatose on the floor. 'Oh my God! What's happened to Mary?'

'This happened,' Angela said, indicating the crumpled telegram she had prised from Mary's grasp and put on the mantelpiece.

'Barry?' Nancy asked and Angela just gave a brief nod because Connie was watching her and she knew who Barry was.

'Ah poor soul,' Nancy said sympathetically. 'And poor you.'

Nancy's words caused tears to prickle behind Angela's eyes because she hadn't even begun yet to deal with the enormity of her loss.

Then Nancy turned to Connie and said, 'Would you like to come and play with our Jenny?'

Jenny was a big girl of eight, but Connie shook her head. 'I need to stay with Mammy. I want to see my Granny wake up.'

'The doctor might send her to hospital so they can help her,' Nancy said. 'And you wouldn't want her to go on her own would you?'

Connie shook her head and Nancy said, 'Well I'm sure your Mom would like to go with her and when your Granny wakes up she'll like it if your Mom is there, but she can't take you with her because they don't let children into hospitals.'

Connie turned to her mother and said, 'Don't they?'

Angela shook her head for tears were too close to risk speaking. Nancy was aware of this and knew it was important to get the child away because Angela was holding herself together with difficulty.

Nancy bent down on her hunkers and said, 'So d'you want to come home with me then? I'm sure I have a spare thruppenny bit in my purse and you could go down Bristol Street with our Jen and buy some sweets.'

Connie smiled and Nancy stood up and held out her hand and Connie took it and as they passed Angela Nancy said quietly, 'Don't worry about tonight, she can stop with us if it makes life easier.'

'Thank you,' Angela said brokenly. 'You are very kind.'

The door had barely shut behind Nancy and Connie when Angela sank to her knees as her legs refused to hold her up and, as the tears flowed, anguished sobs came from deep within her. She cried in deep sadness and despair at the loss of her lovely Barry. It was as if a deep black hole had opened up in front of her for she couldn't visualize a future without him.

Angela had got a grip on herself by the time the doctor arrived minutes later. He said that Mary had suffered a heart attack, which Angela had thought it was and said she had to go to hospital immediately. He asked Angela if she knew what might have caused it and she showed him the telegram. 'Her son?'

'Is he also your husband?' the doctor asked and

441

Angela nodded mutely and he understood her distress and saw that she was barely coping with it.

She travelled in the ambulance with Mary holding her hand and then she sat for hours on a hard chair in a bleak corridor with paint peeling from the walls and illuminated by small high and very dirty windows and she thought about Barry. She wondered how he died and hoped it had been a quick death. She would hate to think of him suffering and thought she would never know.

And she suddenly knew what it was all about. God had enacted his revenge and Barry had paid the ultimate price for her transgression. Mary might pay as well for she wasn't out of the woods yet and they said the next twenty-four hours would be critical and if she pulled through, she had a chance.

Mary made it through the night and as soon as Angela knew that, she went off to the factory and gave in her notice. News of what had happened to Barry and Mary McClusky had flown around the area as it tended to, especially in those cramped streets and so Maggie had heard all about it and told all her workmates as soon as she arrived at the factory and they all felt sorry for Angela.

'Shame about her old man copping it like that,' one girl remarked. 'But I bet she weren't so bothered about her mother-in law. I wouldn't mind a bit if mine popped her clogs 'cos she's a right pain in the neck.'

'Oh it isn't a bit like that for Angela,' Maggie said. 'Her mother-in-law Mary brought her up.'

'How come?'

Maggie found herself telling the whole tale of Angela's

childhood, engendering even more sympathy for her. So when she arrived to give notice everyone, including Mrs Paget, made a fuss of her and said how sorry they were about Barry and his mother and Mr Potter expressed his deepest condolences. He quite understood why she had to leave and said so as he shook her by the hand and said she was one of the best drivers he'd ever had working for him. She left feeling she had been greatly liked and appreciated and though it didn't change what had happened, it made her better able to cope.

Despite how her workmates felt about her though, she knew if Mary died it would be her fault, like Barry's death was, and it caused an ache in her heart every time she thought of this. Overlying it all though was a feeling of guilt that she knew she would always feel and she deserved to. That was her punishment.

Mary didn't die, though they said her heart was very weak and another heart attack would probably kill her. But if she had a stress-free life and no heavy physical exertion she might live some years yet.

Mary wasn't impressed and said she wished they hadn't fought so hard to save her, and this upset Angela for she wasn't sure what she would have done if she had lost Mary too, and she prayed hard for her to pull through, and she said she needn't have bothered, but of course she couldn't argue with Mary and risk upsetting her.

A week later Mary was much better physically so they were getting ready to release her from hospital and the doctor asked her if she had any pain in the chest area. 'I have a throbbing, almost unbearable ache constantly in my heart,' she said. 'There's nothing you can do about it for there's not a physical cause. It's just the tearing pain I have with the loss of another son. I am more than ready to go home. There's worse than me might need this bed.'

Angela knew exactly how Mary felt for her pain too was sometimes agonizing and she got through it, one day at a time. She had told Connie her daddy wouldn't be coming home, but she didn't seem that bothered and Angela tried not to let that upset her. After all she was too young when he left for her to remember him and lots of her friends' daddies were away too. In fact there were few men about generally. In contrast to Connie's reaction, Finbarr and Colm were totally devastated by news of their young brother's death. They sent heartfelt condolences and Mass cards for Masses to be said for the repose of his soul. Even Father Brannigan sounded sincere for a change when he said how sorry he was.

A fortnight after the telegram, a letter came. It was from Barry's commanding officer expressing his condolences. He described Barry as an outstanding young man he had been proud to know for he proved to be honest, reliable and brave, and saying the loss of him must be a grievous one for them to bear. He went on to describe him as a first-rate soldier too and completely fearless in battle. He put his life on the line many times to save comrades and, stalwart to the end, he eventually gave his life to save another and he would be recommending him for a military medal.

When Angela finished reading the letter out to Mary and folded it up she had tears in her eyes, but they were tears of pride. 'Thought a lot of our Barry obviously.'

'And why wouldn't he be?' Angela asked. 'Barry is a son and husband we can both be proud of.'

'He is that,' Mary said. 'Now I wish I could find out what had happened to Stan.'

'Stan must be dead, Mammy,' said Angela. 'I wrote to his sister after we got the telegram to see if she had news of him and in her reply she said that the deal she made with Stan was for no contact.'

'I know that but surely the war changed all that?'

'Not as far as Betty was concerned. Stan wrote to her once to explain he was enlisting and telling her about the money put in trust for Daniel when he is twenty-one, but she didn't reply.'

'So he could be alive or dead and she'd never know?'

'That's about the strength of it,' Angela said. 'We are his point of contact. Any telegram or communication would come here. I don't understand why we haven't had a telegram or anything, but after all this time he must be dead.'

Stan wasn't dead, but he was in hospital, or the loony bin as he preferred to call it. When they collected him up from the battlefield he was unconscious and it was some time before he realized it had been Barry McClusky who had saved his life and so lost his own, and he had wanted to weep, for it was the opposite of what he would have wanted to happen.

He had not got away totally unscathed and they were ages putting his insides back together again and then they had to dig shrapnel out of his body, but he knew he would survive physically. Whether he would ever get over the mental anguish he felt when he thought of

445

Barry sacrificing himself for the worthless person he thought he was, was another matter.

Barry had had so much going for him, a lovely wife, an adorable child, a mother who thought the sun shone out of him and a job he had enjoyed and was good at. His own life was sterile in comparison. No one would grieve overmuch if he had died in the war. He more or less expected death and instead he was still here now because of Barry.

Stan knew they were all worried about his mental state and put some of it down to battle fatigue because he had been in it since the beginning, and he couldn't really explain about the black cloud that hung over him. He only knew it would never disappear. It would always be there because he had inadvertently hurt the woman he loved.

He loved Angela with every shred of his being, though he had never shown it. He was an honourable man and wanted Angela to be happy and knew that what would make her happy was if Barry was to return from the war unscathed. It was his fault that Barry wasn't doing that because he would be alive if he hadn't taken the full force of the exploding shell. Barry sacrificed his own life in an effort to save Stan's miserable skin. However could he face Angela with that on his conscience?

Well he couldn't he decided and he had told the authorities there was no one to inform about his whereabouts, so no one knew where he was, but as soon as he could convince the doctors he was sane enough to be released, he would disappear into the countryside where no one knew him.

*　　*　　*

Through the late spring and summer of that year Mary and Angela coped with the loss of Barry in their own way and Connie helped a great deal and prevented them sinking into serious depression and gradually they didn't so much 'get over it' but rather learned to live with the pain. 'Day to day I can cope as long as I keep busy, but odd things catch you out like the other day someone was whistling a tune Barry used to whistle.'

'I know what you mean,' Mary said. 'Mind how the two of us would nag Barry not to take his socks off and throw them down in the room and he would take no notice?'

'I remember.'

'Well I came upon one the other day,' Mary said. 'It was behind a cushion and I cried bucket-loads and I thought if he was here now he could throw his socks wherever he wanted to.'

Angela smiled ruefully. 'Seems irrelevant now,' she said. 'I crossed the road the other day to avoid the hurdy-gurdy man because the memories of the last time we saw him were too painful.'

The summer drew to a close and the schools reopened and Connie was as keen as ever to go back, especially as Angela drew money out of the savings to buy her some serviceable clothes for school, a thick coat, woolly stockings and stout boots for the winter and when she was all dressed up in her new things to show her Granny she said she was as smart as paint.

Angela hated the slide into the dark nights of winter for since the attack she'd been afraid of the dark. And she hated the way sometimes the mornings seemed reluctant to start the day and it was often murky and grey and sometimes that continued into the day. And that's how it was on Monday 11th November when the church bells began to peal. All the churches around were chiming out the joyful news that the war, which had near annihilated all their menfolk was over at last. The bells had been silent for four years and everyone knew what it meant when they were chiming now.

Factory hooters joined in as people were released from their places of work and thronged the streets, some people singing and a few banging dustbin lids together, adding to the general cacophony. Connie arrived home with Jennifer Webster for the schools had been closed and Jennifer thought her too young to come home on her own.

Even Connie, catching the atmosphere, was excited though she wasn't sure why. Euphoria gripped the crowd and Angela would have liked to have joined them, but Mary had a bad cold and she wouldn't leave her that day of all days, but Connie was allowed to go with Nancy Webster and her children who promised to look after her. 'You shouldn't be staying here with an old woman either,' Mary said. 'You should be off with the rest.'

'I am not staying with an old woman,' Angela retorted. 'I am staying with a mother I love with all my heart. I'd prefer to be nowhere else and I want to remember the man we have lost and Stan too. The end of the war has come too late for us and many more like us.'

'Yes,' said Mary, 'but not for Connie.'

'What d'you mean?'

'Well that's the legacy her father has assured for her because they say this has been the war to end all wars.'

'It's true; they do say that, yes.'

'Well she will grow up without a father, but the carnage has been such that there will be lots of fatherless children and all those fathers will have died so that Connie and the rest might marry and have sons of their own, safe in the knowledge they will not be snatched away to fight in a war. Her generation will not be blighted by war as this generation has been.'

What sense Mary spoke, Angela thought. She'd been feeling so downhearted. She knew that Barry would have gladly given his life to secure a better future for his daughter and in the same spirit she must live with his loss and deal with the guilt feelings that nagged at her almost constantly. Each night she prayed earnestly for the little winter waif she had left behind on the workhouse steps, the baby she still grieved for. And each night she also thanked God that she had Connie and Mary hopefully for a good few years yet, so she was almost content.

ACKNOWLEDGEMENTS

I had trouble with my eyes as I was attempting to write this book and as eyes are extremely important, particularly for a writer, I was very worried indeed. The problem was, almost seven years ago, I had the lenses in both eyes changed as I was growing cataracts behind them. The consultant assured me I would have almost A1 vision after the operations and would never develop cataracts and sure enough, just as he said, I could for the first time read, watch television, work on the computer etc. without glasses. It was wonderful.

Four years down the line, I noticed a slight deterioration in my sight and put it down to natural ageing, but this deterioration continued and I thought that I must have Macular Degeneration. I said nothing, but over the years bought a daylight lamp and stronger and stronger reading glasses. By the time I was writing *The Forget-Me-Not Child*, my eyesight suddenly deteriorated further to the extent I could see very little – including the keyboard, which was a blur – or what I was writing.

I eventually took myself off to the optician expecting to hear her say that I was losing my sight and there was nothing that could be done and I was delighted to hear that that was not the case at all. The fact was, that though the cataracts had been removed, the debris that would have grown behind the cataracts had continued to increase and the best news of all was it was treatable. I had to wait more than three weeks to see a surgeon for laser treatment but apart from daily eye drops and a few floaters, afterwards I was able to see again.

I am always grateful to have such a strong team behind me at HarperCollins but never more than then, for they were so understanding and supportive particularly my editor Kate Bradley and my agent Judith Murdoch. My heartfelt thanks go to them and also Charlotte Brabbin, my publicist Hayley Camis and to Rhian McKay who did such a sterling job on the second copy edits. Writers usually work alone and it is sometimes a relief to know I have a comfort blanket of such reassuring people at my back and I owe a debt of gratitude to you all.

I am also grateful I can rely on the support of the family too: my husband, Denis; my three daughters - Nikki and her husband Steve; Tamsin and her husband Mark; my daughter Beth; my son Simon and his wife Carol and of course the five grandchildren – all of you are immensely dear to me.

But the most important people of all are you, the readers, for without you there would be no point in doing what I do. I value every single one of you, so thank you from the bottom of my heart and I sincerely hope you enjoy this book, it is start of a trilogy. I love it when you write and tell me what you think.

If you liked this book,
why not dip into another one
of Anne Bennett's fantastic stories?

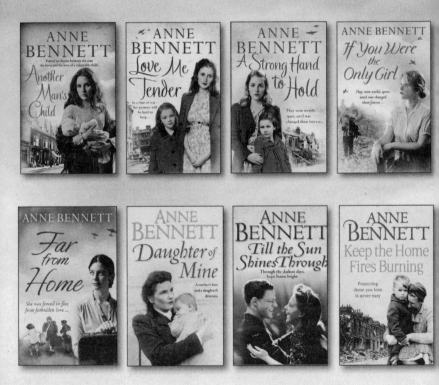

'The beauty of Anne's books is that they are about
normal people and are sewn through with
human emotions which affect us all'

Birmingham Post